Trials of Dusk and Dreams

TRIALS OF DUSK AND DREAMS

FAE DEVILS · BOOK TWO

LANA PECHERCZYK

for Erika Robles,
who saved me from giving up in deadline mode

ADULARIA
HOUSE OF MOONLIGHT
CONNEMARA
HOUSE OF TIDES
WULFENITE
HOUSE OF EMBERS
HELIODOR
HOUSE OF STONE
THE NEXUS
SHADOWFALL KEEP
HOUSE OF SHADOW
AVORLORNA CITY
COURT OF DREAMS
AVORLORNA
THE COMMONWEALTH OF DREAMS

AIRALUDA
HOUSE OF OBLIVION
ETINEFLUW
HOUSE OF PREY
AKAMENNOC
HOUSE OF BLOOD
THE SCHISM
RODOILEH
HOUSE OF FLESH
THE DARK TOWER
HOUSE OF DEATH
NOCTURNA CITY
COURT OF NIGHTMARES
NOCTURNA
THE SUBTERRANEAN OF NIGHTMARES

Part
One

CHAPTER I
WILLOW

Fox stands frozen in stone behind me, having taken the place of Styx—a Sluagh shrouded in mystery. Styx's monstrous form has vanished; no horns curve back from his forehead, no tail lashes behind him. Once bristling with spikes, his olive skin now stretches smooth and unmarred. He towers over me, a naked sculpture of rippling muscle and barely contained power. Like his brothers, his hauntingly beautiful face invites rapturous gazes. But subtle hints of disorder—scarred knuckles, a defiant set to his jaw—suggest he's no stranger to rule-breaking.

Didn't Fox say he was punished for brawling?

Styx's gaze roves over Fox's discarded clothes, his lip curling in disdain. He picks up Fox's embroidered jacket and tosses it carelessly. My heart clenches at the disregard for something so precious to me.

Dazed and confused, I find my attention darting around the temple, desperately seeking something—anything—to make sense of this nightmare. A collection of opalescent butterflies, seemingly alive but frozen in eternal flight, flutters imperceptibly. A small, innocuous-looking acorn pulses with an eerie light in a

crystal box. My gaze lands on a crystal orb swirling with minia-ture stars and nebulae, reminding me of Fox's galaxy eyes when his Sluagh side takes over.

Reality crashes back like a tidal wave. My heart aches to release the grief over losing Tinger and Fox in one night. I feel the phantom imprint of Tinger's vial in my wounded palm, a stinging reminder of my desperation. Yet something in Styx's posture awakens a wolfish intuition, warning of an apex predator in my midst, keeping me alert. When his piercing blue gaze finally settles on me, curiosity and suspicion war in his eyes.

"Who are you?" he asks.

I blink, taken aback. "Wh-what?"

"You heard me."

"Yes, I know I heard you. I just—" I shake my head, confusion clouding my thoughts. "You don't recognize me?"

My wounded fist throbs in time with my broken heart. Blood drips to the dirty temple floor. His gaze sweeps down to my ster-num, and I swear hunger flares in those dark-blue depths before he returns to inspecting the items Fox left behind.

The Nightmare Codex's warning echoes in my mind: *Sluagh are attracted to forlorn and aching souls, so be warned to guard your heart around them. They love to increase the suffering of those already in pain.*

Fear pulses through my veins. Is he eyeing my heart as his next meal? He must know who I am. Fox told them stories about me daily, and for a moment, our Well-blessed bond triggered before he became stone. I touch my marked neck and frown. That sense of connection with the Six lasted only a few seconds, but it was long enough to feel their chaotic magic roar into my veins. Long enough for the mating bond to be confirmed. I've never tasted so much power in my life—not even when I borrowed from the stars to wake an army of undead . . . and Titania and everyone here in Avorlorna.

But all that magic is gone now. With the last of Tinger's wisp faded, my body is hollow, a vessel drained of its essence.

"Are you deaf or dumb? I asked you a question." He is all hard, naked flesh and sculpted muscle as he invades my personal space. His body heat colludes with the stifling temple air, making breathing difficult. I gasp as he presses forward, and my back hits something solid. I reach behind and feel the cold stone of Fox's statue.

Styx snarls in my face and wraps his black-taloned fingers around my throat. "Who the fuck are you, and why is he stone instead of me?"

"I'm Willow," I rasp, struggling to form words under his grip. "He took your place so you'd be free."

"Why?"

"I don't know. It was supposed to be me."

Styx's fingers tremble on my neck as though he struggles to contain his violence. "Am I to believe," he sneers, "that my brother would forfeit his freedom for you—a mere mortal, a filthy dreg of the Cauldron?"

"Trust me, I'm as thrilled about it as you are."

"Somehow, I doubt that." His eyes rake over me, sending an unwelcome shiver down my spine.

My eyes widen. Yeah—he definitely doesn't remember me. He fists my unbound hair and yanks it to his nose, pulling sharply at my scalp. I swallow my whimper, not wanting to give him any more reason to believe I am his prey. He inhales deeply and surprises me with a shuddering, exhaled groan.

"Why do you smell so good?" he mutters. "Did you enchant him?"

Did you enchant me? I almost feel him say.

"I'm your mate," I answer, my voice surprisingly steady. "Your Well-blessed mate."

A pause. "What is that?"

He has a Well-blessed mark beneath his left eye. But if he has no memory of me, then it's logical to think he has no memory of Elphyne or our vocabulary. I must follow the narrative Titania has placed for them here in Avorlorna.

"It's been a long night, Styx." I sigh, fatigue seeping into my bones. "And while I'm happy to meet you finally, it hasn't been without a cost. There's so much to tell you. Goodfellow could be here any minute to carry out Fox's sentencing. He doesn't know Fox tricked him, so it's better we're not here when he turns up."

He drops my hair, but before he lets go of my neck, his thumb grazes over the bite mark Fox left and he narrows his eyes thoughtfully. I hold my breath, hoping he can't sense my fear. In the wild, the scent of fear is everything. It's a signal to attack, to dominate, to feed. Before he steps away, he lifts my upper lip to reveal my teeth. I'm so startled that I jerk back from him and scowl.

"Why did you do that?"

"You have tiny fangs." He flicks my hair away from my ears. "Ears like the Folk. And if I'm not mistaken, your scent and eyes tell me you have a little wolf in you. But you're mortal. I sense it —" He taps my sternum. "Here."

"That's another long story." I shove him away. "Like I said before, we need to leave. Then I can explain everything. Goodfellow—"

"Goodfellow." A growl rips from his throat, aggression hardening his body again. "Who the fuck is that?"

"You don't remember him either?"

My mind races. Something isn't adding up. Fox mentioned Styx was trapped in stone for longer than the others remembered, but how can he not remember Robin Goodfellow?

"If I did, I wouldn't have asked," he grinds out, frustration evident in every line of his body.

Styx's distrust comes from a place of fear, I think. I see it glimmering in the depths of his blue eyes. He knows something is amiss, too, yet he's powerless to understand what.

We assumed he would have his memories because the seal binding his powers had been scratched and dented. But maybe the seals aren't what made them forget. Maybe that's another in Titania's long string of curses.

"When we found you in here," I venture slowly, "your Sluagh form was on display. Do you still have access to your full abilities?"

His skull illuminates beneath his skin. Air caresses my face as his wraith inspects me with an invisible touch, and his eyes turn wholly black. When I don't react, he bares a mouth full of spiky, monstrous fangs and snaps in my face.

"Are you trying to scare me?" I raise my brows, surprised by my own boldness.

"Maybe."

Despite myself, I smile. That's kind of cute.

"I am not cute," he snarls, his features contorting with indignation.

I roll my eyes. "Fox keeps saying I shout my thoughts. When will I learn?"

His skull flickers again as his wraith returns to his body, and he looks away. I almost believe I offended him.

"I mean, if it helps, I was kind of scared for a moment there," I offer. "Truly."

I collect the broken seal from beneath the table where it sits with the others. The smooth stone disc is cracked across the faerie runes.

When I face him again, his otherness is completely gone, replaced by the visage of brooding, chaotic beauty carved from living stone.

Still gloriously naked.

CHAPTER 2
WILLOW

My gaze involuntarily drops to Styx's groin. An unbidden image flashes in my mind—my hand wrapping around his stone penis to steady myself. Heat floods my cheeks. *Please, Well, don't let me broadcast these thoughts.* The last thing I need is for him to know about my accidental statue-groping.

He looks at me, one eyebrow raised.

Shit.

Averting my eyes, I mumble, "Could you put on pants? You're distracting."

"Am I making you nervous, tiny fangs?"

"You wish. I just prefer my men fully dressed."

"Liar. Your heartbeat says otherwise."

"Just do it." My tone is strained. I can't look at him. An extended silence follows.

"I don't take orders from you, mortal, or anyone outside my hive," he growls, his voice a dark velvet that sends shivers down my spine.

I swallow hard, willing my voice to remain steady. "It's snowing outside. Unless you fancy your penis becoming an icicle or for you to be punished for breaking the Old Code again, I suggest you cover up."

"Is that a threat?" he purrs as he draws closer behind me.

The hairs on my neck stand at attention, my body hyper-aware of his proximity. I keep my gaze fixed on the far wall, raising the seal above my shoulder.

"Do you remember how you broke this?" I ask, desperate to change the subject. "The others are still blocked from using their full powers. If you know how to break the seals, stop messing around and do it."

He plucks it from my hand, his touch sending an electric current through my arm. I wait for a heartbeat, then gather Fox's discarded clothing. I bring the fabric to my nose, inhaling deeply. Fox's scent—a mix of spice and mischief—clings to the clothes, offering a moment of bittersweet comfort. The enchanted spectacles weigh heavily in my pocket. Fox said the choice was mine, but is Styx the right one? Maybe it's meant for one of the others in his hive.

"Titania," he snarls at the seal, venom dripping from each syllable. "Where is she?"

"Still sleeping, I think. The Gentle Interlude has begun." I toss Fox's clothing at him, reluctant to part with the comforting scent. "Here. Put these on."

He catches them with a grimace, shooting me a glare that could melt steel. As he dresses, I scan the temple for anything worth pocketing. My last attempt at pilfering ended with a jar of wisps and a close call. This time, I'll be more discreet.

"Once you're decent," I say, fingering a small, intricately carved figurine, "we'll leave, and you can *flicker* us back to Shadowfall Keep."

A derisive snort punctuates his struggle with Fox's too-small breeches. "I do what I want, tiny fangs."

"Are you always this stub—" The words die in my throat as I face Styx.

Fox's breeches strain against his muscular thighs, the waistband gaping to reveal a tantalizing glimpse of his chiseled abdomen. My gaze lingers as he unfurls Fox's shirt with disdain. Each flex and pop of his muscles sends a wave of heat through my body. I was stupid to think he'd be less attractive with more clothes on.

"He dressed like a fucking Radiant," Styx scoffs. "When did he become so ostentatious?"

I bristle at his tone. "He did what he needed to blend in." Privately, I think Fox enjoyed the ornate fashion, but there's no need to fuel Styx's derision.

"If it didn't reek of him, I'd doubt he wore it," Styx mutters, his words laced with suspicion.

His every syllable drips with distrust. It feels like he's waiting for me to say something incriminating, which confirms my suspicion he can't access my thoughts. A flicker of hope ignites in my chest—perhaps the queen-hive bond is still half-triggered, as Fox theorized.

"Well, he did," I retort, unable to keep the defensive edge from my voice.

Discarding the shirt, Styx prowls the temple half naked, inspecting trinkets and treasures with feigned nonchalance. For a few minutes, I do the same. We fall into an almost companionable silence. While he's not looking, I slip the acorn into my pants pocket, then cover the bulge with my cape. He doesn't seem to notice, so I keep hunting for curious items that are smaller and easier to hide than a jar of wisps.

A delicate silver bell sits on a velvet cushion, its surface etched with runes. I can almost hear whispers emanating from it, promising desire and doom to anyone who dares ring it. When I poke it, no tinkling sound comes out. Interesting. Oops. Into my pocket it goes. So do a pair of gossamer-thin gloves that seem to ripple with an unseen wind, their fingers occasionally twitching as if longing to wrap around an unsuspecting throat.

"How long was I gone?" he asks, startling me. I pivot and find him turning over a bejeweled chest the size of his palm.

I gnaw my lower lip, dreading his reaction. "I'm not entirely sure. Fox said you were meant to be stone for only a year, but it's been . . . longer."

His gaze sharpens. "How much longer?"

"Um . . . maybe a few years?"

His visage flickers, and then he is suddenly before me, snarling. "Years?"

"I think so."

"*Years?*" This time, the word is a guttural growl, his face contorting with rage and disbelief.

"I'm sorry. I know it must be a shock." If only he knew about the others forgetting him entirely.

His head dips, body coiling with tension. Then, with a speed that startles me, he snatches a jar of wisps and hurls it against the wall. Glass shatters, releasing hundreds of buzzing energy orbs into the cavern. I duck, narrowly avoiding a collision.

He exhales, the act seemingly cathartic, and throws another jar.

"Styx!" I shriek, dodging a rogue wisp. "Stop! If the queen finds out—"

"Fuck the queen." His eyes lock with mine as he deliberately smashes another jar.

"If one of them hits us—eek!" I dive beneath a table. "We don't know who they belonged to. What if they're from some deranged nightmare? Do you really want those memories hitting you right now?"

He plucks a wisp from the air and pops it into his mouth like candy. "Tastes boring. Like . . . a happy mortal."

From my hiding spot, I ponder. Perhaps the wisps don't affect him because they're a part of his natural diet. When Tinger's wisp entered my bloodstream, I felt dizzy, but then the hive's chaotic magic purged my system. Now I'm empty again. I might not be so lucky if one hits me now.

Styx's feet appear before my table refuge.

"Why can't I access your thoughts?" he asks, his voice unnervingly soft.

"Because I'm your mate," I repeat, swiping my hand out from beneath the table and gesturing toward Fox. "His too. And Legion's, Bodin's, Emrys's, and Varen's. I'm fated to be . . . your skin or something weird like that. Your"—my mouth twists in distaste at the next word—"queen."

He scoffs. "A fantasy. We will never accept enslavement to a queen."

"Good. I don't want to be one." I rub my aching forehead, wincing at my injured palm. Stupid move, breaking that pendant. I'll need to clean the wound before it festers. "Look, I can't control you any more than you can control me. I'm exhausted. I just want to go home."

"You are powerless."

"Because Titania stole my magic!" I crawl out, glaring up at him from my hands and knees. "She ruined my life, stole my magic, and now I'm mortal. Happy?"

"No." A wayward curl falls across his forehead as he meets my gaze. "You could be anyone. You could be the reason Fox is encased in stone."

The wisps have gathered on the ceiling, drawn to the stars beyond. I should be safe now. Pushing past him, I clamber to my feet. "I'm your only way out of this temple. If I'm high on wisps, I can't control the wards."

"How convenient," he drawls, skepticism etched in every line of his face.

Helplessness clogs my throat. We're going in circles. How can I make him trust me? The spectacles burn a hole in my pocket—amongst the other stolen items—but something holds me back from giving them to him. This choice feels monumental, and I can't afford to be wrong.

A dragon's roar shakes the walls, showering us with dust and debris. Oh shit. Time's up.

"The Baleful Hunt," I gasp, shielding my eyes from falling sand. "Goodfellow must be here."

Styx's accusing gaze whips to me, but I don't give him a chance to speak. I grab his wrist, tugging him toward the warded exit.

"The instant we're out," I hiss, "*flicker* us to the Keep. Understand? The *instant.*"

The stubborn bastard resists, and I feel the weight of my failure. I should have forced the spectacles on his face while he was still disoriented. I screwed up again because I can't trust my own judgment.

The shuffle of boots alerts us to Puck's arrival. The auburn-haired Radiant materializes through the temple wall. His lumpy, hairless eyebrows shoot up as he looks at me, then Styx. Instinctively, I step in front of my mate, a futile attempt at protection. More sand falls as the Hunt moves about on his rooftop nest. The dragon is still outside—not hosted within Puck. Probably because the wards only allow humans inside. He was once human, wasn't he?

And if Fox couldn't breach the wards when we were in here last, then it's likely Puck can't communicate with his dragon to warn it we're here. We still might stand a chance of escaping if Styx flickers us to the Keep when we step outside.

A snarl is my only warning before Styx pushes me out of the way. I stumble, blinking in confusion. By some miracle, his other-worldly features remain hidden, but his hand is wrapped around Puck's throat.

"If you kill me," Puck warns, his voice strained but steady, "he'll be forever imprisoned in stone."

Styx's fingers flex as he regards the Radiant with eerie calm. "You're bonded to the Baleful Hunt?"

"And he's right outside. Killing me will set him free, and who will release Lord Fox then?"

"How are *you*, a mortal, bonded to the Baleful Hunt?" Styx's incredulous eyes narrow.

Thoughts churn behind Puck's emerald eyes before he manages a haughty scoff. "I am not mortal."

Styx's grip tightens, but no dragon appears, and no stony power flashes in Puck's eyes. The dragon remains outside. My theory must be correct. He can't call on the Hunt's power from in here.

"*Is he right?*" I project my thoughts to Styx. "*If we kill him, is the dragon released?*"

The muscle ticking in Styx's jaw is the only sign he heard me. He's too enthralled with whatever he sees in Puck's eyes . . . or thoughts. If Cait can't find Medusa's mirror for us, then the Baleful Hunt reversing this condition could be the only way we get Fox out. I refuse to sacrifice another soul to take Fox's place.

"*We have to go now.*" I project my thoughts at Styx. "*If we can knock Puck out, you might be able to flicker us away before the Baleful Hunt spots us.*"

Styx's voice invades my mind, darker and richer than Fox's gentle purr. "*Why should I trust you?*"

"*Because Fox did.*" I inch closer, adding, "*Puck doesn't know your seal is broken. You haven't revealed your powers, which makes me wonder why he's not attacking. I think he's trying to bait you into exposing yourself.*"

"*I know that,*" he snaps. "*The dragon cannot protect his thoughts in here.*"

Ah. So that long look into his eyes was Styx searching his mind.

"*Then you know Puck's right. He's our only hope of freeing Fox. Well, he thinks he is. We have a backup plan back at the Keep.*" Aloud,

I say, "We should leave. There's nothing more to do here. Fox fulfilled the bargain to turn himself in. You're free to go, Styx."

Puck glares at me, and whatever thought passes through his mind makes Styx's lip curl in disgust. His fingers tighten around Puck's throat until his eyes roll. He's losing oxygen. Sensing our window of opportunity closing, I slap my hand against the warded wall, inviting the crawling, itching magic over my skin. I transfer it to Styx and then bolt outside, dragging the reluctant Sluagh with me.

We step into fresh air for a split second, and then the dragon roars. My pulse leaps, I lock eyes with Styx, and I plead in my mind. Relief washes over me as my equilibrium shifts, the familiar sensation of being pulled through space and time enveloping us. He *flickers* us. But when my feet touch wet, coppery-smelling stone, I realize with growing horror that we're nowhere near the Keep. Or if we are, I've never seen this blood-spattered chamber of horrors before.

Cruel instruments of torture dangle from hooks along every wall. A limp, skinless form is nailed to a wooden chair. Its innards are spilled like a butchered animal, but I'm not sure this thing is human. A rotten stench lurks in the blood. My stomach roils as the grotesque reality sinks in.

The Knight Inquisitor strides into the room, wiping blood from his leather-gloved hands. Short, white hair. Black brows. A pale, cruelly beautiful face. Emrys lifts his attention to us, and his eyes widen in shock.

CHAPTER 3
WILLOW

"Y ou're free," Emrys states, his familiar raspy voice tight. In two quick strides, he's before Styx, bloody hands gripping his bare shoulders. "How?"

"Fox used the spell that was meant for me." I cough and attempt to remain standing, but the stench overwhelms my senses. I end up on my hands and knees, fingers splayed for balance as I breathe through the haze of death. How can he work here?

Flashes of death—of undead things rising from the ground—hit behind my eyes. I remind myself that was long ago. I'm in Avorlorna. Not Elphyne. I don't even have my magic. I can't wake up the dead. They can't hurt me. I'm safe.

When my breathing settles, I lift my gaze to find both Emrys and Styx staring at me. Something passes unsaid between the two, and I have the surreal sense that I was wrong. I'm still on that battlefield, still at risk of having my flesh torn from my bones.

Styx stalks to a wall and leans his shoulder against it, oblivious to the sharp hunting hooks dangling above his head from iron manacles. He folds his arms and says, "She claims she's our mate—the hive's one true queen."

I lick my lips and dart a nervous glance at Emrys. For a moment, I fear he'll lie and say he has no idea who I am. He approaches me with a slow, rolling gait. He moves like a wolf tracking its prey.

"Apparently," he replies.

"Apparently?" Styx repeats, brows raising.

"Fox claims she is." Emrys's dark brows knit together. "But look at her—no queen, just a frail mortal shell devoid of magic."

"So she lies," Styx continues. "She trapped Fox into taking my place."

"Search her mind," Emrys suggests, crouching to my level.

Dried blood is caked on his gloves. It's also on his boots, black pants, and white hair.

"I can't," Styx says, scraping a hand through his unruly hair. "She is blocked to me . . . like a queen."

"Queens cannot be trusted," Emrys hisses, lashes lowering as he inspects my face. When interest sparks in his eyes, I know it's not because the curse has been broken. Fox never saw the ugliness, so it's fair to assume Emrys didn't either. His interest is something far more nefarious. I've always felt like he was an inch away from strapping me to his torture chair. It's enough to make me doubt he's the right choice for the enchanted spectacles.

"Which is why I came here first," Styx says.

Emrys straightens to his full, imposing height, yet his gaze remains on my face. I am at his mercy in this lowly position, on my hands and knees.

Scraping on the slate draws my attention to his boot sliding toward my vulnerable hand. The blood-spattered toe lifts and hovers over my splayed fingers, ready to crush my fragile mortal bones.

My heart hammers against my ribcage so hard that I can't breathe. This isn't choking on air. This is lung-squeezing panic.

"Oh, little moth." His sensual lips curve with cruel delight.

"Your heart sings such a beautiful melody. Shall we see what other tunes it knows?"

His boot lowers, and I brace for crushing pain, but nothing comes when Styx asks, "But is she the one who betrayed me?"

Playfulness evaporates from Emrys's posture. His boot slips away from my hand as he glances at Styx. "What do you mean, betrayed?"

"Why do you think I was put in the Cabinet?" Styx's voice drops to a wary tone, eyes narrowing.

The Knight Inquisitor returns his wariness. "What are you implying, Sixth?"

"That the story she told of my sentencing is false, *Third*." Styx pushes off the wall and meets Emrys, toe to toe. "Do you not recall what happened?"

"You broke the Old Code."

Styx's lips flatten. "Did I?"

"Emrys can't remember." I scramble to my feet. "Titania cursed you all. Or the Keepers have. I'm still unsure what's happening with your seals, but your memory is unreliable even when the seals are broken."

Two sets of distrustful eyes swing my way, and I am out of patience.

"And for the record," I continue, "I wasn't here when you were encased in stone. So I can't have been the one to betray you."

At their continued silence, my eyes burn with unshed tears. "I've lost so much tonight," I growl. "I am raw. I am exhausted. I am devastated. I feel like Fox has ripped my heart out with the move he pulled, but I understand why he did it. You lot are a mess. He was at his wit's end trying to unite his hive." A hysterical laugh chuffs out of me. "He tried for five years and couldn't make it work. You need me. Admit it. Return us to the castle to finish this conversation with the others."

"Look at that," Styx drawls. "The mortal with fangs thinks she can order us around."

For some reason, his words cast doubt into Emrys's eyes. I sense his irritation swarming in the air, pulsing against my skin. Then, as quickly as it arrives, it dissipates.

"Return her," he intones as he strolls to his victim and swipes a finger along a limb. He sucks blood from his finger, considering something. When his gaze lowers briefly to my neck—to where Fox's bite mark still marks my flesh—and then darts away, I know he must have felt the mating bond trigger. Fox and Styx both received Well-blessed mating marks matching mine on their necks before Tinger's borrowed mana fizzled out. Emrys's next words to Styx are through a clenched jaw. "Go. Tell the First what happened to the Fifth. Let him decide her fate. I will investigate the circumstances of your capture."

When Styx starts toward me, I realize that no matter whose memories are lost, they still instinctively follow a chain of command.

STYX FLICKERS us to the courtyard before the Keep but doesn't stay to walk me inside. He storms up the steps, his anger palpable in the tense set of his shoulders. A pang in my chest urges me to follow him, to chase him down and ensure he's okay. Waking after years of false imprisonment, finding your brother has taken your place, and the rest have barely any memory of the circumstances surrounding it would be jarring. I dare think he feels lonelier than me.

But exhaustion weighs heavily on my limbs, and even though the enchanted spectacles burn a hole in my pocket, I don't head to Legion's chambers. I return to mine. The closer I get, the stronger Fox's scent becomes, and I remember I won't be able to get inside without him. But when I arrive, his outer door has returned. Frowning, I wrap my hand around the doorknob. Did the castle shift our rooms back last night, and I didn't notice when I woke?

Did it know he wouldn't return?

When I open the door, Fox's cologne tugs at my heart. Our rooms are still attached, but I've been gifted an extra door to enter and leave.

The castle knew he wouldn't return.

Blinking away tears, I pick up one of Fox's crumpled shirts but hurry into my room as if his ghost is chasing me. The jar of stolen wisps casts flickering light onto my collection of treasure . . . including the portal stone back home. Suddenly, I'm back in the temple, Fox's desperate eyes boring into mine, his voice cracking as he pleads with me to understand.

I inhale against his shirt, hoping his scent will banish my doubts. Without him, I have no allies here except Geraldine, Max, and Peggy. Maybe the best thing to do is take them back to Elphyne. At least they'll be safe there.

Varen's hint of honey and jasmine is subtly curled within Fox's comforting woodsy scent. The tightness in my chest eases as I think of him. He might communicate in nonsensical code, but I often see intelligence lurking in his warm gaze. Maybe Fox hugged Varen when he fed him sustenance. Or maybe Varen planted his scent here because he knew I'd return and have doubts.

He might have seen in a vision how distraught I'd be after returning without Fox . . . and Tinger. My wounded palm touches my sternum, a reflex of seeking out the pendant.

My mother often gave me little comforting messages after seeing the future in her prophetic visions. When it came time to live out those moments, I would think of her and smile.

But now I frown. It's not because I don't miss my family in Elphyne, but I feel the pull toward my mates more. They are mine. All six of them.

My head throbs, a war between two loyalties raging behind

my eyes. For a moment, I see my childhood home—the familiar scent of my mother's herb garden and the sound of my father's rare booming laughter. Elphyne pulls at my heart, but Avorlorna tugs at my very being, six new connections humming beneath my skin. I press my palms to my temples, trying to quiet the clash of past and present. The bond is there, waiting to be found again.

Exhaustion crushes me like a tidal wave. I change out of my damp clothes with heavy limbs and slide Fox's shirt over my shivering body. It comes down to my thighs, but it's more than I usually wear to sleep.

I add my new treasures to my growing collection on the table and make a mental note to investigate their magical properties later. The gloves and acorn call to me. Taking the spectacles and jar of wisps, I pad barefoot through the dawn-lit hallways, determined to find the familiar scent that calls to me like home. The sweet, smoky jasmine of Varen beckons me forward.

The castle shifted overnight. The doors have changed positions, but I know which direction to head—toward the Clock Tower. I'm quietly glad it's on the same floor as my room because I wholeheartedly regret not bringing slippers for the journey by the time I reach their wing. The cold seeps in through my bare feet with every step across the stone floors.

Sweet, smoky jasmine lures me through heavy wooden doors into warmed chambers. I pause at the threshold and scan through the dusty, gloomy room. Dawn light joins forces with dying firelight to reveal the room's disrepair. Scratches and nonsensical drawings cover the peeling wallpapered walls. A velvet chesterfield by the bay window is moth-ridden, its clawed legs tarnished. Bits and pieces of broken things litter the floor, suggesting the baby Wild Hunt has been nesting here. A hint of musky animal scent laces the air, yet I see no sign of the troublemaker. The stronger scent comes from the tightly wrapped figure on the four-poster bed, tangled in a blanket.

Relief surges through me, lifting every emotion I've tried to repress since Fox begged me to cherish him. Since I felt his presence slip away. Since he told me to wait for him.

I pad forward, place the jar and spectacles on Varen's bedside table, and then peer down at the softly breathing Sluagh. It's hard to believe he's a creature of chaos and destruction. To me, he is angelic, beautiful, and at peace.

He is in a place I long to be.

New muscle on his pale body confirms what I suspected—Fox fed him. The change in his physique is remarkable. The shadows beneath his eyes are gone, and his cheeks are no longer gaunt, but the hard angle of his jaw remains. Fox might have shaved him last night, too, because the stubble is so fine that it's almost nonexistent. One arm, part of his naked torso, and a cotton-covered left leg are visible outside of his blanket tangle. His biceps are defined. His forearm is thick and corded. He's nowhere near as built as the others, but he is no longer closer to his wraith form than life.

All this from bee bread.

I can understand why he was so disenchanted with normal food.

My fingers graze the cold spectacles on the bedside table. Legion might be the First, but Fox spoke about Varen's visions with unwavering respect. He would be the best candidate for having his memories returned, except that the weight of two seals causes his madness. If the spectacles work, and Varen is still speaking nonsense, I'll be back where I started.

I peel back Varen's blanket, intending to slip into his cocoon, but the tangle is unyielding. I'm almost finished unknotting his twisted covers when I tug too hard on a sheet corner wrapped around an ankle. He mumbles something and frowns. I freeze and wait for him to fall asleep. I'm left with a fluffy blanket, two sheets, and a bath towel. How in the Well's name was he planning on extricating himself from this mess?

Finally, I wrap the blanket over the two of us and shuffle

closer to him. The fatigue I've denied droops my eyelids. To it, I am safe now. To it, adrenaline is no longer needed. My body quakes with the final letdown, and I burrow closer to my mate. That word sounds less foreign the more I think it.

He's so warm and delicious.

He stirs. A husky sigh leaves his lips, tickling my face.

"Shh," I whisper. "Go back to sleep."

"The queen searches . . ." His tone is rough as he squeezes his eyes harder. It's all too real. He knows. I don't want to break the news to him now.

"My room is cold and empty. Please, can I stay here for a while?"

Warm, large hands slide around my hips. His fingers flex as though trying to convince himself I'm real. His breathing becomes sharp and stilted. Panicked.

"Shh," I coo. "Go back to sleep, Varen."

Please.

Don't be alarmed. Let us dream all is well.

He tenses. Fire crackles. The sunlight is growing brighter through the gaps in the curtains. It's an omen, promising a new day already gusting with wind and snow. Still with his eyes closed, Varen glides his hand down my thigh, slips it beneath Fox's shirt, and up my bare back.

The sensation draws a gasp from my lips and a shiver down my spine. He tugs me closer until we're flush, and my head has nowhere to go but to the enticing spot tucked beneath his chin. I have a face full of male neck and collarbone. The smell of him is stronger here. It's sweet, heady, and masculine. It's as warm as his embrace and soothes my frayed nerves.

He gently strokes my back with lazy, repetitive sweeps.

This.

This is what I needed so desperately.

"When it's cold," he murmurs roughly, his chin bumping on

the top of my head, "worker bees cluster tightly around the queen . . . to generate heat through . . . muscle contractions."

My chuckle knocks loose unshed tears. I hug him tighter, screw up my face, and wish I could hold onto the humor for a little longer. It lies and tells me everything is okay.

He continues to mumble more about the hive's temperature being essential to the queen's survival. His factual drone is as soothing as his idle hand, and I relax.

"Tell me more," I sigh out.

"The bees outside the cluster expose themselves to colder temperatures, sacrificing their lives to insulate her."

I pull back to look into his shadowed, sleepy eyes. "What?"

"Shh." He mimics me from earlier. He smooshes his finger against my parted lips and repeats, his body tense, "Shh."

My bottom lip trembles. I don't want to trigger an episode, so I nod and hold my words captive. Mollified, his thumb smears wetness across my cheek. He warned Fox about having sex with me—said that drone bees die after mating with their queen. Fox had laughed it away, joking about his penis falling off, but maybe that was because he'd already decided to take Styx's place. He was diverting me from the truth.

He's not technically dead, but he's not here either.

Another wave of emotion closes my eyes, and I hold my breath in an attempt to stop the sob from breaking free. Varen's lips press onto each of my eyelids, leaving an impression that stays long after he's gone. An ache grows in my lower belly, and there is a need for more of this kind of connection.

He laps away my tears. The raspy and wet sensation all down my face is a little weird but so agonizingly tender and wolfish that I almost start crying again.

"Bees communicate with a waggle dance." He tugs me closer.

"Go to sleep, Varen."

"Honeybees never sleep," he mumbles, his breath warm against my ear. "When a bee finds a good source of nectar, it flies back to the hive and tells the others." A pause. "You are our nectar."

I smile despite myself. "That's better than being queen, I suppose."

"Shh." His fingers trace hypnotic circles over my hip bone, lulling me back into my comfort zone—a place where nothing exists but a warm embrace and dream that one day, none of us will be alone, none of us will make sacrifices.

We'll be a working, functional family. A hive.

We'll be happy.

CHAPTER 4
PUCK

I stride through the vast hallway toward the queen's quarters, fighting the urge to glance over my shoulder. The Sluagh bested me. But all is not lost. I still have the Hunt. Styx could have killed me, but he didn't. Perhaps he is as impotent as the others.

The sense of being watched comes from within, that is all. It is the dragon clinging to my soul with his blackened claws.

"You can't outrun me, fool." The Baleful Hunt's mocking laughter in my mind grates like nails on a chalkboard.

"Perhaps not. But I can send you to your nest at the Cabinet," I retort, suppressing a shiver.

"Oh, but then who will keep you safe? Who will strike fear into the minds of your enemies?"

I focus on the murals hiding behind wild vines on the walls. The longer the queen slumbers, the more feral her magic grows. By spring, thorny botanicals will smother the artwork completely. Tittering wild tiny faeries hide behind trembling leaves, their laughter mocking my failure.

"Be gone, leeches." I stomp my boots and snarl. "Leave Her Majesty's magic alone."

At their inaudible, singsong taunts, I dash a hand through the vines.

"My, my, how far you have fallen, Puck," the Baleful Hunt taunts.

"Don't call me that."

"But that's what they all call you, hmm? That's what She calls you."

My steps falter as I pass her favorite scene. The first Puck, the original Robin Goodfellow, stands on a rock playing the pan flute, his eyes alight with mischief. Flowers adorn his stubby horns, and tiny Folk dance around his furry, cloven-hooved legs. Puck was a prankster, a whimsical practical joker. Always the life of the party. Always making her laugh.

"And when have you made her laugh lately, hmm?" the Hunt mocks.

"Shut the fuck up."

It's not until tittering tiny Folk erupt in peals of laughter that I realize I spoke aloud.

"I would rip that mortal tongue from your throat for your impudence."

"Why don't you?" He thinks to threaten me, but he needs me. Unless another Radiant bonds with him, he is without a host.

"Watching your imminent self-destruction is all the more entertaining."

I inwardly snarl at my baleful passenger and press on. "You seem so sure of that, but you're wrong."

"And why's that, fool?"

"Because I am a survivor."

"Oh, yes, you survived death from that Sluagh rather dexterously. Sheer talent."

Fury simmers in my blood, but I resist the bait. "We are more alike than you think. You should be welcoming me, not threatening me."

"You and I can never be alike, mortal."

"I am mortal no more!" I roar and rip a chunk of thorny vines from the wall. Blood drips from cuts in my hands, but magic knits my flesh. "See? I heal."

"If you say so."

This is pointless. I am the master. He is the dragon. I am—

My gaze snags on the mural I revealed behind the vines. The pearlescent painting depicts a circular table of dragon-bonded Radiants surrounding the queen. They are the Shining Host, the trusted inner circle who counsels her. Each has eyes of a different color, reflecting their elemental dragon. The bonded beasts themselves rise behind each noble, their wings spreading like incorporeal angels.

The Baleful Hunt's presence at the council reminds me that I now have a seat at that table, not the House of Stone. In fact, so long as I have my position ratified, nothing can stop me. I may have connived my way into this role, but don't all faerie revere trickery and devilry? Don't I deserve a place among them?

"Not if you can't stabilize the security of Avorlorna while she slumbers," the dragon scoffs. *"Need I remind you who takes over from the Shining Host if the threat to our safety is deemed too high?"*

The Knights of the Queen's Hive.

Hatred simmers in my gut.

Setting off again, I shut out the stony quips from my mind until I arrive at the open, intricately carved double doors leading to the queen's sleeping chambers. The two guards, both Keepers of the Cauldron, are absent.

I glimpse a flash of pink, yellow, and white and quickly duck behind the door. The light, singsong chattering of Titania's ladies-in-waiting filters out to me.

"Oh, whimsical winds and dancing moonbeams, Moth! When your whispers reached my ears, I nearly mistook you for a changeling of the Unseelie Court." Tinkling laughter ensues, and then she continues. "Your tall tales sound like you have sampled too much faerie wine."

"By my heart, dear Cobweb. I swear it is true."

"A dragon, you say? Bonded to our dear, chaotic Puck? Why, the very stars must have shifted in their celestial dance to allow such an unlikely union."

"Ah, but consider the Puck of old, the true Goodfellow. Now there was a spirit who might have danced with dragons!"

"Indeed, this pale shadow is but a firefly to our dear Goodfellow's blazing star."

"Tut-tut, ladies," Cobweb says. "We mustn't gossip."

A pregnant pause. Then laughter erupts like silver bells, cascading their mirth about the room.

My fists clench so hard that I reopen the thorn wounds, but I hold my breath. There is more to witness here for me to use.

"Heed my words, sisters. Our impudent imposter has pirouetted into a tempest he cannot fathom. The House of Stone seethes with fury."

"They say the newly crowned earl, his blood as old as the deepest caves, means to challenge our faux Puck to a duel."

"No! Surely not! Even the moon would hide her face from such a spectacle!"

"'Tis it not a riot of possibilities? He wouldn't accept the duel, would he?"

"If he does not, he may lose the queen's esteem."

"But the ancient laws are woven into the very fabric of the Old Code. The duel must be walked on two feet alone, from first light to last shadow. Neither claw nor paw may touch the sacred ground. No wings may lift, no winds may carry, and even the gentlest breath of a dandelion's wish is forbidden. Two-legged they must start, and two-legged they must end."

"Then our hapless pretender's fate is sealed, as surely as winter follows autumn."

Hapless pretender?

Never before have I felt so different, inferior, and mortal than this moment, listening to these ladies-in-waiting faeries. I remind myself Titania plucked me from nothing to be her Shadow. I won the trials on my own merit, and she rewarded my bravery with transformation.

"She hardly had a choice, hm? The gods themselves enforce the prize of a dream come true," the Hunt sneers.

The dragon's scornful silent remarks grate on my last nerve. Who gives a fuck how I came to be here, or if I don't speak in riddle or rhyme? I have eons to learn. Time is fluid for me now, despite what those subterranean Sluagh fuckers think. They are my true purpose, my vow to the queen. I promised her I would neutralize the threat of their true identities becoming public, and even if things didn't turn out as I'd planned, I succeeded.

Fox is stone, regardless of his missing public confession about Sylvanar's death. Styx has been released, but there's no indication he is unsealed. If he had access to his full powers, he wouldn't have thought twice about wrenching my soul from my body.

I will keep a close eye on him, but he sounded too confused to be the threat Titania fears. With that dispensed, I can focus on eliminating the Wild Hunt or investigating why the queen fears a silver-haired mortal.

"A mortal with fae ears," the Baleful Hunt reminds me. *"Who seems to have suddenly broken the curse Her Majesty placed on her countenance?"*

"Shut up."

Holding my head high, I barge into the room, satisfied when their tinkling bells clatter into a gasping chorus of discord.

Standing nearest to me by Titania's briar-throttled bed, Cobweb raises a hand to her lace-covered throat. "By the stars! Your arrival, my lord, is as subtle as a pixie in a china shop."

I quickly check my beloved to ensure all is well within her eternally twilight-lit chamber. Gossamer curtains of spider silk shimmer in a nonexistent breeze, casting ever-shifting shadows. She remains unmoved, her hands clasped as she dreams.

It has been only days since her presence graced me, yet the

greenery smothering her bed now emits a pungent scent of wild herbs and moonflowers, making my nose twitch. And those tiny, luminescent, pesky creatures flit among the leaves, tittering and mocking, their glow pulsing in time with her slow breaths.

"Well, well, if it isn't Lord Goodfellow, rolling in like an unexpected storm on a midsummer's eve."

I whip my gaze to Mustardseed where she stands, hip cocked, charm-encrusted skirt askew. Her fists clench around wild weeds. One of the tiny Folk buzzes into her yellow coiffed hair, and she swats it away, never once breaking the formation of her genial smile. Despite what the Baleful Hunt thinks of me, I am no fool. I detect the barb hidden in her voice like a thorn beneath a petal.

"Have you perhaps misplaced your manners in some mortal's pocket," she queries, "or did you trade them for a pair of muddy boots to trample our delicate mushroom circles?"

I glance down and lift my boots. She is right. Mushrooms have grown overnight.

"Yes, my lord," Moth adds as she daintily sidesteps the sleeping Weaving Hunt, now also wrapped in brambles. "Pray tell, what gale of chaos or whirlwind of folly has blown you into our queen's tranquil chamber with such . . . unseemly haste?"

One only needs to glance at her sugary-pink wispy hair wrapped in a beehive to know where candyfloss found its name. Only she utters words laced with poison, not sweetness.

I let the Baleful Hunt shine through my eyes and enjoy watching their charms tremble as they quake with fear. "You three are obviously failing in the one job you have. Look at the state of this room. Soon, she will be swallowed by the very nature that feeds her." I give a dramatic pause, then tap my chin thoughtfully. "Perhaps it is time for Peablossom to return to the palace. She has, after all, heeded my instructions to the letter since she was banished."

Their bevy of apologies sounds like water gushing onto a tin roof. Their attention to my beloved disgusts me. But for them to toe the line, I can't push them over it. I must tread carefully in order to wake without a thorn wedged between my shoulder blades during the night.

"Leave us," I demand. "I will fix your ineptitude myself."

They curtsy and lavish me with empty compliments. As they reach the door's threshold, I say sweetly, "Oh, and ladies?"

"Yes, my lord?" They face me together, their arms linked, their faces holding no hint of the respect they owe me. I was going to let them off with a warning for gossiping, but it's clear they need a reminder of who Titania left in charge.

I summon magic, feel it gush into my veins, and then flick their eyebrows from their bewildered faces. Lumps of multicolored hair land like caterpillars on the greenery. Before their shock morphs into outrage, I waggle my finger and smirk. "Tut-tut, ladies. You mustn't complain or gossip. It lowers the tone, does it not?"

"Yes, my lord."

An irritating itch crawls across my cheek as I wait for their curtsies. I scratch at it absently, feeling something gritty beneath my nails. Frowning, I examine my fingertips, finding a fine, sand-like substance. For a moment, unease trickles down my spine. But no—it must be nothing more than dried sweat or debris from the overgrown vines.

To the ladies, I gesture for them to leave.

"Ensure you return daily," I remind them. "Our queen would be horrified to wake in such subterranean conditions. And ladies . . . we are smiling, yes?"

CHAPTER 5
WILLOW

"Wake up, sleepy wolf."

The familiar voice tugs me closer to the realm of awakening. I shimmy backward, deeper into Fox's embrace. His arms feel so safe, like when he held me in the bath, a warm cocoon I never want to leave.

"Little wolf."

"Not yet," I whine.

His grip tightens around my stomach, and his hard body presses along the length of my spine. The insistent ridge of his erection digs into my bottom, seeking. Hot lips drop to the sensitive spot beneath my ear and give a low alpha growl that has my entire body heating. But I'm a stubborn bitch. I like to play with Fox as much as he baits me. So, I pretend to be asleep.

"Ooh," he purrs into my mind. *"Is that a challenge?"*

Unable to repress my smile, I press my face to the pillow and shake my head. "Maybe I actually want to sleep."

"Pet, I accept."

His hand glides down my stomach. It doesn't have to go far to find the edge of his bunched shirt and slip beneath. The warm

graze of his palm leaves fire in its wake as it glides up toward my naked breast. He pinches my nipple and rolls it between his finger and thumb, tweaking and teasing until a pleasure-filled groan escapes me. Damn it.

"We can't," I pant.

"*Why not?*"

"I've already slept in. I'm sure Bodin said something about training at dinner last night."

"*He doesn't look too upset.*"

Bodin stands beside the bed, looming over us. When did he arrive?

I should feel embarrassed at being watched like this, but that's not the feeling tingling in my body. Bodin's heated gaze tracks Fox's roaming hand to where it squeezes my breast. His eyes darken when I moan.

"*Ask him to join in, pet.*"

A wave of need barrels through me.

"Bodin?" I breathe. "When did you get here?"

His eyes clash with mine and widen. For a hot, arousing moment, I think he'll slip into bed with us. Eyes filled with curious longing linger on my body, but then he clears his throat and steps back. It's then I realize the shape of his body isn't entirely in focus. Shadows blur around his broad shoulders as though they're trying to pull him away. The darkness tries to consume him. Panic flutters in my chest.

Suddenly, the scene shifts. The warm, comforting bed dissolves, replaced by cold stone beneath my feet. The air grows thick with the metallic scent of blood and the acrid tang of fear. I'm no longer in the safety of Fox's arms or under Bodin's watchful gaze. Instead, I stand in a dimly lit chamber, my hands sticky with crimson.

Nero's voice, smooth as silk but sharp as a blade, cuts through the silence. "*Again. Show me what you've learned.*"

I look down, my stomach churning as I see the lifeless body at my feet. A stranger, their unseeing eyes accusing me even in death. But the worst part? The thrill that courses through my veins, the intoxicating rush of power that comes with taking a life.

"Good," Nero purrs, his approval both revolting and addictive. *"You're learning. Soon, you'll be the perfect weapon."*

I want to scream, to run, to wash the blood from my hands and the guilt from my soul. But a part of me—a dark, twisted part I desperately try to ignore—preens under the praise. Revels in the strength coursing through my body.

"No one can ever know," I whisper, horror and shame warring within me. "They'd never understand."

The corpse at my feet begins to shift, its features morphing between those of Geraldine and Max. Once filled with trust and friendship, their eyes now reflect only betrayal and disgust.

"Don't go," I beg, reaching out for them, for anyone who might pull me from this nightmare. But my bloodstained hands only seem to drive them further away.

"You're dreaming, Willow." Bodin's baritone voice cuts through the haze of guilt and fear, feeling cold and wrong in this twisted version of reality.

I struggle against the memory, against the shame threatening to consume me. "Where are you?" I cry out into the darkness, mentally groping for him. "Fox? Varen?"

Anyone?

The nightmarish chamber begins to dissolve, replaced by encroaching shadows. From the corner of my eye, I catch sight of a horrific, disjointed figure—the Cornertwister. No eyes. Gaping mouth. It wants to feed on my fear, and I can't—I can't—I gasp for air.

"My turn," it hisses in my ears, and then I feel its hands picking up from where Fox left off. Cold, dead fingers touch my intimate flesh, and I scream.

"Wake up!"

I jolt awake into Varen's bright room, in his bed, him sleeping behind me. Overcast light filters through the gaps in the curtains.

There is no mistaking Bodin's tall, powerfully built frame as he storms toward me, his jaw clenched and eyes blazing with a mixture of fury, concern, and something else—something raw and vulnerable that vanishes as quickly as it appears. Dressed in his usual work shirt and leather breeches, every taut muscle screams of restrained power. I'm reminded I missed an early morning training session, but his reaction seems disproportionate to a simple missed appointment.

My heart still pounds from my nightmare as I rub my sleepy eyes. "Sorry. I forgot about training," I mumble. "I had this weird dream."

"I know," he grunts, his voice rougher than usual. "I was there."

Shit.

Now that I see him in the warm, living flesh, last night's events return to me. Fox. Styx. Me slipping into Varen's bed from loneliness. And then the nightmare, the blood on my hands, the disgust in my friends' eyes. Bodin saw it all.

Grief hits me hard. I close my eyes against the onslaught of emotions but don't get time to process them. Movement beneath my shirt snaps my eyes open. Varen's hand is trapped beneath Fox's borrowed shirt, toying with my breast. He tweaks my nipple, and my body responds with heat, sending liquid desire straight south.

Bodin's nostrils flare, his eyes darkening as they track the movement beneath my shirt. I glimpse the same heated look from my dream before a scowl quickly masks it. His fists clench at his sides as if he's physically restraining himself.

I glance up at the wall behind Varen's bedhead. No dream-catching web sits there like in Fox's room.

Bodin grumbles, "He doesn't need a web. His dreams are fractured nonsense." His voice has an edge, a hint of something that sounds almost like longing.

Heat flushes my cheeks as I tug the shirt down to cover my nakedness—not that Bodin seems to mind. His gaze lingers every place I try to hide, a war of desire and frustration playing across his features.

"I didn't mean for this to—shit, Varen, stop."

Except Varen must hear the word "continue" because he renews his fondling with vigor.

I give a nervous laugh and pull at Varen's hand. "I think we overslept."

Bodin folds his arms, his biceps bulging.

"You shouldn't sleep here at all." The words come out gruff, but an undercurrent of hurt tightens his voice. His eyes flick between Varen and me, a muscle in his jaw ticking.

My pulse beats harder than a dragon's wings in a storm. I roll and face Varen, acutely aware of Bodin's burning gaze on my back. Varen's eyes are closed, but he growls sleepily at my disturbance and mumbles something unintelligible.

"Honey," I whisper and gently cup his face.

Sleep has artfully arranged his dark blueish-black hair into a sexy, messy style that begs me to run my fingers through it. Warm, lust-drenched eyes flutter open and lock with mine. Instead of slowing his amorous intentions, the sight of me arouses them. He growls low and deep from his chest in a husky, masculine way that makes me breathless. He pins my waist, flexing his hips, digging his erection into me suggestively, hungrily.

My mind blanks. Scrambles. I am struck by how normal he is. How male, sexy, and . . . sane. I almost don't want to stop him, but he probably doesn't know what he's doing. Bodin is right. I shouldn't be here in his bed. Not only is there no privacy protection for my dreams, but it's not fair to Varen. We can't be intimate in the same way I am with Fox. He's too vulnerable in this state, too innocent.

I gently pry his fingers from my hips, kiss his knuckles, and hold his hand as his consciousness fully returns ... along with his heartbreaking madness.

CHAPTER 6
WILLOW

Like many fae, we're part beast—I'm wolf-blooded, while Fox and Styx have tails. Ancient texts hint at the Sluagh's avian origins, which are evident in their wings. Our bond gifted them the power to shed their otherness, no longer relying on glamour. Yet their nature as chaos-bringers, death-dealers, and soul-devourers always lingers beneath the surface.

Varen's eyes dart over my shoulder to Bodin, his expression instantly morphing from amorous to fractious. I can almost feel the panic radiating off him.

"The longer an intruder queen stays," he snarls, glaring at the jar of wisps, "the more her pheromones corrupt the hive."

Intruder? My eyes burn as I pull away. He seizes my wrist, desperate to keep me close.

"Varen, we can't."

His jaw clenches, his grip tightens, and pain shoots up my arm. Darkness drowns the warmth in his eyes, hinting at his Sluagh form—a warning wrapped in madness. My sweet Varen harbors an insatiable beast, and I'm not sure it's meant for me.

What if he doesn't release me? What if he loses control?

I'm acutely aware of Bodin's presence behind me, his tension

palpable in the air. Part of me wants to turn to him for help, but another part rebels against appearing weak.

Varen bares his teeth as he yanks me closer. Hunger hardens his gaze into something terrifying, inconceivable from the man who touched me so tenderly moments ago.

"Let go, Varen," I gasp. "You're hurting me."

"Ren." Bodin's hand clamps around Varen's wrist. He tugs, met with resistance and a snarl. "That's enough."

Varen scrambles off the bed and bolts to the fireplace, muttering self-deprecating words. He plunges his hand into the hot embers and retrieves a coal—the stench of burning flesh assaults my nose.

"Varen, no!"

I lunge for him, but he's too strong. He tosses me aside effortlessly. I stumble against the bed, losing my footing.

Varen lurches to the wall, his eyes wild with panic. He reaches out to start sketching but suddenly freezes, his hand hovering inches from the surface. His expression shifts from frantic to dismayed.

"No, no, no!" he shouts, his voice rising in pitch. "Where are they? Where are my markings?"

He begins tearing at the wallpaper frantically, revealing fresh patches underneath. His distress escalates as he uncovers a clean wall.

"Who did this?" he demands, whirling to face us. His eyes lock onto Bodin, narrowing with sudden suspicion. "You! You're helping him hide them!"

Bodin's jaw tightens, his expression a mixture of guilt and resolve as he moves swiftly, positioning himself between Varen and me.

"We're only trying to keep your room clean, Ren," he says, his voice carefully neutral.

But Varen isn't placated. He spits back, "Clean? The yellow jackets are invading, and you're worried about clean?" He turns back to the wall, ripping off more wallpaper with renewed vigor. "They're coming. They'll destroy everything if we can't see the patterns!"

As Varen uncovers another clean patch of wall, he immediately begins sketching with the coal, muttering about combs and honey. His distraught energy fills the room, making the air feel thick and oppressive.

"If we can't repair the combs," he spits between strokes, "we can't keep the honey." He jabs at the shapes, eyes wild. "The walls are broken. No royal jelly for the bees. Too cold for flowers. No pollen. The bees are dying." More angry slashes. "Too cold. Too cold!"

Bodin sighs and sinks into a chair, his expression one of weary familiarity. But beneath that, I glimpse the toll this takes on him—the weight of being the protector, of always having to be strong.

Blood and charred flesh taint the air. Varen's beeisms shift from outward ramblings to inward arguments. He slaps his head, raging about the deafening swarm. He lurches to another wall, shredding more paper for his frenzied sketches.

"I can't think!"

His cry pierces my heart.

"You're going to leave him like this?" I gesture at Varen, turning to Bodin.

"What would you have me do?" His voice is gruff, but I detect a hint of helplessness. "Restrain him?"

Horror twists my gut. "Is that what you've done before?"

"You've wreaked enough havoc for a year in one day. Let him work through his episode. Then you'll explain yourself."

"What?"

He brandishes a folded letter, a low growl reminding me of his authority.

"If not for this, I'd have ended you in your sleep."

His words sting, but I force myself to look beyond them. I see the fear in his eyes—fear of losing control, of failing to protect those he cares about. It's easier for him to be angry than to admit his vulnerability.

"Shut up!" Varen shouts. I whirl to find him screaming at the wall, spittle flying. "I can't hear through the buzzing wings."

"Varen?" I step closer, aware of Bodin tensing behind me.

"Too loud! Too many. Swarming. Swarming!"

He beats his ears violently, smearing charcoal and blood.

Bodin remains motionless, resigned. He must know about Fox. Why else accuse me of causing problems? Surely, Styx explained.

My nails dig into my wounded palm as I clench my fists. The angry slashes from Tinger's pendant remind me why I broke it.

I'm not nothing. Not some insignificant creature to be crushed or trapped.

I glance between them. Varen, crouched in agony, unhinged. Bodin, pain hidden behind a stoic mask, hardened like Fox's stone form. Titania did this. She's the harbinger of calamity, not me.

She stole my power and summoned them, assuming they were still the monsters she'd bound millennia ago. She shattered Varen's mind. She carved that defeat into Bodin's features.

They're not hers.

They're *mine*.

I'm the fucking giant, and I'll find a way to crush her. Seeing them like this—broken and hurting—ignites my fierce protectiveness. I'm their mate. I want to help and heal them.

Clenching my teeth, I lower myself to where Varen crouches by the wall, rocking on his feet and hitting his ears. I feel Bodin's gaze on me, a mix of concern and skepticism.

"Honey," I murmur. "Look at me."

When he doesn't respond, I raise my voice but keep it steady.

"Varen, it's me. Willow." Nothing. "Varen. I'm here—*look* at me." No response. I scramble for something he'll understand, so I add questioningly, "I'm the queen bee?"

He stops rocking but still clutches his head, face forcibly averted from me. Anguish lifts his brows. I may not want to be a queen, but if that's what he needs to hear, so be it. I repeat the name he gives me, using the narrative of his madness to communicate. He meets my gaze. Acute pain has contracted his pupils to pinpricks. It breaks my heart to see him in such agony.

I gently cover his hands and say, "It's okay."

Stop hurting yourself.

His breath comes in ragged pants. Conflicted emotions batter his expression. He wants me to save him, to help him, but his gaze flicks to Bodin, and suddenly, he slams up a wall between us by looking away. He tries to be strong. To be the kind of male who will be the staunch protector, not the protected.

He almost lets me tug his hands from his bleeding ears, but then his eyes roll, and he resists. "Too loud. Too bright." He starts rocking again. "Too hot. Too cold. The hive is too small for everyone. The walls are breaking. They have nowhere to go without combs holding the honey. *Too loud!*"

He no longer hits his ears but tears at his hair.

Although he says nothing, I feel the weight of Bodin's judgmental gaze on my back.

Calamity, I imagine him thinking. Every time I try to fix things, I make them worse.

No.

I'm not going back to that dark place of doubt and insecurity. Fox showed me I am deserving. Tinger showed me I am valued. My parents trusted me enough to let me go and figure things out by myself.

Nothing grows in the shadows, my mother said the night before I left.

I can do this.

I just need to think of what worked in the past—what helped

me calm down when I was irrational with fear and pain? Aunt Rory used to tell me to look at five things around me and name them. But that won't work here. That's for someone still in the realm of sanity.

The answer comes to me from an unexpected place.

When I was little, my advanced shifter hearing made thunderstorms much worse. Once, a storm battered branches onto my father's wooden cabin roof in the mountains. The wind howled louder than a wolf. Everything felt big. My emotions were big. The danger was big. I scrambled into a corner but could still see the shadows flickering. The gap beneath the door screeched like a banshee. The sprites in the fireplace squeaked and hid beneath their log.

I felt small, insignificant, and powerless to stop the fear growing in my belly.

"Come on, squirt," my father said, thumping the bed he sat on. "Hop on the bed."

"No!" I screamed, blocking my ears.

He was the strongest male I knew, a monster hunter, but there were still so many things he couldn't protect me from.

"Why not?" His growly frown only made me want to shrink.

I can't remember my answer—probably more childish screaming—but what I do remember is that his frown went away, and his eyes lit up with an idea. Somehow, he pulled me onto the bed and said, "If the cabin feels too big, squirt, then we'll make it smaller."

He slung a sheet over our heads and made a cocoon. It muffled some of the sounds, but what completely drowned them out was the rowdy tavern song he sang as I burrowed into his embrace.

"Varen," I raise my voice to get his attention. "Come with me, and I'll take you somewhere the loud swarming won't reach you."

I'm unsure exactly what it is, but something buzzes loudly in his head. It started when I pushed him away.

He tries to ignore me, but I take his hands and order, "Your queen bee needs you to cluster around her. Clustering stops the wings from buzzing."

He gives me another inch, so I tug him to his feet, careful not to let him hurt himself further. We climb onto his messy bed together, and I toss the sheet over our heads. The barrier makes the world seem smaller.

I'm acutely aware of Bodin's presence just outside our cocoon. His concern is almost tangible, but he remains silent, allowing me to try.

"It's just you and me here," I murmur. "No buzzing wings. No swarming. Just you and me."

I hug him close, tightening my embrace as my father once did for me. If we make the world smaller, if we drown out the storm with our own voices, we can take control of reality.

Sweet relief pours through me as Varen doesn't pull away. But he doesn't relax. His muscles are rock hard and frozen, locked in terror against whatever horror rattles his mind. I cup his head and desperately try to remember the lyrics to a song, any song, as he clings to me.

But I don't sing. There's no need. Tension suddenly eases from Varen's posture. He presses his ear to my chest and exhales. Another song has captured his attention—my heart.

I catch Bodin's eye through a gap in the sheet. His expression is a mix of approval and something else—a longing quickly masked. I've inadvertently demonstrated a strength Bodin didn't expect. It's a small step, but perhaps it's the beginning of earning his trust, of proving that I can be more than just a source of destruction in their lives.

CHAPTER 7
WILLOW

Just when I think I'm gaining his trust, the sheet rips away, harsh light assaulting my eyes as Bodin's scowling face comes into focus. My stomach drops when I see what he's clutching in his fist.

"I know how that looks," I say, my gaze locked on the jar of wisps. Uncertainty gnaws at me—did Fox tell them about it? About everything that happened with Lord Sylvanar and Puck? "But it's not what you think."

"And what do I think?" Bodin's expression hardens further. "That you manipulated Fox into taking your place in the Cabinet and stole wisps from the queen?"

My heart sinks. "Is that what Styx told you?"

His eye twitches. "Styx?"

Dread unfurls in my gut. "You know, Styx—your Sixth? The one I was supposed to exchange places with?"

"So you admit it."

Shit on a wisp. This is spiraling fast. I notice Varen scowling as my pulse drags with my grief.

"Fox lured me into Titania's temple," I try to explain, "saying we needed to investigate the seals. But the moment we entered, he—"

"Save your excuses for the Knight Commander." Bodin cuts me off with a wave toward the chamber doors.

Doubt prickles my skin, but I need to face this head-on. And I have the enchanted spectacles—it's time I chose who wears them. I retrieve the brass object from where I left it last night.

Bodin rifles through Varen's closet and tosses a coat at me. "Cover yourself."

My stomach growls audibly. "Can I at least grab something to eat first?"

"No." His tone brooks no argument.

Varen shoots Bodin a disgruntled look on my behalf but doesn't relapse into his bee-obsessed mania. He watches curiously as I button his coat over Fox's shirt. The fashion is similarly decadent but with touches of blue. I smile inwardly, imagining Fox curating Varen's wardrobe. I can't picture Bodin doing it. Maybe Legion, but his personal style is far more tame. As Styx put it, everyone else in the hive has far less ostentatious tastes.

Bodin takes advantage of Varen's distraction, wiping blood from his ears with a cloth and inspecting him for injury. When I finish buttoning, Varen turns to Bodin's dangling braids and tugs on them playfully. I might have giggled if worry wasn't gnawing at my insides.

"Is he okay?" I ask, unable to keep the concern from my voice.

Bodin answers with a noncommittal grunt, then rinses the bloody cloth in a bowl on the washstand beside the fireplace. A collection of grooming tools catches my eye. I touch the sharp razor blade, frowning at the metal. It's a stark reminder that something is off in Avorlorna. Magic feels different here. Wilder. Perhaps I'll get answers once someone dons the enchanted spectacles.

"Let's go," Bodin says gruffly.

I offer a mock salute. "Lead the way."

"Stay here, Ren," he orders Varen, then jerks his chin toward the door. "You're fortunate the Nexus has closed for a day of silence after the loss of Earl Sylvanar. Otherwise, your tardiness would have consequences."

As I step into the hallway, I pivot and wave goodbye to Varen. "And where is the study today?"

Bodin slams the door, cutting off my view of Varen, and strides away without answering.

Right. I guess we're heading in that direction—toward their private chambers. Bodin's tall, broad-shouldered form moves with taut purpose, a steady reminder of my precarious situation. I hurry after him barefoot, clutching the wire spectacles like a lifeline and silently praying to the Cauldron's deities that the enchantment will work.

The cool air would be unbearable without the coat. Fox's scent is fading from his shirt, but Varen's coat smells strongly of him. I grab the collar and inhale deeply as we walk. The scent settles something within me, and I can't help but smile. Despite everything, I still feel I belong here. This sense of rightness proves it. The warmth, the fuzzy buzz deep in my soul—it's how I feel with my kin, my family. My thoughts flit to my parents, brother, and little sisters.

I bet those rascals are tearing the house apart without someone to watch them. I'm always finding them in places they shouldn't be. The twins have some kind of secret, silent language that helps them collude and get into mischief. A few weeks ago, I caught Hazel standing guard at my bedroom door while Holly rifled through my nest of valuables. At first, I was outraged, but part of me felt a surge of pride. They'd been watching their big sister and Tinger, taking notes on our thieving ways and putting them into practice.

I wish I'd brought more items with my family's scent, but I inhale Varen's again in their absence.

Bodin glances over his shoulder and stops abruptly. "What are you doing?"

"Nothing." I quickly release the collar. He can't understand, not until his memories return. Averting my gaze, I realize we've stopped before a section of wall that looks different from the others. An iron padlock dangles from a knob on a reinforced door.

"What's in there?" I ask, pointing.

"Nothing," Bodin replies curtly.

I touch the door, and telltale magic tingles across my skin. "Is this the Clock Tower?"

"Let's go." He starts moving again.

My curiosity is piqued. "Cricket warned me never to go inside the Clock Tower. Why?"

Bodin responds by descending a nearby staircase.

"I'm just curious," I persist as I jog to catch up. "Are the locks meant to keep you out as well?"

Each question I fire darkens his mood further. I don't think it's because I'm annoying him, but maybe because he genuinely doesn't know the answers. His brow furrows in frustration, and a flicker of fear passes through his eyes. If he's aware of his unstable memory, it must be terrifying.

We reach the landing a level below and continue along the corridor, passing the cellar kitchen. Hearing our steps, or perhaps Bodin's huffs and grumbles, Geraldine, Max, and Peggy turn their attention to the open doorway. We don't stop. They're clustered around the central counter, facing Marina, who's in full gossip mode. Maybe she's heard about Fox.

When I catch Geraldine's concerned gaze, I have my answer. They know.

A flash of my nightmare hits me behind my eyes. It was warped, wicked, and oh so wrong. All I know is that I'm left with a lingering sense of guilt and shame.

To avoid awkward questions, I quickly wave and force a smile.

Geraldine jumps off her seat, but I shake my head. "See you all for lunch."

I feel her wary eyes following us long after we've turned down another hallway. That human is smart. My false bravado wouldn't have fooled her. The House of Stone Tower burned to the ground last night. Now Fox is suddenly missing. We're back at the Nexus tomorrow to resume training for the exhibition trials. Goodfellow will likely turn up and be bonded to the Baleful Hunt.

We continue onward to a room near the public entry of the Keep. I'd assumed Legion's study would be near his bed chambers or by the library on our level. Maybe the castle shifted it during the night.

Bodin raises his fist and raps sharply on one of the carved double doors. I turn and survey the landscape outside the windows overlooking the courtyard. It snowed again last night, leaving a thin, fluffy blanket of white on every surface. Mist obscures the gate of twisted, enchanted, thorny vines. Not long ago, I watched Fox wave his hand, causing those vines to crack and snap open for our entry. I realize now that security beyond that gate seems lacking. Either people are too afraid of the fae living here, or more hidden protective measures are in place.

A cocktail of familiar smells wafts through as the door opens, revealing who's inside: smoke, cedarwood, leather, absinthe, bergamot, and spice. I turn to enter and sigh as warm air hits my face, comforted by the knowledge that three of my mates are within. The more I say that word to myself, the more it feels right . . . and wrong. It's like I'm living in a future no one else has reached yet. An impatient frown creases my brow, and I slip my hand into my pocket. I touch the spectacles to reassure myself that this won't end with them abandoning me again.

No evil queen is stealing my magic and summoning them away. She's slumbering in her Ivory Palace until Imbolc, just under two turns of the moon from now.

The worst we have to contend with until then is Puck and his inflated ego.

Bodin steps forward, then halts abruptly, and I collide with the solid wall of his back. Male voices filter out of the room.

"Fuck," Bodin grunts. "You took too long. Now we have to wait for the military reports to be delivered." He sighs heavily. "Leaders from around Avorlorna send updates on the state of security during the Gentle Interlude."

His arm sweeps back, his hand resting protectively on my hip. A spark of warmth blooms where he touches. The gesture surprises me. Legion's abrupt order to enter makes him tense, but then he releases a breath and gives a disparaging head shake that rattles his braids. They tickle my face. I have the urge to yank on them as Varen did, just to see how Bodin will react, but he steps forward and ushers me inside.

CHAPTER 8
WILLOW

The warm study is larger than I imagined—like a ground-zero war room. Nero had one like this in his private top-floor conservatory. The association makes me shiver uncomfortably. I wonder if we'll ever be rid of war or if this volatile trait is a permanent fixture here on earth.

Four bookcases flank the left wall like soldiers. A blazing fireplace warms a sitting area on the right. Smack in the center of the room, facing the door, is the Knight Commander's oversized yet simple wooden desk. A tapestry map of Avorlorna hangs behind him. Red and blue pins sporadically mark what I guess is enemy activity.

Legion sits like a king, head bowed as he pores over one of the many documents before him. Emrys looms behind him, gloved leather hands clasped at his front. His black military uniform is spotless, crisp, and clean. It isn't easy to reconcile this version with the one Styx dropped me into earlier this morning.

Speaking of Styx, he lurks in the shadows between two bookcases, nose stuck in a book, pretending not to notice my arrival. It's a lie because we all see each other—my mates and I. We sense it in the minute shifts in the atmosphere. Their comforting scent fills my lungs. It feels so right in here, surrounded by four of them. It feels safe despite the other strangers doing business with the knights.

Two ruddy-cheeked city guards sit in the guest chairs at Legion's desk, waiting for him to read their report. Both have elfin ears, brownish hair, and pale skin. A third unfamiliar male waits in the sitting area, arms folded and glaring impatiently at the guards as though they stole his time slot. His afro hair is cropped close to his scalp. No jewelry adorns his dark fae ears. He keeps his chiseled face in profile, eyes locked on Legion. I'm taking a stab in the dark and guessing he's a House of Stone Radiant. That style of plain clothing was precisely the type Sylvanar favored.

If he's here and decidedly unhappy, it's likely about the lord's death—perhaps he's the new earl.

I want to slink into the shadows with Styx, but Bodin slams the door behind us with such force that my spine rattles. Multiple sets of eyes snap my way. A scratching and wet gnawing sound fills the silence. It seems to be coming from somewhere near the bookcases. The sound stops abruptly when I glance in that direction. My nose twitches with another detected scent . . . raw meat. Maybe Emrys brought some of his work home after all.

The House of Stone Radiant takes in my presentation with disapproving raised eyebrows. I fight the urge to comb my wild strands into order. Varen's coat comes down to my knees, and I am shoeless. If I'd known there would be people here, I'd have fixed myself before entering the room.

One of the two guards cants his head curiously at me. I lock eyes with him and startle. It's Briar—the guard who was kind to me when I arrived in Avorlorna. The last I saw him, he sent me up and away on a Dandelion Drift.

"Briar?" My lips stretch into a warm smile.

He does a double-take and hesitates.

That gnawing and grinding wet sound grows louder again,

coming from the same direction as before. I glance that way again, still seeing nothing unusual.

Confusion pinches Briar's brows. I guess he would see so many people passing through those gates that he wouldn't recognize me. Still, I'm so excited to see a friendly face that I rush toward him, heedless of his growing alarm, grab his shoulders, and grin stupidly in his face.

He laughs nervously. "Um . . . have we met?"

"It's me, Willow O'Leary-Nightstalk." I squeeze his shoulders. "I was the last exhibitor through the gates before it closed for the Gentle Interlude."

"Willow?" Shock splashes over his features, and he cups my elbows, holding me at arm's length so he can inspect me with rapt attention. "Ah, 'tis a joy to see you again. Alive and no longer afflicted by your unfortunate countenance. I must say, you are even more remarkable . . ." Appreciation darkens his eyes as they dart over my face. "How? Wha—wait. Was I correct in assuming you are of the Folk? Captain Sorrel, did I not tell you?"

The captain rounds on me and gasps. "By the Holly King's horn! So you were indeed a trixie-pixie after all. What a cracking jest—almost as good as when he turned the entire Court purple for a week!" He then nods knowingly to Briar. "Glen has truly outdone himself this Interlude. I am eager to see what the crafty lad comes up with for the Solstice Ball."

Briar gives his captain a mollifying look before turning to me and rolling his eyes. It seems the captain thinks everyone is having a jest. I almost want to meet this Glen fellow.

I smile back. "I'm still mortal, sorry. Just no longer cursed."

"It was a curse?" Briar's eyes widen, then soften as he grazes his knuckles on my cheek. "'Tis a travesty to hide such beauty."

His touch lasts a second, and then Bodin shoves him away from me and snarls, "You overstep, guard."

"Ill-mannered swine," Emrys sneers as Briar stumbles into the desk, knocking a report from Legion's hands.

The temperature drops as if the fire has been doused, yet it crackles and burns brightly as before. No one dares breathe. That scratching, gnawing sound has even stopped. The captain's lips flatten at his soldier. Briar's panicked eyes shutter, and he slips on a practiced mask of forced politeness.

"I should not have touched her. You have my deepest regrets." His apology does not affect Bodin's temperament or his fist, which slowly tightens at his side until his knuckles crack.

"Bodin," I whisper harshly. "I touched him first. The fault is mine."

His dark, angry eyes simmer. Fear flips my stomach. That look is unhinged. Primal. What's worse, as I glance around the room, it seems no one will stop him from hurting Briar. The House of Stone Radiant watches it all with amusement from his seat by the fire. Just when I think Bodin will ignore me, he warns Briar through his teeth, "Do not presume such familiarity within our house again."

A small shadow breaks loose from the bookcases—the baby Wild Hunt streaks toward Briar, his fangs out in a snarl. I glimpse blood on his skull muzzle and realize the little dragon must have been eating meat—that was the gnawing sound. And he's still hungry.

"No!"

I tackle the tiny monster as he launches into the air, wrapping myself around his slippery-scaled body. Curved, bony horns almost hit my face, but I dodge. We tumble to the ground. Razor-sharp fangs snap at my face, testing my dominance.

This triggers an alpha urge within me, and I slam him to the ground, growling darkly in his face, "Stop it now." Black, wide eyes roll my way, and I reinforce my command: "He is *not* yum-yums. Do you hear me?"

The baby Hunt whines and thrashes beneath my solid grip. My muscles strain under the weight of his resistance. I almost lose control. Has he grown another inch overnight? He is no longer the size of Tinger but more the size of my sisters in cub form. And just like them, he is strong-willed and mischievous. Unlucky for him, I have four years of practice corralling those little monkeys into obedience.

"So help me, baby Hunt. If you don't submit, I won't feed you scraps under the table. Do you understand?"

The coiled tension relaxes beneath my fingertips. The dragon twists his slippery body. Before I can stop him, he's upon me, licking my face and whimpering apologies. The smell of raw meat on his breath is pungent. I cast a nervous glance around and wipe drool from my face with the back of my hand. The House of Stone Radiant watches with avid curiosity. Briar's jaw has dropped. Bodin's nostrils flare, and his eyes flick to Legion, whose expression has gone cold.

I guess I shouldn't have done that. Manhandling a dragon isn't something an ordinary "mortal" exhibitor—even an esteemed Shadow—would do. This faerie society has laws and codes about acceptable behavior and etiquette according to societal classes. They even have rules about handling dragons. Not only have I arrived in attire decidedly not presentable, but I've behaved out of line amongst superiors. Peablossom would be horrified. Heat floods my cheeks. At least I didn't flash my naked ass at anyone this time.

I don't think so. Shit. Did I?

"Out," Legion clips, his eyes on me.

Biting my lip, I collect the spectacles I dropped sometime during the tackle. Who knows what punishment I'll receive for this? But as I straighten, I frown. It's not me being kicked out. Bodin already ushers the others outside.

"You don't understand, commander," the House of Stone Radiant protests. "Goodfellow already has Titania's vote by proxy."

"That sycophant's been planning this for centuries," Emrys

growls to Legion. "He's positioned himself perfectly—the queen's advisor, now a dragon host. Two votes already in his pocket."

Legion's jaw tightens. He nods with understanding. "If Goodfellow gains control of the Shining Host, he'll have the power to rewrite our laws, restructure our defenses, even alter the Old Code itself. All while Queen Titania slumbers."

The Radiant's eyes bore into Legion. "The House of Stone stands with you, commander. But we need your support. Your vote could be the difference between maintaining order and watching Avorlorna descend into chaos."

"I am well aware of the dangers to Avorlorna, Ser Larkspur," Legion grinds out, eyes flashing.

Bodin takes the earl's shoulder and guides him forcibly to the door, but he breaks away and slams his hand on Legion's desk. "We don't have time for this to wait," he insists. "The Shining Host convenes at moonrise. If we don't act now, it'll be too late."

"You are dancing precariously close to breaking the Old Code protocols."

After a beat of tension, the earl composes himself and plasters a fake smile on his face.

"Good day," he says, then inclines his head. "Your careful consideration of my visit has been most appreciated."

His smile falters when he looks at me. Then he strides out.

"Ensure he is escorted out of the Keep," Bodin instructs the captain.

The gloomy hallway swallows the Radiant's appeal as the captain tugs him away. Briar's eyes lock with mine, and then Bodin shuts the door in his face.

CHAPTER 9

BODIN

The bastard guard dared touch what is ours.

My blood boils with fury. I want to rip out his heart, suck the marrow from his bones, and obliterate the space he takes up in this world. A rage like no other infests my soul . . . and it's all because of her, our Shadow.

I glance at my brothers, noting the growing distance between us. We're hiding secrets when once we were so in tune that we melded our minds, our hearts beating with one desire. Now, with Puck's machinations threatening to tear apart the very fabric of Avorlorna, we should be united. But she's here, and I can't focus.

Keeping secrets is pointless if this intrinsic part of me hasn't changed despite Titania's curse. Legion will always be driven by the need to control. Emrys will always let pain rule his mind. Varen—even caught in madness—will always play with his puzzles. Fox will poke and lay traps to test our affections. Styx will always be restless, always hungering for the warmth we cannot give him.

I am the Knight Marshall of the Queen's Hive. I should be dependable, lethal, loyal, and adaptable. I should blend into soci-ety's vital surface and never reveal my true nature. I should be forgettable, not this loud, boisterous, hungry nonsense infecting me whenever she is close.

But the clouds in my mind make it hard to remember why I must be these things. The political machinations blur and fade while she remains in sharp focus. A distraction. A danger. Just like . . .

The thought eludes me. My nostrils flare as I inhale to steel my patience at this infuriating state of mind, but Willow's scent lingers like the sun's warmth after dusk. It refuses to allow me a moment's peace. Always there. Always around the corner of the night, whispering a promise of its return.

You'll never escape your true nature.

A flash of memory: golden feathers crushed in my fist, blood on my hands. A little canary silenced forever. But it wasn't a canary, was it? The truth slips away like sand through my fingers, leaving only guilt and the overwhelming need to protect.

The earl's words echo in my mind: "One more vote and Puck controls everything." The weight of our responsibility crashes down upon me. I should be strategizing and planning our defense. Instead, my eyes are drawn to her wild silver hair, her bare feet.

I remind myself I am the quiet ebb of water. I am dismissed until I perceive a threat. Then, and only then, will I rise like a wave and crush the danger, dragging it beneath the surface before our society's joyful mien and manner are indistinguishable from the beasts.

My rage stills for only seconds while I stare at our Shadow. The wildling flaps its wings and circles her legs. Her existence shatters Titania's illusion of decorum.

Look at her—wild silver hair unkempt and akimbo from her tussle with the dragon. Varen's jacket buttoned unevenly. She strolls around the castle without undergarments, sleeps in Fox's stolen shirt, and invites herself into beds other than hers. She leaves a piece of herself wherever she goes. She is the picture of chaos, of flames flickering brightly, and she couldn't give a fuck.

She is the wildest creature I know. When I stumbled into her unguarded dreamscape and found her in Varen's bed, petty jealousy overwhelmed me. Ever since, my cold, hard body has craved her soft warmth.

Darkness cannot understand sunshine.

I have forgotten much but know I cannot hold back when taking what I want. This intrinsic hunger is carved into my being. Sometimes, fractured memories bubble past the seals binding us and pop into my mind. I've caught enough to know I cherish possession more than any other war prize.

I hunt. I chase. I keep . . . and . . .

"Ignore my warnings all you want," a faceless queen hisses at us, at me, at the crushed sunshiney feathers in my fists, "but you'll never escape your true nature. The result will be the same. You will always be drawn to bright, sparkling, warm things because you wish to possess, study, and be like them." Blood spatters on my skin. Drips onto the floor. "Darkness cannot understand sunshine. It can only consume it the way night swallows day."

The memory fades, leaving me shaken.

I am the Second, the Knight Marshall, the protector, and I have allowed this hive to fall apart. It feels like I have held dusk's breath within my lungs for eternity, hoping and hungering for the sun's return.

It never came.

Not until Fox planted his pussy-wet lips on my own and breathed scalding, sweet life into me.

She is a calamity, ripping apart five years of stability and control in five days. She is a natural disaster, a force of destruction, and a danger in my world.

I will always ache to possess the wild, untamable thing with the brightly burning soul. I will always hunger to learn what makes it so appealing. I will pick it apart and flay it with my passion and need. And I will always, always consume it until nothing is left but my grief and regret.

Crushed golden feathers in my bloody fist.

The wildling curls around Willow's ankles, snarling at me as if it knows what I'm thinking: *Snuff out her brilliance or bathe in it?*

Either way, she won't survive me. I killed something bright once, something I was meant to protect.

The thought leaves me unsettled.

As does the realization that I've let my guard down in my fixation on her. Puck could be moving his pieces while I stand here, distracted. I am the Knight Marshall. I must protect. But from what? From whom? The curse clouds my mind, leaving only the certainty that she is the key to everything.

And she has distracted me once more.

CHAPTER 10
WILLOW

It feels like a strange dream inside Legion's study. Only a week ago, my problems revolved around avoiding babysitting duties and deciding which house to rob next. Now, I'm back in the middle of a war, caught between politics. The only difference is no one is using me as a tool. And I am mated to six demigods. Bodin's possessive reaction proves our connection is trying to push through Titania's enchantment.

He glares at me with expressive eyes, yet the rest of him is hard and unyielding. I should be angry—he shoved Briar. But as I look into his eyes and find vulnerability beneath the violence, I want to know why he tries to hide it. What happened in his very long life that shaped his personality? It's hard to believe this reaction is born of Titania's recent false narrative. It's something else, something deeply experienced.

Emrys hasn't moved an inch since the door closed. His rusty-colored eyes are always filled with so much bitterness. Styx lurks in the shadows between the bookcases, still pretending to read. Why do they distrust me so much? This version of them doesn't even know me. So what did the other queens do to them?

And then there is Legion. He watches me, patiently, steadily. He is the First, the Knight Commander. He is too beautiful, enigmatic, and sophisticated to go unnoticed on a battlefield. The buttons on his double-breasted silk waistcoat accentuate his broad shoulders and athletic frame. His black silk shirt sleeves are rolled casually to his elbows, revealing muscular forearms as they rest on his desk. Long, silken hair falls from a widow's peak. His skin is so pale and luminous that it reminds me of carved crystal. It was he who reached for me on that battlefield and locked elegant fingers around my ankle.

He who called me nothing.

And I called them monsters.

But I don't think that makes Legion appear so sad and haunted. He probably doesn't even remember now that Fox is gone. No, he seems to be the type who cannot be shaken from his foundations. Once he wants something, he takes it. He does not care if he must wait eons for the right time or opportunity. His hidden torment comes from somewhere else, and I want to know where. I want to banish it from his eyes so he is free to smile.

Just once.

"Willow." A warning tone deepens his voice. He never once lowers his eyes from mine.

"Yes, Legion?" I return, blinking innocently. Maybe I also want to ruffle his control. Ignoring the rules always felt so liberating to me before. They should all try it sometime.

"Sir," he reminds me curtly. "I am your Lord Knight Commander. You will address me—all of us—as sir."

Baby Hunt bares his fangs at Legion, whose brows raise incredulously. Laughter peals out of me. Does Legion's arrogance come from this false identity, or was he born with it? He clearly believes even a baby dragon with "wild" in its name should act tame around him.

"Aww, you little terror cutie." I scratch the soft scales around baby Hunt's skull. "You can't help being protective when everyone here is a big fat grump." He thumps his hind leg, tongue lolling in pleasure as I deepen the scratch. "But I love you. I promise you yum-yums as soon as we get out of here." When my stomach growls, I add, "I'm starving too."

"Bodin," Legion clips.

A grunt behind me warns of Bodin's approach. He scoops up the baby dragon and tosses him outside the study before closing the door. He turns to me and arches an eyebrow as if to say, *Checkmate.*

The sounds of destruction travel through the gap beneath the door. They should have let me entertain the dragon. At least we would have saved the furniture.

Bodin stalks to where Styx lurks and retrieves something I can't distinguish. He unwraps strips of shadow to reveal the jar of stolen wisps. Holding my gaze, he crosses to Legion's desk and drops it with a thunk.

All eyes narrow on me. After a moment, I ask, "You all remember you can't get into my head, right? Styx can only project his thoughts to me or listen to mine . . . well, apparently, I shout them anyway. The point is, I'm not a mind reader. If you have a question, ask it."

A fee-lion seems to have caught their tongues because they're baffled by my statement. I collect the jar and slide my butt onto the desk, crinkling the papers as I get comfortable.

Styx finally leaves the shadows and walks to stand beside Bodin. Every instinct in my body wants to look at him—to inspect his clothes and compare them to Fox's "ostentatious" fashion sense. Instead, I swing my legs and inspect the little balls of trapped magic.

"Why do you think Titania is hoarding these in her temple with the treasures?" I muse. "More importantly, why aren't any found in nature? Where have all the wisps gone?"

Silence.

I glance up and catch multiple gazes averting from my bare legs. Someone clears their throat, and a smirk tugs at my lips. They can't fight their attraction to me even when they're magically bound to forget their true natures. There is a saying in Elphyne—the Well wants what it wants. It means we can't fight fate. If the Well blesses a union, there is no stopping it. My parents fought their attraction to each other. My brother fought his attraction to Laurel. Leaf—the most stubborn Guardian of all, fought his fate so hard that he sent himself on missions in the opposite direction of my mother's psychic guidance to find his Well-blessed mate. He was happy being broody and lonely for the rest of his life. As it turned out, his mate Nova turned up anyway. She was someone he loved and lost centuries ago.

"All streams lead to the Wellspring," Styx mutters, then realizes he spoke aloud and faces the war map with a scowl.

"Listening in on my thoughts?" I tease him, mind to mind.

Sensing I've made his brother uncomfortable, Emrys snarls and snatches the jar from my fingers.

"Explain yourself, Shadow." Legion frowns at my legs. "And kindly remove yourself from my desk."

So polite. So faerie. Ugh.

Some possessive part of me wants to get a rise out of him. It wants to obliterate that faerie decorum. It belongs to Titania and her stupid, fake rules and stupid, fake pleasantries.

Styx shoots me a curious sideways glance, and I assume he heard my thoughts. In the temple, he became quite impish when I warned him not to break the jars of wisps. He broke more.

"I'm quite comfortable here, thank you," I answer Legion and swing my legs.

"Give me one turn of the hourglass with her in my chambers," Emrys promises darkly.

"Your *bed* chambers?" My eager tone makes him balk. I almost laugh. I don't think I've ever seen him confused or awkward like this.

"Give me half a turn," Bodin offers with a growl. "That's all I need to crush her insolence."

I pretend to consider it. "Well, crushing sounds kind of hot if it involves me between the two of you."

"Thirty seconds," Styx counters.

"*Crimson*, Styx." I laugh, shaking my head in disbelief. "Thirty seconds?"

"One second," he corrects, baring his sharp, monstrous fangs.

"*I hope you last longer than that,*" I tease, mind to mind.

"What?" He blinks.

"*In the bedroom,*" I explain, waggling my brows. "*You're going to need to last longer than one second—correction, longer than thirty seconds—if you want to keep up with me. Fox could go all night.*"

His gaze dips to my swinging legs.

"Enough," Legion snaps, gripping my calf to halt the next swing. "Remove yourself from my desk, Willow, or we will do it for you."

Our eyes collide. My whole world starts in that connection but ends where his warm grip zings electricity into my limbs. I see a hint of desperation in his expression and remember what brought me here. Fox is gone.

"Fine." I sigh, sliding from his desk and onto a guest chair. "Explain what?"

"Everything," Legion replies. "What happened with Fox? How did you release Styx if you have no magic? How did you get out of the temple?"

Emrys slams the jar onto the desk. "Why did Bodin find that by your side as you slept in Varen's bed?"

"Were you planning on returning to"—Bodin pauses as he pulls a crumpled letter from his pocket, unfolds it, and scowls to read—"Elphyne?"

"With Varen?" Legion adds, his brows puckering. "Were you going to take him with you?"

"Whoa, whoa. One outrageous claim at a time." I blink

rapidly, processing which of their questions to tackle first. Wait. "What's in the letter?" I ask. "Did Fox write it?"

He didn't write *me* a letter. He let me believe everything was fine until it wasn't. No one answers.

"You clearly know what happened." I gesture at Styx. "He's here. Fox isn't because he blindsided me. He . . ."

Cherish me.

His angst-ridden voice crashes into my mind. I squeeze my eyes closed against the memory, but it's no use. *Cherish me. Cherish me. Cherish me.* Each time it repeats, I remember new details. His voice broke with emotion. He was afraid. Doubtful. I hold my breath and wish away the agony. I pray to the Well, and my tears don't spill.

"Show me," Styx whispers into my mind.

I shake my head. *"It hurts too much."*

Instead, I slip my fingers into my pocket and grip the spectacles until they cut into my wounded palm. The pain grounds me. It reminds me of my purpose.

"These are for you." I hand Legion the spectacles. "A gift from Fox."

Bodin intercepts, stealing them. Just like that, the illusion of my control vanishes. I snarl and launch at him, but he holds the spectacles high over his head. He is an immovable mountain of muscle. Every ounce of my training to disarm someone like him flees my mind. All I can think is that Fox honored me with that choice. It was a gift. The right is mine.

"Don't put them on," I warn, jumping for the prize, but he keeps jerking them out of reach. "They're not for you."

"I am the Knight Marshall," he snaps, dark eyes flashing. "Gifts go through me."

"They're probably cursed," Styx adds, circling me like a hungry wolf. "She's hiding something from me."

The door bursts open. Varen storms in and heads straight for

Legion, the baby Hunt hot at his feet. He slams his palms on the desk and shouts, "We're out of honey!"

I've never been happier to see him. Bodin's hand briefly lowers in the distraction, and I jump, snagging the spectacles. I dart around the desk, intending to throw myself on Legion and shove them on his face.

But my steps falter when I find him already watching me, ignoring Varen's continued demands. Does he know? I make a split decision and drop to my knees, a silent plea in my eyes as I look up at him.

By now, the others have caught on to what happened. Varen distracted them. Styx *flickers* to Legion's side, his eyes bleeding into black. Small conical spikes erupt over his brows and knuckles, and he bares a mouth full of razor-sharp fangs. Bodin and Emrys crowd closer, ready to protect their First at a moment's notice.

A Nightmare once called Legion a prince. Right now, with all of us centered around him, I have no doubt they were right.

Fox showed me a book filled with their history. These Sluagh are six of the original seven born of the Morrigan—the Cauldron's deity of chaos. He alluded to King Oberon owning and controlling them once. But that's not the type of royalty I think the Nightmare spoke of. They can't all be princes of the underworld. Fox and Bodin weren't called princes.

I look into Legion's beautiful, expressive eyes and see the heavy burden of leadership. I see a cunning, ruthless male willing to do anything to protect the innocent people of Avorlorna. I see a blue, glimmering teardrop beneath his left eye and am reminded of the goodness inside of them.

He might be arrogant, abrupt, and bossy, but his brothers respect him—even if they don't remember why.

"Fox enchanted these." I lift the brass spectacles higher. "So the wearer can see through Titania's forgetting curse—or whatever makes you forget who you really are. The enchantment works only for the original wearer and can't be transferred. He also said the choice is mine." I feel a dash of guilt when Styx recognizes them from the temple. He probably wonders why I didn't choose him. Or Emrys. Or Bodin. I can't look any of them in the eyes because the only answer is there can be no room for disobedience. "I choose you, Legion."

CHAPTER II
WILLOW

Legion delicately takes the spectacles, his eyes narrowed. His finger tentatively pokes through a circular space for the eyes. Unlike the spectacles old-worlders wear for correcting blurred vision, these have no glass lenses. A perplexed look crosses his features.

"Fox said to pretend they're a fashion adornment." I shrug. "That no one will suspect they're enchanted because of the brass, and you're—"

"A Guardian," he finishes.

"Yes. No one knows what that blue mark means."

"She's obviously lying." Styx tries to snatch them, but Legion glares and holds them away. Disgruntled, Styx folds his arms and explains, "I can't see into her head, so how can we trust her?"

"I'm sorry, Styx," I sigh. "The only reason I didn't choose you in the temple was because I don't know you yet." I cast a nervous glance around the room. Varen has fallen silent and watches me curiously. "I don't really know any of you yet."

"You think I'm jealous?" Styx bares his fangs, flashing that devilish side of him again. "I couldn't care less what you think of me."

"Hush," Legion murmurs.

Styx's expression drops. "You can't be considering this."

"She freed you from your prison," Legion reminds him, then points to Fox's crumpled letter in Bodin's hands. "In his own words, he absolves her from wrongdoing."

Love for Fox swells in my heart. Of course he wouldn't leave me without ensuring they wouldn't blame me. He probably repeated the same offer in the letter that he did in Titania's temple—he gave me the choice to take the wisps and use them to return to Elphyne. I dash a tear from my eye.

"Legion," Bodin warns. "Think about this with a clear head."

"It is imbued with powerful magic." Legion turns the spectacles over, angling the brass to catch the firelight. "It feels like us, like Fox. Perhaps we can make more."

"I agree with our brother," Emrys snaps. "This female is naught but an interloper. Perhaps your lack of memories is a blessing when our history is full of suffering."

"Hiding from the truth is not the answer," Legion returns, gaze shifting to the map behind his desk. His finger taps on the brass frames as he considers the pins, marking enemy activity. "Our war is with Nocturna, not Willow O'Leary-Nightstalk from Elphyne."

Before anyone can stop him, Legion looks at me, slides the spectacles on, and doubles over in pain. Black silken strands fall to shield his face, and his trembling hands clench and press against his forehead. He emits little shallow grunts as if breathing hurts.

I lurch forward, horrified.

"It shouldn't hurt!" I cry. "I'm so sorry. I—"

An unseen force—Styx's wraith—wrenches me away.

"What did you do?" His guttural snarl holds an edge of panic.

"Remove the spectacles," Bodin barks, barging into the space. Emrys is already there, gloved hand groping for the brass frames.

My arms are pinned, squished to my body. It's as though Styx stands behind me, clamping me with his hands. Varen shouts something about the buzz and covers his ears. Baby Hunt howls. It is pandemonium.

Emrys latches onto Legion's long hair and yanks his head back, exposing his neck and face. His dark eyes are wide. Sweat dapples his skin. Every tendon and muscle is pulled agonizingly taut. He seems paralyzed with pain. Bodin tries again to pluck the spectacles, but Legion's hand jerks up, blocking him.

"Wait," he grunts. "I remember."

I wish I could feel relief. But what if this process kills him? What if it does to his mind the same thing that happened to Varen? With Puck's scheming, we can't afford that.

Eons of history return to him through the enchantment. Hundreds and hundreds of years. Thousands. Tens of thousands. The past five years probably occupied only a thimble-sized space in his mind.

My heart pounds hard as Bodin hesitates. What if it doesn't work? What if they kill me right here, right now? I am a fragile mortal compared to them—even with their powers dimmed from the seals. Styx's wraith only needs to sneeze, and he would break my bones. The Sluagh himself paces wildly alongside the desk.

A sense of foreboding fills me when he stops and stares, chin dipped, looking at me through dark, wavy locks like I'm dinner. I hate knowing nothing about him. I hate that I'm still no one to him.

"Please don't," I whimper and struggle against his wraith. "Let me go."

Suddenly, the pressure against my arms falls away. Styx's eyes widen. His complexion turns ashen as his skull briefly illuminates, and his wraith returns to his body. I don't think he called his wraith back.

For a moment, I'd forgotten the lesson Fox painstakingly learned when I almost drowned. They can't use their magic on me unless I give my permission. It's part of the queen-hive bond.

I rub my sore arms and say, "I am already partly bonded with the six of you. Titania isn't your true queen. I am. You can't harm me with your magic. You can't force your way into my mind. You can't *flicker* or heal me without permission."

Fear flashes in his eyes, and it breaks my heart. He hesitates, but I can tell he believes me. He's probably piecing together the evidence. I reach for him, but he steps back.

"Styx," I whisper. "I'm not like the others, I promise. Like it or not, we're all in this together. None of us had a choice. Give me a chance."

His doubt vanishes, and he is again the picture of violence. "Perhaps I can't use magic directly on you, but you are mortal. I can still crack open your ribs and feast on your heart."

"This might be true." I shrug. "But pointless. You just said it— I am mortal. Titania stole my magic. I can't hurt you even if our bond allowed it."

"What do you mean, allowed?" Bodin asks, eyes narrowing.

"It means that I am your mate. We are equals. Even if I had magic, I can't use it to entrap or hurt you any more than you can with me. The worst we can do is steal each other's magic without permission." I roll my eyes. "I know this because my mom complains that my dad does it sometimes and surprises her."

"Clarke." Legion rests his head against closed fists, his shoulders sinking.

"Yes!" I gasp, heart soaring. "And Rush. You remember?"

He nods, trembles, and breathes with stilted gasps but keeps his head in his hands.

A frown pinches my brows. I can do nothing for him now except wait it out.

Fox said he had to constantly remind them of the truth—but it worked. Maybe that's all I need to do now. Turning to the others, I show them my wounded palm. "When Fox activated the spell in the temple to swap with Styx, I broke the glass containing Tinger's wisp—"

"Who is Tinger?" Bodin barks.

"My friend from Elphyne. That one drop of his mana filled me with enough power to trigger our bond. You all must have felt it as I did. Your magic poured into me from six different places. My mating mark turned blue—like your Guardian blessings. The same mark appeared on Fox's neck and Styx's. But when Tinger's magic waned, I was left empty again. The bond faded."

At their confusion, I deflate and scrub my face. Maybe this won't work coming from me.

Legion makes a pained sound that draws our attention. He is hunched over, seized. His fists are clenched so tight that his fingernails cut his palms. A trickle of blood winds down each wrist, following the path of a distended vein until it hits a folded black cuff.

I fall onto my knees before him and gently place my hands over his fists. He vibrates with tension and continues to give low, shallow grunts of pain with each hissed intake of breath. What is it that hurts him so much? What memories are causing the pain? Or is it simply the load of so many, so fast?

"Legion," I whisper. "I don't know if you can hear me, but we're all here if you need anything."

All here except Fox.

I tighten my grip on his hands—but they're much larger than mine. It feels as ineffectual as a mouse gripping a lion.

"Try to breathe," I add. "Inhale deeply and exhale slowly. It might take time to adjust to your memories."

His hands flip to capture mine and squeeze. Hard. I try not to gasp from the pain. Instead, I repeat my instructions. Slowly, breath by breath, he stops trembling. Through the curtain of his hair, his long, thick lashes lift. Our eyes lock. The power of his recognition is visceral, robbing me of breath. Every doubt I've ever had about our connection, about me, about the world is washed away under the weight of his emotion.

"You came." His hoarse whisper sounds almost awed, baffled,

as if I am too good for him—for them. As if he's the one who is awkward and unsure of himself.

A tentative smile touches my lips. "To be fair, I came because I wanted to kill you all."

Styx snarls at the threat.

"But you didn't." He gives his Sixth an amused, affectionate glance. It reminds me of a look Rory once gave me when she found me hiding from Alfie and his friends playing Kiss-Chasey. I told her boys gross me out, so I hid. *Just wait,* her look said. *One day, you'll think differently.* Legion's gaze suddenly darkens on me, and he lowers his voice. "So, you and Fox . . ."

A blush rises to my cheeks. I bite my lower lip and nod. Some kind of peace settles in his eyes. There are no words to describe how he makes me feel at this moment. After suffering from eons of memories, it is the knowledge Fox and I found comfort in each other's arms that gives him relief. It tightens my chest, connects us, and sings all at once.

His gaze hardens as he turns my palms face up.

"No one has healed you," he mutters darkly, staring at the puffy wounds left by Tinger's pendant. "May I?"

On my nod, he traces a finger in circles around my wounds. Magic itches my skin as it heals, sending shivers throughout my body. When it's done, he helps me to my feet.

"This is ridiculous," Styx snaps. "She has ensorcelled you. It's obvious."

The others look at me with a mix of caution and curiosity. The warmth I glimpsed in Legion leeches away until he is the same indomitable leader as before. Except for the blood streaking his forearms, a few stray hairs out of place, and the spectacles, which I might add, only serve to make him even more attractive.

He lets go of my hands and scolds, "Don't wait so long next time to ask."

"Yes, sir." I give him a salute, and his lips flatten. But I'm sure I glimpse a dash of that affectionate amusement before he locks it down and faces his hive.

"Willow," he says quietly. "Go get cleaned up and find something to eat. I'd like a moment alone with my brothers."

CHAPTER 12
BODIN

As I lean against the door, my eyes catch on a painting hanging slightly askew on the opposite wall. I cross the room in two swift strides and adjust the frame, aligning it perfectly with the others. The simple act releases tension within me.

With Fox gone and *Styx* returned, even my thoughts feel untethered. The castle itself seems made of transient thoughts, as insubstantial as mist. But at least our Shadow has left and taken her intoxicating scent with her.

Legion releases a strangled, furious sound. Tension coils in his posture. He stares hard at his desk, the reports and the war map pinned to the wall behind him. Then he looks at us in turn, and his demeanor grows incandescent and dark.

He is not one to lose control of his emotions. Even in my gut, where I know our history is stored, I feel this statement's truth. So when the room dims as his fury sucks the light and his fists tremble, I take a step in Varen's direction, the weakest among us. He sits by the hearth, lost in a puzzle of his own making—strips of kindling and bones, leftovers from the wildling's snack.

Legion sees my protective move, directs his gaze down, and

roars his fury. He swipes his desk clean of papers, quills, inkwells, and the jar of trapped wisps clatters to the floor. Then he braces himself against the desk, head bowed, breathing ragged.

This is not control. This is catastrophe with its claws in all of us.

Amidst a sea of scattered papers and spilled inkwells, I lock eyes with Emrys, then Styx, a slight tilt of my head conveying my concern.

My muscles coil, ready to spring into action at the slightest provocation.

"Pay attention," Legion's harsh, guttural voice cuts through the tense silence. "Because I will only say this once. If *any* of you allow our queen to suffer again, I will disembowel you and string your entrails over the mantlepiece until you have learned your lesson. Understood?"

I blink, stunned into silence. So many parts of that statement don't make sense.

"Hardly fair," Emrys drawls, "considering our current afflictions prevent us from following your decree to the letter."

Legion's hand hits the desk. "Do not belittle your intelligence by feigning ignorance of my true meaning, Emrys."

"I have a question." Styx raises a hesitant hand. "What suffering are you talking about, the cut on her palm?"

Legion glares through the curtain of his hair, jaw clenched until Styx's facetiousness fades. Only then does he straighten, fix his shirt, and calmly reply, "For eons, the word suffer has only had one definition: *us*."

Stupid question, Styx. He hears my thoughts and rolls his eyes, then continues aloud.

"Let's say," he waves his hand around. "For shits and giggles, and unless you want me to dip into your mind . . . be precise, brother."

"The most recent incident is her wounded palm." His eyes

turn inward, self-deprecating. "I admit, I was also to blame. It is unforgivable."

The others stare at him, holding their peace. Perhaps out of fear or respect. Not me.

I fold my arms and say, "If you admit to this oversight without your memories, how are we expected to uphold this impossible task?"

He drops into his chair, his expression defeated for a moment before he gathers his composure.

"Which is why," he growls, "I now give this order as your Knight Commander, your First, and your Last." His emphasis on the final word drops the temperature in the room to arctic. "If any of you willingly or negligently allow our queen to suffer, then there will be consequences."

A low growl builds in my chest, my teeth aching to elongate into fangs I don't have. I swallow hard, forcing the sound back down. Even Varen looks up from his mystery puzzle, wary.

The dragon takes advantage, slinks out from beneath a couch, and tentatively bites a bone. Varen snarls at him and snatches it back. A tug-of-war ensues, and I walk over to break it up.

Styx strides to the desk, fearlessly meeting Legion's gaze. "The mortal is not our fated queen."

"Stop fooling yourself," Legion mumbles, retrieving the fallen jar of wisps and turning it over in his hands. "The sooner you fall in line, the better."

"Perhaps it's time to step out of line."

Legion levels his stare on our Sixth, darkness flickering in every corner of the room. "Is that a challenge?"

A pause. "Maybe."

"Styx," Emrys warns, "do not test him."

"Why not? He is impotent, as you all are. Not me. For once, I am—fuck!" Wings erupt from Styx's back, ripping apart his dark shirt. Dismayed, he glances over his shoulders. "Why are they fucking doing that? Our wings never used to do that!"

"Be thankful it is not your tail."

"This could happen with my tail?"

"Maybe you instinctively keep it shifted away like your horns and spikes." Legion slides his fingers beneath his spectacles, rubbing his eyes. "We started bonding with Willow the moment we first touched her five years ago. We've absorbed her ability to shift forms. Fox was the same. Before her, our wings were always out, simply glamoured away."

"That makes sense," I cautiously reply, my mind racing to process this new information.

Shifting, as opposed to glamouring, provides numerous tactical advantages. Improved stealth capabilities, easier movement in tight spaces, and better ability to blend in with mortals when necessary. But it also means we'll need to develop new fighting techniques to compensate for the sudden appearance or disappearance of wings in battle. Kinetic energy from the shift could be useful.

At Styx's disgruntled concession at the logic, Legion's eyes fill with patience. "You will all feel confused and conflicted until we break the seals. So you must do as I instruct until we are whole and united again."

"Don't we anyway?" Distaste twists Emrys's lips, but he gives a reluctant nod.

"You know where I stand," I reply.

"By the door?" Styx snarks.

My fist clenches. "Do you wish to sleep bruised tonight, brother?"

"You'd have to catch me first."

I take a threatening step toward him. He grins and *flickers* across the room to stand by the fireplace. He can outmaneuver me with his seal broken, but inevitably, mine will be too. Fortunately, the fool still recalls how precarious the sixth position is in the hive.

The true meaning of my thoughts slips. I grasp to catch it, but it's gone. I am left with only a strange sense of guilt and walk backward, creating distance between us until my spine hits the door.

Legion turns to Styx. "Is there anything you recall about how your seal was broken?"

"As I told you before, I last remember feeling like I walked into a trap."

Legion mutters darkly, "I sent you on a mission—the Interlude had just begun, and like now, rogue Nightmares were surfacing. You were being petulant as always, wanting to go off alone for some reason. Emrys, you broke the news about his punishment for public brawling."

"Did I?" His dark brows knit.

Legion waves him off. "You won't remember much. The enchantment keeps sending your memory in circles."

"I think I would remember something like that." He scowls, grinding his jaw.

Emrys prides himself on being direct. These clouds in our heads are likely causing him more distress than me.

"There was no brawling," Styx snarls. "They lied, and you left me there to rot."

We all look at each other, fear skating down our spines. It feels odd, foreign. Fear has no place in our world except within the hearts of our victims, the wicked souls we feast upon. I roll my shoulders, trying to shake off the unfamiliar sensation.

"We forgot." Legion's tone is flat as he studies his hands. "And it is unforgivable."

Legion's admission of guilt catches me off-guard. For a moment, I see not our unshakable leader but a vulnerable, flawed being. The urge to step forward, to shield him from the others' gazes, is almost overwhelming. Instead, I straighten my posture, drawing attention to myself and away from his moment of weakness. The hive needs strength now, not vulnerability.

"We will continue to investigate," Legion promises Styx, then looks each of us in the eyes. "The end of our suffering is finally within our grasp. Our queen is with us . . . and by some miracle, she looks fondly at me—even at you miscreants." That last bit sparks amusement in his eyes. When we don't laugh, he deadpans. "You've all lost your humor, it seems."

"Perhaps you need to work on your jokes," Styx returns sourly, although his lips twitch.

Legion looks to me for help, but I show my palms in surrender and mutter, "What would I know about humor?"

"Jokes are a muttonheaded mortal pastime," Emrys huffs and idly takes a stick from Varen's makeshift honeycomb diagram to poke the embers with.

"I find them fun," Styx counters.

Varen launches to his feet, snatches the stick, and glowers as he sinks down again. Emrys gives an exaggerated apologetic look, then purposefully sits on the sofa beside Varen and starts poking holes in his diagram's logic. The ensuing bickering grinds Legion's jaw but strangely brings music to my heart.

"And what of the earl's warning?" I ask. "The Shining Host convenes at moonrise tonight."

Emrys gestures at the map of Nightmares. "What of that?"

Legion's eyes glitter as he taps his finger on the jar of wisps. "Leave Puck up to me."

"So, he survived." Styx rolls his eyes. "I should have killed him, but Willow didn't want me to reveal my powers."

"She was right to stop you," Legion confirms, eyes landing on Varen. "Puck won't have control of the Baleful Hunt for long."

"Tonight, then." I nod.

A fierce protectiveness surges through me. We may be fractured, our memories in tatters, but our bond remains unbroken. Whatever storms lie ahead, I will be the bulwark that shields my hive from harm.

It's not just duty—it's who I am.

CHAPTER 13

WILLOW

Getting cleaned up in Fox's shower doesn't take long. The scent of his soap lingers on my skin, comforting my frayed nerves. Still, being near water makes my heart race, so I avoid the bath. Not wanting to be alone with my thoughts, I dress quickly in leather training breeches and one of Fox's shirts, its fabric soft against my skin. I wrap a woolen shawl around my shoulders, its warmth a poor substitute for his embrace.

My wolf side perks up, nostrils flaring. My friends are still in the kitchen, but Marina's gossip has given way to the clatter of meal preparation. The salty aroma of broth makes my mouth water. As I approach, I hear the rhythmic thud of Geraldine peeling potatoes, the scrape of Peggy's wooden spoon against the pot, and Cricket rummaging in a sack beneath the butcher block. The mood has plummeted since I last passed by; tension hangs thick in the air.

"Hi," I say, forcing a smile as I step into the kitchen. "Is it too late for lunch?"

Cricket's hands collide in a sharp clap as she turns, her smile

faltering as her gaze meets mine. "Not at all, love. I was just telling your friends—" Her jaw drops, eyes widening.

"Is everything okay?" The hair on the back of my neck rises, sensing the sudden shift in the room.

"I . . . ah . . ." Cricket stammers.

"Your face," Geraldine blurts, her eyes darting between mine. "It's . . . I mean . . ."

Fear squeezes my heart, cold and sharp. My fingers fly to my cheeks, but the curse is gone. My skin feels smooth beneath my touch, except for my left side's faded scars.

"I broke the curse," I mumble, suddenly feeling exposed, like a nerve stripped raw.

"A curse?"

"Titania placed it on me." I can't meet their eyes now. Tears prick at the corners of my vision, threatening to spill over. How can I explain the way the curse was designed to make me look as ugly as I feel? I haven't told them what Nero made me do, that he's the man who destroyed their world, what else I woke from the dead, the people I killed.

I still feel shame and self-loathing . . . but also a dark part of me thrills when I hold someone else's life in my hands. I fear it's something intrinsic and not just learned from an evil man. What if it's me? What if I'm born with that ugliness? What if they think I'm a chip off Nero's block? After all, what kind of person is the perfect mate to six demigods of chaos?

My new friends would turn on me if they knew the truth.

Without Fox here, it feels like I'm missing a vital piece of myself. The urge to go to him thrums beneath my skin, a constant, maddening itch.

"Sit down, poppet." Cricket slides a stool out for me, its legs scraping against the stone floor. "Tell us what happened."

"Yes, please do." Marina's worried tone draws my gaze to her painting. The mermaid's iridescent tail slaps anxiously against her rock, creating ripples in the painted water. "Tell us what happened to dear Master Foxy-woxy."

The sky behind her, usually a vibrant blue, is now overcast. Rain pours in gray sheets, churning the once-turquoise ocean into a tempest.

"Are you okay?" Geraldine asks me, her brow furrowed with concern.

"I don't know," I admit. The stool creaks as I settle onto it. Cricket places a steaming bowl of stew before me, its rich aroma a welcome distraction.

I launch into an explanation of events covering Titania's theft of my magic, the Six's true identity, that they're my mates. We're at war with Nocturna because Titania stole the Six from Oberon. She was the first in a long line of slaver queens designed to contain their chaotic powers, but they are changed after their time in Elphyne. I tell them about the Guardian teardrop and how they've been blessed and are responsible for ensuring magic flourishes. I tell them of Fox's sacrifice—his love. My friends' scents shift subtly as they react to my story—fear, concern, confusion.

After I finish, I fill the stunned silence by eating, trying to eat away my guilt over leaving details of my sordid upbringing out. I'm scraping the bowl with bread when someone finally speaks.

"So Fox destroyed the House of Stone Tower," Geraldine says warily, and I nod.

"What does that mean for us?" Peggy scowls at the pot she stirs.

"What do you mean?" I ask.

"I think she means," Max adds, "are we in trouble?"

"Why would you be in trouble?"

"Well," he replies, "will we be more of a target now? Will other Houses come for us by association?"

Heat rises to my cheeks. I can only imagine how fearful they'd be right now. Everything I do has consequences beyond my own safety. I shake my head. "No one knows except us."

They all let out an uneasy exhale.

"Although . . ." I bite my lip as I recall the reason the earl was here. "Puck seems to have gained somewhat of a political advantage."

"So we're fucked?" Geraldine asks.

"Fox's bargain silences Puck from revealing the truth."

"So we're not fucked?" Max nervously questions.

"Correct me if I'm wrong," Marina pipes up from her painting, "but don't the trials make you all fucked regardless? Unless you win, of course."

"*When* they win." Cricket throws her dishrag at Marina. It slides off the painting and falls to the floor. "A little tact wouldn't go astray."

"I'm sorry," I mumble. "This kind of thing is going to keep happening. I have enemies here—the biggest enemy of all, just because of who I am to the Six. For being born, really. The danger won't be over until . . . well, not even after the exhibition. You might survive this, but maybe it will be worse. If you want to leave, I can still activate that portal stone to Elphyne."

The words leave a bitter taste in my mouth. Part of me—the lone wolf—wants to push them away, to shield them from the dangers that seem to stalk my every step. But another part, the one starved for genuine connection, aches at the thought of losing them.

Geraldine snatches up Cricket's fallen dishrag and hurls it at me. It hits my chest with a soft thwap. "Stop trying to get rid of us."

"We'll be fine." Max's hand lands on my shoulder, warm and reassuring.

I cover his hand with mine. "I don't want secrets between us."

I wince. It's not a lie, but I'm too cowardly to share them all.

"Not to throw water on it, milady," Cricket interjects, her

brows arching, "but do the masters know we now know their secret?"

"Um . . ." My stomach drops. "Maybe not?" Panic flashes across their faces, and I quickly add, "But don't worry, I'll deal with it. Legion is wearing the enchanted spectacles Fox made. He remembers we're mates, so I should have a little sway when it comes to protecting you all."

That appeases them, and they settle into silence as they finish the meal prep. I wash and dry my dishes before sitting and staring at them, wishing there was more I could do to keep them all safe.

"Are you all okay?" I test. "Is there anything I can do to help you feel more at home here? I help myself to everything and go wherever I want, but the same won't work for you. It must feel foreign here and so different from your old world."

The words tumble out. Part of me still can't believe they want to stay, that they accept me.

I used to stumble across my mother wistfully speaking with her girlfriends about things they miss from their time. Even after twenty years, that longing hadn't passed. My heart aches to hear the pain in their voices, especially when they speak about friends or family they'll never see again. My gaze swings to Peggy, who lost her adult daughter. A part of me wishes that I could bring them all back, but even if I had my powers, the Well—the deities of the Cauldron do what they want. They always have. We're just pawns in their battle for dominance.

Geraldine sighs and sits next to me. "I'd be lying if I didn't admit there was a time we all thought it was easier to be dead than alive. But we're fine, babe. Honestly, this is heaven compared to what we've been subjected to. You've made such a difference in our lives already."

She pauses, her eyes growing distant. "Sometimes I wonder about my family back in Chicago. If they survived the nuclear winter or are somehow down in the subterranean. It's hard not knowing."

Max nods, his voice soft. "I miss my dad's terrible jokes and our Sunday barbecues. But being here, with all of you . . . it's like we've found a new family."

"Yeah, love." Peggy sniffs and shrugs. "But I still miss my daughter. And the bloody Corgis back home, their barking, their cuddles. Even their messes in my azaleas." She laughs, tears in her eyes. "I think I even miss the smell of dog shit. Sounds bonkers, right? But I'm learning to appreciate the magic of this place too."

"Maybe," I suggest hesitantly, "we could find a way to honor your old lives here? Could we set up a small memorial garden for Peggy or find books from your time for Max? Or ask Cricket to make those sugar cookies your mother made, Geraldine."

She blinks. "When did I tell you that?"

Heat hits my cheeks. "When I met you."

Their faces light up at the suggestions, and I feel like I'm finally doing something right. We might be in a strange, dangerous realm, but we have each other. And maybe, just maybe, that's enough to build a new home for them.

As for my family, I'm still working up the courage to contact them. Guilt has a way of holding me back from doing what's right, especially if it involves making an apology. I'm only beginning to understand the pain I've caused them. I just want to be in a good place when I talk to them, so when I reveal I'm not coming home—not yet—I don't crumble under the weight of that guilt. If all I can give them is my happiness, then I want it to be irrefutable . . . with all my mates by my side.

Peggy sniffs and shrugs. "I kind of feel bad for the Nevers in the tournament now."

"You mean, since the other Nothings are dead," Geraldine adds wryly.

I rub my eyes. "Fair point."

"You're right." Peggy scrubs a hand over her short hair. "I can't believe how callous this place is making me."

"You're not callous," Geraldine points out. "It's just hard to think about what we've lost sometimes because we're in survival mode."

Marina pipes up, waving her comb at us. "Isn't it Yule this weekend? My Captain Rubal Jackam loved Yule. He would hoard his most favored treasures from his journeys and then give them to me at Yule."

Geraldine's brows pucker. "Yule. Like Christmas?"

I nod, a wistful smile touching my lips. "My mom and her friends still celebrate Christmas in Elphyne." Sadness squeezes my heart when I realize I won't be there with them this year. And my friends won't be with theirs. "I'm sorry you won't be spending this tradition with your family, those who never"—my throat clogs—"woke up with you."

"No one blames you," Peggy says, coming over and giving me a maternal hug I want to sink into. "We all know you're not a bad person."

"You say that because you know me. But if anyone else found out I'm responsible for them being here, they might not think the same way." Before I overthink that problem, I quickly move the topic to planning gifts. "Maybe we can find something after classes. Providing the week's training doesn't ruin our bodies."

We fall silent and ponder our options when Peggy pipes up. "Actually, hun, there is something you can help us with."

"Name it," I return.

"Well . . ." She looks at her two friends, who give her a nod of encouragement. "We want to be of more use around the castle. The weekends and nights might be boring if you're off with your dark dreamboats. Perhaps you could give us tasks to help with the upkeep?"

"Dark dreamboats?" I flinch. "I don't know what that means,

but it sounds like something Fox would eat up and never let you forget. Please don't call him that, or I'll never hear the end of it."

"He's a scoundrel!" Marina shouts, waving her hairbrush at them. "He'll love it!"

We have a giggle amongst ourselves. Their laughter, their easy acceptance . . . it soothes something inside. It's nice to talk about Fox as though he's not dead. I bask in the warm and fuzzy feelings my friends give me. They're so different from what Alfie or any others have given me. Sadly, even Rory always erected a wall between us, no matter how much she tried to care for me. It saddens me that some people never discover this feeling, but I hope it can be waiting around the corner for anyone. They just need to step outside their comfort zone first.

"So . . ." I grin and drop my chin into my hand. "You want jobs around the castle, huh? What do you think, Cricket?"

"Thank our lucky stars the Cauldron has finally provided." She grins back at me. "I've been asking the masters for a little help. Poor Finch is run ragged around the grounds. And with the rooms changing nightly, goodness, it's a tough job keeping things pristine. We're lucky none of the visiting gentry get to the upper levels." At my curious look, she adds, "The Knight Commander's study is always on the lower level. Almost as if the castle doesn't want anyone snooping around, you know?"

"That is weird," I muse, then tap my chin as my thoughts return to Finch needing help. Wait a minute. "Peg, didn't you own a farm or something?"

"Close enough, hun. I bred Corgis. I'm not afraid of good, honest work."

"Stables." Cricket nods to herself. "Lord Bodin will need a hand there. He doesn't like Finch helping out because my love has little experience with animals."

"I'd love to help." Peggy flexes her knee. "Since Lord Fox healed us, I feel like I'm twenty-five again."

I snort at them addressing my mates as lords. It's weird. But then again, I've been mixing with elite society and royalty all my life.

Peggy mistakes my laugh. "You don't think I should?"

"Sorry, I was thinking about something else." I smile sheepishly. "You helping Bodin is an excellent idea. It's not like anyone portals around here, so animals are an important mode of transport."

"Sold." Max smashes his fist in his hand, then points to Peggy. "Stable help to the lady with the new good legs."

"What about us?" Geraldine asks me hopefully. "Max and I don't have transferrable skills from our time. He's a math teacher, and I was in retail."

"Hmm." I tap my lip but come up short. "Cricket?"

"Not sure, love. I can always do with extra help dusting and cleaning."

I hold up my finger. "Also, I've wanted to rejuvenate the conservatory. There's space for sparring, and it's much warmer there than outside in the snow. On another note, Peggy, do you know anything about raising bees?"

"Bees?"

Cricket and Marina both give me a sad look, but I think it's a good idea. "Varen loves bees. Maybe he'd have something to tinker with if we make a beehive. Plus, we would have more honey."

All he does is puzzle over his honeycomb problem. It distresses him.

Peggy nods. "My daughter and I tried our hands at raising bees when she was young—pre-corgi days, of course. I could give it a go."

"Really?" I clasp my hands hopefully. "There are loads of books in the library upstairs. Maybe they've got some information to help you. Also, maybe now that I think of it, Geraldine, you and Max can help me root around for information on the enchanted spectacles Fox made. Or even see if we can find some information about the seals or the Keepers or . . . the Baleful Hunt. There's a lot about this world we don't know."

"It would be our honor." Max gives me a valiant, sweeping bow. When he raises his head, his eyes widen at something over my shoulder, and he scrambles to stand beside Geraldine and Peggy. "Sir."

I turn to find Bodin, his arms folded and eyes narrowed. He dismisses them and looks at me.

"Training. Now."

I bristle at the command, but a part of me—the part starved for connection—thrills at his presence.

"Alright, you heard him," I say to the others. "No rest for the wicked. Time for training."

"Just you." He stops me as I try to slide past him.

I lift my chin and look him in the eye. "If I train, they train."

Bodin pauses, fists flexing at his sides. But I refuse to lower my gaze.

"Fine," he says.

The smile stretching his wide lips isn't as satisfying as I thought. It's more like a wolf's smile before he eats his meal.

When he leaves, Max mumbles, "Why did he look happy?"

"Because he's a sadist," Peggy returns.

"No," I groan. "That's Emrys."

"The Knight Inquisitor?" Geraldine gapes. "Please, lord. Don't let it be him."

CHAPTER 14

BODIN

Snow crunches under my boots as I stride into the frost-encrusted courtyard, our Shadow and her three mortal friends trailing behind. The biting cold nips at my exposed skin, but I ignore it. My focus remains razor sharp: hone these mortals into something resembling competent fighters. Perhaps even teach them a lesson about nature.

It is unforgiving and relentless. The winter cares little for warmth or emotion. It will not bow to a heartfelt plea. Willow will not perform at her best if she worries about their safety. The sooner she learns to cut the distractions, the better.

"Two laps," I bark, marching toward the stables where weapons for sparring await. "Now."

To their credit, no groans erupt as the exhibitors shed capes and other cumbersome clothing before beginning their jog. As I retrieve the weapons—likely rusted or moldy after this morning's revelation about Fox—I seize the opportunity to assess our new house inhabitants.

Peggy, the older woman with cropped hair and a stout figure, moves slower than the others but with unwavering determination. Geraldine, the younger female with ebony curls, appears

frail, yet her eyes blaze with inner fire. But the third friend, the male, sets my teeth on edge, especially when he murmurs something that makes Willow toss back her head in laughter before she loses her breath and continues running.

A low growl builds in my chest.

"Enough!" I shout, pointing to the weapons laid out on a patch of gravel peeking through the snow. "Pair up and join me. You and you together," I order, singling out the male and Willow. "You two." I nod to the others. "Pick a weapon each."

Their ragged breaths cloud the air as they amble toward me like a herd of disorganized, lazy boars. The man—Max, I recall with distaste—shivers visibly, rubbing his arms. Weak. Tentative. A liability.

I begin my lecture, voice carrying across the frosty courtyard. "Mental resilience and physical awareness are crucial. You must ground yourselves in the here and now, even when every part of your body screams with cold."

Pacing before them, each crunch of snow punctuating my words, I continue: "The first trial involves escaping a nightmare dreamscape. You'll face anything from Terror attacks to psychological warfare. Know yourself—your fears, desires, capabilities, and breaking points. You may confront twisted versions of yourself or loved ones. Remember what's real."

I fix them with a hard stare, lingering on Willow. Bile rises in my throat when I shift my attention back to her companions. They're dead weight, distracting her from self-preservation.

"The second trial," I continue, "is straightforward: a physical threat. Terrors can break, burn, and bleed like you. In a nightmare dreamscape, defeating them depends on self-knowledge. In the flesh, exploit their weaknesses. Be fearless. Strike without hesitation—even if they wear a familiar face. Understood?"

They nod, but something flickers in Willow's eyes before she masks it, fidgeting with her sword hilt. My jaw clenches. That weapon is inadequate. I make a mental note to retrieve—and improve—her homeland blade from Peablossom at the registration building.

"Finally," I growl, "you'll infiltrate the subterranean through a watergate. This combines the first two trials with unknown dangers. It's enemy territory. Many don't return."

"Watergate?" Willow interrupts, eyes wide. "As in . . . swimming?"

The fear in her voice twists my gut. Fox's letter, read five times this morning, emphasized her water phobia. "A short drop," I explain, softening my tone despite myself. "Then you emerge in the subterranean."

"Define 'short,'" she presses.

"Puddle-sized," I admit. When she falls silent, I continue: "The key to winning the final trial is to stay focused on your goal —retrieve the assigned item and escape. Run from Terrors, ignore pleas for help, hide in shadows if necessary. Understood?"

They nod again, determination etched on their faces. My gaze lingers on Willow. She stands tall, silver braid catching weak winter sunlight, but tension radiates from her stance.

"Now," I command, "show me what you've got."

The couples spread out in the courtyard. The evergreen trees and pale spires looming behind the rear boundary fence are a reminder the Ivory Palace is always nearby. I fold my arms, assessing as they enter a lazy, sloppy sparring match—more witty banter than actual combat.

Rage boils within me. I scoop up a clump of snow, compact it, and hurl it at Max's head. It connects with a satisfying thud.

"You're not taking this seriously," I snarl.

Fear flashes in his eyes. Willow's jaw drops in outrage, but before she can protest, baying and snarling erupts from the stables. The wildling attempts to breach the locked doors. He won't get inside. The doors are floor to ceiling and locked tight. An idea comes to mind, and I turn back to them. "The next lazy attempt at sparring or disrespect earns you stable-mucking duty. Understood?"

They mumble assent.

"'Yes, *sir*' is the correct response," I snap.

The sparring intensifies. I circle, observing. Geraldine's footwork shows promise, but she telegraphs every move. Her wide stance leaves her vulnerable. Peggy swings her weapon like a club —all force, no finesse.

I grasp Peggy's wrist, demonstrating a smoother motion. "Too much force leaves you unable to adapt."

"Sorry," she mutters. "Long way from breeding Corgis." At my arched brow, she elaborates, "Dogs. From the old world."

"She's great with animals." Geraldine sniffs, wiping her nose. "Told me how humming when she works helps calm them. Right, Peg?"

"You can't sing a Terror to sleep," I growl, kicking out to widen her stance. "Balls of your feet. Loose knees. Better."

Laughter draws my attention. Willow beams at Max. My eyes narrow inhumanly at the back of his brown-haired head. I stride over in time to catch what might not be evident to Max but is glaring to me: Willow pulls her punch at the last moment, sparing Max's pain. Fury ignites within me. I stride over, seize Max by the scruff, and deliver the blow Willow couldn't—blood sprays, painting the snow crimson.

He cries out, covering his nose. Willow shouts at me before I grab her viciously by the collar, twisting it and tugging her so close that our noses almost touch. Her scent—wild, defiant— floods my senses.

"You think you're doing them favors?" I hiss.

"They're my team. My allies. I can't do this alone."

"Protecting them from harsh realities teaches nothing."

"You didn't need to make him bleed," she snaps, eyes flashing despite her trembling lip. "You didn't need to break his damn nose."

My tone softens, but my grip remains firm. "He'll face far worse from creatures more violent than me."

Guilt works in her gaze. She knows I am right. Coddling them is worse than lying to them. It's sending them to their death with a blindfold on.

"You're taking out your frustrations on him," she whispers.

It hasn't escaped my notice that she allows this dominance. Her arms hang loose, her body limp. But the fire in her golden eyes promises defiance. It stokes a hunger within me.

"For good reason," I growl.

"Jealous much?" Her eyebrow arches.

I release her, blinking. "Absurd."

"Sure." Her lips curve sardonically. "Just like you weren't jealous of Briar. Or even Varen."

Other males' names on her lips ignites something primal within me. Varen, I can accept. Any in our hive, fine. Never another. The thought startles me. I turn away, her warmth lingering. My body betrays me—pulse-quickening, muscles tensing with the desire to pull her close again.

Red stains the snow. The mortals huddle together, simpering. I've gone too far, I realize. But I must keep her safe, even from herself.

Still, I can't be everywhere all the time. I move to heal Max's nose. Willow might be right. She needs allies, a team. But a selfish part of me wishes she only needed me.

CHAPTER 15
WILLOW

Bodin dismisses Max to the sidelines and pairs off Peggy and Geraldine. His intense gaze locks onto mine. "Willow, you're with me."

Feral energy surges through my veins as I meet his challenge head-on. My chin dips, mind already plotting strategy. His eyes narrow, searching for hesitation. I won't give him the satisfaction.

The steel blade feels foreign in my hand—useless against Sluagh, as I learned with Fox. But it'll do for now.

"Draw first blood," Bodin challenges, "and I'll allow you to come to Burn After Reading tonight."

A harsh laugh rips from my throat. "*Allow* me? As if you could stop me."

His lips thin, the silence more damning than words. Realization slams into me—without Fox, without my magic, I'm at their mercy. Doubt claws at my gut as I glance at my friends.

Bodin's voice cuts through my thoughts. "They're a distraction. You'll lose because of them."

"Fuck you," I snarl. "They're my team. You wouldn't know anything about that, would you?"

"Neither would you," he snaps. "Trusting is as new to you as it is to me."

His words sting, hitting too close to home. I shove the feeling aside, focusing on the challenge. This cold, possessive Bodin grates on my nerves. The Knight Marshall—unyielding as stone.

"What do you win if you draw first blood?" I ask, eyeing him warily.

Something hot flashes in his gaze. "Your obedience."

I roll my eyes. "Boring."

Unless it involves him pinning me and marking me.

"Fine," he grinds out. "If I win, training starts an hour early. Just you and me before the others."

Triumph swells in my chest. He's willing to train my friends alongside me. Mostly. "Deal."

We circle each other, frigid air crackling with tension. Our audience grows—Peggy and Geraldine have stopped sparring, and I spot Legion, Styx, and Emrys arriving at the courtyard's edge.

Bodin jerks his chin toward the stables fifty feet from the others. "Let's move further back."

"Scared, old man?" I taunt, following.

He scoffs. "Of a little girl playing warrior? Hardly."

"Don't want them to see you lose?"

Impatience flattens his lips. "I'd rather not heal another imbecile today."

I see him target a spot by the wooden boundary fence separating the courtyard from the stables and the larger boundary wall. When we're close, I lunge. He barely dodges, my blade whispering past his cheek.

"This little girl might surprise you," I hiss.

Our bodies clash, a tangle of limbs and steel. Each movement flows into the next, a deadly dance. Wet snow seeps through my boots, chafing my skin. I ignore it, pushing my advantage. He hits the fence. His brows lift as he glances back to see what he bumped into. I use my smaller frame to slip past his guard and press against him, throwing him off balance.

"Distracted?" I breathe, lips grazing his ear.

He growls, spinning us. My back slams against the fence, our faces now inches apart. Our chests heave in unison.

"You wish," he snarls, flashing teeth. But there's a new light in his eyes. He's enjoying this.

I grin. "I think you're the one wishing, Bodin."

He grunts, pushing away. We resume our deadly dance, trading blows. Neither gains the upper hand. My muscles scream, bones brittle with cold. For a moment, doubt creeps in. I surprised him earlier, but eons of battle experience live in those hardened muscles.

"You've been holding back," he accuses. "Time to stop playing games." He tosses his sword amongst a pile of nearby weapons, then beckons with bare hands.

"Who says I'm playing?" I mirror him, ducking under a powerful swing to dance on my toes.

My muscle memory kicks in, movements sharper. My fingers itch to take the kill shot—or at least draw blood, but he's my mate, whether he admits it or not. I don't want to hurt him. And others are watching. If he keeps averting my attacks, I'll have to dig deeper into that dark place.

Suddenly, he catches my wrist, yanking me against his chest. His arm bands around me, breath hot on my ear. The heat of his hard body presses against my rear end, and all I can think of is him—hot, male, spicy *him*.

"When you pull your punches," he says, "that's playing."

His scent overwhelms me. I struggle to focus on the stables ahead. He has me caged, and part of me doesn't want to leave. It aches for this embrace to be real. I don't want to return to that dark place where I did terrible things.

"Show me," he challenges, grip tightening. "Show me why we

chose you as our Shadow. Why Fox writes such . . . glowing praise."

His hips flex into my rear, digging a hardness I can only assume is one thing. His hand slides down, igniting heat I refuse to acknowledge. Our backs are to the castle. No one sees his hand gliding lower. My lashes flutter under the weight of my hormones. I just want to drop—to show him my belly and let him take me. He is a force of strength surrounding me, and I ache for more. Fox has been gone for mere hours, and yet I crave touch. What is wrong with me?

"Maybe I don't need to prove anything," I whisper as his palm reaches my stomach. "Maybe you need to trust I'll do what's necessary when it matters."

"Or you're afraid of what you might reveal. You won't act because you're being watched."

His words strike a nerve. Anger and determination surge, drowning self-doubt. I snap my head back, connecting with his face. Pain explodes in my skull, but I face him, ready to defend.

He wipes his nose. No blood—the fight's not over. A wide grin transforms his face into something breathtaking. Damn him for looking so good, smelling like my personal sanctuary. He's my opponent, not my . . . whatever. No, screw him and his stupid perfect body. Perfect eyes. How *do* his eyes always look bedroom-ready? It must be those long lashes, that lazy stare.

I wonder what his actual bedroom looks like.

Heat floods my cheeks. I groan, shaking away the thoughts. He's my mate; of course, his scent affects me. He must feel it too.

I take a moment to let that sink in. I can use this.

Grinning, I assess his frame. Immortal or not, his anatomy remains predictably human. That semi-hard length between his legs . . . yeah, he's turned on. The Sluagh might not have been sexual beings before they received their drop of light magic, but they're definitely sexual now. Fox taught me his cock works like any hot-blooded male's.

"Giving up?" he taunts.

"Just getting warmed up." I strip off my outer layer, leaving only a thin shirt. I unbutton the collar, glaring defiantly.

"Some kind of warning?" His lips curve. "Gloves off?"

I reach behind to grab the wooden fence, stretching and putting on a show. No sword means my body takes the hits. I refuse to lose to a cramp. His dark eyes roam my body. I'm acutely aware of the effect on him . . . and my watching mates. They've stilled. Good. Let them underestimate me.

After finishing stretching, I roll my shoulders, crack my knuckles, and attack. My movements grow precise and deadly. Bodin matches me blow for blow, and our dance intensifies. I brush against him, making small feminine sounds, but he resists admirably.

"I've seen how you fight when no one's watching," he says between strikes. "It's not just training. It's instinct."

I falter, his words hitting home. This is why we moved—away from prying ears. He knows I hide my true self from my friends. He pushes me to embrace my darkness. I get it. I went there when I first met them—when Ignarius made me fight Dahlia. I almost killed her. In class! Max was a little scared of me. He admitted it.

It's not Bodin's choice.

He presses his advantage, backing me toward the fence. "Why hide what you are?"

"You don't know me," I snap, redoubling my efforts. I twist and turn, channeling all my strength into each move. My eyes never stop assessing—how his guard drops when he attacks. Every detail fuels the cold fire of strategy in my mind.

"I know enough. We need that part of you to survive what's coming."

"You don't need that. Nobody does," I growl, circling warily.

I feint left, watching his reaction. His movements are powerful but predictable. He's used to being the predator. But the view from the top can be skewed. He forgets the underbelly is as vulnerable as the heart. I could slice him open. I've done it before —Wellhounds, people, even teenagers getting in my way.

"Hiding your strength endangers everyone," he insists, voice hoarse.

The weight of my past, of what I am, threatens to crush me. Bodin glances at our audience. I seize the opening.

I run and leap. Eyes wide, he catches me instinctively, hands on my bottom. I yank his braids, throwing him off balance. He stumbles but doesn't let go . . . probably instinct. Or because— *oops*—more of my shirt buttons have somehow popped during our fight. Smirking, I hook my legs around his waist, drawing us flush. Our bodies press together, lungs heaving, skin burning despite the cold. His gaze drops to the pillows of my half-exposed breasts squashed against him. A moan escapes—his or mine, I'm not sure.

Our eyes lock. The world melts away, leaving only us and this sizzling, demanding thing between us. It's that needy place in my chest—and between my legs. Bodin wants me to embrace my instincts, but some are more powerful than killing and death. There's life. The need for a pack. To care. My family tried teaching me, but I wasn't ready until Fox. Now, I need to teach the remaining five Sluagh that we're stronger together.

Darkness consumes us the moment we forget that.

Styx's voice shatters the moment. "Looks like our little queen's got you wrapped around her finger, Bodin!"

Bodin's eyes widen. He drops me, shoving away. I use the momentum, spinning into a low sweep. It's misdirection—my hand swipes a dagger from the snow. As he jumps to avoid my leg, I rise, blade whistling toward his face.

He grabs my wrist, twisting. I cry out, more surprised than hurt. His grip loosens, concern flashing across his face. Quick as lightning, I reverse the hold and slash his forearm. A thin red line appears.

"First blood," I pant triumphantly.

Anger and admiration war in his eyes.

"You tricked me," he growls, glaring at my gaping shirt.

"I used your weakness against you," I counter. "Isn't that what you've been teaching?"

The crowd erupts—mostly my friends cheering. But I focus on Bodin's indignant flush, his heaving chest.

He lunges, knocking me down. Ice bathes my back. He pins me, a force of nature. I glimpse a hungry snarl before his teeth graze my neck. A soft gasp escapes me, my body arching instinctively.

Yes. Mark me. Admit you want this.

Admit Fox is right. My heart is right. We teeter on the edge of something dangerous and thrilling. Then reality crashes back. He jerks away, breath ragged.

"Enough for today," he grumbles, avoiding my eyes. "See you tonight."

"If you still want me to come earlier to training, I'll do it," I add, surprising us both.

Our eyes briefly meet, and then he stalks away, leaving me breathless and confused on the ground.

CHAPTER 16

PUCK

I pace outside the Shining Host's grand chambers, my footsteps echoing off living crystal walls. Gilt doors carved with faerie revelry scenes stand closed before me. Dragon-bonded scents seep through—ozone and brimstone mingling with laughter and heated arguments.

"*What are you waiting for?*" the Baleful Hunt growls in my mind. "*Moonrise was five minutes ago.*"

I straighten my emerald doublet, its silver threads catching the light. "*Patience. An entrance is everything . . . unless there's no one to witness it.*"

The dragon harrumphs. Chalky smoke curls from my nostrils.

"*No snide quip? No scathing retort?*" I smirk. "*Perhaps you're learning from me after all.*"

He yawns, stretching within me. Restless claws scrape my insides. I contain him through sheer will, gritting my teeth. I must ratify this bond. The Shining Host could strip everything from me in an instant.

Tasting magic on my tongue, I thrust open the doors and stride in, chin high.

The chamber unfolds—a masterpiece of faerie architecture. Cobweb curtains shimmer between towering crystal columns pulsing with inner light. A circular moonstone table sparkles at the center, surrounded by six ornate chairs carved to represent each dragon. The queen's throne, woven botanicals blooming with starlight, sits empty. The Weaving Hunt perches behind it, incandescent light shimmering around its dozing form.

What a joke. The Weaving Hunt weakens yearly; its once-iridescent scales are now dull. Titania thinks she can hide the problem behind clouds, but I see it. And the Wild Hunt—supposedly the other High Dragon—is a mere hatchling in hiding.

The Baleful Hunt's seat remains vacant. He resides within me now, a constant pressure behind my eyes. But I refuse to unleash him again, not after what happened at the Cabinet temple. I'm lucky to have escaped with my life.

"Why did they let you go?" the dragon prods. *"Seems curious to me, considering who you faced."*

I've wondered that myself. All I can think of is the Shadow. She holds some kind of power or influence I'm not privy to. But also, they're not foolish enough to leave a dragon without a host. *"Even they were aware of the dangers of a rogue, unbonded dragon."*

It's well documented that dragons left unchecked and unbonded will grow wild and destructive. If the Sluagh had killed me, the Baleful Hunt would have instantly sensed the bond breaking. If another host has not taken precautions to take over immediately, control is a slippery slope, leading to disaster. For all these Radiants know, I saved them untold drama.

One more vote is all I need.

The chamber buzzes with bickering and gossip. No one spares me a glance.

I survey the remaining dragon-bonded:

The Fever Hunt smolders behind Marquess Ignarius, smoke and lava oozing from a scaled hide. The dragon's eyes glow like embers, reflecting its bonded's fiery temperament.

Beside them, Lady Nivene argues with the Marquess, her voice fluid as the Dread Hunt coils behind her like a serpent. Water droplets sizzle when they meet the Fever Hunt's heat nearby.

The Hollow Hunt's luminous form watches with unblinking eyes, moonlight dancing across its ethereal scales. Its mistress, Duchess Selene, whispers with the Knight Commander— Legion is a dark presence leeching her radiance. Today, he sports a rather absurd change in fashion. Round brass spectacles adorn his nose, partly hiding his perfectly shaped black brows. The old-world fashion throws me. He's not the type for gaudy accessories. His structured cheekbones and jaw are enough decoration. Radiants don't need spectacles. Their vision is perfect.

Whatever fashion statement he makes, he poses the greatest threat to my power play. Not his rabid runt of a wayward dragon but his very role. The knights could impose martial law at any hint of danger to Avorlorna. All he needs is proof to back up his claim.

"*Fool,*" the dragon scoffs. "*He doesn't need proof. He is the danger.*"

"*Silence.*" I force a smile through clenched teeth. Any minute now, they'll notice me.

"*You'll botch this without me,*" he grumbles. "*You don't even grasp the dragons' true purpose.*"

Lady Nivene's melodic voice cuts through the chatter. "You know, Puck, your dragon should be present during these meetings." She gestures to the Dread Hunt, its wings extending in a show of dripping power, irritating the Fever Hunt as more droplets sizzle on its tail.

The two glare at each other. I have the sense if they were ever to be freed from their bondages, they would rip each other to shreds. Or fuck.

"Do you doubt that I hold him?" I step forward and let my hold on the dragon slip for a second. The Baleful Hunt's stony gaze echoes from my eyes. The chalky scent of rock permeates the air.

I glance at the empty dragon nest behind Legion.

"Where is the Wild Hunt?" I ask. "Why does nobody seem to care about its existence or lack thereof?"

As usual, they ignore my reference to the missing hatchling.

Duchess Selene purses her lips. "Before we ratify this turn of events, you must explain."

"Explain? What's to explain?" I throw up my hands, pointing to my eyes where the Baleful Hunt's presence swirls. "Isn't it obvious?"

Lady Nivene raises an eyebrow. "My, my, Puck. Did you forget to bow before addressing the Shining Host? Or perhaps you left your manners in the old mortal realm?"

Lord Ignarius snorts, brimstone intensifying. "Tell me, imposter, do you always stomp about like a bull in a china shop, or is this a special performance for us?"

Laughter ripples around the table. Heat floods my cheeks.

"I wasn't aware we'd invited a court jester to our proceedings," Lord Ignarius stage-whispers to Lady Nivene. "Though I must admit, his lack of grace is rather entertaining."

Selene's lips twitch. "Perhaps we should provide our colleague with a guidebook on etiquette. It seems he's more accustomed to entertaining mortals than addressing nobility."

Anger bubbles within me. I force a smile. "My apologies, esteemed colleagues. I was simply eager to begin our important business."

"Did you murder Lord Sylvanar?" the Knight Commander's voice cuts through the air.

He stares at me steadily, dark eyes unreadable behind those ridiculous spectacles. What's he playing at? He knows I'm bound by Fox's bargain not to reveal the truth. Unless . . . perhaps this Shadow of theirs has caused a rift, and the spymaster never told his commander the whole story.

"No," I answer simply, meeting his gaze.

"Good enough for me," Lord Ignarius grumbles, holding out his empty chalice. "This bickering is tedious."

They return to their conversations, ignoring me again. I slam my chalice down. "We have business to attend!"

But they're lost in their own world. Lady Nivene wrinkles her nose. "The stench of mortals has permeated even the highest towers. I can scarcely enjoy my morning nectar without hearing their incessant wailing."

"I put the mewling ones to work," Lord Ignarius suggests dryly. "My tower is sparkling."

Duchess Selene sighs dramatically, pressing a scented handkerchief to her forehead. "Three of my prized moonbloom gardens were trampled yesterday! Is no one to speak of the dissenters rioting through our midst?"

I listen to their complaints and see opportunities forming. These self-absorbed fae and their petty grievances . . . if I play this right, I might just get what I need.

"My esteemed colleagues," I begin, infusing my voice with honeyed charm, "let us not forget the very essence of who we are. We are the Fair Folk, the Good Neighbors. Our realm is one of beauty, revelry, and eternal joy." I gesture to Titania's smiling portrait overhead. "We must ensure that we uphold our values, even in these . . . challenging times."

I pause, letting my words sink in. "The dissenters clamor at our doors not because they wish to disrupt our peace, but because they yearn for a taste of our perfection. But we cannot let their disruptions mar our festivities."

"Do you really think festivities are appropriate considering Sylvanar's death?" Legion interjects.

I mentally sigh. He's always trying to bring the mood down with reality.

"He's right," the Duchess remarks. "It is one thing to celebrate in the face of rioting peasants, but it is another to do so when one of our own is lost. Is it not more pertinent to hold a wake than to focus on festivities?"

"Why can't we do both?" I suggest.

"And what do you propose, Puck?" Lady Nivene asks, leaning forward with interest. Her sea-salt perfume wafts toward me.

"Leave the rioting people to me," I reply, grinning. "I have a plan that will not only quell their discontent but also provide us with the grandest spectacle Avorlorna has seen. And as to the wake, why not do it at the Solstice Ball during the revelry? We should celebrate life, not death. Otherwise, we draw closer to the subterranean ways, do we not?"

Murmurs of agreement travel around the table.

Legion challenges, his voice low and threatening, "And what of the increasing danger in our midst? The Nightmares cropping up from watergates that should be frozen but aren't?"

I falter for a moment, caught off-guard. *"Why does Titania even want the knights here?"* I think. *"They belong with Oberon in the subterranean."*

"Because if she controls them," the dragon tells me, *"she controls the Wild Hunt."*

"A mere hatchling," I scoff inwardly.

"The hatchling," he warns, *"will soon feed on souls, and once he has no more, he will feed on us."*

"Surely five dragons can overpower one."

"Four," he corrects. *"The Weaving Hunt is nothing but dreams and starlight."*

"What does that mean?"

But the Hunt goes quiet. I refocus on the Shining Host, determined to win their approval.

"My friends," I say, my voice low and conspiratorial, "I assure you, I have plans in motion to address these . . . nightmarish intrusions. But to implement them fully, I need your trust, your support." I look each of them in the eye. "Together, we can ensure that Avorlorna remains a shining jewel, untouched by the darkness threatening to encroach upon us."

I speak of grand festivals to distract the masses, enchantments to soothe their discontent, and illusions so beautiful they'll forget their hunger and strife. I promise each dragon-bonded something they desire—more power for Lord Ignarius, finer silks for Lady Nivene, rarer books of magic for Lady Selene. Finally, I declare, "Now, it's time to ratify my position within the Shining Host as the Baleful Hunt's new bonded Radiant."

They stare at me, their dragons alert behind them.

"As the queen's proxy," I announce, standing tall, "I am the first to put forward the motion." I move to the side, affecting a different posture. "And I, Lord Robin Goodfellow, second your motion."

All we need is one more.

"If you are with me, you know what to say." I look to each of the Host expectantly, particularly Lord Ignarius. But he remains stubbornly silent, suddenly fascinated by his wine glass.

No one raises their hand. Fury bubbles within me, threatening to burst forth in a torrent of chaos magic.

Until Legion raises his hand, his voice cutting through the tense silence. "Aye."

The chamber falls silent, all eyes turning to the Knight Commander. There's only one reason my enemy would vote me in. Mutually assured destruction. He knows I know his knights are Sluagh—that this very war is likely over them, despite what lies Titania tells the rest of the kingdom.

When he doesn't share my triumphant grin, I realize that while I may have won this battle, the war between us is far from over.

WILLOW

Flames crackle in the upper-level castle library as I give my friends a tour at Geraldine's request. She's already compiled a list of research topics to help us win the tournament and bring Fox back.

"Knowledge is power," Geraldine declares, waggling her finger in my face as I stoke the fire. "And your Radiants have a wealth of it tucked away here."

An hour into our study session, exhaustion takes its toll. Peggy slumps over a reading table, lost to sleep. My muscles scream, a testament to our grueling day. I stand by the crackling fireplace, careful not to set my dress alight before I arrive at Burn After Reading later. Max yawns from his spot on the floor, book drooping in his hands. I shift a teetering log away from his direction with the poker. An ember could fly out at any moment.

Bodin's earlier attack on Max still haunts me. Though healed, the inner scars linger—mostly mine. Max brushed off my apology. He defended Bodin and scolded me for pulling punches. "The Terrors won't," he'd said, determined to survive these trials with me.

That truth in my kind friend's eyes stung. It's one thing to take a punch; it's another to witness me coldly gut an innocent person. I might have to if other exhibitors attack us. Max is right. Bodin is right.

"You should rest," I tell Geraldine as she disappears behind a bookcase. "We're at the Nexus tomorrow. I have to go to B.A.R. tonight, but I can survive on little sleep. Take advantage of the extra hours."

Her black curly-haired head pokes out. "We'll go to bed when you leave. I need to feel . . . useful."

"I understand that." I set the poker aside, my mind wandering to the peculiarities of metal in Avorlorna.

As Geraldine returns, she finds me lost in thought. I seize the moment to check in.

"Hey, are you all okay after today's training?" I ask softly.

Geraldine's shoulders slump. "Mostly. But Peggy . . . she's struggling. She's been talking about her daughter more, wondering if she's alive somewhere in Avorlorna or Nocturna. Her head's not in the right place, and she's worried she'll distract you. Or get herself killed."

My chest tightens. "Bodin is pushing too hard, scaring you all."

"The trials will be terrifying," Geraldine admits. "Maybe preparing us now is for the best. We could use this time to study the Nightmare Codex and learn what monsters we're up against."

"The Codex at the Nexus isn't accurate," I remind her. "It had false information about the Sluagh."

Geraldine's eyes spark with determination. "Then we'll find a better source. There must be something in here to read. Max and I can do our own research."

Pride swells in my chest. "That's brilliant. Your due diligence could save our lives."

She beams at the praise, and I feel a flicker of hope. Maybe we can face this together after all. My gaze returns to the metal poker, and I remember how Bodin gave us steel weapons.

"Magic in Elphyne flows purely for every fae," I explain, voicing my earlier musings. "We've even had a human born without access to the Well, who was then blessed. I asked Bodin a few days ago why the Folk can use metal and still cast magic. He said ancient faeries are only allergic to pure iron. Industrialization changed the rules, and the Folk were slumbering during that time. When I woke Titania and the rest, they missed those changes. They don't know the rules have shifted."

"The Chaser chains . . . they're metal, right?"

"Yeah." I scratch my chin, brow furrowed. "The charms are like mana stones back home. Once magic is infused, it can exist isolated from the Well—or the Cauldron's Wellspring, whatever we call it here."

"Wait." Geraldine's eyes widen. "You said a human was gifted with this magic in Elphyne. Do you think we"—she swallows—"could receive the same gift if we start following these rules?"

My heart cracks. Sid's gift came at a terrible price—the Guardian initiation ritual, a living nightmare. Eighty percent of initiates die. The Six have the blessing but are pawns in a divine game. I've never heard of any other humans born in this time suddenly receiving it. Like my mother, most humans woke up with magic. Some never realized they had it when they lived on desecrated soil, like in Crystal City, because their access was blocked.

Nero habitually stole manabeeze—wisps—directly from living bodies. Geraldine's eyes are still hopeful as she waits for my answer. What if she had magic, but now she doesn't? It could explain all the jars of wisps inside Titania's temple.

I wince, a chill seeping into my bones. "What if you've already been given access to the Well?"

"What do you mean?"

Shit. The deeper my friends are embroiled, the greater the danger. If my suspicions are confirmed and Titania discovers it, Geraldine is dead. It's bad enough I'm keeping secrets about my past. She'd never forgive me for hiding this. I'd want to know if it were me.

Taking a steadying breath, I dive in. "When we met, you told me about the Nevers, Nothings, and Chasers. The Nothings were easy to explain—imperfect, disabled, old, scarred." I gesture at my face. "They didn't fit Titania's vision of a dream faerie society. Chasers, too—they're mortals or lesser faerie chasing Radiant power. But you weren't sure about Nevers. What if they're called that because Titania stole their magic, like she did with me?"

Geraldine hugs herself, staring into the flames. "We'd remember having our magic stolen, wouldn't we?"

"Not if she didn't want you to. She's a master at altering reality." A full-body shiver rattles my spine when another thought occurs to me. "Did I ever tell you about the man who kidnapped me?"

She stills. "No. I mean, we all guessed something horrible happened to you but didn't want to pry."

I nod, eyes unfocused with oncoming memories. "He was"—the man who destroyed your world—"an evil human. He stole his daughter's wisps during 'treatments.' Rory woke from your time with mana, powerful and ageless like the Folk. After treatments, she'd return cloudy-minded and forgetful. More aged while he looked younger . . . but remained mortal."

"I'm listening."

"Magic depletes in one of three ways: using it yourself, a Well-blessed mate borrowing it, or forceful, stolen depletion—like what happened to Rory. The former two ways rejuvenate naturally, but the latter cuts a fae's lifespan to mortal levels. When Rory had no more to give, she aged. What if Titania did the same to humans who woke from the old world? What if being a Never means they'll never have magic again?"

"You're saying I could have been like you—" Geraldine shakes her head. "I mean, like your mother was?"

Guilt floods me as I think of how, by learning to be his

weapon, I indirectly aided Nero's theft of magic from my own people. As a Reaper, Rory went on missions specifically to steal from Guardians so Nero could portal with forbidden metal—bringing guns and ships into Elphyne.

"It's a theory," I admit, rubbing my neck.

Geraldine's eyes harden. "Then that bitch stole from us. Made us mortal."

I hug her until the tension eases from her shoulders, then return to brooding at the fire, longing for my old fire-sprite friends.

"We don't know for sure," I remind her. "But she tried enslaving the Six instead of asking about their Guardian teardrops." My gaze darts around, following the flickering light. "She might not have needed to steal anyone's magic if it still flowed abundantly in this land. Five years is enough time for magic to fade with all the metal used here."

The saddest part? If it meant escaping Titania's chains, I wouldn't put it past the Six to deliberately let magic fade. Fox's words echo: *"We will devour the world if it means keeping you safe."*

"None of this is in the books." Geraldine frowns at the shelves. Max's soft snoring joins Peggy's between fire crackles. "I found only a small section on the Sluagh, as you mentioned."

"Maybe Titania wanted it that way. This Keep is enchanted. Fox collected some items himself, but everything else could be her design."

"Where would he have gathered authentic books? In Elphyne?"

"Titania and Oberon brought many treasures into their original slumber," Legion answers, startling us as he enters with Bodin. "Then they brought them back into this world when they woke. Fox raided the Ivory Palace whenever he could."

Legion cuts an imposing figure in his tailored black winter coat. Brass spectacles perched on his nose add to his austerity and catch the flickering firelight. Bodin's presence is equally commanding in a black shirt, open at the collar. It's the same cut as his work shirt but somehow more decadent. Maybe silk. The laces are open enough to reveal a tantalizing glimpse of a smooth, muscular chest. It's hard to look away. There's something about the clothes he prefers that makes my blood heat. Everyone else covers up in this cold, but not him.

"Are you wearing that?" Bodin frowns at my outfit.

Having been to Burn After Reading, I know my low-cut dress is tame compared to typical attire.

"You will don a cape," Legion states.

"Have you not been there?" I counter. "It's warm."

"Then you will change into something . . . more."

My brows rise. "You directed Peablossom to make this dress—my whole wardrobe, in fact."

He clears his throat. "That was before."

"Before what?" I tease, though I know exactly what he's alluding to, and it makes me all hot and prickly and giddy inside.

"You are being deliberately obtuse," he says, without real bite.

I shrug, smirking. "My other dresses are similar. We don't have time to change. It's almost midnight. Oh, and Cait said her offer still stands. Mean anything to you?"

Dodging the subject clearly irks him. But instead of snapping at me, he turns his piercing glower on Geraldine.

She quickly averts her eyes, fear spiking her scent like spilled pepper. I bump Legion's shoulder, glaring at him and Bodin. *Be nice,* I mouth. Today's training scared my friends enough. If this is more possessive, protective bullshit like earlier, I won't stand for it. My friends don't need to feel unsafe in their own home. Because that's what this is—their home. The Six will have to learn to coexist.

Bodin looks perplexed by my annoyance, but Legion's expression smooths into something more approachable. Geraldine keeps her head bowed through our silent exchange.

I squeeze her hand reassuringly. After an hour of researching the Sluagh's monstrous origins, I don't blame her fear.

Legion eyes Peggy sleeping at the table and Max by the fire. "Unfortunately, your friends may no longer lodge at the castle."

"What?" I gasp. If that's his version of "nice," we need a serious talk.

"It is not safe." Bodin scowls at my rising emotion. "They should move to the House of Shadow Tower at the Nexus."

"Absolutely not." I slice my free hand through the air. "You tried painting them as dead weight this morning. It didn't work. I won't let you do this."

Geraldine steps back. "Maybe I should leave you to discuss—"

"No," I snap, making her flinch. Shit. I didn't mean to sound so bossy, so I force myself to gentle my tone. "It's not safe for you there either. Please stay."

"Willow," Legion warns.

"If they sleep in the tower, so do I."

His eyes flash. He and Bodin share a tense look, clearly holding something back. But I must work with what I know since none of the Six besides Bodin have spoken to me since their little *family* meeting.

"If you have something to add, say it," I challenge. "I've told them everything."

Almost.

"That's the problem," Legion counters dryly. "If they know everything, they're targets."

"It's too late. They're already targets. I can't un-tell them. I wouldn't even if I could."

Bodin growls in frustration. "It will take too long to train them to my standards. I cannot keep you all safe. This is untenable."

Geraldine clears her throat, drawing our attention. She blushes. "May I suggest something?"

Legion gives a curt nod.

"The other Houses have flowstones and charms for their

Chasers. Perhaps you can give us something to protect us from spilling your secrets?"

"Brilliant idea," I breathe. "But will charms work for you if you're Nevers?"

"We were Nothings first. And the charms worked when Fox gave us some."

"Yes," I agree, remembering. "But we discarded them after Sylvanar . . . well, the point is, they're gone now. We need to source appropriate stones, right? Aunt Peaches said each type has different magical capabilities."

I channel my best pleading eyes at Legion and Bodin. Bodin's scowl deepens, but Legion rubs his forehead, considering.

"I can find stones to work with," I offer. "Just tell me what you need. I'll hunt around at B.A.R. while you deal with Cait."

Bodin whispers to Legion, "This invites trouble."

"I can still hear you," I sing, tapping my shifter ears. "And correction—this invites help. More of us working toward the same goal is better. Geraldine's already found valuable information. They're looking for more accurate information on the Nightmares. She also raised an excellent point about the wisps in Titania's temple—what if they're stolen from humans who woke from the old world?" I tap my chin. "Come to think of it, Styx did say a wisp he gobbled tasted like a happy mortal."

Geraldine shoots me a look. Technically, I came up with the stolen magic theory, but she was there brainstorming. Semantics. I know she'll have many more clever ideas. When we met, she timed routes between towers, always prepared. She has a unique perspective. She needs time to absorb knowledge first. I have faith in her. Besides, I won't leave them to face more assassination attempts. Their earlier comment today about them being targeted after Sylvanar's death nags at me.

They're safer here. If Radiants hunting the Wild Hunt fear entering Shadowfall Keep to kill the dragon, it's the safest place for my friends.

"And," I continue, "Peggy used to work on a farm. A dog farm. She wants to work in the stables. Cricket's already agreed and is excited for help around the castle."

Bodin stares at Legion, all storm and grump. "If I must prioritize our Shadow's wellbeing, having another take over my home duties will free up time."

He pauses, clearly holding back more.

I can't stop my grin. "Wouldn't it be better to have allies I trust when the trials start?"

Legion sighs in capitulation, followed by Bodin's grunt of agreement.

"Very well," Legion concedes. "We will source flowstones ton—"

Squealing, I launch myself at him, planting a kiss on his cheek. He stiffens, pushing me away. Odd, but I probably surprised him. Before he can complain, I do the same to Bodin. Their flustered looks make me want to do it again. Instead, I say goodbye to Geraldine and head out.

These Sluagh have been known to lie. I don't want to give them the chance to change their minds.

CHAPTER 18
BODIN

Styx meets us in the snow-encrusted front courtyard, dressed in only threadbare breeches. No shirt. No shoes. His hair is tousled, fingers stained with charcoal. A smoking cigarillo of something decidedly not tobacco dangles from his mouth, its sweet, cloying scent making my eyes water. Judging by his half-mast eyelids, it's not his first indulgence of the night. A flash of irritation sparks through me. We need him alert, not lost in a haze of artificial bliss, especially considering our Shadow's penchant for calamity.

I shouldn't have challenged her during the training session. Now, I have to deal with distractions.

I pluck the offending item from Styx's lips and stomp on the embers, watching them die with grim satisfaction.

"Why did you do that?" His thoughts slur into my mind.

"You need your wits tonight," I return, my tone brooking no argument.

Calamity's voice cuts through the tension. "Aren't you cold, Styx?" she asks, rubbing her arms vigorously before blowing on her hands. A puff of breath escapes her lips, arousing the air into a misty cloud.

She adamantly refused Legion's third attempt to have her don something less revealing. Now, she clearly regrets her decision but is too stubborn to admit it.

"Nope," Styx answers, his speech a poor imitation of mortal cadence. He's likely been eavesdropping on the thoughts of old-worlders all day. Goosebumps break out on his flesh as we speak. "I'm just your transport. Don't need a coat."

"Or clothes, apparently," Willow says with a snort.

"You can talk." Styx prowls around her, his gaze a physical thing as it assesses her revealing attire. "Not much left to the imagination, is there?"

His steps falter as he circles behind her, his gaze sweeping down to her shapely behind. Sensing his pause, she glances over her shoulder. He quickly scowls, but not before I glimpse the raw need in his eyes.

Those two are more alike than they care to admit. They'll be thick as thieves once he overcomes his distrust. Trouble loves company, after all.

Legion shares a derisive look with me, no doubt sharing my sentiment.

"Let's go," I growl, stepping closer to Styx. His skin is like ice as I take hold of his closest arm. Maintaining an excellent grip is imperative to avoid being thrown when *flickering*. Legion does the same, standing behind Styx on the opposite side.

Styx smirks at Willow's dubious stare and beckons her with two hands. "Time for a hug, fangs."

She hesitates.

He drops his arms. "What now?"

"Just wondering where I should—ahem—hold on?"

"Anywhere you want," he purrs. "I'm not precious."

Her snort of amusement confuses him. I'm about to bark for them to hurry, my patience wearing thin, but then she steps forward. Willow encircles her arms around his waist and presses her body flush to his front.

He's not the only one taking a hitched breath at her scent, at her maddening nearness. My senses have been heightened all day since our sparring session. My cock grows hard until I feel it press against Styx's thigh. If he notices, he doesn't reveal it.

Remembering Legion's warning from earlier today, I splay my hand on Willow's lower back and tug her flush against Styx. Her suffering is the last thing we want. She squeaks in surprise.

"Hold onto her," I growl to Styx. "Tight. And if you fuck this up because you're stoned, then you know what will happen to your entrails."

Styx's face pales. Legion's lips curve. Willow's lips part, brows furrow. Before she can question my comment, Styx slips his hands around her waist, and the world *flickers* around us.

The scenery changes with every blink, a dizzying kaleidoscope of places and times. For a moment, I catch glimpses of unfamiliar landscapes, echoes of laughter, and flashes of golden feathers spattered with blood.

When we land, I am thoroughly disoriented. The heady air is humid and thick with the scent of night-blooming jasmine and exotic spices. A rhythmic beating of drums competes with my galloping heart, the primal rhythm sending vibrations through the soles of my feet. I step back, frowning at the familiar breezy curtains dangling between low-hanging branches, their gossamer fabric shimmering with an otherworldly radiance. Bonfires flicker in the distance, casting long shadows that dance and writhe like living things. A gathering crowd laughs and converses, their voices a melodic hum punctuated by occasional bursts of tinkling laughter. Some kind of grassed dais is being set up for dancing, its surface sprinkled with luminescent petals that glow softly in the fading light. A pole at each corner connects lanterns swinging on chains overhead.

"This isn't the meeting spot," I growl, suspicion coiling in my gut like a serpent.

"This is *inside* Burn After Reading." Legion's voice is tight as he scans the shadowy trees on the outskirts. The brass spectacles perched on his nose catch sparks of light from flying sprites nearby, momentarily transforming his stern visage into something otherworldly. My gaze snags on the tiny sprites, their wings leaving trails of glittering dust in the air, and I'm transported to another place for a heartbeat. But the memory slips away like smoke through my fingers.

I grip the back of Styx's neck and squeeze hard, leaning in to whisper harshly in his ear, "Why did you *flicker* us straight inside?"

The other mortals and Radiants do not know this true location. It is a secret Fox imparted to us. Styx could have blown our cover if anyone noticed and then later evaded the memory-stealing enchantment on the exit.

"More importantly," Legion adds, his eyes shrewd. "How did you know where to go? This place is spelled to be hidden. The meeting point I gave you was not."

Styx *flickers* out of my hold, reappearing beside me with a disgruntled expression. "Relax, no one is watching."

He glances around, searching. A gentle breeze carries the familiar sweet, cloying scent of magic-laced cigarillos, and realization dawns.

"You were already here," I accuse.

He gives an infuriating shrug.

"Go home, Styx," Legion orders, anger tightening his voice. "We'll find our way back."

"Nah. Think I'll stay." He lazily scratches his abdomen, a predatory glint entering his eyes as they land on Willow. "I'm feeling peckish."

Before we can remind him of the incident with Fox and the dangers of feeding here, he's gone, melting into the crowd of gaudy revelers like a shadow at noon.

"Is he always like this?" Willow asks.

"I don't know," I grind out.

Legion says, "Yes."

"Okay, then." She snorts. "Have you been here before, Legion? You weren't clear earlier."

His expression becomes a mask of inscrutability as he walks toward the crowd, his hands in his pockets, the picture of powerful nonchalance. Willow rolls her eyes at his back and mumbles something about being obtuse.

I ensure she follows him while I take the rear. A few steps in, she flicks her golden-eyed gaze over her shoulder and asks, "Do you remember coming here?"

I shrug. My mind can't focus enough to think. She looks breathtaking beneath the sun's dying light. It was midnight at home, but sunset here.

A rose-gold glow lingers on her silver hair, cascading down her back like a waterfall of starlight. The same glow paints her curves with alluring highlights, deepening the shadows and accentuating every tantalizing line of her body. She's a living masterpiece, and I'm torn between the desire to protect her and the urge to claim her as my own.

Willow huffs at my lack of response and continues walking ahead. The sway of her hips becomes a hypnotic dance, drawing my gaze like a moth to a flame. I'm so mesmerized that I fail to notice Legion dropping back to walk beside me until he murmurs, "Our queen is beautiful, is she not?"

"Mouthwatering." The word escapes before I can stop it, raw and honest in a way that surprises even me.

He makes a sound of appreciative agreement.

My tension releases when we fall into silence, admiring the treasure ahead. Every step she takes is a temptation, every glimpse of smooth, bare flesh a siren call. She is a dichotomy—both the moon and the sun, night and day, two opposites that shouldn't exist together but do.

"I don't think she knows how alluring she is," Legion mumbles darkly. "The dress is a problem."

"I agree." It is the epitome of trouble in that tantalizing body. "Do we order Peablossom to redesign her wardrobe?"

Legion's jaw works. "That is the smart choice, however ..."

"Hiding her beauty would be a crime," I finish.

We share another gaze. Despite the lack of our hive connection, he knows exactly what I'm thinking.

"We will have to think of another way to stake our claim," Legion muses, eyes taking in the roaming gazes sent Willow's way. "Without her magic, the mate bond will not be visible. And Puck will be a problem for a while."

"The meeting did not go well?"

"It went as expected."

"Hm." So Legion voted Puck in as the next member of the Shining Host. "And now?"

"Now we let him do his thing while we do ours."

Our gazes settle on Willow as she walks and looks around with curiosity. I catch her hand snake out whip-fast and nab something dangling from a Radiant's belt. It disappears into her fist so deftly I'd be forgiven into thinking my eyes deceived me.

"She should not be so brazen," I growl.

"Let her enjoy the anonymity," Legion says. "Every eye in the kingdom and beneath will be watching her soon."

"I will mark her somewhere all can see." The surge of hot possessiveness is sudden and brutal.

"Not yet," he replies calmly, studying her with bright curiosity. "We have much to make amends for. Fox opened her fragile heart to us, but to keep her trust, we must take care of her, listen to her desires, and give her what she needs."

"Then it is fortunate you have the spectacles," I grumble begrudgingly. "You are the best for a job requiring patience."

If it were up to me, I would eat her alive. I would start my meal between her legs, where that tantalizing scent is strongest, then—

He grabs my arm. "Not I, brother. You."

"Me what?"

"You will see to her desires."

"I know nothing about her needs." I only know what I hunger for.

"So ask her." He cocks his head. "Listen. If necessary, I will fill in the gaps."

"She is a distraction," I remind him.

"A good one."

"We don't know the meaning of good."

"You've simply forgotten." His lips curve. "She will remind you." His eyes deviate with a low warning growl. I follow his line of sight and realize that while we've been admiring Willow, so has every other hot-blooded male in the vicinity.

My fists clench at my sides. I should have noticed she was being watched. There is no such thing as a *good* distraction.

Flashes of gold from her sun-kissed hair shine in my eyes. In the darkness of my blink, I see yellow feathers spattered with blood. An unbearable feeling of grief paralyzes me, and I don't know why.

Legion's attentive eyes search mine. "What's wrong?"

"Nothing."

"We may not share minds, Bodin, but I know you well enough to see that is a lie."

"I said I'm fine." I sharpen my gaze on our surroundings. The burn of his attention paints the side of my face, but I keep walking. Our conversation has caused a gap between Calamity and us.

I may not have full access to my memories or gifts, but I can still do my job. I can still protect. I can instill fear into mortal minds with a single glare. And those leering at her? They've seen me in action on the battlefield. If not, they've heard about me. They'll stay away from us if they know what's good for them.

It's been a while since I visited this place, but my vague memories always end in debauchery and trouble—the former for other patrons, but the latter for me. At the time, I believed my lack of interest in sex was battle weariness. My emotions were too frayed.

My gaze inadvertently gravitates to Willow's swinging hips. One whiff of her scent makes me hard. But her mouth, voice, and taste make me obsessed with wanting more. It seems irrational for a single person to affect me so viscerally so soon after meeting.

Despite what Legion believes, this is the danger I must contain—for once it is let out, there is no holding it back. She will be crushed, like the gold feathers I often see behind my eyelids. The thought sends a chill down my spine, a premonition of tragedy I cannot shake.

We approach the bar with the turquoise thatched roof. Willow pushes through imbalanced, intoxicated wastrels with practiced ease and walks inside. A male with an open shirt and lustful eyes tracks her passage. He smacks his hand on his companion's chest, then jerks his chin toward her.

I pause beside them and stare down. Suddenly, Legion's order to prioritize her safety isn't so off-putting. The first male lifts his attention to me and curses, then lowers his gaze appropriately.

"Bodin," Legion calls from somewhere in my periphery. The bar, perhaps.

"Look at her again," I warn the men, "and I'll pluck out your eyes with my teeth."

The stench of urination fills me with satisfaction. Legion calls my name again, yet I keep my stare planted on my targets. One twitch in her direction, and I follow through with my promise.

"Sir, we're so sorry, sir." The sour, stinking one drops to his knees.

"Move," I grunt.

They scramble out of my way, and I stalk to the bar, rolling my shoulders to ease the tension.

This place has been known to harbor outlaws amongst the shady-dealing Radiants. My suspicions are confirmed when I lock eyes with a bulky, muscular mortal with buzzed hair and sharp eyes. His posture is relaxed, dwarfing the couch he sits on in Cait's reserved area at the end of the bar. He holds an open book in his large hands, but I have no doubt he's committed every corner of this grimy establishment to memory.

Another mortal reclines on the opposite couch, smoking a cigarillo and deftly flipping cards. His short blond hair is slicked back, and he wears a stylish silk shirt and buttoned vest. He reminds me of Fox. Not for his appearance, but for the deft skill in his hands when he flips the cards and catches them. A distraction, so no one sees their death until it's too late.

A third male with black hair and feathered wings arrives. Warning bells go off inside my gut. I don't know why, but the wings—yes, the wings. They're uncommon in Avorlorna. And yes, the tattoos. They wrap around his athletic, leather-covered figure. The skin markings and scars are outlawed according to the Old Code's mandates on pristine appearance. Something in his psychotic blue eyes rattles my nerves.

Recognition flashes across his face with a dash of spite when he looks at me. He knows me. Or perhaps us—the Sluagh— because his gaze drops to the blue Guardian teardrop beneath my left eye, and that spite deepens to hate. He sits beside the big brute, and the two quarrel as the wings occupy too much space.

They're no threat for now. But the nagging feeling that I'm missing something crucial lingers, an itch I can't scratch.

I arrive at the bar in time to see Legion handing a small, heavy sack over the counter. Cait smiles warmly at Willow but levels narrow emerald eyes at him and ignores the sack. She rests her curvaceous behind against the rear shelf, raises wordless, dark brows at Legion, and purses her lips when he fails to respond.

Willow glances between the two with a frown. "What am I missing here?"

I am wondering the same thing. The petite barmaid is part

cat, part soul stealer. Originating from the subterranean, she cannot be trusted. The glowing jewels dangling from her nose chain and choker are entrapped souls she controls, a grim reminder of her power.

"One hundred wisps." Legion jingles the sack. "As agreed upon with Fox."

The pointed black ears poking through her auburn hair twitch, a telltale sign of her interest despite her feigned indifference. Legion places the sack down on the bar with a sigh.

"Anyway—" Willow bumps Legion aside, grins, and leans excitedly on the bar. "Hi, Cait! I brought two tall, dark, and brooding friends." She narrows her eyes at us and taps her lips, considering. "They both fit the descriptor, so I'm not sure which one you referred to last time I was here."

"Good to have you back, O'Leary-Nightstalk. I see you didn't need my help after all." Cait's emerald eyes take in Willow's face with a flash of respect. "I knew you wouldn't, but I hoped you would. A soul like yours is hard to come by."

CHAPTER 19
BODIN

A warning growl slices through the air, low and menacing. Not mine. Legion's countenance hasn't shifted, only his hand. It is now an inch closer to Cait across the bar. It's all she needs to understand the threat.

"Relax," Cait purrs at him. "I was never going to go through with it. Her soul is already taken."

"You were going to what?" Willow gapes. "Wait. Taken by who? You?"

Cait's smile turns feline, all sharp teeth and secrets. She points to a bottle behind her. "Another Screwdriver tonight?"

"Um. No." Willow pats her flat belly nervously and shakes her head. "Last time, it didn't go down well."

"Hm. Not for anyone, it seems." Something in Cait's eyes flickers—almost fondness, I think. But it's gone before I can be sure. Instead, she shifts her gaze to Legion's face. "You realize I'm the one who told Fox where to look for the enchantment for those fancy, useless pieces of decoration on your face."

"Does he owe you?"

"He's a friend. Sometimes friends help each other out for free."

I scoff. "Cait Sith doing something for nothing?"

"You're not the only one who was changed by Oberon's rule." Her eyes darken, pupils narrowing to slits. "Continue to judge me for my actions back then, and I will do the same to you."

Did we know her before?

Displeasure flattens Legion's lips, but he answers, "Noted."

At my frown, Cait jerks her thumb at me and asks Legion, "Is it true, then? He remembers nothing about your Canary? None of them do?"

What?

He flicks a concerned look my way before returning to her. "Fox told you?"

"He had no one else to talk to," she replied. "Despite what you think you remember about me, it's wrong. And as I mentioned to Willow, my offer to talk stands."

His reply is lost to the sudden roaring in my ears. A wave of heat engulfs me. My vision wavers as yellow, bloody feathers flash across my mind. I sway on my feet and grip the bar to keep my balance.

"Bodin?" Willow touches my burning forearm, and I flinch.

She tries to hide her hurt at my reaction by looking away, but I see it lurking in her posture. I can't seem to do anything right today. I try to breathe through the unsettled feeling, but the air in here is stifling. Who the fuck needs it to be this warm, and where the fuck are we that I hear the ocean?

I tug at my collar, but the laces are already untied and loose. If I remove any more layers, I'll look as reprobate as Styx. Fuck.

Legion tells Willow, "I noticed a fresh tray of food head outside a moment ago."

Her golden eyes widen. "I *am* kind of hungry."

"I'll take her," I growl through a clenched jaw. Anything to get out of this place. Even the noises seem amplified. Bottles clank, laughter shrieks, and drumming music vibrates my bones. I push off the counter and check Legion is comfortable with the Cait Sith.

"I will be out shortly," he explains. "See to her needs."

"Naturally." The response rolls off my tongue in a familiar way. Legion gives me an odd look, but then a firm nod. I tail Willow into the balmy night air. Outside, she takes one whiff, grabs my hand, and tugs me as she hunts her meal. With my head still swimming, I allow her to guide me around haphazardly placed lounge settees cordoned off with flowing banners and torches.

The air is stifling, yet her warm touch is not. I find myself tightening my grip and focusing on that connection to drown out the horrible, unnamed emotions still churning within me.

Those occupying the settees range from misbehaving Radiants to desperate mortals, drunkards, and those conducting shady business that likely goes against Old Code mandates. Some eat luscious foods; others drink elixirs and concoctions like they're water.

I never understood the appeal of such sustenance. The taste is bland in my mouth. I'll eat if I must or if I forget my true diet, but it is somewhat lackluster. Still, it fascinates me. I hate not knowing why it is so delicious that these people will eat or drink until they burst or cannot walk straight. The music grows louder as we approach dancing and musicians on a raised grassy dais decorated with wild botanicals.

Willow catches the waiter just before he heads into the throng. She taps him on the shoulder. The slim, sparsely dressed male with gold glitter around his eyes swings around to face us, his tray held high. When he looks up at my face, he almost loses balance, but I steady the tray with my free hand and say, "My Shadow would like your sustenance."

"Shadow?" he squeaks.

"Hi." Willow waves. "That's me. Do you mind if I grab a few?"

The waiter blushes at her, his cheeks turning a deep crimson. "Oh. Yes. Um, here."

His assortment of food seems to be a mix of bite-sized meat and juicy little balls of fruit. Willow pops a meaty morsel into her mouth and then collects as many as she can in one hand while the other still holds mine. Helpless desperation crosses her expression as she glances between her full hand and the plentiful tray.

"Give it to me." I relieve the waiter of his tray. "Bring a drink for her to wash this down."

He's more than happy to scurry away, nearly tripping over his feet in haste.

"Sorry," Willow mumbles through a mouthful. "I'm hungrier than I thought. I'll be quick, I promise."

With us caught between the sprawled settees and raucous, dancing throng, she attempts to swallow as much as possible. Every time she licks her lips, she leaves sparkles granted by the nearby torchlight. But she shovels more food into her mouth . . . while still holding my hand.

I raise the tray out of her reach. Her scowl of defiance is a direct line to my cock, and it baffles me. Something primal in that gaze calls to my slumbering, like-minded instincts. They unfurl and take notice. They want more. They want to hunt—just as they did at the end of our sparring session. When I next speak, my voice is hoarse. Tight.

"Let's take this to a table," I suggest.

Relief courses through her eyes, and she nods. I scan and locate a nearby group of people standing around a tall, round table. Perfect. Three strides, and we're there. I glare and part my lips, intending to growl them into submission, but am pleased when they scamper away first. But the fools leave a mess, and the surface area is lacking. I relinquish Willow's hand for the opportunity to swipe every glass and plate to the floor. Once every crumb has gone, I gently lower the precious cargo but almost lose it all when the waiter appears and startles me.

"The drink, sir," he squeaks and holds out a glass filled with a vibrant cherry liquid.

"Oh, you're too kind." Willow grins at him, flashing her tiny fangs.

He blushes again and bows. Hm. Prompt and appropriately subservient toward our Shadow. And I don't wish to pluck out his eyes with my teeth.

"Your name?" I demand.

"Ah . . . um. My name, sir?"

"Yes."

Willow's smile is kind as he fidgets and flusters. It makes me realize I am frowning, so I relax my jaw and brows. I do something with my lips and cheeks that could be considered a smile. It's nowhere near as approachable as hers, but at least it's not a death stare.

"It's okay," she says. "You can tell Bodin. He won't bite. Much."

She winks at me, pops another morsel into her mouth, and something fizzes in the region of my lower belly. Now I'm frowning again. Fuck.

The boy's eyes widen, and she quickly explains, "He bites me. Don't worry, I meant *me*."

"Your name, mortal?" I remind.

"Colin, sir." He bows again. "Recruit rank. I woke up during the last Interlude, sir."

I give the male a once-over. Not much to look at. Scrawny. Hardly any muscle on his bones. No charms. I sniff in his direction. Younger than I first thought.

"Are you a Never?" I ask. "Or not industrious enough to gain yourself a charm by now?"

Willow's next morsel pauses halfway to her mouth. Her eyes narrow on me as if I've said something displeasing.

"I, um . . . I guess I'm what they call a Never," he says, voice pitched high as though it's a question. "I can't use charms."

"Then why are you here? Everyone knows this sordid open-air brothel is where the mortals curry favor with Radiants in turn for charms."

"I want the coin, sir. Cait pays me well, and I need every advantage I can get for the trials."

Unfortunately for him, she will soon leave to hunt for our enchanted mirror, closing this establishment down.

"Are you buying weapons?" Willow asks him, now fully invested in the conversation. He nods, and she adds, "What House are you with?"

"House of Embers," he grumbles, his shoulders sinking.

"Figures," she snorts. "How old are you, Colin? If you don't mind me asking."

"It's fine. I turned sixteen last month. I think." He scratches his head. "It's hard to know the exact date these days."

"You're only a baby," Willow gasps, dismayed.

"No, I'm not." He scowls but quickly dips his head. "I just hit puberty late."

"How many exhibitors are under eighteen?" she asks, almost to herself.

"A few of us, I suppose," he answers. "At least ten in the House of Embers. We have the biggest group of youngies." He snorts at himself. "That's what I call us. Cos we're young. Get it?"

It's the oddest thing. Willow smiles, yet her eyes shimmer with unshed tears, and she seems to have trouble answering. So I fill the silence for her. This banter is becoming long-winded, and I have a reason for initiating conversation with the youth.

"You snuck up on me," I state gruffly.

"Sir?" His sour fear hits my nose.

"Someone with your skills is more useful trained as a Phantom for when the Interlude is over." For when the war renews.

"Me?"

"That's what I said." Perhaps I was wrong in my assessment if I must constantly repeat myself. At his blanched complexion and Willow's echo of surprise, a nervous roll in my gut makes me second-guess myself. So I add, "Unless you . . . actually want to compete in the trials?"

"No!"

My brows raise.

"I mean, no, sir, I don't want to participate in the trials. I'd very much rather learn to be a Phantom. I'm only here because . . ." He looks nervously at Willow. For guidance, I realize. She seems to soothe the fractious fear so often witnessed in mortals around me.

"Speak freely," I say.

"It's just that, sir, us Nevers don't often get promoted to anything beyond recruit. That's what they tell me, anyway. And the thought of working on a farm or indentured servitude doesn't appeal to me—"

"Whoa, whoa, whoa." Willow holds her hand up. "What do you mean indentured servitude?"

His eyes widen. He looks at me, so I put him out of his misery and remind Willow, "Nevers—like Cricket and Finch—must contribute to the good of our nation by either serving the Folk directly or working on a farm and supplying a tithe of produce and resources."

Her jaw drops. "I didn't know that." She closes her lips. "I mean, Max mentioned something about a farm. And Cricket did say she . . ."

The troubled look in her eyes concerns me. "Willow?"

"It's just that I'd made assumptions based on brief conversations. I thought all the mortals were in Nocturna or at the Nexus."

"Oh no," Colin offers eagerly. "There are thousands of us up here, too. In fact, I think mortals outnumber the Folk. Right?"

He looks to me for confirmation, but I am still stuck on Willow's troubled face and ask, "Did you not know?"

"I did not."

CHAPTER 20
BODIN

In the following silence, I consider plucking the youth's eyes out after all. His words put that sadness in Willow's eyes, killing the light.

"So, can I be a Phantom without being able to use charms?" he asks, oblivious to my mood.

Indeed, the Radiants usually promote those who can use magic, but this year is different. The Knights of the Queen's Hive rarely have time to worry about recruits or where they're from. We're too busy to deal with low-level matters.

"A Phantom is what I say it is," I growl. "Only the queen's knights deal with military matters."

"What about Lord Ignarius?"

"I will deal with him. You will move into the Shadow Tower."

"How will I—"

I rip the House of Shadow emblem from my shirt pocket, eager to finish this conversation. "Take this. When you leave this establishment and find it in your possession, you'll know to find me at the House of Shadow Tower."

It is well-known that if one finds a mysterious stone the

morning after visiting this establishment, they should take it to the House Radiant.

"Yes, sir." He nods vehemently but pauses expectantly. Waiting for something?

"What?" I ask, bristling at the awe in his eyes.

"I'm waiting for you to dismiss me, sir."

I give an approving grunt. Good start. "Tell me what's in the drink, and then you are dismissed."

"Cait said it's a Cosmo."

What the fuck?

Willow chuckles and mentions something about her aunty and cocks and tails—which makes me even angrier at the youth —but then she takes a sip, and her pink tongue drags slowly along her plump bottom lip. A moan of satisfaction slips out of her.

I shoo Colin away.

Emrys could have a point about our memories. I'm unsure if I want them at all if they're full of images of her with other cocks and tails.

Six cocks in our hive are enough. Two tails are already too much. They knock things over all the time, cause a mess, and . . . the thought of her with others . . . Violence. That's the only response I'll have. I blink away the concern and glare at our surroundings, checking for signs of any other lurking eyes that need plucking out.

A ginger-haired mortal watches us from a few yards away. The Court of Dreams Shadow must be drinking the palace water to believe he has the right to look this way. A sliver of shadow peels away from mine and starts snaking its way across the grass toward him. The sound of her voice stops my assault in its tracks.

"How many do you think I subjected to this fate?"

I call the shadow back. "Subjected?" I ask.

She's swirling the cherry-colored drink with her finger, that sadness back in her eyes. "Some would say I kidnapped them from their families."

"The mortals?"

"Geraldine, Max, Peggy . . . they had family in the old world. A family that, for some reason, never woke. Or maybe they did and were tossed down below before they could reunite. How much suffering have I caused without even knowing it?"

"You did not kidnap them." My hand covers hers, stopping its next smear across the glass. "Nor did you knowingly cause their suffering. The gods have a lot to answer for. Not you."

Her eyes search mine. "But maybe I want to have an answer."

"Then that makes you . . ."

"What?" she asks and licks her finger.

"Good."

"Ooh yum." She smacks her lips, distracted by the taste. All thoughts empty from my mind. "I'll have to tell Cait she nailed this one. My aunt Laurel would be impressed."

"This is the aunt who enjoys multiple cocks and tails?" My brow raises, and she bursts out laughing, then pats my cheek with affection.

"What they say about you is so wrong."

"Hm?" How does she do that? Smile crookedly and pout at once? Wait. My gaze flicks up to hers. "What do they say about me?"

She lobs a berry into her mouth and crunches. Juice squirts, and she covers her mouth awkwardly. The liquid runs down her chin.

"What do they say?" I growl, snatching her second helping of berry.

"That you're a villain." She rolls her eyes. "That you eat babies —what a lot of *katuri*-shit. Maybe you were bad once, but you're not now. You're all a bunch of softies."

"Katuri?"

"Elphyne flying bird-beast? You really don't remember?"

Red spatters on yellow feathers.

I shake my head.

"*Crimson*, I miss home," she murmurs, eyes downcast. "I can't go back yet, but I wish ..."

"What?" Tell me so I can remove the sadness from your eyes.

"I wish I didn't leave without saying goodbye properly." She scratches her head and exhales. "I should have said goodbye. Should have felt confident enough to come here even if my father didn't want me to. My mother knew I would. She approved."

A feeling washes through me, both unsettling and familiar. "Would you like to speak with them?"

Hope glimmers in her eyes. "You would help me make a blood-bond communication through the water?"

I blink. "I'm not sure what that is. My question was simply curiosity."

"Oh."

Speaking with family outside of Avorlorna could pose a risk, especially considering I remember nothing about such dangers but ... she is suffering.

"Perhaps," I say, "if you tell me what to do, I can help."

Too overwhelmed with emotions, she simply nods.

I'm not sure how long I stand there, trying to catch more of that familiar feeling, but when Willow next speaks, her sadness shifts to something closer to home.

"Colin is too young to die," she murmurs, searching my eyes. "You saved him. Thank you."

"You might think differently when you learn what a Phantom does."

Her tone drops, a hint of steel underlying the question. "Why?"

"Eat your food, Calamity." I shove a berry into her mouth. The soft brush of her lips against my fingertips sends an unexpected jolt through my body.

Willow's eyes widen, but she accepts the berry, chewing

thoughtfully. Her gaze never leaves mine, a silent challenge in those golden depths.

"You didn't answer my question," she says softly after swallowing.

I consider deflecting again, but something in her expression stops me.

"Phantoms," I begin, choosing my words carefully, "are essential to our operations. They gather information, infiltrate enemy lines, and sometimes . . . eliminate threats before they become problems."

Willow's brow furrows. "So, you've basically recruited Colin to be a spy. And possibly an assassin."

I nod, watching her reaction closely.

"I suppose in times of war, such roles are necessary," she says slowly. "But he's so young . . ."

"Youth can be an advantage in this line of work," I explain. "People underestimate the young and let their guard down. And Colin has already shown an aptitude for stealth."

Willow nods, but conflict clouds her eyes. "I understand the logic, but it doesn't make accepting it any easier. He should be . . . I don't know, learning a trade, falling in love, living a normal life."

Her words stir something within me. "Normal is a luxury we can't afford, Calamity. Not with the threats we face."

She looks at me, really looks at me. "And what about you, Bodin? What's normal for you?"

The question catches me off-guard. Flashes of blood, violence, and duty flicker through my mind, interspersed with newer, softer memories—all of them centered around the female before me.

"I . . ." I begin, then falter.

Willow reaches out, her hand resting lightly on my arm. "It's okay. You don't have to answer that. I shouldn't have pried."

Her touch is warm and grounding. I find myself leaning into it almost imperceptibly. "No, it's a fair question. I'm just not sure I have an answer."

But I want to.

She nods, understanding in her eyes. "Well, I'd like to hear about it when you figure it out."

I watch as she sips her drink, her throat working as she swallows. The sight stirs a savage hunger in me that has nothing to do with food. I think it's at this moment I realize Legion is right. She is a distraction, but a good one.

CHAPTER 21
WILLOW

Bodin stares at me from across the round table, tense and looking like he wants to say something. I hope he'll open up about what's worrying him, but he abruptly presses another berry against my lips. His gaze darkens hotly when I open, allowing his offering partly inside.

"Nibble the tip." His gruff voice sends shivers down my spine.

We're mere yards from the music and dancing, yet the noise and crowd melt away. Why is he so mesmerized by my mouth? It can't be that enticing . . . can it?

"Tell me what it tastes like," he murmurs, nudging the berry deeper.

I bite down, and juice bursts, trickling with abundance down my chin.

"Oops." I try to catch the spill.

"Gentle," he scolds, brushing his thumb along my chin to catch the drip. He licks his thumb and brings the berry to my mouth again. "Once more. But savor it. Yes, like that."

My second nibble is softer, allowing the juices to pool on my tongue. There's something in how he looks at me, eyelids heavy, pupils blown, breath shallow. I feel an echo of it myself, low and

hot in my belly. Lower. Between my thighs. I press them together with a moan.

His eyes crinkle. "That good, huh?"

I nod.

"What does it taste like?" he asks.

"Sweet. Tart."

His brows pucker. "What is sweet and tart?"

"You don't know?"

"Most things taste like dirt to us," he explains absently, tossing the crushed berry, licking his fingers, then finding another ripe one on the plate. "Fox plays a game sometimes to guess what it's like for those more alive than us, but . . . ah, this one. Here."

"Why?" I stubbornly avoid his advance. "You seem alive to me."

"It is not the same." He scowls. "It's hard to explain without my memories."

His expression shutters, and I feel like I've lost him. He turns his vigilant gaze to the crowd and asks, "We shouldn't dawdle. Where has Styx gone?"

"He's on the dance floor," I grumble, then blush when he gives me a questioning look.

How has he not noticed Styx with his arms up, his muscular torso glistening with sweat as he stares at the stars and sways hypnotically to the music? Every female in his vicinity can't take their eyes off him and his body. Chasers circle like sharks. Yet he's oblivious to all of them as he sucks on that heady cigarillo, lost in his own world, nodding to himself every so often as if he's . . . I gasp.

"Is he sneaking into people's minds?" I ask.

"Naturally."

I smile despite myself. Fox was averse to entering minds without consent, but something about Styx doing it makes me think he's just curious about these people, their customs, and their desires.

The dance floor is filled with mortals. The flute and rhythmic drums keep pulling into familiar glimpses of tunes I recognize from my time in Crystal City. Rory had an old tiny brick that played music, and Nero had something he called a granniphone —no, a grandmaphone. No, that's not right either. Whatever it was called, it recorded music for later play. The nightly shows at dinner featured music from the old world. They used old-world songs to remember humanity's history. I liked that part of their society—they honored the beauty they lost.

Kind of like the way my mom and her friends continue to have their cocktail tradition.

Of course, Nero used our love of music as propaganda. He forced my aunt Melody to sing certain songs so he could evoke the mood he required before grandstanding about the so-called Tainted Fae. Tears prickle my eyes, and I shake myself a little.

I have to stop blaming myself for what happened. If I hadn't been in Crystal City, Queen Maebh would have killed me. Melody would never have met her Well-blessed mate, Forrest. Multiple matings afterward wouldn't have happened either. How can I put my suffering before the love of so many couples? Events were even manipulated so my parents would find each other because of my prophesized birth.

I was kidnapped, alone, and made to murder animals and innocent people, then bring them back to life so they could murder more under my direction. But now I'm here, searching for redemption and my happily ever after. A tugging in my chest lifts my gaze to Bodin. His eyes are closed, his brows pinched, and he sways as he did at the bar.

Concerned, I touch his hand. "Are you okay?"

"I'm fine." He tugs his hand away and resumes a listless search of the crowd, but his eyes have lost the spark they gained when feeding me berries.

I probably look like a mess. I'm sticky, covered in juice, but he seems to like that. A wicked idea forms in my mind.

"Tell me what's making you frown"—I rifle through the fruit and hand him a round, plump berry that smells divine—"and I'll let you do to my mouth whatever you were fantasizing about earlier."

The impact of our eyes clashing steals my breath. The intense wave of lust and longing from him nearly bowls me over. It smells spicy, male, and good. He slowly removes the berry from my fingers and inches closer, but I shake my head.

"You go first," I say.

His arrogant, frustrated growl floods my lower belly with desire. That shouldn't turn me on, but it reminds me of how he pinned me beneath him after our sparring. The way he dominated me triggered every wolfish instinct in my body.

Stay strong, Willow. He needs to learn to share. How can I help him? How can we bond if he can't share his worries?

"Bodin?" I press. "If you let me in, maybe I can help."

He cups the back of his neck, stares at the berry, then rushes out his words. "I keep seeing things in my head. It makes no sense and leaves me ill."

I glance around to see if anyone is within earshot, but the music is loud enough to cover us. "What do you see?"

"Yellow feathers. Blood. In my trembling hands."

Cait questioned Legion, *Does he know about your Canary?*

Nero forced me to kill birds and then bring them back to life. At first, I refused. After a while, he threatened to use Rory as the practice subject. That's how he lured me into my first kill . . . I was trying to protect her.

The death of an innocent, no matter how small, is harrowing.

My lips part to ask more, but he pushes the berry into my mouth. I'm unsure if it's my surprise clamping down or his trembling fingers squishing, but it bursts. I groan appreciatively. It's the juiciest one yet. He swears again at his ineptitude, but I laugh as rivulets run down my neck and tickle.

"It's fine." I lick around my lips. "It's just juice."

"I hope so," he grumbles, wiping his hands on his shirt. "I don't recognize this delicacy."

"It was an accident." I grip his arms to stop his fussing. "What are you worried about?"

"What if I poisoned you because I—" He bites off his words and frowns at my lips. "I should . . . taste it to see. Maybe."

"You're going to poison yourself too?" I laugh too easily.

His mood is anything but amused as he dips and swipes his tongue along my lip. Warm, wet, male. He tastes—*oh*. His tongue pushes into my mouth, and now he's kissing me, slow and deep. I am dazed and disoriented when he breaks away.

I chase his lips, but he mutters darkly, "It won't kill you."

"What won't?"

"The berry," he explains, still close, breath warm on my face. "It's not going to kill you."

"You sure?" That was dumb, Willow. Use your words. "Maybe you should check again."

A glint in his eyes. His lips curve, lighting up his face in a way I've never seen before. Butterflies riot in my stomach as he leans in again but hovers an inch from my mouth. The heat of his body, the smell of leather and spice mixed with male—it turns my insides liquid. His hand curves around my nape and controls me so I'm pinned as he drives his tongue in deep. His plundering kiss is dizzying, drugging, and it fries every cell in my brain. He kisses nothing like Fox. Fox was enticing, seductive. Bodin is taking, claiming.

I exist as the object of his fascination, and I'm okay with that. More than okay.

I fist his shirt and tug him closer. He growls, hand slipping up into my hair and clenching tight, holding me still so he can finish how he wants. When he pulls back, we're both panting hard. My lips are swollen and tingling. A pleasant warmth has spilled through my body, loosening my limbs and heightening my awareness of every hot, mouthwatering inch of his square jaw, thick neck, and taut tendons. Fuck, that vein—that smooth, velvety skin. It reminds me of a hard, rigid cock, and now I want to see what his looks like. My eyes dip down to the bulge in his pants. No one will notice if I get on my knees now.

A low, appreciative growl rumbles from the base of my throat. My knees weaken, and I try to drop, but he holds me steady, a concerned look in his eyes.

"What was in that berry?" he muses.

"It's likely a grape from a faerie vine, not a berry." Legion appears like an apparition at our table. Whoa. I blink. He's also looking mighty sexy with those brass spectacles framing his long-lashed eyes. Such beautiful, soulful eyes I can get lost inside.

Styx arrives also, all lazy, puffy-eyed, and messy-haired. He searches the tray. "Any left?"

"Styx!" I squeal. He gives me a dubious look. I tug myself from Bodin's arms and throw myself onto him. "I'm so happy to see you."

"The effects are mild," Legion drawls, steadying me when I stumble. He holds me at arm's length and searches my eyes. "More a loosening of the body than the mind. Still, don't eat another."

"I feel fine." I grin, all warm and fuzzy. "This is nothing like what Milford drugged me with."

Someone snarls viciously, but I can't tell who. They're all suddenly furious.

"Lighten up, guys." I toss a grape at Bodin, the scowliest. "Or we'll never get out of here alive."

He catches it before his face. Styx's lips twitch. Legion's gaze hardens as he scans me from top to toe. "This is problematic."

I roll my eyes. "I'm not that bad."

"You smell like a berry." He frowns. "Instead of . . ."

"You?" I boop his nose, grinning when his frown deepens.

"Precisely. You need to smell like us." His nostrils flare. "Fae have heightened senses."

"I'm well aware of that." I point to my ears.

"So then you're on board with us covering you with our scent?" This coming from Styx surprises me. I partly think he's mocking me, partly testing me.

I shrug. "Actually, I think that would be comforting. I've been secretly stealing your clothes . . . Especially Fox's."

"Agreed." Legion nods. His eyes already tell me he's formulating the best way to have them all set up a roster for who marks me and when. Whose shirt I can borrow next. I have to admit, I was teasing them at first, but now they're staring at me so Well-damn seriously.

Wolves have glands on their paws. They also mark by—ew. "No one is allowed to urinate on me. Got it?" I scold a little too loudly. "Just in case you were confused."

"No confusion here." Legion's eyes glimmer with amusement. He gently directs me back into Bodin's arms. "You are the first queen we're biologically compatible with."

"Not a queen," I correct. Wait. "Biologically compatible?"

"Yes," he says simply.

A thought occurs to me. "That means I should probably go on some kind of birth control, right? Do they have that pink elixir my aunts take here?"

Legion tenses. He takes a noticeable step away from me, but I don't think I offended him. He seems to be composing himself. It's good to see him being affected by the same things that affect me. The more I see these little genuine tells of emotion, the more my old, misguided thoughts about the Sluagh disappear. These little moments, these little looks cast my way, remind me of the fondness shared between my parents. I can only be a good sign I'm heading in the right direction.

"Cait is honoring her deal with Fox," Legion notes, returning to business. "She leaves tomorrow."

"That's good news," Bodin replies, eyes flicking to me with thought. "What is this elixir?"

Legion stares at me. Something like longing flickers in his eyes before they turn cold, and he returns to Bodin. "I will ask her about the elixir."

"Um. Thanks?" I wave my hand. They're talking about me like I'm not here.

All eyes land on me. Stare.

"You have juice all over you," Legion notes, and I laugh.

This feels good. I like it.

CHAPTER 22
WILLOW

"Do you think anyone will notice if I steal a few Chaser charms on the dance floor?" I ask absently. "So many of them dangle unprotected, ripe for the picking."

Styx deadpans and replies, "We can't repurpose charms already keyed to others."

"I knew that." I blush.

He gives me an unimpressed look and then scours the crowd, ignoring me. It both riles me and confuses me. My emotions have been hard to regulate since the mate bond connected but then disconnected. It's like my hormones are bouncing back into me, furious they have nowhere to go for relief. That scent-marking thing is starting to feel like a really good option for more reasons than my perversive fantasies.

My heart soars when a familiar tune comes on, and the mostly mortal crowd cheers. Grinning, I look at my companions and shout, "It's my aunt Melody's song! She used to be famous in the old world."

"I remember." Legion's lips twitch.

"This is a sign," I groan. "Who wants to dance with me?"

I look at them expectantly, my grin still on my lips.

Legion shakes his head. "I don't dance."

"Neither do I," Bodin grumps.

"I do." Styx sidesteps Legion to walk toward me, but then smashes his shoulder against mine as he passes. "But not with you."

I watch him stroll into the dancing crowd, and my grin broadens. I should be angry at his mercurial behavior toward me, but I'm not. Melody's song is on. I stare at the remaining two.

"Come on," I plead. "This is the last night we get to mingle like this in public! It will be fun."

They don't move, so I start walking backward, trailing my finger down my neck and dipping into my juice-covered cleavage before sucking my finger suggestively.

"Guess I'll find someone else to dance with, then," I tease.

Legion palms Bodin between the shoulder blades, and he stumbles toward me. It's hard to fight my triumph, but when Legion strides behind him, expression hot, I raise my arms and thank the stars in the sky.

I wind around the loners, skirt the main thriving mass, and climb onto the grassed dais. Alfie's familiar russet hair is a few yards away. His green eyes lock with mine and fill with emotion before hardening as he takes in who is behind me. Dahlia and Becky are beside him, cheering and singing along to the music. Two other female Chasers I don't recognize listen avidly to something he says. My first thought is that he's boasting he knew Melody, but then I remember he hasn't told anyone where we came from. While he never went to the extremes I did, he's as ashamed as me about our past. Or maybe he's just ashamed of me.

Legion tugs my shoulder.

"Just here," he barks, pointing to a spot near a pole.

Fine with me. I'd rather stay far away from that *floater* anyway. With a sigh, I lift my chin and inhale deeply, taking the scent of my mates into my lungs. I lift my hair off my neck. The sensation feels so good on my skin. But it feels even better when I let it all cascade down and leave my hands swaying in time to the music as I saw Styx do earlier. I close my eyes and remember Melody trying to cheer me up last year before she celebrated Christmas with the other old-worlders.

"Sugar, give me a song, any song, and I'll sing it for you." She *squishes her curvaceous body next to Forrest on the sofa in the Guardian's house.*

"That one you sang when Uncle Forrest stole you away from Crystal City."

"By John Farnham?"

I nod. She gives me a coy look from beneath her platinum-blond wavy hair and starts tapping a beat on a porcelain saucepan between her legs as she sings, "We have the chance to turn the pages over..."

"Behind her." Legion's gruff order draws me out of the memory.

"What am I to do?" Bodin returns, sliding around to stand behind me.

"Brace her. Stop her from falling off the dais."

Warm, steady hands land on my hips. Bodin presses the length of his body against my spine.

"This feels awkward," his deep voice vibrates through my back, but I'm moaning at the tingling sensations.

"Feels right to me." I move to the music, swaying my hips, falling back into my memory. While I scowled too much to dance that day with Melody, I'm making up for lost time now. I'll have to tell her one day that I remembered. That I danced, thinking fondly of her.

"Sway your hips in time with hers." Legion's voice grows huskier, quieter. "Yes. Like that."

If I could stay here forever, I would. It feels so good leaning against my warm pillar of strength, to feel safe enough to let myself go without being too drunk to know my name. The effects of that grape are mild, as Legion predicted, and not muddling my thoughts. I just feel ... happy.

It would be my honor to catch you. Fox's voice swims into my mind. My eyes flutter closed, and my grin turns wistful as the music sinks into my bones. I reach behind to rest my hand around Bodin's neck. His breathy growl of approval tickles my skin, tightens my nipples, quickens my pulse.

"You missed a spot." Legion's deep voice is closer this time. Softer. Is that desire I detect in his tone? A wall of heat envelops my front. My breath hitches. I open my eyes and find his dark eyes hooded behind those brass rims. He's not dancing, just soaking me up like the sun on a cold day. Only Legion could stand where everyone else dances and command attention with his presence, his beauty.

He gathers my long hair to one side, then trails a finger down the side of my exposed neck. "Here," he tells Bodin softly. "Clean up your mess."

Hot lips land on the skin beneath my ear. I gasp as a shiver runs through me. Legion's gaze collides with mine, holding me captive as he traces another sticky rivulet down my neck, over the mounds of my cleavage, to the dip in the middle and taps. "And here."

Bodin twirls me to face him and pushes me back. Legion tugs me hard against his body, trapping me with a strong arm beneath my breasts, lifting them like an offering to Bodin's lips. The low-cut V-neck collar is not built for such actions. The pillows of flesh almost burst from their confines. My sensitive nipples drag precariously close to the edge of the fabric.

Bodin swallows my gasp, kissing me hungrily.

"No," Legion growls. He grips Bodin's knot of braids and forcibly guides his mouth back down to my decolletage. "Lick every last drop of your mess."

"How do you know it's mine?" He chuckles, dragging a raspy tongue over my cleavage.

"I saw you." A breathy, rough confession. "I stayed back and waited, watching you."

Bodin groans and shoves me harder against Legion. Every swirling, open-mouthed swipe of his tongue feels like he devours me. He inches closer to my aching nipple. My world centers on that point. Please. Yes, there. Lower. With a moan, I arch into him, wanting to guide that friction. Bodin nips me. My hitched breath makes him look up at me with smug male eyes.

"I said lick, not nip," Legion scolds, his breath tickling my ear.

"She likes it." Bodin nips me again, and I moan. "See?"

Hypnotic music swirls like his tongue. Hands, warm and large, slide around my hips to my belly.

"Bite her lower." Legion's quiet demand is hot on my jaw as he cranes for a look over my shoulder. "Through the dress."

His long hair falls forward, tickling my exposed skin, adding to the overwhelming sensations. Through the dress, Bodin takes my nipple between his teeth and gently clamps down until pleasure floods me. I cry out. He suckles until his saliva dampens the dress. A breeze washes in and cools the spot, adding to the sensations threatening to overwhelm me.

"More," I beg. Whimper. Try to guide Legion's hand where I need it. Lower. Through the slit of my dress. "Please."

"No." He tugs his hand away from me, voice cold. "I refuse to touch you this way."

A confusing swirl of arousal and anger swamps me. They crowd me between their bodies. Legion's reticence doesn't make sense. My heart sinks. He's tensed every time I touch him. Now this. All I can think is that he's rejecting me, even when he directs Bodin's lips to my neck and adds, "But I will not leave you wanting."

I might have walked away to protect my feelings, but Bodin's tongue swirling on my sensitive breast is insistent, hungry. I fall back into that place of need, spiraling fast into hot desire, forgetting about the cold body behind me.

To anyone else, it might look like we're slow dancing, my head thrown back against Legion's shoulder, and Bodin's face buried in my neck. Their shoulders meet on my exposed side. The pole obscures most of my left. So no one sees the hand snaking up my thigh, burrowing beneath the split in the dress. It's Bodin's hand, but Legion is there too, covering his, directing him—they move in tandem to tug aside my soaked panties.

I gasp at the first swipe along my folds.

"Yes," Legion rasps to Bodin. "Into her tight heat."

We groan in unison as Bodin's finger enters me, stretching me. Blood roars in my ears as he leisurely pumps in and out, following every direction Legion utters. I vaguely recall Fox's confession—that he waited for me to have sex. They all waited. *You are the first queen we're biologically compatible with,* Legion said earlier. Their only experience in eons of existence comes from sensual voyeuristic moments stolen while in their invisible wraith forms. They watched and learned from others. They saved these precious first moments for me.

CHAPTER 23
WILLOW

The enchanted spectacles returned Legion's memories. Now, he's using them to teach Bodin how to pleasure me. He won't touch me, but he won't leave me wanting. My confusing, diverting thoughts are pushed aside when Legion guides Bodin's slick fingertip to my swollen clit. I release a long, deep moan.

"She is most sensitive here," Legion instructs. "Lick, tease, play with this."

"Nip?" Bodin asks.

"Yes," I plead, but they're not listening to me. They know they have me. I am theirs.

Bodin increases his speed, deepening his pressure, and I cry out as more pleasure builds within me. I fist his shirt and pant, "Again."

"Mm," Bodin grunts in agreement. "Most sensitive."

They mutter amongst themselves, hotly discussing how to test my desire, how to explore my body for erogenous zones, and how to ensure I come hard and hopelessly in their arms every time. Through the fog of desire, I register the changing tune. This new song is slower in tempo, as if the musicians tapped into our

mood. I feel so good. Legion's fingers trace lazy circles on my collarbone. His eyes focus downward as Bodin's hand moves beneath my dress, his finger finding a rhythm, building hot, coiled tension within me.

My lazy lashes flutter open. My lust-drunk gaze wanders aimlessly.

Most people dance closely, like us now—bodies entwined, hips gyrating, and mouths clashing. As if reading my mind, Bodin's mouth falls to my neck again. He licks and laves hungrily. Legion's hand fists in my hair. Inadvertently, my gaze lands on a familiar face—only yards away from the dais. Alfie's red hair looks black at night, but there's no mistaking the dark swathe of jealousy in his eyes.

A wave of irritation suppresses my desire. What right does he have to look at me like that? Even now, he stands amongst a bevy of mortal and fae females. Charms sparkle on his swinging Chaser chain. I almost think he'll storm over here and demand I am freed, but a blond female tugs his face to hers and kisses him. He returns the kiss with passion but keeps his eyes on me.

I feel nothing. No spike of envy, nothing beyond the chagrin that the sight of him interrupted my pleasure. Bodin growls at my inattention, captures my mouth with his, and swallows my protest as he withdraws his finger from my clit. I whimper at the loss, but then he calls on the shadows to hide us from view and plunges two into my pussy so firmly that I lift onto my toes. I am shoved back against Legion.

"You're ours," he growls, biting my lower lip hard enough to cause pain.

I feel Legion move behind me, perhaps searching for the source of Bodin's troubled claim, but then Bodin's thumb finds my clit. Every time his fingers enter me, filling me deliciously, that thumb hits my sensitive nerves. Sparks fly. Heat unfurls. I am thrown back into this heady world, caught between two walls of hot-blooded male. Legion might refuse to join in, but his erection digs into my back. His breathing is as labored as Bodin's, watching as I'm worked closer to climax, tighter and tighter. I whimper helplessly, thrusting into him, chasing my high.

"Harder," I gasp. Beg. "And my . . ."

Bodin kneads my aching breast with his free hand. Grunts, gasps, into my mouth.

"I want to taste her. I want—" He rams his hard length into my hip, and I moan. He's thick and needy for me.

"Yes," I pant, reaching down to stroke him. "I want to taste you too."

"Not here," Legion warns. "At home. But she comes first." Then, more softly, "Always."

As if he's punishing my mouth for denying his cock, Bodin drives his tongue deep. Legion's shoulder against my head perfectly supports him as he dominates me. I feel devoured. Owned.

Fair warning, love. Bodin's going to love this mouth.

Legion's grip tightens over Bodin's hand on my breast. Heat fires from my nipple to my womb. My orgasm rips through me so intensely I see stars. A hot, salty mouth swallows my hoarse cry. Wave after wave of ecstasy crashes through me. I soak Bodin's fingers. The wetness is slick down my thighs, but I can't stop thrusting into him. I am almost embarrassed, chasing the throes of sensation, except I know he loves this. Legion, too, despite his hurtful words. They're eating my moans with their stilted breaths, almost whimpering themselves.

Bodin slowly drags his fingers from my still-quivering pussy. Hot, bedroom eyes become black as he slides a glistening fingertip along my parted lower lip. I taste myself, and it makes something snap within him. An animal, a beast, stares out at me.

Then he licks his wet finger and growls, "You taste good."

"Like what?" Legion's quiet demand is laced with hunger.

"See for yourself." Bodin winks at me as he offers his hand to Legion.

A wave of something hot barrels through my chest. He saw how Legion's rejection hurt me. Is this him pushing back?

Legion's grip tightens painfully on my arms. His erection digs into me so hard it hurts. I gasp at the flash of pain. Then Legion releases an arrogant snarl at Bodin's challenge. Holding my breath, I half expect Legion's hand to plunge between my thighs, to wet his own fingers, or for him to walk away stubbornly with nothing. It seems like something he would do. Instead, he grabs Bodin's hand and leans over my shoulder to suck on his glistening thumb—the same one that worked me to climax.

Seeing Legion react to my taste is my new favorite thing. I watch, mesmerized, as he licks my arousal from Bodin—inches from my face. When he's done, he draws back. Takes a moment to breathe through flared nostrils. Not the savoring Fox did, but a gathering of decorum. As if he's about to lose all sense of control. Shadows hide my dark angel's eyes, then he moves to my side to show me his glare. But scowling eyes only make him look sexier.

"What?" I shrug innocently, my lips twitching in amusement.

"I'm unsure who has marked who now," he grumbles.

"Does it matter?"

His lips curve, eyes knowing. "Calamity, indeed."

My smile drops when Bodin's shadows fall from around us and a path directly to Styx is revealed through the dancers. It's as though swaying limbs synchronized to make way for this moment. Unmoving, he stares at me—at *us*—with a dead expression while two women paw and grind against his body like he's covered with an aphrodisiac. One is a gorgeous, tall brunette wearing a sparkling negligee for a dress. The second is a redhead dressed in what seems to be pearlescent body paint. I know because every swipe of her hand and body leaves residue on Styx's naked torso.

He glances between Bodin, Legion, and myself and then turns away, but not before I catch the flicker of pain in his eyes. Left out.

Forgotten. Guilt slams into me hard as a wave of people hides him from view.

"Fuck." Bodin frowns, scrubbing a hand down his face.

Legion answers with a growl of disapproval. "I forbade him."

"Forbade him what?" I ask, heart racing, eyes searching among the shadowy, moving heads for another glimpse of Styx.

He hasn't gone far, but now has his tongue deep down a woman's throat. The painted female still crowds him, her hands deep inside his pants. But it's his posture that cuts me to the core. His shoulders are slumped and tense at once.

For a moment, I don't see Styx. I see Fox feeding on Irisa. That moment on the sofa when his arms were spread wide along the backrest, and his head thrown back, staring at the sky, waiting for her to finish using his body for release. I see his shame because he thought feeding made him a monster. The act produces some kind of erotic byproduct that has their victims hardly knowing what's happening as their souls are seduced out of their mouths. There is no other way to gain sustenance for Sluagh except to murder, and Fox never wanted me to see it—any of it.

I see red.

Fury burns the last vestiges of desire from my body. My feet are crossing the dance floor before I can stop myself. I have no conscious thought driving my actions, only rage. Rage that the Six were created to feed like this. Rage that the act produces an aphrodisiac, forcing them to subject themselves to unwanted sexual advances.

"What is it, then?" I asked Fox. *"What is true freedom for you?"*

His sad eyes collided with mine. *"Unconditional love."*

Two feet away from Styx, my rage erupts. I grab each female's hair and yank backward, shrieking, "Get off him!"

I smash their heads together. Make their noses bleed. Someone shouts, "Fight!" and then pandemonium erupts.

CHAPTER 24
WILLOW

When I throw one woman into the crowd, the raised grass-covered dais becomes a battlefield. Heightened emotions flick from lust to anger as others join in.

I go for the brunette first. She's fae. Magic makes her the most dangerous. She barely has a moment to breathe before I push my thumbs into her eye sockets. Her scream is lost to me. The roar of blood in my ears drowns out all sound. There is nothing but my fury and something else . . . something darker and horrid.

Someone behind me rips my hair. I twist, moving with predatory focus, pounding my fist into her throat to incapacitate her airways, then into her face for no other reason than I want to destroy every inch of it for daring to touch what is mine, for adding to the never-ending cycle of Styx's shame, for giving him what I can't.

Not just the sexual attention but the sustenance.

"He's mine, bitch." I pound and pound my fist into her face. He's my *mate*.

Envy.

Tears burn my eyes. I hesitate, my fist hovering in the air, my

164

lungs heaving as I straddle the groaning half-naked woman while a brawl rages around me.

Envy.

That's the name of the darker, insidious feeling clawing my heart. I hate that my mates have to feed like this. I hate that it has to be with other females and never me. I want to be the only one who ever touches them this way.

I want to protect them from all the shame, the disgust, the self-loathing. Titania has made them fit in here, but the moment anyone discovers their true nature, they'll be hunted and feared.

Someone bowls into me, knocking me off the limp, bloody woman. I bounce to my feet and round on a man, an unhinged light in his eyes as he drinks my bloody fist in, and my upper lip curls. My fist pulls back, but someone catches it and flattens themselves against my back.

"Now don't be greedy, fangs," Styx purrs into my ear. "Save some fun for me."

I twist, and our gazes lock. Amusement and something deeper, darker flickers in his eyes. Something I've wanted to see pointed in my direction. Something I need as much as I need air. Then he is gone, prowling around me and joining the fight.

The unhinged man was prepared to take me on. Fear shoots into his eyes at the terrifyingly beautiful Radiant, slightly more unhinged than him. There's no stopping Styx. He is a brutal force of efficiency, taking down my attacker. Fast, violent, repetitive strikes eliminate the threat. It's over too fast. Styx pouts and then grins when more attack. He takes down man after man joining the fight. Any strike is captured, reversed, or broken. Bones snap —cartilage crunches. Screams curdle.

Deadly poetry in motion.

My lips curve almost as broadly as his, and when his next opponent stumbles into me, I trip him up. That's when Bodin and Legion appear, dark scowls on their faces as they try to form a ring of protection around me. Like knights bowing before a queen, they close ranks. But it's not the fight, not my behavior, that bothers them. It's Cait shrieking about this not being the right place for fisticuffs. She and her security staff charge toward us.

"I'm sorry," I mutter. "I shouldn't have done that."

"Get her out of here," Legion orders Styx, shoving me into him.

We collide, fall, and clash in a tangle of limbs against three other brawlers, crashing to the dais. Shadow surrounds us and then suddenly the grass beneath me is replaced by soft, crunching snow. We emerge from shadows inside the courtyard of Shadowfall Keep so fast my head swims.

I land roughly. The ice cools my senses. Blood on my hands. The daunting realization of what I did hits me with guilt.

Strong hands jerk me to my feet. I stare into Styx's wild eyes and can only apologize again.

"I'm sorry. I shouldn't have done that."

"You're *sorry*?" He blinks, confused.

I can't look him in the eye.

He growls and advances on me. Anger emanates from him in waves. I back up until I hit the trellis against the castle's façade. Rose petals fall on me. His hand—bloody hand—grips a slat beside my head. Short conical spikes distend from each blue, gore-covered knuckle. The rest of him is still flesh-toned, normal. But that one glimpse, that dangerous difference, makes him a killing machine. And I encouraged it.

His biceps flex, a reminder of the strength and skill I just witnessed. He dispatched man after man without breaking a sweat. And now he's crowding me, hard muscles still twitching with adrenaline.

"You're sorry?" he snarls in my face. "But I thought this is what you wanted."

"To hurt people?" I gape, frowning. "I couldn't help myself, I couldn't—"

"What's the matter?" He guides my palm to the hard bulge in his breeches. "You don't like this?"

His hips flex, punctuating his question. Heat pools between my legs, awakening every desire Bodin claimed.

Giant black tattered wings erupt from his back and spread so wide they block out the moonlight. His skin darkens to a bluish hue. More spikes appear over his brows, shoulders, and collarbone. And those horns—long, twisted, and sharp. He gnashes his fangs in my face. "You don't like what you see?"

I don't flinch. I hold his gaze steadily with mine. His broad chest heaves with ragged breath, still with one arm gripping the trellis, waiting for my response. I suddenly realize what this is all about. When I called them monsters, Fox felt ashamed. He tried to hide his tail, horns, and wings. He thought I was afraid of him. Styx's otherness is much more pronounced. Of course, he'd feel the sting of my hastily thrown words.

I open my mouth, but Styx bellows furiously and shakes the trellis, showering more petals.

Now I flinch. He overheard my thoughts. "I don't think you're a monster."

"You think I care what you said?" A cruel smile twists his lips. "That I care what I look like?"

"Fox did."

"I am *nothing* like Fox," he growls, eyes flashing. He presses his finger between my eyes. "Get that through your head."

My jaw drops. I don't know what to say. There's so much anger in him. So much pain. If it's not from that, then what's it from?

"I'm your mate, Styx," I state. "You can't scare me away."

Something in him changes. He softens just enough to melt against me, trapping me against the trellis again. The hard length of his erection digs into my hip. He wants me so badly, but like Legion, something holds him back. Unlike his First, Styx lets his emotions out to play. He idly toys with my hair around my ear, anger still simmering in his dark gaze. I let him catch his breath, let him trail his finger along my jawline. But when his eyes lock with mine, he's nowhere near calm—just contained.

He nuzzles my cheek with his nose, dipping his chin, scraping my skin with the spikes over his brows. I gasp. But it's from surprise, not pain. He wields himself with finesse, dancing on the knife's edge of rough. I hold my breath as the sharp scrape moves back up.

"Let's get this straight, fangs." His voice is intimate and deep as his lips move against my cheek. "We might both have horns and a tail, but I know how to use mine."

Something lashes about my ankles, tugging me off balance—his tail. I want to see, but he crowds me with his wings, arms, and body being my world.

"He's the cute one." He drags his tongue up the side of my face. "I'm the bad one."

"Still not scared," I breathe, less sure than last time.

"You should be."

CHAPTER 25
WILLOW

I am trapped between Styx's indomitable body and a castle. The night is cold, but I feel none of it—only heat—as his teasing tongue starts a leisurely exploration of my cheek, tasting, kissing along to nibble my earlobe. "I'm not going to love you like they do."

At first, my heart sinks when I think he's rejecting me—just like Legion. But something in his tone gives me pause. I see the image of his dejected face after Bodin and Legion made me come. He felt left out, and then I publicly claimed him with violence. Something he seemed to enjoy. And then I went and apologized for it, taking it back.

Maybe he's not angry because he's ashamed of his otherness, but because he'd hoped to find a mate who loved him as he was. Someone who doesn't like to hide behind shadows, but someone who shouts their emotions from the rooftops.

I push him back to look into his eyes. "You think I'm sorry for claiming you?"

A flash of that hurt. Then it's gone. "I don't care what you think."

"Then why did you ask if I liked what I saw?" My eyebrow arches as I take his still-hard erection and squeeze. "Admit it."

"You admit it," he groans breathily, thrusting into me.

"I mean, it's okay." I lick my lips, fingers clenching around his length as if I'm testing the girth. "A little on the small side."

His brows raise, then slam down as he growls, "You won't say that when I'm pushing into your tight hole."

"Maybe."

He tenses. I stifle a smile. His buttons are too easy to push.

"Maybe?" He pauses. Thinks. Then his lips curve wickedly. "I mean the *other* tight hole, fangs."

Hot, liquid heat snakes through my body as his palms glide around my hips, heading toward my rear. My heart races. I know where he's going. I can stop him. But I don't want to. I hold my breath as his fingers curl between my buttocks, pushing against the dress's barrier until he hits my back entrance, making me whimper.

"There?" I whisper, a little turned on. A little nervous.

"Scared yet?"

"No."

I stroke him through his pants. They're looser with his tail out. Must have ripped through the seam when he shifted. But it gives me the freedom to pump harder, faster.

He makes a strangled sound deep in his throat. His entire body exhales against me. His wings rustle and settle into a beautiful mantle along his shoulders, talons like draconic pauldrons. The dark, silken lengths spread out behind him on the snow as he gifts me with a moment of trust, a gentle interlude. This feels more like an embrace now, his chin resting on my shoulder. His fingers on my ass gather my dress in slow, walking increments. His tail loosens its hold around my ankles and slides up my legs, lifting my dress for his fingers to slip beneath.

"Your ass is mine, Willow," he mutters hoarsely, breath hot on my ear. "When you're ready to admit it."

"Admit what?"

"That you're our queen."

"Mate."

He chuckles. Kisses me. Gives a breathy groan when I pump him harder.

"First, I'll lick it." His finger strokes along my inner thigh, inching toward my slit. "Then I'll rim it." His tongue traces circles on my cheek, winding closer to my lips. "Then I'll stretch it with my tongue." He licks along my lower lip. "I'll make it fit," he whispers against me. "And you'll love it. You'll learn to love it."

My heart stutters. I fist his hair, yank his head, and force him to meet my eyes. The black is gone. The spikes, horns, and the blue skin are gone. There is no mocking amusement, either. Just blue, vulnerable eyes and a handsome face overcome with longing. His expressionless mask slams up—and he's gone, leaving me clutching cold air.

I close my eyes and try to work through what just happened. My chest is tight and aching. It's that place I always react when my mates are near. I rub it, hoping to ease the pain, but it refuses to budge. It needs to be fed, to be touched. Styx has left me bereft. Empty.

That wolfish part of me is an emotional, irrational bitch. Right now, she wants to howl with indignation. She wants her pack. She aches for their comforting warmth. That bitch can also be a possessive, feral predator when she sees her mate suffering. Unfortunately for me, she also isn't that smart. She acts on instinct. She hurts things. People.

Flexing my aching fists, I pace in the snow and welcome the numbness climbing up my limbs. My crunching footsteps hurtle me into the past, to another time I paced in the snow with Rory by my side. I was eleven and had been in Crystal City for five years.

"*Stop crying, Willow,*" *Rory growls at me.* "*Before he hears you.*"

"*But it's cold. I want to go inside.*" *I stumble to a halt, my tears turning to ice on my face. "The other kids are learning to dance, and I'm—"*

"Hush." She crouches before me and takes my shoulders, gripping me hard as she hisses, "He's just over the hedge, sitting on the bench by the fountain."

"But Alfie and—"

She shakes me until my teeth rattle and my tears renew. Pain and guilt enter her eyes, now glistening like mine. "I'm sorry," she whispers, tugging me close and cupping my hair with her gloved hands. "Willow, learn this lesson. Learn it now and learn it good." She holds me tight and strokes my hair. Her voice wavers with sadness. "Dispose of emotions, or he will use them to exploit you. He will find your friends, punish and even kill them to make you obey. Trust me, darling. It's better to keep a clear mind and focus on the task at hand."

"I hate him."

"No . . . even this emotion is wasted. He can use it against you too. If it's not him, then it's your enemy using it. Emotion is the key to finding your weak spot. Lock it all down. Erase it from your mind. Only then can you fly free."

"But that feels wrong."

"You'll learn to love it." She gives me a sad smile, eyes glimmering as she looks at the wall keeping me from my home. "And at least the world will still turn."

"What do you mean?"

She deadpans, "I meant, at least you'll still be alive."

I look at my bloodstained fingers turning blue under the moonlit sky. I was never good at following Rory's rules. My emotions are too big. Too demanding. Whether it's love, hate, or anything in between—it's there, smack bang in the center of my chest, begging for a connection I don't know how to make. I fall hard onto my ass, my head in my hands.

I don't know how to be a wolf. I don't know how to be fae. I don't know how to be human. I certainly don't want to be a queen. So how the fuck can I be what Fox wants me to be—their source of unconditional love? How can I reunite my hive if I keep causing trouble?

If I lose my temper like that outside of Burn After Reading, I put a target on those I'm trying to protect. Not just on the Six, but Geraldine, Peggy, and Max. Anyone I care about will suffer because of me.

I'm so glad they weren't there to witness that. So grateful no one will remember because that darkness only scraped the surface of what I'm capable of. Bodin said he was open to helping me make a blood connection through water to speak with my parents, but I can't let them see me like this. I can't do it.

I'm not sure how long I sit there staring at my numb fingers, but when rustling and crunching announce Bodin's arrival, I pretend to do what Rory taught me. I dispose of emotion and face him with thinly veiled bravery.

He helps me to my feet with pity in his eyes.

"Styx was here," I say, teeth chattering. "Then he went."

"He's smoothing things over with Cait."

Relief drops my shoulders. I don't know why that makes me feel better, but the thought of him being alone doesn't sit right. "And Legion?"

"Ensuring Styx does as he's told." He lifts my swollen knuckles and inspects the wounds. "May I?"

I shake my head and tug my hands, hiding them behind my back. I deserve to feel the pain. The woman I beat up, the one whose eyes—I squeeze my eyes shut. *Lock it all down.*

His long-suffering sigh reminds me of a parent. It's a sigh one gives when dealing with a child . . . a naughty and irritating pain-in-the-ass child.

"I'm sorry, I messed up."

I used to be annoyed at hand-signing my sorrys and thankyous in Elphyne to avoid a Well-enforced debt. But now I understand why the Well does this. Words are empty. For an apology or gratitude to mean something, actions are needed.

"Messed up?" Confusion flickers over his face. Is that a dark blush staining his cheeks?

"Not us," I clarify. "I'm sorry that I started a fight. Sorry I hurt people. Sorry I forgot to hunt for stones we can use as charms. I messed up."

He takes me by the shoulders and pins me with his dark gaze.

"No matter what I do," I whisper, "I keep hurting people. Life just feels like . . ." My mind reaches for an appropriate explanation, but I come up short.

He grazes his knuckles against my cheek. "We are all wisps, floating aimlessly—"

"Yes!" I exclaim. "Exactly. The moment I think I've figured things out, meaning either darts away from me or it slams into me with insanity."

"You didn't let me finish," he scolds. "I was going to say, searching for a home. You did nothing wrong tonight."

"But Styx . . ."

"Is more wounded than you will know." A small smile touches his lips as his knuckles move to caress the old scars on my face. "What you did tonight was . . . no one has *ever* fought for us like that. I feel that truth in my bones, even if I can't remember. Knowledge that deep, that right . . . let's just say, if you call that hurt, then I will wish upon the stars for it nightly."

"Lies," I accuse, despite my lips curving. "What do you really wish for?"

"I wish for you to get warm and have a good night's sleep. Tomorrow, you're back at the Nexus." He places a vial in my hand. Folds my fingers over it.

"What's this?" I ask, but when I look, I recognize the pink elixir. It must be from Cait. "I guess this means you're not firing me as your mate?"

"No, Calamity." His eyes heat. "We're keeping you."

CHAPTER 26
PUCK

When I emerge from Titania's chambers, dawn brightens the sky—even the Baleful Hunt slumbers within me. Today, I did not force the chambers to be weeded. I stood there and watched them choke her, only to remember that nature gives her power. Eventually, the scent of chalk and smoke caused the Keepers to force me out.

I claim a paltry hour of sleep before the page boy wakes me for the day ahead.

The pretty, young male attending me bustles about my chamber, setting down the breakfast tray and laying out my outfit for the day. I admire his delicate beauty for a moment—the sweep of glossy black hair over his forehead, the blush painted on his cheeks, the berry stain on his lips.

His mouth and tight ass provide the perfect relief while my beloved slumbers, and I am denied yet another night without release. I stroke myself beneath the thick blanket and moan as pleasure teases me. But I am late as it is.

Groaning at denying myself, I toss the blankets off and slide my legs over the edge of the bed. The boy rushes to my side and kneels. As he glides a slipper onto my foot, I fail to resist the

175

magnetic pull of his silken hair and slide my fingers through. He gasps as my fist clenches, and I yank down, drawing his face up. Those berry-stained lips part, but the thick swaths of black brows shadowing his wide eyes make my heart flutter.

I see multicolored eyebrows flinging from the ladies-in-waiting and landing like slugs. They will rue the day they called me an imposter. I tug down my waistband and release my aching member. The page boy's lips part to receive me.

"*You aim too low,*" the dragon quips in my mind. "*Aim higher.*"

"Sir?"

"Shut up and let me—" I aim higher, rub my tip on his silken brows, and groan. Feels so good. So much softer than the queen's inner walls. "Suck my balls," I gasp and pump my length. Like a good little page boy, he does as he's told. The more his saliva wets me, the more I slip and glide along his soft, velvety face. Each time my tip hits his brows, I am closer to climax. When he grips my behind and rubs his face along my length like a cat, I come hard. Thick squirts of sticky white paint his luscious brows, and I groan triumphantly. Everything pales in comparison to this moment. Never has my queen wrung such pleasure from deep within my soul.

I tip his chin up and gently smear my release, styling his brows into wispy shapes, wondering why this simple act fills me with such satisfaction.

"*It is power,*" the dragon answers in my mind. "*You were not born to serve. You were born to dominate.*"

"Changed your tune now?" I mock.

"Pardon?" the boy asks.

"Not you," I quip.

"*Perhaps.*" The Hunt's claws pluck at my mind. "*Perhaps you showed me last night what you're made of. Perhaps I now see great things are ripe for our taking . . . if we work together.*"

I allow the page boy to dress me, but as he moves to wipe his brows, I scold him.

"Leave it," I bark, then soften my tone when he startles. "I wish to be reminded of how well you serve me when I see you today. You may clean the rest of yourself, though." I grimace at the sand on my legs. "And me. You've left dirt everywhere."

Five minutes later, I am dressed and walking outside the palace to meet with the Court of Dreams Shadow. Something heavy has lifted from my shoulders.

"Alfred," I greet. "What news from last night?"

Already in his exhibitor uniform, his appearance is pristine and prepared for the day. He gives a slight, reverent bow. The young man reminds me of myself. He has ambition, strength, and a clever mind. When his eyes meet mine again, I catch a flicker of anxiety.

"Did the charm work?" I flick the latest addition I've gifted him to his Chaser chain. Having had enough of the secrecy surrounding that feline bitch's establishment, I took it upon myself to find a workaround. Titania's private library has many interesting resources with old faerie magics. The more I find, the more I feel I don't need her assistance.

"It worked." He scowls. "I remember everything. Not that I think it will matter after last night."

"Why?" I gesture for us to start walking toward the Nexus.

"Burn After Reading has closed. Permanently."

I stop. "What? Why?"

The loss gnaws at me. Without it, the delicate balance I've maintained threatens to crumble. As we walk, I notice whispers behind cupped hands and darting glances from staff. Are they plotting against me?

"They fear your power," the dragon hisses. *"Show them why."*

I clench my fists, resisting the urge to lash out. Not yet. Soon.

The Shadow sighs and rubs his face. "I don't know. I asked around, but no one had an answer."

"Then how do you know?"

His gaze darkens as it swings to the dark spires of Shadowfall

Keep peeking over the Ivory Palace walls. "I overheard one of *them* mention it."

"Them?"

"The knights."

"Ah, yes." Of course. I knew that. "And did you see the Knight Enforcer? The one called Styx?"

"Yes." He frowns. "He and their . . . Shadow started a brawl, but I failed to glimpse signs of a Nightmare form. Are you sure they're—"

"You doubt me, Shadow?"

"No, sir." His gaze turns inward as it lingers on the dark Keep's spires.

"He's holding something back," the Baleful Hunt remarks. *"He cannot be trusted."*

"You think no one can be trusted."

"Often, I am right."

"Is there something else?" I ask my Shadow. "About last night?"

He hesitates, then says, "If there is no B.A.R., how will we earn charms?"

He has a point. While that establishment was a thorn in my side, without it, Radiants have no way of stacking the odds in their favor to win the tournament. I am sure I will hear about it from the Shining Host. I glare at the overcast sky and continue stalking through the courtyard. The snow has lessened overnight, and the soggy ground has ruined my shoes.

I muse, "The Folk are already fractious with this strangely warmer weather. The mood is sour, and the Solstice Ball is in two nights' time. It should be a time for revelry, not rotten sentiments. Ask Glen to prepare a special trick. Something to wow even the most cunning of Folk."

We need something big to shake things up. My mind races with possibilities, each more outlandish than the last. Perhaps Ignarius had a point. Public executions? Forced humiliations?

The old me would have balked at such ideas, but now . . . now they seem almost reasonable.

"Yes," the dragon purrs. "Now you're thinking like a true ruler."

When nothing is to occupy their minds, the Folk—from the tiny to the tall—grow curious, antagonistic, and entitled. They will come out of the woodwork against Titania's edicts and ruin the carefully constructed decorum of control.

"Perhaps a little rivalry," Alfred suggests. "Some challenges with charms offered to the winners?"

I rub my jaw, a smile stretching my lips. Burn After Reading was the perfect place to conduct dealings that went against Titania's rigid Old Code. But if I can bring this practice out into the open, perhaps offering the exchange of charms and favors within the existing tournament structure, I will be seen as a benevolent leader on all sides.

I stop by a fountain before we leave the grounds. "A series of challenges and a leaderboard. We will announce it at the Winter Solstice Ball."

"That makes sense," he replies thoughtfully. "Revelry and rivalry. I like it."

"Of course, it makes sense," I retort flatly. "I came up with it."

I catch sight of my reflection in the fountain. For a moment, I swear I see granite scales pushing beneath my skin, my eyes glowing with an otherworldly light. I blink, and it's gone. But the hunger for power, for control, remains.

CHAPTER 27
WILLOW

Despite sleeping well in Fox's bed, I stumble into the courtyard, bleary-eyed and miserable at the crack of dawn. Last night's events weigh on me, leaving an odd mix of irritation and dissatisfaction.

The urge to be with my mates grows stronger each day. Wolves aren't solitary; we run in packs, sleep in piles, nuzzle, and touch. Crystal City suppressed these instincts so thoroughly that I feared I'd killed that part of myself. Five years in Elphyne with my family, and with Tinger, flirted with reawakening it. Now, after bonding with Fox, being close to my mates is an itch I'm desperate to scratch.

Bodin seems to have warmed up to me, but Legion avoids my touch. Emrys glares with loathing. Styx remains a puzzle. And Varen . . . he's complicated.

At least I have friends. My frown lifts when I spot Geraldine and Max waiting on the frost-encrusted grass. They wear exhibitor uniforms with warm, fur-lined capes. The cool air has glazed their eyes and painted their cheeks and noses pink. Clouds bloom from their lips as they warm their hands with breath. I hug my woolen cape close and ask, "Where's Peggy?"

They exchange a glance.

"Still at the stables," Max answers.

"I didn't know she'd started working there."

Geraldine pulls a book from beneath her cape. "The Knight Marshall woke her early to demonstrate her daily chores."

"Oh." My brows knit. "That was fast."

Geraldine presents the book. "Max and I found this in the library."

I take it, gasping as invisible ants seem to crawl onto my fingers. "It's magic," I whisper. "I can feel it."

"Maybe that's why we never noticed it before." She shares a look with Max. "We didn't know it was magic."

"You think it was hiding?"

"Read the title," Max urges.

"*The Secret Commonwealth of Faeries, Elves, and Fauns* by Leonardo da Vinci." I open the cover, admiring the elegant hand-written title. Flipping through, I find sketches and diagrams of faerie creatures with detailed scientific explanations. "I'm not sure why it feels magical," I muse.

"It's actually in Italian," Geraldine explains. "But you can read it, so that might be what the magic is."

"Italian?"

"A language from our time." She scratches her head. "I know a little but can't read much. It took forever to figure out the title. But if you can read it, maybe the book has changed the words to something I could read. I showed you because the author is a famous artist and inventor from . . . well, many years before even we were born. Weirdly, I found another book in the library with the same title, written by a monk about four hundred years later."

"A copy?"

"I think he copied it, claimed it as his own, and cut anything the church deemed heretical. This version likely has accurate facts. Leonardo was renowned for documenting what he saw." She sighs. "I wish I could read it. I could help more."

"Give me your hands." I gesture for them to touch the book. "I'll try to transfer the effect to you, as I did with the wards at the Cabinet temple."

We hold our breath as I focus on the crawling ants' path. It's unfamiliar magic, nothing like I've sensed before. When nothing happens, my confidence wavers. Maybe it only worked at the temple because Titania used my stolen magic with hers. But that doesn't explain how Chaser charms work for anyone. Another person with these charms can still activate magic; no wisps are needed. Concentrating harder, I search for a connection to make the wild magic recognize them. It comes when I think of my friends' hard work and the warmth it stirs in me.

Max and Geraldine gasp as the ants latch onto them.

"You did it!" Geraldine flips through the pages excitedly.

A warm heat fills my chest. I think it's pride. It feels good. A small hope starts to build—maybe I can learn to repurpose other people's magic. Titania stole mine, after all.

Max points out an anatomical diagram of a Nightmare, eliciting sounds of awe from us all.

"I'll take this inside," Geraldine says. "Don't want it ruined or stolen at the Nexus."

As she leaves, Max turns to me. "You just bent an ancient spell to your will. Could you do that before?"

"I wouldn't call it bending to my will. I just wanted the book to recognize you like it did me."

He arches an eyebrow. "I rest my case."

"What case?" I look around, confused.

He laughs. "Sorry, it's just a saying. Means you proved my point."

"And your point is?"

"That you have magic, or at least the potential for it."

I shake my head. "I don't. I'd feel it."

"But you will." He smirks knowingly. "I bet you'll get it back or find another way."

I give him a hesitant look. "I was sort of thinking I could learn to repurpose magic."

He snorts. Claps me on the back and nods. "Only the greatest thief in the world would call it repurposing."

"Ha! Now you're flattering me." I narrow my eyes and waggle my finger. "What are you up to?"

"Nothing." He blushes when Geraldine appears at the door again. This time with Bodin. Seeing him in the official House of Shadow uniform sets my heart racing. Now I'm blushing too.

Max's eyes follow Geraldine as she approaches, grinning at him. His expression softens, then clouds with doubt.

"She's amazing, isn't she?" he murmurs.

I nudge his shoulder. "Why don't you tell her how you feel?"

He shakes his head. "Look at her. She's way out of my league. Besides, with the competition heating up . . ."

"Max," I interrupt, "life's too short for regrets. Especially here. Tell her."

"Maybe."

"Think that book has useful information against Titania?" I ask absently, pretending not to ogle Bodin as he strides toward us. *Well-damn,* he scrubs up nicely. His black military-cut coat hugs broad shoulders and a narrow waist. Creased pants complete the ensemble, but they're tight against his muscular thighs. His clean-shaven jaw and the sides of his head accentuate glossy braids knotted tightly at his crown.

"It had dragon pictures," Max points out. "Nightmares. Faerie. It's got to be more accurate than what they tell us at the Nexus."

"Speaking of which, we're late, and Peggy's still not here." I face the gates, dread coiling in my gut at the thought of crossing the moat. Is that flowing water I hear?

"She's not coming."

Bodin's deep voice snaps my attention back. His rich leather-and-spice scent curls my toes. To keep from ripping his collar and sinking my fangs into his neck, I bite my lip. Bad move—his eyes darken and fixate on my mouth.

"Why isn't she coming?" Max's question breaks the spell.

Geraldine looks expectantly at Bodin.

"I've tasked her with my duties here while I'm"—Bodin's eyes flick to me—"reassigned to conduct training at the Nexus."

"Won't that hurt her chances in the trials?" I ask.

"Peggy's withdrawn from the exhibition." His gaze slides to Geraldine and Max. "The offer extends to you. There's work here at the Keep."

My heart plummets. I hope this isn't just another ploy to keep my friends from weighing me down. "But they'd be safe from deportation to Nocturna?"

Bodin nods. "They're no longer Nothings. We need trusted staff."

My eyes narrow. "You mean you need them here so other Radiants can't pull secrets from their minds."

"That too," he admits.

Max and Geraldine are stunned.

"It's safer here," I say, trying to mask my disappointment. Facing the Nexus without friends is daunting, but better than risking their lives.

"What if we want to win?" Geraldine asks.

"You think you can beat our Shadow?" Bodin grumbles, gesturing at me. "There is only one winner."

I bristle at the implication I'd hurt them to win. "I know people die a lot in the trials, but many still survive, right?"

Doubt flickers in his expression. Before I can retort, Max puffs out his chest. "Who says it can't be a team effort?"

"Only one dream becomes reality." Bodin's eyes meet mine—a warning to them, a reminder to me. Win and free Fox. That's what matters.

"We don't care about the prize." Geraldine touches her new scar-free face, then meets Bodin's hard gaze. "I don't even care if I get scarred and wounded again. Willow needs allies. It's not like you can enter the trials to protect her."

"How do you not care about the prize?" His eyes narrow.

"It's not like Titania can actually turn back time."

"She can't?" I gasp. "I thought this was an all-encompassing wish."

"We've been looking into it," Geraldine replies. "There are parameters to the prize. Isn't that right, sir?"

I catch a glimmer of respect in Bodin's eyes as he nods. Not just for their loyalty, but for Geraldine's cleverness. "Naturally, it must be within her power to grant."

She turns to me and explains, "Titania can't even raise our loved ones from the dead—that was you, not her. So if we can't have our family back, we make the most of this one." At my teary eyes, she adds, "Shit happens, Willow. We need to move on."

Bodin produces small onyx skulls on delicate chains from his pocket, pinning them to their uniforms.

"This charm," he explains, "blocks mind-reading and eaves-dropping on private thoughts. Wear it always outside the Keep. Touch to activate a silencing ward. Anyone you want to be included must touch you or activate their own ward."

When it's my turn, I ask quietly, "Where did you get these?"

His eyes meet mine briefly before he goes back to focusing on pinning. "Styx gathered them last night."

My heart clenches. "He did?"

Bodin's fingers linger on Fox's embroidered shirt beneath the pin. His brows furrow, and his eyes close with a sharp breath. Worried he's having another dizzy spell, I reach for him, but he steps back. "Let's go."

The gate's vines crack open. As the others start walking, I hesitate. Bodin turns, his frown deepening.

"Must you cause trouble so early?" he growls.

"We should talk about last night," I murmur, scowling as I pass him. "And this isn't trouble. It's toeing the line."

I want to win as badly as he does. I want Fox back, and I'm not sure I trust Cait and her Rogues to find the mirror in time—or deliver it to us if they do. This means the only other options are convincing the Radiant bonded to the Baleful Hunt to release him from the stone or winning the trial and wishing for it. The thought twists my gut with anxiety.

Max and Geraldine wait ahead at the rope bridge spanning the moat. My heart leaps when I realize my ears are right—the moat isn't completely frozen. Water flows between chunks of broken ice.

Bodin stops beside me. "Interesting."

"Shouldn't it be solid?" I ask, my voice trembling.

"Yes." He scans the skeletal trees, whistling sharply as he spots a raven. It caws and lands on his outstretched hand. After a moment of eye contact, the bird caws again and flies over the Keep's walls.

"Keep walking," he instructs.

Geraldine and Max cross the bridge, but fear locks my limbs.

"Everything okay?" I ask, glancing after the raven.

"I've alerted the commander about the moat."

He tries to hurry me along, but I resist with a nervous laugh. "I didn't know the birds worked for you. Peablossom said they belonged to the queen."

He frowns. "A misperception we encourage. Ravens have always belonged to the Morrigan."

"Right. And she's your mother. Right."

He blinks. "You're stalling."

"No, I'm not."

"Yes, you are." Concern fills his eyes. "Fox's letter mentioned you might still have a phobia."

"He did?" I frown. "How long was that letter?"

His hands slide around my waist, lips dipping to my ear. "Long enough to detail how he tried to help you overcome this fear."

I squeak as he hoists me over his shoulder, crossing the swaying bridge with a warrior's easy grace. I glimpse Geraldine and Max on the other side as his stride swings me. First, they're giggling, then walking ahead. I tell myself the heat in my cheeks is from hanging upside down. It has nothing to do with Fox's letter or with wondering what else he thought was important enough to write.

On solid ground, Bodin slides me down his body. His hands stay on my hips as he searches my eyes.

"Do you truly regret last night?" he asks.

It takes a moment to gather my thoughts. We're so close. His heady scent fills my senses. His warmth, his hard body, muscles flexing beneath his coat. Damn, he's strong.

"Yes," I admit. "I shouldn't have hurt those women."

"Those women?" He blinks, confused. "I meant what I did with you. What I tasted."

"My only regret with you was that it didn't last longer." I trace his bottom lip.

A low growl rumbles in his throat. His nostrils flare, and he curses softly. "How can I focus enough to protect you? It's impossible."

"So give in." My lips part as he sucks my finger into his mouth. "Why fight it?"

His teeth clamp down. Ouch. I yank my hand back, scowling.

"Because distractions get you killed," he says.

I roll my eyes. "You seem to remember well today."

"Perhaps because all I can think about is how you tasted on my fingers and how much better you'll taste directly from the source." With a frustrated growl, he strides ahead down the wooded path.

Smirking, I jog after him. He's already slowing. "That's not really why your memory seems better, is it?"

He gives me an amused look. "When Styx shifts out his otherness before me in the morning, it helps anchor my memories during the day."

Geraldine and Max are frowning at a tree trunk covered in crudely carved symbols—moons, stars, and other strange glyphs.

Bodin curses, quickly ushering us past.

"Graffiti," he mutters. "Coded messages of dissent."

"What does it mean?" I ask.

He shakes his head. "Nothing good."

"You can read them?"

"No. But they're appearing all over, usually before a riot. Probably a call to action."

"Riots?" I share a concerned look with my friends.

"Keep moving," Bodin says. "Change is coming, whether the nobility wants it or not."

CHAPTER 28

WILLOW

At the Nexus, the air shimmers with an unnatural stillness. Earlier in the week, grief hung heavy in the air. Today, laughter tinkles like crystal. Fae nobles twirl in dazzling gowns, their faces masks of practiced joy. But beneath the veneer, I catch flashes of strain—a trembling hand here, a too-wide smile there.

As we pass the registration building, a commotion catches my eye. A cart laden with exquisite delicacies—glistening fruits, aromatic pastries, and meats so tender they seem to melt—is being unloaded. Bejeweled, well-dressed Radiants oversee the delivery.

"More supplies for the ball, I suppose," Geraldine mutters, her voice tight.

I notice a group of Chaser workers, their glamour flickering to reveal gaunt cheeks and hollow eyes. One reaches for a fallen grape, only to snatch their hand back as a Radiant's polished gaze sweeps over them.

"Don't look," Max warns us under his breath. "Noticing too much can be dangerous here."

The stark divide between abundance and want knots my stomach. How had I missed this before?

It's worse when we get to the heart of the Nexus—a new House of Stone Tower gleams, pristine and unmarred. There is zero evidence of rubble. Even the grass bears no scars. It seems impossible, illogical, and absurd that they managed to build a tower in the span of a few days. No one questions it. They just murmur about the incredible power of the Radiants and continue on their way.

"It's like it never happened," Geraldine whispers, her voice tight with disbelief.

Max nods, his eyes hard. "Welcome to Avorlorna, where inconvenient truths vanish faster than morning dew."

The week passes with a surreal air of normalcy, if such a thing exists in a tournament designed to train mortals as war fodder. Bodin escorts me to every class. Goodfellow doesn't show. No one mentions the House of Stone debacle, their deaths, or their Shadow and Sylvanar. No one mentions Fox.

The House of Tides runs the morning Magical Defense and Counter Magic class. Much of what they teach is useless to mortals without charms. The message is clear: trust your Radiants and know your place. It reminds me of what Colin said— young mortals never achieve a better station than recruit. I worry he hasn't turned up at the House of Shadow.

Max splits off to take a different class than Geraldine and I. Bodin waits until we're safely inside before leaving to do whatever the Knight Marshall usually does. We file into the House of Moonlight Tower classroom for medical training and sit in the second row.

Lady Selene commands the center of the room, her pale tartan dress shimmering like liquid moonlight. The Hollow Hunt gleams in her unnerving, luminous eyes as she surveys the settling students. Heath, her tall and slim Shadow, sits behind her with a box of medical supplies. Alfie, Irisa, and Becky huddle nearby, whispering. Alfie's gaze darts to me, a silent promise of unwanted conversation. I'll need to bolt after class to avoid him.

"Good tidings, precious dew drops," Lady Selene's melodic voice fills the air. "To understand the importance of battlefield triage, we must first grasp the concept of empathy and perspective. Let me share a tale as old as the stars: the fable of The Two-Faced Moon."

Her eyes, luminous with the Hollow Hunt's glow, sweep across the room. "In a realm long ago beyond mortal understanding, the moon was a living entity with two distinct faces: one radiant silver, basking in adoration, and one shadowed, often forgotten or feared. The silver face grew vain with constant praise, while the shadow face bore the weight of neglect."

I lean forward, drawn in despite myself. Geraldine's eyes widen with interest beside me.

"This imbalance," Lady Selene continues, "caused chaos in the world below. Seasons shifted unpredictably. Tides behaved erratically. Rhiannon, a lesser-known fertility deity, heard the moon's plight. 'Why do you wobble so?' she asked. The moon shared its woes, speaking of its divided nature and the chaos it caused. 'Balance,' she said, 'is not achieved through dominance or neglect but by recognizing the worth of both sides.' Only when the moon learned to rotate fully, integrating both faces, did harmony return. Now the beings on earth celebrate the full cycle, finding beauty and wisdom in both light and darkness."

She pauses, letting the message sink in. "Just as the moon learned to embrace both its faces, we too must recognize the value in all aspects of ourselves and others, especially in times of crisis. True strength comes from balance and understanding the light and shadow within us all."

I shift, acutely aware of my hidden darkness. This fable reminds me of home, of how Queen Maebh drew too much from the inky side of the Well and ended up creating a taint in the magic source. That taint warped my intention to wake an army of undead, instead waking so many more. Imbalance can tip both ways. We can't eradicate the dark. We have to learn to live with it.

Lady Selene's gaze lingers on me as she transitions. "Now, we practice. Empathy and perspective are our most potent battlefield tools. Pair up."

Alfie's voice cuts through the rustling. "With all due respect, Lady Selene, empathy has no place on the battlefield. This is my fifth year. Sentiment only gets you killed."

A chill runs through me at his familiar mindset.

Lady Selene turns, her expression serene but her eyes sharp. "Ah, young Alfie. Five years, yet wisdom eludes you. Have you never relied on a comrade? Never drawn strength from shared struggle?"

Alfie's smugness falters. His gaze flicks to me, then darts away. Lady Selene continues, her words shimmering. "Empathy isn't weakness. It binds a fighting force and anticipates ally and enemy. Without it, we're solitary moons, forever half-shadowed."

The class nods. Alfie flushes, tapping an odd rhythm on his Chaser charm. My spine tingles—what's he doing?

"Now," Lady Selene says, "let's begin. Remember—understanding others helps us understand ourselves."

Heath approaches with supplies.

"Ready to play doctor?" Geraldine winks, nervousness beneath her smile.

"Sure," I say. "That's an old-world healer, right?"

Her expression falters. "I forget sometimes you're not really one of us."

I resist tugging my hair over my fae ears.

She quickly adds, "I meant an old-worlder. Not friend."

"I get it. Don't worry."

But as we clear space to work, I feel less connected to her than I should. We settle on the floor amidst bandages and sour-smelling elixirs. Medicinal herbs mingle with Avorlorna's sweetness.

"Okay," I start, faking calm. "You've got a sprained ankle. What's your name?"

Geraldine quirks an eyebrow. "Um . . . Geraldine?"

I nudge her. "Pretend you're a stranger."

She ponders. "Call me Scary Spice."

"Weird name, but okay."

Nearby mortals chuckle. I assume it's a funny reference from her time and want to ask, but we're ushered back into the exercise. Caring for another soothes me as we practice treating different injuries. It's a return to basics, a reminder of the empathy often lost in quick fae healing. I guess that's why the Folk have fables about it.

The door bursts open. Puck saunters in, his grin chilling me. Slicked auburn hair and green embroidered silks set off his stony gaze and chalky skin. White powder dusts his shoulders.

"Someone's got a bad case of dandruff," Geraldine mumbles.

Lady Selene's smile tightens. "Your presence always brings . . . illumination, Lord Robin Goodfellow. Though one wonders if it aligns with Rhiannon's teachings of balance and harmony."

Puck grins wider. "Why, of course I'd be delighted to take over your lesson."

Her jaw drops, then closes. The Baleful Hunt's eyes flash, and she forces a smile.

Interesting.

Now that he is dragon-bonded like her, she seems to fear him. Or at least is wary. She walks out of the way as he circles the room. He stops by Geraldine and me, his opaque eyes taking in our lesson.

"You know," he announces to the class, "sometimes the one wielding the blade is most qualified to treat the wound. Isn't that right, Nothing?"

The world lurches. I'm in a dark room, blood-scent thick in the air.

My own voice, younger and hollow, recites mechanically:

"Femoral artery severed. Ten seconds: Massive blood loss begins. Twenty seconds: Blood pressure drops precipitously. Thirty seconds: Consciousness fades. Forty-five seconds: Brain activity ceases. Sixty seconds: Heart stops."

A whimper from the figure before me, bound and bleeding. My hands, slick with red, hold the blade that caused this suffering.

"Good." Nero nods. "Now make it happen. Show me you understand."

"Willow?" Geraldine's voice snaps me back. Her warm hand grounds me. "Are you okay?"

I blink rapidly, banishing the phantom scent of blood.

"Fine," I lie, unable to meet her eyes.

Under Puck's tutelage, the lesson quickly escalates. Mock injuries become severe—crushed throats, eviscerated bowels. My earlier calm evaporates.

Heath offers gentle guidance amidst the tension. A commotion across the room draws my attention. Irisa kneels on Becky's throat, pretending to be in a battle. Becky struggles, tapping Irisa's knee.

Lady Selene quickly moves across the floor, saying, "Remember the moon's lesson. In the darkness, we find light's seeds. In pain, healing's potential."

As the lesson nears its end, Puck claps his hands. "Let's make this fun, shall we? One final test—a real wound to treat."

Lady Selene's eyes flash. "Ser Robin, we tread dangerous ground. Rhiannon teaches growth through reflection, not forced trauma."

Puck's look silences her. "Sometimes, true learning requires sharp reality."

"Balance is not achieved through dominance or neglect, but by recognizing the worth of both sides."

"Are you saying we must recognize the worth of Nightmares robbing our people of children?"

Her lips part. No words come out.

"Hm." He gives her a scathing once-over before addressing the class. "Sounds exactly like something a dragon-bonded would say. They've never fought in the belly of a battle, have they?"

Hesitant murmurs of agreement spur him on.

"It's hypocritical, isn't it?" he sneers at Lady Selene. "They preach about empathy, but do any of them feel our wounds when we're sliced open by the enemy? This is why I will be your first member of the Shining Host to enter the thick of battle with our prevailing exhibitors."

The voices of agreement grow louder, encouraging. I have to admit, Puck has a way of capturing approval without really proving himself. He's a slimy sucker who doesn't deserve this praise. Maybe that's why I blurt out a fault in his claim. "How can you be the first? Aren't the knights—"

"They have no working dragon," he snaps, cutting me off. Visibly flustered, he quickly points to Geraldine and me. "You two demonstrate a battle wound. Make it real—needing stitches. This is battlefield triage, after all."

Lady Selene protests, "We didn't practice suturing."

"I saw some playing with tourniquets and needles."

"That's—"

"Well, then this really will be an absolute lark." Puck laughs and sniggers ripple through the room.

The walls seem to close in, and I feel like I'm underwater. But as Puck's challenge hangs in the air, a new resolve crystallizes. I may have been forged in cruelty, but I won't let it define me. Not anymore.

I accept the dagger he gives me but offer it to Geraldine. I'd rather be the wounded one, not her. Unfortunately, the tremble in my hand cannot be stilled. My voice sounds less sure than it should when I say, "You take the lead."

Her eyes widen. "You trust me to wound you like that?"

"Of course."

"Is the Shadow afraid to get the job done?" Puck sneers. "If you don't make it realistic, I'll do it for you."

Geraldine glares at Puck, then pushes the blade to me and says, "You're not afraid, are you?"

Yes. "No."

"It's okay," she whispers, squeezing my fingers on the hilt. "I trust you."

Ten seconds: Massive blood loss begins.

Tension heightens. Eyes filled with morbid excitement and trepidation watch me. With shaking hands, I mentally map out Geraldine's anatomy.

"Let's not take all day," Puck drawls.

"Fuck him," Geraldine mutters. "You've got this."

Twenty seconds: Blood pressure drops precipitously.

Her uncertain tone spins my head. Fear or doubt in my knowledge? My trembling hands might nick a vital spot if I don't pull myself together.

Thirty seconds: Consciousness fades.

I point the blade at various spots on her body, murmuring to myself the safest places to make a deep wound.

"Upper thigh, away from the femoral artery," I mutter, eerily calm. "Outer biceps, avoiding brachial. Lower abdomen, shallow to avoid peritoneum ..."

Geraldine's eyes widen, shock and confusion flashing. "Willow, how do you—"

I don't let her finish. With a swift, precise movement, I make a deep cut on the back of her upper arm. Her sharp cry of pain tightens my throat, but I hold her steady, hold her like I did my victims as they bled out in my arms. The blade parted flesh with sickening ease, and blood wells up quickly, trickling down her arm in rivulets.

Forty-five seconds: Brain activity ceases.

Time seems to slow as I assess the wound. My hands move

with practiced efficiency, applying pressure that makes the bleeding appear worse than it is.

"Significant blood loss," I announce loudly, my voice clinical and detached. "Possible muscle damage. Will require immediate attention and sutures."

I catch Geraldine's eye, slightly shaking my head. She understands and plays along with dramatic winces and moans. It's not hard—all wounds hurt—especially the ones where friends lie.

I take a tourniquet and strap her upper arm like we were taught, but then I hesitate. I'm a killer, not a healer. I can't stitch wounds. My mind whirls, trying to remember the techniques from this lesson. Heath swoops in with a needle and thread, steadying my hand and guiding my stitches. Geraldine's eyes hold pain, confusion, and dawning realization of my inner darkness.

Sixty seconds: Heart stops.

"Well done, Shadow," Puck's sarcastic voice cuts through. "The blade wielder truly is *most* qualified to treat wounds."

I hate him with a passion bordering on insanity.

I finish bandaging, the dressing unnecessarily tight for show. The trust in my friend's eyes has been replaced by something else —not fear, exactly, but a new wariness cutting deeper than any blade.

"Willow," she whispers, barely audible. "What aren't you telling me?"

Lady Selene ends the lesson, saving me from answering. Guilt and fear storm inside me, and I am the first to leave down the winding stairwell. Geraldine catches up, eyes stark with pain.

"I get it—you can't talk about your past," she says. "Just promise me you'll make things better."

"Bodin's just outside," I mumble. "He'll heal you."

"That's not what I—"

She stops when Alfie and his entourage approach, descending the stairwell with Puck behind them.

"Let's go." I grab Geraldine's good hand and hasten my exit.

Bodin pushes off the wall and immediately demands an explanation of why he smells blood. I quickly point him in Geraldine's direction. It's not until he's halfway through healing her that I remember something odd from the lesson. Alfie tapped his Chaser charm minutes before Puck turned up and singled me out with a challenge highlighting my violent skills.

How much has Alfie told his mentor about me?

CHAPTER 29
WILLOW

Max joins us on the way to combat class at the House of Shadow Tower. Geraldine's just finished recounting the medical lesson, and he shakes his head. "How do they expect anyone to survive long enough to join their war?"

"They don't," Bodin grunts behind us.

"Have you seen Colin?" I ask.

His worried look chills me. What's happened to the teen?

Bodin arrives first at the tower. Instead of allowing us entrance, he stands guard, arms folded, inspecting each arriving exhibitor like an enemy.

"Are we going in?" I ask quietly.

"When it's safe," he replies.

I retreat to wait with the others, hugging my cape against the cold. Most of us are eager to prepare for the Winter Solstice Ball. Flyers around campus detail proper attire, etiquette, and expected rituals. It's also Yule, and we're expected to bring an offer to the gods representing hope, resilience, and the promise of the sun's return. Since we're exchanging gifts at home, I've wrapped a few stolen treasures but need time to finish.

Tonight, the dragon-bonded Shining Host gathers for the first time since the Pageant of Prowess. The ball is meant to celebrate the longest night and herald the next stage in the Gentle Interlude. For us exhibitors, it means we are about to get serious with training.

I hope so. Nothing we've learned will prepare us for the trials less than two moon turns away. Soon, I'll likely go into heat, forcing me to miss classes or risk being mobbed by every male nearby. Bodin will hate the added attention. I can just hear him complaining about my calamity. I've been too nervous to discuss it with Legion, who's busy dealing with Terrors appearing around Avorlorna.

A shriek pierces the air, followed by a crash inside the tower. Bodin's jaw clenches, but he remains still until someone speaks to him at the door. He glares at me, clearly saying, "Don't go anywhere," then repeats it to the crowd before slipping inside.

Geraldine whispers, "I know we're not supposed to gossip, but this is weird, right?"

Max tenses. "That sounds like—"

"A Terror inside," I finish, surprised by my certainty.

Geraldine raises an eyebrow. "How do you know?"

I shrug, uncomfortable. "I'm not sure. It just . . . feels right."

Max grins, nudging me. "See? You're learning. That special dusty tome is coming in handy after all."

My smile drops when I hear Alfie call my name.

He stands slightly aside, half-turned as if ready to bolt. In the growing darkness, his red hair looks almost black.

"You'd better see what he wants," Max mutters. "I'll stay here with Gerrie."

I don't want to risk drama. It's been a long, dull day, and I'm ready for it to end. I haven't spoken with Alfie properly since my walk of shame around campus. He probably thinks we're still friends, despite all I learned about him at B.A.R. I take a few surreptitious steps back in case my babysitter watches from a window up higher.

Keeping my gaze ahead, I settle beside Alfie and wait for him to speak. His nearness makes me sick. It's like I sense his duplicity in the air.

"Are you well?" he asks quietly.

"Fine."

He pauses. "It's been hard to catch a private moment with you lately."

It's because you're an asshole. "I've been busy."

"I saw you a few nights ago," he murmurs. "At B.A.R."

My lungs seize. *Play it cool, Willow.*

"Oh?" I reply.

"There's something I need to tell you. About that night."

I relax slightly. His tone sounds worried, not accusatory. "What is it?"

"The enchantment didn't work for me," he admits. "I remember some things and thought you should know that your Radiants took advantage of you."

My brows knit. "What do you mean?"

"I saw you." He clears his throat. "I saw you caught between two of them on the dancefloor."

Is this a test? Does he still think we're engaged? Or is he probing to see if I'm willingly involved with the Six?

"What do you mean, caught?" I ask.

"Tell me you're not involved with them," he whispers.

"Alfie, what did you see?" I glare, hoping he misreads my anger for fear.

He hesitates, then leans closer. "They drugged you and forced themselves on you. *Sexually.* I saw it all."

Shock courses through me.

I was definitely a willing participant, but also, how the fuck did he see anything? Bodin and Legion had taken special care to hide the details from anyone around us, except maybe for the part where they licked me off Bodin's fingers. I guess that's not hard to interpret.

Wait. *He* sent me to Milford, a known abuser who drugged his conquests. Now he's acting concerned, playing the virtuous knight. Does he think I'm clueless?

"So you watched it happen?" I test him back. "And yet did nothing to help me?"

"I couldn't." His eyes widen. "There were two of them."

That sick feeling continues to churn in my stomach. He mistakes the source of my expression. I want to start poking holes in his story, to ask him what he was doing on that dance floor himself but remind myself I don't give a fuck about him anymore. He's already whispering how he's gaining Goodfellow's trust, has more charms than ever, and will get me out of the House of Shadow if it's the last thing he does.

"They even manipulated you into maiming two innocent women," he continues. "You went wild and attacked them for no reason while they laughed. You weren't yourself."

Not myself? That night—apart from the fight, well, half the fight—I was happy. It's the happiest I've been in a while. What did I look like before that he couldn't recognize that person was me?

"Alfie, I'm fine." I show him my healed fists. "If I was brawling, wouldn't I be wounded?"

"They erased the evidence." He looks at me like I'm dumb.

The tower door opens. I step forward, eager to escape, but he grabs my arm.

"You're beautiful again, Willow. Haven't you asked yourself why?"

"What are you insinuating?"

"I don't need to. The evidence is in the mirror. It's in the way they follow you around like lecherous freaks."

Rage burns cold inside me. "Now you're saying I'm a slut who traded sexual favors for beauty?"

"That's not what I meant." His grip tightens.

"I'm sure you've done deplorable things for those charms, Alfie," I hiss. "You've been here for years. I'm not rubbing your face in it, am I?"

"So you admit it?" He scowls. "You're fucking them."

"Shh! Keep your voice down," I say with a glare.

"Why? Are you conducting a forbidden affair with your Radiants?"

"I was cursed, you *floater*," I snarl, fisting his shirt. "And I broke it myself. That's why I'm not ugly anymore."

I shove him away and return to Geraldine and Max as Bodin reappears. His eyes narrow at my expression, but I look away.

Just as we're about to enter, Peablossom's voice resonates from our pocket stones. *"Hark, cherished blossoms of Avorlorna!"* Her singsong words ring out with an otherworldly timbre. *"I bear tidings most wondrous and fair!"*

The crowd falls silent, enraptured by her melodic tones.

"Our most luminous and benevolent Regent, Lord Robin Goodfellow— now graced as the Shining Host of the illustrious Baleful Hunt—has, in his infinite wisdom, crafted a glorious opportunity for the advancement of our beloved exhibitors. This boon comes in light of recent whispers on the wind."

A collective gasp, like a breeze through autumn leaves, ripples through the crowd.

"The Winter Solstice Ball, that most enchanted of gatherings, shall feature an announcement to dazzle and delight. Thus, your daily learnings are suspended for this turn of the sun. Return to your dwellings and adorn yourselves in finery befitting our revelry. Embrace this unexpected boon of freedom!"

When no one moves, she adds with a lilt of forced merriment, *"Off you flutter, dear ones! Embrace the dance of chance and change. And remember, as surely as the stars shine . . . we are ever smiling."*

The crowd disperses excitedly, but beneath the surface, anxiety simmers. Exhibitors wear smiles that don't reach their eyes.

I push closer to Bodin. "What just happened?"

His jaw tightens. "Goodfellow."

The fucker hadn't filled his meddling quota after all.

CHAPTER 30

WILLOW

Dusk settles as we approach the Ivory Palace for the Winter Solstice Ball. The crisp air carries notes of pine and frost, mingling with the heady aroma of spiced wine wafting from within. The soft crunch of snow beneath our feet and the distant tinkle of enchanted bells add to the winter symphony. My breath forms small clouds in the frigid air, and I shiver, pulling my shirt tighter around me.

When we read that the ball included costumes, the team thought channeling something nostalgic would be great. Geraldine wears a swashbuckling pirate ensemble, Peggy is in a rose-adorned bathrobe, and Max wears something called a "Jedi Knight" robe, but I think he just stole a Keeper of the Cauldron's robe and ripped off the emblem. I'm secretly proud of him. I have zero creativity apart from the little acorn pinned in my hair. The stolen treasure is the perfect understated adornment to complement my other stolen prize, Bodin's work shirt and trousers.

It's cold, but *Well-damn,* it feels good to be out. Tonight, I finally get to have fun with my friends.

Our excitement wanes as we near our destination, replaced by a growing unease. Goodfellow's sudden decision to move the

ball from the Nexus gnaws at my mind, but curiosity overtakes suspicion as the decorations come into view.

The palace gleams like a fallen star, its spires reaching heavenward. Delicate ice sculptures line the path, refracting light from countless floating lanterns. Garlands of winter blooms and shimmering frost adorn every window, transforming the palace into a winter wonderland—the air thrums with anticipation and magic.

Our haphazardly sourced costumes are a stark contrast to the glitz and glamour.

A group of giggling gentry strides past us down the path, their servant hurrying to catch up and lift their dress trains to avoid falling in the snow. I glimpse hollow cheeks and sunken eyes when the servant glances at me. The contrast jars—opulence and desperation side by side, separated by an invisible line. A pang of guilt twists in my gut as I think of Colin. His continued absence weighs on me.

Dream webs sparkle between hedges, casting intricate shadows on the snow-dusted ground. Only the pathway to the Cabinet of Curiosities remains dark, an ominous entrance into the maze holding my mate for ransom. A tug pulls at my chest, halting my steps. Bodin's touch warms my back, urging me onward.

"But—" I start, barely above a whisper.

"Later," he interrupts, his stern look swinging toward the palace. The others are already a few paces ahead.

Being this close to Fox without seeing him feels like a betrayal. My chest aches with a mixture of longing and guilt. How can I be here, about to celebrate, while he's trapped in stone? And yet, the warmth of Bodin's hand on my back sends a confusing thrill through me.

"Let's just get this night over with," he grumbles, his breath clouding in the cold air.

Unlike us, he wears his usual black House of Shadow attire

and a tailored suit. It should be comfortable, but he shifts from boot to boot, betraying his unease.

"You look nice," I whisper, trying to lighten the mood.

He meets my eyes, surprise flickering across his features. I meant it. The simple, black attire becomes him. It's rare to see him out of his rough work clothes. Now I've seen him look all dashing twice. All those hard muscles are hidden in sleek darkness, but his lethal prowess feels more apparent.

I reach out, gently touching his hair. Someone has changed the tiny braids to tight, twisted rolls. No, wait. There's something wound around them. I take a length and roll it between my fingers. He inhales sharply, watching me intently. The thin sections are braids on the scalp but morph into something else further down that's kept in place by a glittering thread. Black skull-shaped beads are clamped on regularly, tingling with power against my fingertips.

"You have charms," I murmur, curiosity and concern warring.

A muscle flexes in his jaw. "She tries to stifle us, but we find ways of growing stronger."

"Who did your hair?" I ask, unable to keep the edge from my voice.

"I'm not telling," he returns, amusement in his eyes.

"Why?" Jealousy runs through my veins, hot and unexpected. Then suspicion follows. It better not have been a female. Maybe I could handle Cricket touching him, but one of the ladies-in-waiting? No way.

The line moves forward, and we're suddenly faced with Cobweb and Moth. It takes every ounce of self-control not to burst into laughter. Their eyebrows are missing, replaced by comically elaborate arches adorned with sparkling gemstones.

"Bejeweled locusts" is my first thought as I take in their attire. Emrys's disdain seems to be rubbing off on me. Cobweb's lips curl in a sneer as her gaze travels from my borrowed trousers to Geraldine's eye patch. Moth lets out a delicate, mocking laugh.

"My, my," Moth coos, "did you mistake the Winter Solstice Ball for a peasant's costume party?"

I clench my fists, biting back a retort. We may look out of place, but we're far from powerless. Bodin's low growl beside me is a reminder that we're not to be trifled with.

Behind the ladies, I catch a glimpse inside the ballroom. Fae and exhibitors sparkle brightly. Not a single dark dress or costume is in sight. The air thrums with wild, raucous energy barely contained. Laughter and music intertwine, creating a dizzying symphony of color and sound.

Goodfellow stands on a glittering dais, hands on hips, scanning the crowd with a pleased expression. His eyebrowless face looks almost as comical as the ladies-in-waiting. The glitter in his stockings makes his enormous codpiece stand out like a sore thumb. But I notice the stony gaze the most, a coldness that doesn't match the festive atmosphere.

With a start, I realize the Baleful Hunt is not at its post guarding Titania's temple. Nor was it there during class today. My heartbeat kicks up a notch. Maybe I can visit Fox, after all.

"Your offerings?" Cobweb's voice drips with disdain.

Moth titters. "Oh my."

"This won't end well for you," Cobweb adds, smirking when they see we have nothing in our hands.

I curse inwardly, remembering too late the fae custom of bringing gifts to curry favor with the nobility. Each offering, carefully chosen, can influence alliances and tip the scales of power. Our empty hands might as well be a slap in the face to the Court.

Bodin's growl rumbles low. "Threatening our Shadow?"

They pale. Stammer. Curtsey.

He grumbles some more, annoyed, and directs us inside.

More snickers follow us as we enter the ballroom. My cheeks burn with embarrassment when we reach Peablossom at the refreshments stand. She moves and adjusts the flower arrangements to catch the light just right. Her dress is a supernova of light, twinkling more than the stars decorating her pastel-blue hair. My friends start sampling the food, oblivious to Peablossom's smile dropping when she glances at us.

"Dearest confection." She refits her smile, but it's tight. "Why are you wearing that monstrosity?"

"What do you mean?" I ask, confused.

Geraldine balks. "I thought this was a fancy dress ball."

"Oh my, when I spoke of costumes, I envisioned regalia, not the garb of jesters." Peablossom's lips purse. She scolds Bodin quietly, long enough for him to appear abashed, before he growls something back. The clamor and music are too loud for me to pick out their words. But we've clearly fucked up somewhere.

"Um. So it's not a costume ball?" I ask. Blood drains from my cheeks when I take in all the other exhibitors wearing formal and extravagant clothing.

An unhinged laugh peels out of Peablossom.

"Are you alright?" I ask her. It's been a while since we've had a moment together. Puck's new power would surely cause waves in the palace staff.

She doesn't hear my concern. That wild look in her eyes grows. "Alas, the sands of time fall too swiftly for alterations. You must grace the pageant just as you are, dear heart."

"It's fine," Bodin adds, scowling at the ballroom. "We don't need a pageant for a sponsor. She has us."

"I'm afraid, just like the moon's attempt to capture the sun, the parade is not negotiable, sweet Bodin." Peablossom's tone gentles for him. "Whether you seek charms or not for your Shadow, the points alone are simply vital to gain a temporal edge in the trials. The leaderboard is already afoot and hanging on the wall for all to see."

She gestures at a tapestry on the far wall between two ice sculptures shaped like the Holly King's jovial, wintery face. A space in the center is marked from one to ten for names.

"Points?" his brow furrows.

"I explained this last week." She cocks her head, perturbed. "Do you not recall? Such boons are bestowed only outside of one's own House. This is why I worked on her wardrobe so tirelessly."

So, having six Radiants in the House of Shadow means nothing to us. We'll have to gain favor from other Houses.

Bodin's expression darkens with frustration as he realizes his memory has failed him again. The apologetic look he gives me breaks my heart. It's not his fault, but his self-disparagement tells me he thinks it is.

"I will speak with Legion," he offers, stepping away.

"Fear not." Peablossom halts him by taking his wrist. "I will swoop in like a swallow and save the day again for my cherubs. No need to lay another burden on our Knight Commander's silken head."

"We will owe you," Bodin mutters.

"Add this to the tally and just remember . . ." Unreadable emotion flickers in her eyes. She swallows and directs the next part to me. "Just remember your allies at the end. Off you all go, into the line. Chop-chop."

"Even me?" Peggy balks, looking at Bodin. "I thought I'd forfeited."

"Forfeited?" Peablossom squeals. "Goodness, no, dear. There's a long process for that."

"It's started," Bodin assures her.

"Perhaps adhere to the customary steps," Peablossom advises gently. "Align yourself with the others, and by the time the next gathering beckons, you shall have gracefully exited the Nexus system."

Peggy's eyes lock with mine. Something about her fluffy gown makes her seem old and vulnerable. I squeeze her shoulder and say, "If Bodin said he'll get you out, he will. Don't worry."

I trust my mate to follow through with this. If he doesn't, I'll live up to his nickname for me. We start walking toward the dais at the front of the room, but Peablossom stops me.

"I'll catch up," I tell them, watching them shuffle onward with remarkably less vigor than we arrived with.

With a covert look at my pin, Peablossom says, "Such a captivating trinket adorning your hair, Shadow. Pray, where did you acquire it?"

Oh shit. She called me Shadow. I'm in trouble.

"Um."

"I gave it to her," Bodin says.

Peablossom gives him a dubious look, clearly not believing him. "Are you aware of its unique properties?" His eyes widen. She looks at me and raises her brows. "Are you?"

"No."

"Hm. You are lucky indeed." She purses her lips, taps the acorn three times, and then claps her hands, ushering me forward to catch up with the others. Bodin escorts me through the decadent room of haughty, fine-dressed Radiants studying us with veiled curiosity. When we reach the mob of raucous exhibitors, he hands me to my friends with a regretful look, but he can do nothing for me now. All Radiants must gather in their House groups to assess the exhibitors and vote, so he leaves to join the rest of the House of Shadow.

Before I can ask if Peggy's okay, elevated music takes on a suspenseful tone and brings goosebumps. Mustardseed flutters around the exhibitors and plucks Shadows out to stand in a separate line. I look back at my friends, worried, but Geraldine says, "Team Shadow for the win."

In other words, don't worry about them. If I win this stupid pageant, then we all win.

CHAPTER 31

WILLOW

The air thrums with anticipation as we line up beside the dais, facing the crowd. The rest of the exhibitors remain behind us and back toward the door like second-rate citizens. I find myself sandwiched between Dahlia and Irisa, feeling decidedly out of place in Bodin's borrowed work clothes. At least it smells like him. When I'm bustled, I drop my nose to the shoulder and steal a whiff of his comforting scent. Instantly, I feel better.

Dahlia tosses her raven hair, the movement releasing notes of smoke and cinnamon. Her dress, a masterpiece of flame-colored silk, clings to her curves like liquid fire. Dark eyes rimmed with kohl regard me coldly, red lips curled in a perpetual smirk. She shares a look with Irisa on my other side, who examines her pearlescent nails with feigned disinterest. Her ethereal gown ripples like water with every breath. Her skin, the color of sun-kissed sand, seems to glow from within. I hate that she's so beautiful. I hate that she's the one Fox let dry hump him after he nibbled on her soul.

This simmering note of possessive jealousy is only getting

212

worse. The urge to complete our mating bond crawls beneath my skin. I won't feel satisfied until it's done, until my Well-blessed mating mark is back, and I can sense each of my mates through the bond.

Alfie stands before Dahlia at the front of the line beside the dais, a vision in an iridescent suit that seems to capture and reflect every color in the room. He practically preens, his coppery hair perfectly coiffed, a dazzling smile plastered on his handsome face as he waves at the crowd like a king.

"How exactly does the point system work?" I ask, trying to keep my voice casual despite the knot of anxiety tightening in my chest.

Dahlia and Irisa exchange a look, their eyes glittering with malice.

"Wouldn't you like to know," Dahlia sneers, her voice as sharp as her stilettos clicking against the marble floor.

Irisa adds with disdain, "Maybe if you'd bothered to dress appropriately, you wouldn't need to ask such basic questions."

I bristle at their tone, heat rising to my cheeks. "Women should be lifting each other up, not tearing each other down."

They roll their eyes in unison and turn away, the subtle rustle of their gowns a whisper of dismissal.

From behind me, a deep, warm voice chimes in, rich as honey and just as smooth. "Don't mind them. The point system is actually quite simple."

I turn to see Heath, the tall, thin Never Shadow from the House of Moonlight, lining up behind me in a second row. He might have no capacity for magic, but his natural good looks are spectacularly exotic. His silver ensemble shimmers like starlight, his skin almost luminescent in the soft glow of the chandeliers. Beside him stands a new face—a muscular man with kind eyes nearly the same hue as his warm amber skin. This must be Corey, the new Shadow for the House of Stone.

Corey's smile is genuine, revealing dimples that soften his strong jawline. His outfit, a masterpiece of intricate stonework patterns, seems to pulse with an earthy energy. "Each Radiant has a certain number of points they can award," he explains, his voice hinting at a lyrical accent. "The more influential the Radiant, the more their points are worth."

Heath nods, the movement causing the light to dance across his blond hair. "The trick is to appeal to their fae nature. They love wit, beauty, and just a touch of chaos."

"Exactly," Corey agrees, a mischievous twinkle in his eye. "Show them something unexpected, and you'll have their attention."

"The only unexpected thing I can do right now is strip down naked," I joke.

Heath blushes. "I wouldn't call that unexpected. Most of us have already seen you nude."

"Good point." I chew on my lower lip. Guess I'll have to come up with something else.

"Thanks for explaining," I mumble to Heath and Corey, then face the front.

With nothing else to do, I scan the crowd idly and hopelessly wait for Peablossom to save the day. If she doesn't help me, it could be a blessing. I'll be in the same position as my friends. Receiving a false leg-up seems just wrong. It makes me feel like a puppet again.

A familiar flash of brunette hair and green grabs my attention. Further back in the room by the refreshment table, Briar is chatting away with his captain and a rotund fellow—a curly-haired member of the Folk who speaks with a dramatic, animated expression. From his illustrious blue and gold embroidered attire and lack of charms, I assume he's a Radiant. The captain hangs on his every word, suddenly bursts out laughing, and claps him on the back. Briar smirks but is less impressed.

Could this be the infamous Trixie-Pixie-Glen, whose pranks

once turned the entire Court purple for a week and whose favor can make or break a fae's social standing?

"And now, the moment you've all been waiting for. Let the revelry and rivalry begin!" Puck's voice booms from resonance owl statues high in the ballroom rafters, rattling the ice sculptures. "Let us turn our ears to the enchanting whispers of our beloved Shadows!"

"Alfie, my dear," Puck sings melodically, inviting him to the dais. "You need no introductions. You are known far and wide, a steadfast, modest, and mirthful jewel in our Court of Dreams—Titania's pick to triumph in the exhibition. What magic do you weave to be such a delight?"

Alfie flashes a dazzling smile. "Why, it's simple! I just imagine everyone in their underwear . . . made of cotton candy and dandelion seeds!"

The crowd roars with laughter. Alfie gives a flourish, then skips off the stage.

Actually skips.

I cough with surprise. Irisa grimaces at me with disgust.

"Sorry," I mumble, tapping my throat. "I just vomited a little bit."

Dahlia moves forward. I shuffle gratefully along the line. Then realization hits. I'm next. And I have no plan.

"Dahlia." Puck leans in, voice tinged with curiosity. "Now whisper us a secret. What is your heart's desire should you claim victory?"

She pauses thoughtfully and tosses her raven hair. I detect a faint tightening of her posture when she answers with a broad grin. "I'd ensure everyone had a charm to make them as naturally stunning as me. Then, no one would need to fear deportation to the subterranean. World peace through fashion!"

Laughter erupts from the crowd as if the plight of mortals is a big joke, but quiet murmurs of support break out from the exhibitors. From the sour look on Ignarius's face, I don't think she was supposed to say that. But her own House can't sponsor her points, and she still hasn't lived down how a Nothing made her look inferior in a class. Could this be her attempt at currying favor amongst the mortal exhibitors? The more she has on her side, the less competition she'll have during the trials.

It's a great strategy, if not a lie. She cares nothing for those being deported.

Then it's my turn. I step onto the stage and try not to vomit for real.

"Ah, Willow, our first *Nothing* Shadow." Puck's smile turns cruel, his stony eyes somehow glittering maliciously. He leans in close, his voice a silky threat. "Tell us, what's your strategy for the trials? How do you plan to survive in a world that was never meant for you? After all, you've had plenty of practice, right?"

The crowd falls silent, and the mood suddenly grows heavy. I feel the weight of countless eyes on me, waiting for my response. Fuck Alfie for blabbering about my history. I instinctively seek out my mates' familiar, comforting faces and find them standing together at the edge of the room. Legion's expression is calm. Bodin's is steady. Even Emrys and Styx hold no mocking glint in their eyes.

"Tell him to eat a bag of dicks." Styx's velvety voice slides into my thoughts, and I almost burst out laughing.

"Sounds like something an old-worlder would say," I send back. *"You've been spying again, haven't you?"*

"Maybe."

It's nice to hear his voice in my head. I haven't spoken to him since our encounter outside of the Keep. I thought maybe I'd scared him off.

"Have you . . . *nothing* . . . to say for yourself?" Puck taunts, still leaning toward me. He's close enough that I smell chalky granite, a scent I'm beginning to associate with the Baleful Hunt.

Strange that I never noticed it this strongly with Sylvanar.

"I . . ." I begin, my voice barely above a whisper. He rolls his eyes like I'm an amateur and points to the resonance stone receiver in his hand. I lower my lips to get closer and reply, "I just want my team to survive."

Dissatisfied moans wash through the crowd.

"*Bravo. What a riveting response,*" Styx teases me.

"*It's not like I've had time to prepare for the questions,*" I shoot back, glaring at him. "*And it's not like you're helping me.*"

His reply is a little hesitant, almost tentative. "*Do you want help?*"

"*Duh, of course I want help from my mates.*"

Puck's smile tightens, a predatory gleam in his eyes. He gestures at my clothes. "And your, ah . . ." A pause. A smirk. "Unique outfit choice?"

"*Tell him you're wearing Bodin's clothes in public because it's making him hard, and it's hilarious because he keeps having to adjust himself, and—*"

"*Not helpful, Styx.*"

"*Fine. Then tell him to go and eat two bags of dicks.*"

A genuine smile stretches my lips. I can see why Fox spoke so highly of Styx. I bet those two get up to mischief when together. I can't wait to be a part of it.

"It's comfortable," I answer with a shrug, earning nervous laughter.

Peablossom's blue hair bustles through the crowd and into the front row before me. She mimes for me to tug on Bodin's shirt laces and swings her hands down and out to the sides. Then she taps her head.

"Are you well, Lady Peablossom?" Puck scowls down at her.

"Oh—" She laughs nervously. "Just reminding our dearest confection to smile."

Puck narrows his eyes at her. I'm already smiling, so I don't think he buys the excuse. When he turns back to me, she widens her eyes and points again to the dress where the laces would be.

"Pull the laces," Styx explains, mind to mind. *"And wish for a fancy dress."*

"Why?"

"Just do it."

I grin widely at Puck's sardonic face, my heart pounding so hard I'm sure everyone can hear it. What am I doing? But there's no backing out now. With a deep breath, I swing the laces in an arc, wish for a fancy dress, and silently pray I'm not about to make a complete fool of myself.

There's a hot, prickling, burning sensation in my hair. I almost think the acorn is on fire and move to pull it out, but then magic shimmers around me, like a thousand tiny fireflies dancing across my skin. I tense at the sudden sensation, the air around me crackling with energy and the scent of ozone. Peablossom mimes for me to tug the laces again. When I do, it's like I tug Bodin's shirt clean off my shoulders. But in reality, his clothes transition into a gown woven from twilight. Stars glimmer across the bodice, and a cape of shadows trails behind me. My hair lifts off my neck and twirls into a magical updo. I can't see it, but from the gasps echoing around the ballroom, it's either horrifying or beautiful.

Even Puck looks momentarily stunned.

"Behold," Peablossom announces, "the true face of our trials —beauty rising from adversity!"

Impressed murmurs grow loud. A chorus of applause breaks out amongst both exhibitors and attendees. Puck recovers quickly, his smile turning mocking. "How . . . quaint. A new dress. Is that all?"

Peablossom's eyes widen. "Oh, she's not done. She worked on this next part for days, didn't you, Willow?"

I stare at her blankly, secretly about to soil my pants. "Sure."

With another flourish, Peablossom gestures to the crowd. Suddenly, Bodin's work clothes materialize on someone else— Glen. The rotund, curly-haired 'Trixie-pixie' fae beside Captain Sorrel.

"Oh!" Glen exclaims, examining his new attire with shock.

Then, one by one, each Radiant and lesser nobility in the room suddenly wears a copy of Bodin's black work clothes. A hush falls over the crowd. Everyone turns to Glen, the Court's unofficial arbiter of humor and revelry. He sizes me up, I guess, working out if he approves. Then he tips his head back, bellowing a laugh so hard it shakes his curls and belly.

The crowd erupts into raucous laughter, the sound vibrating the floor beneath my feet. When Puck calls for silence, the noise drops to an excited chatter. The mood is well and truly elevated as Puck faces me, his expression a battlefield of warring emotions —impressed, annoyed, and something darker, more dangerous. His eye twitches. His voice drips with sarcasm as he asks, "And how, if you would be so kind, did a Nothing achieve such a marvel? Or should we be asking who's really pulling your strings?"

Peablossom stares at me, her smile tense. I lean toward the resonance stone, my mind racing, my eyes darting all over for inspiration. *Wit, beauty, and just a touch of chaos.*

I shrug and say, "Glen made me do it."

The ballroom explodes with guffaws and cheers. Glen, ever the performer, looks mildly surprised at first. But when he realizes he's been given the credit for this magnificent stunt, he takes a dramatic bow, and the applause grows.

I hike up my new ballgown and exit off the dais. With Peablossom's help, I've inadvertently positioned myself as not just a powerful magic user but as someone who can play along with the most beloved prankster in Avorlorna. I hope that wasn't a mistake.

Peablossom rushes over, knocking the gentry out of the way with her giant skirt. She takes my shoulder and tugs me to the side, eyes gleaming. "You were spectacular," she gushes.

"You mispronounced 'you.'"

She blinks. "Did I?"

I laugh. "You should have said 'I' because *you* were spectacular."

"Oh no, dearest, I mispronounced nothing." A coy look crosses her face. "You're the one who thought to bring such a precious adornment for your hair."

I raise my hand to test my new updo. My fingers land on the acorn. A spark zips into me, and I gasp, eyes wide, then snatch my hand back before anyone notices.

"Can I . . .?" I let my question trail off as another round of applause erupts, and Irisa sashays off the dais toward us. I didn't bring the charm that provides a secrecy barrier around us.

"Did you know," she says, "that acorns bring luck and prosperity?" Peablossom smiles with pride before licking her thumb and wiping my cheek like my mother used to. She gives a self-satisfied sigh and tells me to mingle before my luck runs out. Then she leaves to corral my Radiants into doing their duty and voting mindfully.

Not wanting to stand there and be gawped at beside Irisa, I decide to head to the refreshment table. I catch glimpses of my friends' faces, still waiting further back in line. Awe. Confusion. And something else—something bitter they're trying to hide that makes my stomach drop. Guilt hits me like a physical blow. This wasn't how it was supposed to go. We were meant to be in this together, and now . . . now I've left them behind. I wanted to stand with them as a team. Instead, I've been elevated above them, thrust into a spotlight I never wanted.

At the refreshment table, I'm stopped by Captain Sorrel and Briar, congratulating me on a job well done. More Radiants start moving toward me. Their eager eyes quicken my pulse. As the captain continues to ponder about the intricacies of my prank, I smile and nod vacantly but reach behind my back and fumble around the table. I'm sure I saw a butter knife moments ago. My fingers hit something cool, hard, and long. *Success.* I quickly hide it within the folds of my skirt.

"Excuse me," I blurt, fanning my face with my free hand. "I need to visit the . . ."

I don't finish because I'm already rushing toward the exit, aiming for the maze, hoping Peablossom is right and my luck won't run out. Good luck rarely smiles upon me. I may as well make the most of it.

CHAPTER 32
BODIN

Nothing is worse than feeling like sinking while standing on solid ground. My inner turmoil comes not from the argument unfolding before me but from being forced to remain here and listen to tedious bewailing while lecherous suck-ups mob our Shadow. I itch to leave. Especially now she wears something other than my clothing. How will other fae know to back the fuck off without my scent surrounding her?

Earl Larkspur of the House of Stone, face flushed with indignation, will not shut up. Two nobles eavesdrop nearby, their eyes gleaming with barely concealed interest. Perhaps I can use scaring them off as an excuse to leave.

"Unacceptable," Earl Larkspur hisses at us. "Days of inaction. The Old Code—broken. There's an order."

Legion's jaw tightens. "I understand—"

"Do you?" The earl's voice rises. "Nightmares invade Heliodor. In three days, we've caught—"

"Don't lecture us," Emrys snaps, leather creaking as he clenches his fists. "We know the situation."

Tension thickens the air like a poisonous fog.

"This isn't the place for such conversations," I tell the earl.

He ignores me and fixes Legion with a dark look. "Where else, when you banish us from your Keep?"

I scan the ostentatious ballroom for a glimpse of silver hair, hyper-aware of potential eavesdroppers. Those two nobles must see their death on my face because they quickly scurry away. We are not free, though. Puck breathes the same air, and his presence is a constant threat.

The earl's words chill me: "It's as if this kingdom crumbles in Titania's absence."

Frustration knots in my chest. I should patrol, especially with the Baleful Hunt absent. Babysitting our Shadow is having a knock-on effect. Legion rubs his temples, shadows deepening under his eyes. He hasn't fed, likely too busy in my absence and giving his rations to Varen or Styx. Our Sixth's insatiable appetite unnerves me, and Legion coddles him—lets him get away with everything. Even now, he's managed to slip away from his duties.

A nearby lord's laugh grates against my nerves. The Ivory Palace's opulence suffocates.

"Stray Nightmares plague Avorlorna," the earl says, folding his arms. "Heliodor suffers most. Thirty good souls lost to Nightmares from unfrozen watergates in days."

I clench my jaw, bristling at the loss of life.

The earl continues, voice rising, "Without the Baleful Hunt's regular sweeps of Heliodor territory, the House of Stone is vulnerable. We are the kingdom's source of resonance stones. What would happen if we suddenly lose our communication network during a war?"

I snort. "You think to question our intelligence?"

"The Shining Host must address this charlatan's suggestions." The earl gestures at Puck's grandstanding on the dais, his fury barely contained. "Martial law should be imposed during Titania's slumber. Either you agree, or I challenge Goodfellow to a duel tonight."

Emrys's eyes flash with a dangerous glint, his voice a low,

menacing purr. "Tread carefully, you preening peacock. Threaten us again, and you'll learn the true meaning of peril."

The earl's skin pales, and the scent of his fear blooms. It is truly interesting how these Folk harbor fear of us Sluagh deep within their bones when their minds recall nothing of our origins. Then again, it makes sense. When my mind clouds, my body still remembers certain things—my hunger for blood, a persevering feeling I am not eating well, and the need to be with my hive. I inadvertently search for Willow, but the rest of the exhibitors seem to be winding up and spilling from the dais, filling the room.

Legion calmly tells the earl, "Martial law during the Gentle Interlude is a fool's dream and perilously close to talk of treason. We must prove without a doubt the risk to our safety is real." He pauses for effect. "The increase in attacks could be from one Terror or multiple."

"You know as well as I do that it is not a single, rogue Terror."

"My point is, we need overwhelming evidence first." Legion's stern expression holds enough weight for the earl to read between the lines. "Perhaps your soldiers should bring some of those indispensable resonance stones and capture some of these attacks."

"Yes, well," the earl says woundedly, "that . . . is a good suggestion."

The topic of conversation changes to more benign things— the leaderboard and point system. Legion manages to secure some points for our Shadow in return for one of us voting for his Shadow. Finally, Earl Larkspur leaves.

Legion immediately turns to us, lowering his voice. "You know what this means?"

"Naturally," Emrys agrees darkly.

"Have I missed something?" I ask.

Legion nods toward the dais. "He carries the Baleful Hunt within him."

Puck turns a bird to stone with his eyes, eliciting laughter from his admirers as the clump of stone falls with a thunk and cracks.

"Ask for something more challenging!" he boasts, his voice carrying over the music.

Emrys growls, echoing my anger.

"Yes," Legion says grimly. "As I suspected would be the case, the temple is unguarded and will likely remain so for the future."

The implications hit hard. I'd assumed Legion voted him in because it was the simplest way to control the Hunt for now, but the fool regent is too afraid to let the dragon out for air. Despite what he believes, Puck is not fae. Titania is not a goddess. Her wish-granting parameters are contained within her natural abilities of deception. This is only one of the secrets we hold close to our chests, waiting for the right time to reveal. Until then, the Baleful Hunt will slowly eat Puck from the inside. That danger his grandstanding poses will eventually fizzle out on its own. In the meantime, with our Shadow's ability to transfer magic, we have free access to the Cabinet.

"This is another reason you voted him in," I put to Legion.

"Yes."

Something like hope stirs and falters in my chest. "We can bring Fox home. We are not meant to be divided."

Legion's grim eyes meet mine. "Find Styx. Then our Willow. Emrys and I will defuse the situation with the House of Stone nobility." He pauses. "We can't afford a Radiant duel now. Not with this idiot's new layer of trouble in trials and training."

I nod, heading back to where I last saw our Shadow. She is gone. Styx wanders the refreshment table, poking food and licking his finger clean.

At least he is clothed. Like us, he wears all black—a small mercy amid gaudy costumes.

"What are you doing?" I ask.

Styx glances at me, mischief in his eyes. "I saw our mortals do this."

"But why are you?"

"Taste testing, I suppose."

"It's all dirt to us. Why bother?"

"Curious," Styx says, squishing a frosted cake, his finger going knuckle deep. "Oh, soft, wet," he muses, licking his finger clean. "They say this is sweet." Then he gives me a dark look, his voice deepening. "Did she taste like this too?"

Possessive anger surges, then ebbs. Memories flood back—my fingers inside our queen; the soft glide, the sleek sensation; her sweet, musky feminine scent. And yes, the taste when I ran my tongue up and down my finger. The carnal look in Legion's eyes when he did the same.

I clench my fists, fighting for composure.

Styx watches me, waiting for an answer. But there are no words to explain her taste. How can I compare it when I have nothing to compare it to, not even the tastiest soul of the most heartbroken innocent? Nothing can compare to her essence. I hunger for it, even now.

Distraction.

Calamity.

Blood on yellow feathers.

"Styx," I say roughly, "we need to find her. Trouble's brewing, and Puck left the temple unguarded. We can retrieve Fox."

"Unguarded." His eyes lock with mine. "Has this happened before?"

I shake my head. "Not with this kind of carelessness. If it had, we'd have done the same for you." My gaze catches movement outside, a twilight shadow sneaking away from the ball. "I take my eye off her for one minute—"

"Tell me what she tastes like first," he urges.

"Like the sun," I say low. "I can't explain it otherwise."

Closing my eyes, I see blood. Yellow feathers. A familiar yet unknown woman's mocking voice: *"You can't outrun your past. Your true nature. You'll always hurt what you hold dearest."*

"What's wrong?" Styx asks, concerned.

I rub my temples. "I'm remembering. Blood . . . feathers . . . always yellow. An old queen, maybe. Saying we'll always kill. That love isn't for us. It's our nature to destroy."

Styx stares hard, then sighs. "Canary's death isn't your fault."

Peablossom's familiar pale-blue hair cuts a line toward us through the crowd.

I grab Styx. "We need to go. Now."

We quickly head outside.

"Don't tell me that's her," Styx growls as we arrive at the exit in time to see a figure running toward the hedges.

"Fuck. The last time she broke in, a resonance stone captured her image. Puck used it to blackmail Fox."

Styx's eyes blacken, fangs descending. The transformation chills me, sharpening my memory and purpose. I am Sluagh. The Second. Willow is ours.

"We should kill Goodfellow now," Styx hisses, distorted. "Why not let me feast on his soul? He's no challenge. Fox could've taken him easily."

"Perhaps," I reply. "But hasty actions have dire consequences. And we have someone more important to consider."

Inside, Peablossom shrieks, "Oh my word, what in the Cauldron's name happened here? Who did this to the food?"

Ribbons of shadow swirl around, hiding us from view. Styx grins at me, mouth full of sharp teeth, both terrifying and exhilarating. He covers his mouth to stop a laugh. Before we *flicker* away, he shouts, "It was Glen! He finger-fucked the food."

We vanish amidst an uproar of outrageous and aimless protests.

I can't shake the feeling we're walking a razor's edge. Our

queen is potentially in danger, and here we are, barely containing our monstrous nature before our enemies.

The irony stings—we're meant to protect her, yet we might be what she needs protection from.

CHAPTER 33
WILLOW

I creep through the maze leading toward the Cabinet, the scent of night-blooming jasmine heavy in the air. I have no idea if my luck still holds or how much of my pageant experience was Peablossom and how much was the acorn, but I tap the adornment in my hair three times in the same way she did, just in case.

Moonlight casts eerie shadows across the hedges, transforming dead statues into looming threats.

Gravel crunches softly beneath my feet as I dart through the now-familiar pathway, wary of hidden resonance stones. I push down the feeling of heartache tearing at my insides, growing louder and more painful with each step toward the temple.

My grip tightens around the knife I stole, its cool surface a meager comfort in my sweating palms. It may be as blunt as a pancake, but it's better than nothing. The absence of a proper weapon feels like a missing limb, leaving me exposed in a way that sets my nerves on edge.

The bone sword I brought from Elphyne is too cumbersome, too conspicuous. But I can't take Rory's dagger back. Geraldine shouldn't even use it—the metal disrupts magic.

As I approach the temple, my wolf senses strain, picking up the faintest sounds—the scurry of a small creature in the underbrush, the distant murmur of the ball, the steady drip of water from somewhere unseen.

Two looming figures step out from the shadows. My pulse races, and I strike out. Before the butter knife hits, I see it's Bodin and Styx. My strike loses power, and the blade impotently skates off Bodin's chest. His brow arches as he glances down.

"A butter knife?" Horror dawns on his face. "This was your defense plan?"

Styx sniggers, and I swing the blunt blade, pointing at his face. "Don't underestimate me."

"Wouldn't dream of it, fangs."

I narrow my eyes at him. "What are you both doing here?"

Bodin's brows lower, his expression a mix of concern and something darker. Styx smirks, then catches himself, his face sobering.

"You had the same idea as me, didn't you?" I ask.

"Almost." Bodin's gaze flicks to the temple. "You should have waited for us."

"You were busy."

He grunts, unhappy with my response, but they need me. He can't send me back. "We're going to bring him home."

My heart soars. "So, not just a visit?"

"Puck seems to be refusing to let his Hunt out for patrols."

"Why?"

Styx replies, "He's afraid someone will come and take his dragon from him."

"Or," Bodin says, "the Hunt is using him for its own purpose. Whatever the case, we must take advantage of this opportunity."

"Do we have time?" Hope and anxiety war in my chest.

Bodin's hand slides over my shoulder, warm and large. "We do if we work together."

"Okay. What's the plan?"

"Take us inside," he says. "Styx and I will push Fox toward the exit, and Styx will *flicker* us home."

"Fox isn't too heavy?" I ask.

Styx gives me a skeptical look. "You're seriously asking me that?"

I shrug, assessing his frame. Sure, they're both strong males, but how much of their strength is within the normal realm of fae? "I don't know."

"Don't worry your pretty little head about me," he scoffs, strolling toward the temple.

"Styx," Bodin warns. "Only Willow can sense the warded entrance."

The cocky bastard keeps searching for the entrance, but all he can see is rock. I wait a few minutes, arms folded, foot tapping, before Styx turns to me with a stubborn smile and says, "After you."

I roll my eyes but can't help the small smile tugging at my lips. Despite the danger, despite everything, there's something comforting about their presence. We're in this together, for better or worse.

"Alright, let's do this," I say, moving toward the temple entrance. I take both their hands and use my foot to connect with the entrance. Once the itching sense of magic crawls over me, I let it spill to them and take us through.

The first sign something is wrong is the darkness. With hundreds of jars of wisps, it should be bright. When my wolf eyes adjust, I'm stunned—the jars of wisps and treasures . . . all gone. All that remains is Fox's statue, tables with ancient carvings, and the thick discs sealing the Sluagh's full powers.

"What happened?" I whisper, the eerie silence pressing in around us. "The wards haven't changed."

Bodin scans the room. "There is only one person apart from yourself, Willow, who has access to this temple."

"Puck."

"No wonder the Baleful Hunt no longer guards it," Styx drawls, his voice tinged with dark amusement. "There's nothing to guard."

At first, I try to help push Fox toward the exit, but I'm more of a hindrance. The two take over, but it's slow going. I occasionally poke my head outside the warded exit to check, but it remains empty. Eventually, Bodin orders Styx to shift.

Styx's wings erupt from his back, tearing his shirt to shreds.

"Fuck!" he barks, scowling down at his exposed chest with embarrassment. He plucks fabric scraps from his skin, discarding them carelessly, but can't seem to reach the trapped shreds at his back.

Bodin sighs. "Pick up your trash. Leave no traces of our visit."

I quickly volunteer to help, kneeling to collect the discarded pieces. When I offer to untangle the remaining shirt from his wings, Styx refuses, a blush darkening his cheeks.

"Let me do it," I insist softly. "It'll be easier for me."

He doesn't stop me from stepping closer. I set to work, hyper-aware of his gaze on my face. His hand, warm and large, curves around my waist, anchoring me.

"Done," I murmur, our eyes locking.

"I'm still getting used to shifting," he says in my mind.

I give him an understanding smile and reply, *"My claws used to catch and rip things before I was used to it."*

Bodin clears his throat, breaking the moment. "Willow, you touch both Styx and myself as we push. Styx—"

"I know, I know," Styx interrupts, his voice still intimate.

He gently moves me aside, undoes the buttons on his breeches and slings them low on his hips, then fully transforms. Horns, spikes, blue-tinted skin, tail. His skull briefly illuminates, and then his wraith exits his body with a rush of wind against our faces. Bracing his hands on Fox's middle, he quickly flaps his taloned, silken wings, creating a buzzing sound. He pushes the statue with casual ease toward the exit.

He is a sight to behold. A force of strength, muscle, and—dare I think it—divine.

I help them exit through the wards. Outside, Styx's otherness fades, leaving him almost vulnerable as he buttons his pants.

Bodin stares at him, annoyed. "You could have saved us a lot of trouble if you did that at the start."

Styx shrugs and swipes his hair from his eyes. He won't look at me, leaving me wondering if he's embarrassed, ashamed, or angry to show me his true form. The portraits he sketched of himself in Elphyne had a sense of self-disparagement. The name Spike had been scratched out and replaced with Styx. The other night, he went to great lengths to convince me he's unashamed of this form, but I'm not convinced.

"Everyone needs to touch me for this to work," he grinds out, his earlier playfulness replaced by intensity. "Get close."

I step forward, placing one hand on his shoulder and the other on Fox's cold stone chest. Bodin moves to the other side, his warmth a stark contrast to the chill of the statue. He tries to encircle me and Fox but can only cover so much surface area.

"You sure this will work?" Bodin checks.

Styx's response is a glare cut from steel.

Before we *flicker* away, I lean in closer to Fox. The rough texture scrapes against my cheek as I press close.

"I miss you," I whisper. "We're going to fix this, I promise."

I press my ear to his chest, amazed to hear a faint, slow heartbeat, like a distant drum. My eyes burn with unshed tears.

"Ready?" Styx asks, his voice uncharacteristically gentle.

I nod, tightening my grip. "Ready."

The world blurs, colors and shapes melding in a dizzying swirl. When everything solidifies, we're standing in the dining room at Shadowfall Keep, Fox's statue still cold and immobile between us.

"We did it," I breathe, relief and determination mingling in my voice. "We brought you home."

Part
Two

CHAPTER 34

WILLOW

I wake with a start in Fox's bed, my hand instinctively reaching out, seeking him. The absence of his warm body beside me is a physical ache that settles deep in my chest before I even open my eyes.

Of course, we argued about which room to put him in when we returned to the Keep. Styx wanted to draw a mustache on his face "to go with his ostentatious fashion." Emrys suggested the vegetable garden to scare away the ravens. Baby Hunt cocked his leg and peed on Fox, which made Bodin lose his ever-loving mind. Varen left, probably because of the chaos. Legion just wanted them all to shut up. Ultimately, they made sense of it when I suggested he remain in the dining room where his hive would see him daily. We hoped that gazing upon his stony face and expression of heartbreak would keep his memory alive, unlike what happened with Styx.

I close my eyes, remembering the faint heartbeat. He's still in there, still alive. The thought of him possibly aware but unable to move, to speak, to live is almost too much. Styx said his memory was hazy before he was imprisoned in stone, but does that mean Fox isn't suffering?

I sit up, pulling my knees to my chest. The room still smells faintly of Fox—that mix of moss, woods, and musk that's uniquely him. It's both a comfort and a torment.

A wave of loneliness overcomes me. An ache grows deeper inside my chest, and I rub my sternum as if to dispel the feeling of loss. Wolves need to be with a pack, and in the absence of my family back in Elphyne, I need to be close to my mates.

I need the reassurance that I'm not alone.

I need to feel wanted.

Varen is my first thought. But he has no dream web, and I triggered his manic attack the last time I slept in his bed. I don't want to cause trouble and discomfort.

Bodin is grumpy with me for running off without him and attempting to break into the temple alone. I get it. It was stupid. But love makes us do silly things. I'm not sorry.

Styx still doesn't trust me. Emrys scowls at me constantly. And Legion, the one person in this group who should know what mates are to each other, avoids me. *I refuse to touch you this way,* he said. The more I think of those words, the more I feel wounded and need comfort.

My new friends have suffered enough because of my actions. I can't lump my emotions onto them too.

So that leaves me with Fox. He's a stone statue, but his heart beats steadily inside. Maybe curling up at his feet will let me fall into a dreamless sleep.

I gather Fox's black embroidered blanket around my naked body and ease off his bed. It's become my own. The dream web must work well enough because I've had no complaints about rogue dreamscapes infecting the hallways. I tiptoe through the connecting door to my small room. Having six domineering mates is both a blessing and a curse. I'm a glutton for tactile company, but I'm no fool. There will be times when I need my own space.

Now is not one of those times.

I run my finger along my collection of stolen items. Last night, one of Bodin's hair beads joined the mix.

I collect a scarf I wore last week and head to the dining room at the end of the wing. Each step on the cold floor feels heavier than the last. But still, I press on. Because even a stone Fox is better than being completely alone.

When I enter the dining room, festive smells assault my nose—a potent mix of pine, cinnamon, and the lingering scent of mulled wine. A shadowy old-world Christmas tree stands by a window. My friends helped me decorate it. Cricket and Finch even added their decorated Yule log as a centerpiece on the empty dining table. It's dark, the room bathed in the ethereal glow of faerie lantern lights that dance along the walls like captured starlight. It must be somewhere between dusk and dawn, that liminal time when the veil between worlds grows thin, but I've lost track of time. All I can think of now is how impossible it seems to get Fox back.

I pad over to him, my bare feet silent on the floor. Placing my hand on his cold, hard chest, I feel the faintest thrum of tingling magic beneath the surface, a cruel reminder of the life trapped within. We dressed him in pants and a shirt. I add my scarf around his neck, thinking that smelling me close might be nice for him.

When I look up at his beautiful face, my lips curve at the curly charcoal mustache Styx drew—such a brotherly thing to do. Despite being born of the same mother, I didn't see the Six as siblings. They weren't biologically made in her womb, and all appear different based on the traits of each slaver queen. But the more time I spend with them, the more their fractiousness and camaraderie reminds me of my behavior with my kin.

I consider wiping the mustache off, but it's fun to imagine Fox discovering what's on there when he reanimates.

A low hum from somewhere in the dark room instills a deep sense of unease. I guess the sound of the fey lines, the magical energy coursing through Avorlorna, is more potent now in winter's heart. It moves the carriages and probably helps keep the watergates frozen.

I look into Fox's opaque eyes, those heartbreaking eyes frozen in a moment of sacrifice, and I'm taken back to when he told me why he was turning himself to stone in my place. The memory washes over me, as vivid and painful as if it were happening all over again . . .

He slams his palm on Styx's solid chest. *"I ate Sylvanar, Willow. I ate his Shadow. I'm the fucking monster! I made it worse."*

I step away from Fox as the truth dawns on me. I shouldn't be here. I should be far away from these people I care about. Fox is in this situation because of me. He said it himself—he tried to be something other than himself to prove he was no monster. Monster: that stupid word I slung in the heat of battle five years ago.

The further away I step, the more the sounds of that battle ring in my ears, adding to the pulsating sense of fear and regret already clinging to me. My bottom bangs into the dining table; my hands fly out to steady myself. The blanket falls from my shoulders, and cold air rushes in, tightening my bare nipples.

I close my eyes against the onslaught of more battle memories. I don't want to be back there. I don't want to remember all the horrible things I did, but there's no escaping them.

The sounds of undead creatures clawing their way out of dirt scrapes in my mind. Immediately, I think about Max, Geraldine, Peggy, Bob . . . Colin. Where is Colin?

I hug the blanket. The room seems to spin. The faerie lights blur into streaks of cold fire. The scent of death and decay, a memory from that battle, fills my nostrils.

What if he's dead? What if he's like Bob? Someone killed him because he's weak. Here I am complaining about pageants and lessons; people are still dying in the shadows. Just like they're suffering outside the city gates.

Panic starts to climb; my heart races. The ringing of blades clashing in the distance becomes guttural growls of the undead biting into my side. My hand flies to that side of my face, where I feel an echo of the scars they left behind.

I almost feel the rough, rotting flesh against my skin, hear their teeth gnashing, and smell the putrid decay.

Even if I manage to reclaim my magic from Titania, I'm only good for killing and raising the dead, creating suffering.

The thought settles over me like a shroud, cold and suffocating. Memories of my time with Nero flood back, unbidden and unwelcome. The countless lives I took, the bodies I raised, all under his command. The room seems to darken, the shadows growing longer, reaching for me with grasping, accusing fingers.

"Run," someone whispers to me. *"Run now. Run far, far from these people before you make it worse."*

The whispers grow louder, harsher, seemingly closer. Dread builds, and my pulse gallops. I gather the blanket around me as if that can save me from my own mind.

"Run, run now."

That's when I realize the pulsing sense of fear, the hum, the whispers . . . they're not coming from my mind—the very air around me ripples and shifts. A shadowy, spectral figure with a mirror-like surface appears. It's vaguely humanoid but doesn't seem to hold a shape. Its eyes are swirling vortexes of fear and regret. Tendrils of mist emanate from its body.

The temperature plummets. My breath comes out in visible puffs, and goosebumps race across my skin. The lanterns flicker and dim, as if recoiling from the creature's presence.

When one of the tendrils snakes toward me and touches my bare shoulder, Fox whispers, *"Fucking monster! You made it worse!"*

I'm having a nightmare.

I must still be in Fox's bed. His dream web might be defective without him. But the cold is too real, the fear too palpable. I can smell the Terror's presence—a mix of decay and ozone, tinged with the metallic scent of old blood. I can see it before me with crystal clarity.

I try to back away, but my legs won't move. Once a comfort, the blanket now feels like it's suffocating. The Terror looms closer, its form shifting and writhing, a kaleidoscope of my worst fears.

"This is real," it whispers, its voice a meld of all the people I've failed—Rory, Bob, my mother, father. "You can't run from what you are."

I open my mouth to scream, but no sound comes out. The Terror's tendrils reach for me again, promising to drag me into a void of endless regret and fear. Images flash before my eyes—the faces of those I killed under Nero's command, their eyes accusing, their mouths twisted in silent screams. The secrets I've kept from Geraldine and Max, the horrors I inflicted, threaten to over-whelm me.

But then, oddly, its voice becomes female. She mocks, she taunts, she's . . . not looking at me anymore but at Bodin, standing only a few feet away in his Sluagh form, staring in horror at his bloody, taloned hands. His wings are out. His eyes are wholly black.

"Bodin?" I gasp.

He looks up, wide eyes clashing with mine. Shame contorts his face. He tries to hide his hands behind his back, beneath the mantle of his tattered wings. He walks toward me, but the Terror senses him too. Its tendrils unfurl and head toward him. It's trying to suck him into my dream.

This is bad.

Very bad. If he gets lost in here, he might never come out.

"Bodin, no! Don't come any closer!" I shout. "I'm dreaming. This is a nightmare. You're in my dreamscape again."

He pauses. Panic washes over his features. I've never seen his eyes filled with fear like this before. He glances between the Terror and me.

"It's an Echo Wraith," he says. "Don't listen to it. Wake up. Wake up now."

I try to shake myself awake, to pinch myself. I try everything but can still feel the cold press of the floor beneath me. I still smell the pine and mulled wine. This feels so real, so visceral.

"It's not working," I say, my voice trembling. Whispers of regret, of my past, the blood, the undead clawing at my skin—I feel like they're right here with me. I can't see them but hear them and smell them.

"Bodin, you need to go," I plead.

"That's right," the wraith whispers. *"Make him run. Make him run away from you where he's safer."*

"Where are you sleeping?" Bodin shouts at me, his voice strangely sounding distant and down the hall. It's almost like he's not here.

"I . . . I guess I'm in Fox's bed. As usual."

Wait, how can Bodin's Sluagh side be out? The whispers laugh at him. That cold dread on his face increases. We both realize our mistake at the same time: He's not entering my dreamscape—I must be entering his. Or . . .

"Our dreamscapes have clashed!" I gasp.

"Impossible," he grunts, shrewd eyes darting about, looking for answers.

I know I'm right. I feel it in my bones, in the tingling of magic crawling along my skin. I never noticed it before, but it's there. And it's different. Darker. Thicker. More pungent and lethal.

"Where did you fall asleep?" I ask Bodin. "In your bed or somewhere without a dream web?"

He doesn't answer, but the horror dawning in his eyes tells me all I need to know. He's not in his bed.

"Bodin," I say, barely above a whisper. "Wake up."

Come for me. Wake me up too.

We lock eyes, then he disappears, leaving me alone with the

Nightmare and its tendrils, its misty wisps locking around my wrists and stinging like regret.

The room seems to stretch and distort, and the walls melt like wax. The Nightmare's grip is ice cold, seeping into my bones. The scent of fear—my own and remnants of Bodin's—mingles with the pine and wine, creating a nauseating cocktail.

"*You see?*" the Echo Wraith hisses, its voice a chorus of every doubt I've had. "*Even in dreams, you bring nothing but danger. You don't belong anywhere—not in the waking world. Not in nightmares.*"

I struggle against its hold, but the more I fight, the tighter it grips. The whispers grow louder, a roar of regrets and fears drowning out my thoughts.

"*They're all going to leave you.*"

The wraith's form shifts, becoming a mirror image of myself —but this version of me is covered in blood, eyes wild with the same feral hunger I felt when Nero commanded me to kill. It grins, revealing sharp teeth. "*This is who you really are,*" it taunts. "*A killer. A monster. Just like Nero made you.*"

"Bodin!" I scream, hoping against hope that he can still hear me. "Hurry!"

CHAPTER 35
BODIN

I jolt awake, muscles coiled tight. Straw crackles beneath my palms, grounding me in reality. *Where am I?* A pitiful whine cuts through the darkness . . . followed by snuffling . . . heavy breathing. The pungent musk of horses and manure assaults my nostrils—the stables.

My gaze darts around the dim space, seeking familiar anchors. Heart hammering, I drink in each shadowy shape, desperate to prove this isn't another nightmare. Inevitably, my gaze locks on the cage housing the Wild Hunt pup. Its liquid black eyes bore into mine as it whimpers, pleading for release.

The little bastard pissed all over Fox's statue. But that's not why I've imprisoned it. No, the real reason is far more terrifying.

Phantom echoes of a woman's taunting voice slither through my mind: *"You'll always kill the fragile, beautiful things you long to covet, to keep, to treasure."*

Shame lances through me as I recall Willow witnessing my terror. The Echo Wraith barely had to scratch the surface to find my deepest fears. I've exiled myself here because those blood-soaked golden feathers morphed into crushed strands of moonlit silk in my last dream—Willow's hair.

The memory of Styx's words haunts me: I once killed a bird, a canary. But the visceral sensation lingers—the sickening give of delicate bones collapsing within my fist, the crunch that still echoes in my nightmares. The soul-crushing realization of what I'd done. Something so small, so fragile, so trusting . . . it must have been a cherished pet. There's no other explanation.

In my desperation to possess that bright, beautiful thing, I destroyed it.

I scrub my face with a calloused hand, glowering at the caged pup. Its presence reminds me of my fear—that I might somehow hurt it too. And if I did, how could Willow ever accept me?

A chill races down my spine. She's alone in the castle, at the mercy of a Nightmare made flesh. The Echo Wraith must have slithered through a nearby watergate, drawn by our fears like a moth to a flame.

In my misguided attempt to protect her by keeping my distance, I've left her defenseless.

Fool.

My mind races, grasping for a strategy. Two things weaken an Echo Wraith: strong social bonds make it harder to isolate its victim, and light. If only Willow had been safely ensconced in my bed . . . or Varen's . . . or anyone's. She'd have been overlooked.

But I can't change the past. I can only act now. Since I can't conjure sunlight from my dark shadow magic, I need the real thing. I unearth a wooden torch from a nearby haystack, wrapping the end with more fuel-soaked rags before grabbing a flint.

The wildling whines again, clawing at its cage. It's resourceful —it always finds a way to escape. I weigh my options, desperation clawing at my insides. I can't let harm come to the wildling, but one Echo Wraith isn't strong enough to kill it. The dragon might even help. The pest has a unique bond with Willow.

"Let's go," I growl, unlatching the cage. "Your queen needs us."

We race toward the castle, the frigid night air whipping

around me. Each pounding step on the frozen ground sends shockwaves through my body. For the first time in memory, I feel the biting cold.

"Hold on," I mutter, a desperate prayer carried on ragged breaths. "I'm coming."

WILLOW'S terrified scream curdles my blood as I reach the conservatory door. I slam it open, every thought fleeing except one: protect her.

Her scent hits me, and I *hunt*. This is what I was born for, what I'm made to do. I race through the castle, taking stairs two at a time, following the tugging ache in my chest to where her scent is most potent. The pest has disappeared, probably sniffing for scraps somewhere behind. But I can't wait. I keep moving.

My footsteps slow as I approach the dining room. I force my lungs to steady, willing my heartbeat to silence. My senses stretch, hyperalert, probing for danger within. A quick peek around the doorframe, and I exhale in relief.

Willow is pressed against the wall behind Fox's statue beneath the faerie lanterns. Our clever queen found the safest spot—closest to her mate, where his heart beats quietly within the stone, and near the room's only light.

The Terror, a dark echo, wobbles in my vision, its incorporeal body rippling. The side closest to the lights solidifies in patches, revealing its weakness. It has power only in darkness, in shadows. There, it's incorporeal and impossible to fight.

I wedge the torch between my knees, striking flint over the fuel-soaked end. Flames erupt, heat searing my face as I stride in, torch held high. Willow's eyes lock onto mine, her relief palpable and echoing in my heart.

Our bond deepens, but the Terror persists, assaulting her

fears, regrets, pain. Wispy tendrils lash out, seeking any part of her to latch onto. It thinks itself invincible, uncaring of my approach. Wait. Willow's skin reddens, welts rising where tendrils touch. This isn't a dreamscape. This is real.

The Wild Hunt pup—either too stupid or too young to grasp danger—chooses that moment to burst in. It tears through the room with caged-animal excitement, toppling a chair before backtracking, distracted by food scents. Its clumsy rampage creates chaos under the table, splitting the wraith's attention. I seize the moment, sliding to Willow's side.

Two golden, tear-filled eyes lock with mine. The impact is visceral—her gratitude, relief, and raw emotion are unlike anything I've ever felt. I've guarded my hive for eons, but no one has ever looked at me like I'm their entire world.

No one except—

"*He trusted you,*" the wraith taunts, its voice a sinister whisper. "*You were his whole world.*"

A tendril finds my bare foot. I snarl, hissing as I swipe the torch. It recoils, prowling just beyond reach, calculating. I have mere seconds.

"This isn't a dream. Are you hurt?" My hand roams, checking for injuries beyond the welts. She's ice cold. Shivering. Practically naked save for panties and a crumpled blanket on the floor. Silver hair cascades, barely covering her. Welts mar her skin every-where. My calloused, unworthy hands gently rub her arms, moving across her hair—and find something wet.

Blood.

The sight of it, stark against her pale skin, ignites a primal rage within me. The Echo Wraith will pay for this violation.

CHAPTER 36

WILLOW

Bodin's grip tightens on me, his eyes widening with alarm.

"You're wounded," he mutters.

I frown, piecing together the last few minutes. Bodin's dream form had vanished, and the Terror attacked. Instinctively, I'd searched for a weapon.

Rory's ghostly voice had echoed in my mind, challenging the wraith's. *"Stay focused. Adapt or perish."*

The Terror hurled memories at me—regrets, guilt—but I've lived in that space for half my life. Guilt feels like an old friend now. Fear and panic morphed into something stronger when I thought of Rory.

She reminded me of my strength.

"This will make you stronger," she'd whispered. *"This will hurt now, but one day you will remember . . . remember."*

And I did. My training flooded back—the breathing techniques, the laser-sharp focus—shoving everything from my head except my target. Rory's dagger wrapped as a gift for Geraldine beneath the Yule tree.

"One problem at a time," Rory's voice guided me. *"What takes the highest priority? What's going to kill you first?"*

The Terror wouldn't cause immediate death. Its power came from my fear. So I had lunged for that package, ripping the paper off. My fingers closed around the familiar hilt, and I slashed at the Terror. It shrieked as Rory's magic-cutting metal made contact. Something wet splashed my face. We both recoiled.

I gasped, stumbling back until I hit the wall near Fox. His faint heartbeat thrummed in my ears like a war drum, anchoring me. The Terror hesitated to attack, and that bought me time until my Sluagh found me.

"The blood's not mine," I tell Bodin, aiming for confidence. Relief washes over me as I look at him. "You're really here."

The wraith prowls beyond Bodin's light, seeking an entrance.

"I should have been here," Bodin mutters, shaking his head. He gathers the blanket from the ground, wraps it around me, and then tugs me against his chest.

Something crashes against the tree, shaking ornaments. Bodin tightens his grip on me and arcs the torch toward the tree, illuminating the scene.

"Another Nightmare?" I whisper, my heart racing.

The baby Wild Hunt bursts from beneath it and claws up my body, flapping its wings for momentum.

"Now is not the time for cuddles," I admonish the dragon, catching it and glancing at the wraith with panic. We lock eyes— its vortexes swirling, trying to hypnotize us and trap us in a torture chamber of our regrets. It's trying to lure me out of our haven and into the danger zone.

Bodin's hand covers my face, blocking my view.

"Don't look at it," he growls.

Heart kicking, all I can muster is a nod and drop my chin. He removes his hand, and I lower the baby dragon. It settles eagerly at my feet, a string of drool dangling from its maw.

It dawns on me—he's waiting for a signal.

"There," I point in the Nightmare's direction. "There's your yum-yums. Go get it!"

The little dragon's high-pitched yowl of excitement pierces the air. It spins unnaturally fast and launches across the floor, leaping into the Terror's dark sanctuary. Flashes of purple, skull, oil-slick scales, and screeches escape the shadows. My jaw drops as the wraith steps into the halo of light. The previously transparent body is peppered with corporeal, dripping wounds. It shrieks and writhes, trying to throw the vicious dragon off.

"What the fuck is this?" A voice cuts through the chaos.

Styx steps out of flickering darkness, dressed in low-slung cotton pants and nothing more. His black wavy hair is messed up. Shadows dot his collarbone, shoulders, and above his brows—his Sluagh form close to the surface.

"The Terror attacked Willow," Bodin explains, his voice tense. "I was about to take it down, but the wildling seems to be enjoying himself."

Styx prowls around the monster as it fends off the dragon's attack. He seems unhurried, not worried—even a little excited at the prospect of a fight. He casually takes in the battle, then his gaze swings back to land on the blood in my hair. I clutch the blanket tighter as his eyes bleed to black, lips parting to reveal sharp, spiky fangs.

More footsteps thunder toward us in the hallway.

Emrys jogs into the room. I hardly see him in the castle; I'd forgotten he was here. He wears loose cotton pants similar to Styx's, but his muscular torso is riddled with black ribbonlike tattoos. A thrill glimmers in his eyes as he takes in the scene.

Legion arrives next, fully clothed in a dark, tailored suit. He must have come straight from his study but still wears the spectacles.

Finally, Varen is the last to arrive, his eyes wide and filled with panic, his hair and pajamas ruffled from sleep.

"Contain it," Legion decrees, his voice cutting through the chaos.

As my mates advance on the Terror, it stops still, despite the dragon still mauling it. The air crackles with tension. It knows when it's outnumbered. It flings shadows and unseen magic, shrieks in a way that makes my bones ache, and then leaps through a stained-glass window—smashing it. Two seconds later, we hear crunching outside as it hits the ground.

"Stop it!" Legion barks, his voice thundering through the room.

Styx disappears. I rush to the window and glimpse a flying dark-winged shadow—stark against the snowy moonlit ground— closing the gap to the Echo Wraith. Ahead, the half-incorporeal body jerks as though it's been shot by an arrow. Then it convulses and slumps to the ground.

The shadowy winged silhouette lands gracefully and takes shape as Styx in his Sluagh form. As he stalks his dying prey, his great draconic wings fold and settle on his blue shoulders. The wind catches the tattered, silken membranes, and they billow behind him—like his hair. His blue-tinted face tilts up toward us. Moonlight slices along his curved horns, his brutal profile. The flickering light of his skull is blinding in the gloom. I wince at the brightness. When I look again, Styx is gone. Only the Terror's drained and visible corpse remains. No blots rise.

Did Styx feed on its soul?

Emrys shoves me out of the way and looks down. "Imbecile."

Bodin smothers his torch with shadow. "What has he done now?"

"See for yourself," Emrys replies. "Our impulsive brother has robbed us of answers yet again."

"He killed it," Legion grumbles, shaking his head.

Emrys and Bodin lock eyes, something worrisome passing between them.

"We want it dead, don't we?" I ask.

Emrys glares at me, his coppery eyes burning so intensely that I gasp and step back.

"Amateur," he spits, his voice dripping with disdain. "Your naivety is as dangerous as it is irritating."

Bodin growls, stepping between us. "Don't speak to her like that."

Emrys's laugh is mirthless, sending chills down my spine. "Or what? Can't you see what's happening? How did it get in here?" He turns to me, his gaze accusing. "Did you invite it in? Are you so desperate for attention that you'd risk all our lives?"

"Why would I invite a Nightmare in?" I retort, my voice trembling despite my efforts to stay strong.

"It was me," Bodin admits, his shoulders slumping. "I'm the one who dreamed without a web. I was out in the stables."

Emrys sneers, his body coiled with tension. When his muscles harden, the black lines on his body seem to strangle him. He pauses, considering this new information. "None of that matters," he finally says, his voice low and dangerous. "It was here in the flesh."

"Why did Styx kill it?" Bodin asks, frowning. "He knows better than that."

"See what I mean?" Emrys takes a menacing step toward me. "She's infected our senses. It's almost as if Styx *wanted* to sabotage our safety."

"Or maybe he was just afraid!" I shout back, anger rising in my chest. "That thing got into our home. Don't we have wards for this?"

"That was Fox's job," Bodin returns, another splash of self-disparagement crossing his face.

"Then we'll find a way to train Styx with the knowledge," Legion suggests, exhaustion slumping his frame. "At least it's dead. Go deal with the corpse. If Styx ingested the blots, then . . . bring back what you can salvage. And where is that damn dragon?"

Emrys gives me a scathing look as he strides away toward the exit.

My plea halts him in his tracks. "I didn't do anything wrong. You have to believe me."

He opens his mouth and shuts it when Legion glares a warning at him.

"You, of all people, should see what's happening," Emrys snaps back at his leader, voice thick with resentment. "You have your memories. You should be able to smell the effect she has on us, on all of you. It lingers and wraps itself around your very being. It's poison, slowly corrupting us all. For *Nicnevin's* sake, you almost fucked her in front of strangers at Sith's establishment! What happened to your vow?"

Legion's eyes flash with guilt as he glances at me. When he looks back at Emrys, his expression hardens. "I made a mistake. It won't happen again."

"What vow?" My heart races. If this is about me, I need to know. "Legion?"

"In a honeybee colony," Varen mutters, his eyes unfocused, "when a foreign queen's pheromones are introduced, it can cause chaos and aggression among the workers. The hive becomes unstable, vulnerable to outside threats."

"Your rambling won't help now," Emrys snaps at him.

"It's not rambling," I retort, anger flaring. "Sometimes, he says things that make sense. He's one of us."

Emrys stares at me, then steps close enough that I feel the heat radiating from his body. I ache to move into him, to hug him and tell him it's okay to be angry and hate. I've been there, and it's a lonely, horribly empty place. But he's not alone anymore. Whatever hatred he's holding onto, we can weather it together.

But then his voice drops to a dangerous whisper, and my compassion flees. "You think you're one of us?" he sneers. "You know nothing of what we are, what we've endured."

I reach for him but barely brush his skin before he hisses and flinches away.

"Don't touch me," he snaps, baring his teeth. "Don't *ever* touch me. You are not one of us. Never will be."

The fear in his eyes stops my heart. He's afraid of me, of a tiny brush of my fingers. His vulnerability lasts a fleeting moment and then it's gone beneath his armor of seething hatred.

Varen raises his voice and grips his hair, pacing by the door. "When a hive is under attack, guard bees release alarm pheromones. This rallies the colony to defend against intruders."

"Precisely," Legion sighs, humoring him. "And now we are defended."

It seems to mollify Varen, disrupt Emrys, and quieten the room. But inside, I am boiling with something indignant. Something that won't stay down.

"Stop calling me queen!" I shout, my cheeks burning. All the emotions I've stifled surge to the surface. "I'm not your queen," I clarify, forcing my tone to soften despite wanting to shake sense into them all. Instead, I meet each of their gazes in turn and set my jaw. "I'm your mate. It's completely different."

I adjust the blanket and tug my hair aside, revealing Fox's bite scar on my neck.

"We're all connected," I say, "whether you like it or not, but I am not your queen. I'm not here for the same purpose as the others. I didn't lure the Nightmare in. The thought of controlling you, manipulating you—or anyone—makes me want to puke."

I spent half my life being controlled and manipulated. Why would I subject anyone else to that suffering?

Emrys narrows his eyes. "You can't help it. It's in your nature."

"Maybe nature can change," Bodin offers quietly.

He receives a hiss of contempt in return. "Keep dreaming."

Legion's gaze flattens on Emrys. "Go deal with Styx and the Terror. Channel that anger into something useful for once."

Emrys looks at me, then at the dragon licking drops of spattered blood on the dining table leg.

"Deny it all you want," he says to me, "but you already control the beast. We will never be free so long as we have a queen."

He leaves without a backward glance.

Legion turns his stern gaze to Bodin. "When I give you an order to meet her needs, I expect you to follow it. Sleeping in the stables is not meeting her needs."

He takes Varen and walks out.

Bodin looks at me. I can't read his expression, so when he storms off with a curt, "Follow me," a stubborn urge to plant my feet takes over.

The room feels colder and emptier now. Tension lingers in the air like a thick fog. Emrys's words echo in my mind, reminding me of my outsider status. Yet, beneath the hurt, determination grows, and warmth spreads through my chest.

They came for me. All of them. This should be a good thing, a sign of our bond growing closer. But they're all acting like . . . My mind scrambles to find the right words.

A memory surfaces—an overheard conversation between my mother and her friends during one of their cocktail catch-ups. I'd been hiding in the larder not long after returning to Elphyne when their laughter and chatter drifted in.

"God, men can be so . . . ugh," my mom had said, slinking into the room with her friends Laurel, Melody, and Silver.

Their conversation flowed with the fruity cocktails they mixed, full of old-world clichés and playful complaints about the men in their lives. I remember the sound of ice clinking in glasses, their drinks' sweet scents, and their laughter's warmth.

"Sometimes they just need some help dotting the Is and crossing the Ts," Melody says, reaching across the counter to squeeze Mom's hand.

"And killing the monsters," Laurel adds with a wink.

Silver nods solemnly. "I might be good at killing, but when the shit hits the fan, when I need protection, there's nothing Shade won't do to keep me safe."

The memory fades, leaving me with a bittersweet smile.

As Bodin strides away down the hall, I realize this family needs help. Unlike me, this family has lost their memories. Legion can only do so much on his own. Since Fox removed himself from the picture, I've been waiting for Legion or any of them to guide me forward. I'm not their queen. I don't control or have power over their actions and lives. I want to be their equal, their mate. I want respect.

That means I need to start pitching in, tackling problems head-on, and proving I'm not like their slaver queens.

Bodin stops, turns, and realizes I'm not hurrying after him. A baffled expression crossed his face, and I burst out laughing.

I need two things to survive this: more cocktails and a regular venting session with my friends. When Bodin, my all-powerful demigod mate, returns to me with a nervous glint in his eyes, I realize I need a third thing . . . honesty.

"Let's go," he grunts.

"Not until you tell me—"

The Clock Tower bell tolls. The floor trembles. Oh, shit. The castle is changing its structure. Walls drag and slide. Blocks of stone come at me. I'm going to be crushed.

CHAPTER 37
BODIN

"Careful!" I bellow, yanking Willow against my chest. Her blanket snags in the moving stone, threatening to drag her along. She yelps as the floor tilts.

"I've got you," I growl. "Let go of the blanket."

She releases it, and I haul us both into the doorway's refuge. Wind gusts past as a stone wall sails by, rock grinding in a deafening roar.

I twist, pressing Willow's spine to the thin doorframe. My arms cage her, shielding her from harm. Glancing around, I see walls shifting beyond our sanctuary. We're trapped.

Air continues rushing in, circulating her unique, musky scent in our cramped space. It stirs something within me that I'm unprepared to examine.

"Are you okay?" I ask her.

Wide, expressive eyes meet mine, and she nods. "Thanks to you. Are we safe here?"

"If the castle wanted to move this doorframe, it would have by now. We're secure until the walls finish shifting."

"How long?"

"Could be minutes. Could be an hour."

Her eyes widen. "Stuck in this tiny space?"

"Yes."

It's not even safe to call for Styx until the castle stops moving. Darkness envelops us as a moving wall blocks the lantern light from the dining room. Sometimes slow, sometimes fast, the transformation always demands stillness. One misstep could mean being swept away by the castle's whims.

I might survive the moving walls, but she's mortal. Fragile as a bird in my hand. The thought chills me.

"It'll be okay," I promise. "I'll protect you."

The blanket is gone, lost in the castle's walls. If a wall comes too close, nothing will remain of her fragile body.

"Don't move an inch," I instruct, voice low and rough.

"Why?" she asks warily.

"Always so defiant. Even in the face of death."

"I believe you'll keep me safe." She scowls. "Just wondering why I have to remain completely still. Will the walls come in here? Will they—"

"I'm removing my shirt for you to wear. In case the bricks get too close."

"Oh."

My gaze drops to her lips, pursed in frustration.

"That makes sense," she admits, eyeing the moving walls warily.

I try to remove my shirt, but the cramped space makes it difficult. I have mere inches to work with.

"Let me help," she offers. Her palms slide up my front, and my breath hitches. Every ounce of awareness in my body focuses on that point, seizing it, claiming it, drawing her into me as if she's intangible too.

I swallow hard.

Does she have to sleep in the nude all the time?

Hunger builds within me—craving, obsession. I should tell her to stop when her fingers work at my collar's laces, but words fail me. All I can do is brace myself against the doorframe around her, ensuring I'll take the brunt of any impact.

Her nimble fingers set my skin ablaze. My eyes flutter closed.

"Okay," she murmurs. "Arms up higher."

I comply, sliding my hands up the frame to above her head. Her touch skates along my sides as she lifts the shirt. I hold my breath, fighting arousal. If I let it in, there'll be no stopping me. I'd crush her with my want, demolish her with my need.

I call her Calamity not for her actions but as a warning—a reminder of what I'll do to her if I lose control. How did Fox manage? How does Legion resist? Thoughts of her taste consume me. I want to explore every inch of her mouth. *Stop. Empty her from your mind.* My fists tighten against the doorframe, creaking the wood.

"Bodin?" she whispers. "Are you okay?"

I want to fuck your mouth. "I'm fine."

"You don't look fine. You're sweating."

Because it hurts to hold myself back. "It's hot in here."

"You never get hot."

Only around you. "You done?"

She makes a disgruntled sound but finishes removing my shirt with clinical attention.

"Got it," she says, then adds under her breath, "jackass."

"What?" I glare down at her.

"Nothing," she replies with a sweet smile that scatters my thoughts.

Those fuckable lips invade my dreams nightly. If I'm not having a nightmare about bloody canary feathers, it's those fucking lips wrapped around my cock, hot against my throat, sucking on my earlobe, whispering the filthy things she'll do to me.

I know she can take it. I know she wants it. The worst part is that I know how eager she is to explore it. With me. With us. She needs to feel close, to sink into us as much as we do with her. The gods wouldn't have given us anyone different. But they have fucked-up timing.

This thing between us has to wait until our hive is whole, until we're invincible.

"Put it on." My command is too guttural, too thick with emotion, and I shut my eyes again. It's dark now in our little hide-away, but her skin is luminous, as if lit from within. Sometimes, I think it's a trick of the eyes. Even the shadows can't contain her for long. Our Calamity, she shines for us.

Catch our falling star.

A memory. A voice.

I sense movement beneath me as she puts on my shirt, but then she curses and jostles to the side. My eyes snap open, fearing she's been caught, but she grabs my belt to steady herself. Her fingers dig into my waistband, brushing against the sensitive tip of my erection. I suck in a sharp breath.

"Sorry!" she gasps, but doesn't remove her hand.

Which means she felt it. She knows I'm hard for her. For a moment, I can't move.

I glance down and see her silver head dipped, her shadowed shoulders swathed in my shirt. At first, some deep possessive part of me preens to see her wearing my clothes again, knowing my scent marks her again. But then I realize what she's looking at.

"Willow?"

"Yes, Bodin?"

"You need to remove your hand from my pants."

"Am I making you uncomfortable?"

I detect a note of challenge in her voice.

The air between us is electric, charged with tension and unspoken desire. Every breath, every twitch, sends sparks into my body. I'm caught between the instinct to protect her and the overwhelming fear of hurting her.

"If you don't," I growl, fighting for control, "I might do something we both regret."

"Like what?"

"Always testing, aren't you?"

"Questioning, I think you mean."

I huff, almost laughing. Shaking my head, I count the striations in the wooden doorframe above her and remind myself of my duty. Protect. Don't destroy.

She slips her hand from my pants, but relief doesn't come. We're too close to escape the heat, the awareness prickling my skin.

"When the castle finishes," I say through gritted teeth, "I'll take you to your room."

"You mean Fox's room?"

"Yes."

"I don't—" she begins, then stops.

"What?"

"Nothing."

I drop a hand to her chin, lifting her eyes to mine. "Finish your sentence."

"I don't want to be alone," she admits, golden eyes flashing.

My grip tightens before I catch myself and let go.

"The wildling can sleep with you," I offer, returning my gaze upward.

"No," she replies. "No, thank you."

"No?"

"I want it to be you. I'll feel safer."

I arch an eyebrow, doubting her reasons. But before I can challenge her, she gasps.

"The baby Hunt!" she cries. "What if the castle—"

"The little beastie is fine," I grumble. "It has a knack for getting out of tight spaces."

"You sure?"

"As sure as the sun comes up in the morning."

"Okay." She relaxes, but her concern for the dragon touches something in me. Her capacity for care, even for a creature others might fear, reminds me of why she's different from the queens we've known before.

We don't speak while the castle moves, grating and rushing around us. It's taking its time to decide on a structure tonight.

"Bodin?"

"Yes, Calamity?"

"Why are you avoiding me? Why does Legion refuse to touch me?"

I swallow.

"Emrys doesn't surprise me." She sighs. "He's always had some kind of burning hate for me."

"Ignore him. It's not about you."

"Even Styx, I understand." She gnaws at her lip. "That was about me."

"What do you mean?"

"I mean . . . I called you all monsters in Elphyne. Maybe he hates me because of that too."

"He won't remember that," I point out pragmatically. I don't. "And he doesn't hate you."

"He doesn't?"

The hope in her voice melts my heart. "No."

"Then what is it?"

I stare down at her. The curve of her cheeks, her scent mingled with mine, makes this hard to resist. I growl at myself, and she looks up, confused. "You keep doing that—growl."

"Ignore me too."

"See? That's the thing. I can't." She digs her fingertips past my belt again. "I won't."

"You should."

"You keep saying dumb things like that too. We're mates, Bodin. It's too late to ignore this."

I close my eyes, fighting against the surge of desire her words ignite. I can't risk hurting her. I can't risk losing control like I did with the Canary, especially since I can't remember exactly what I did.

CHAPTER 38
BODIN

illow's fingers sink deeper behind the waistband of my pants.

I move to tug her back out, but a stone block grazes my elbow. I return my hand to the frame, angling my body to take the hit instead of her, but it doesn't come. And she doesn't appear to notice. Her head is dipped, her breath hot against my bare belly.

"Why are you avoiding me?" she repeats.

"Are you talking to my cock?"

"Maybe he'll actually give me answers. He seems more honest than you."

I squeeze my eyes shut. Every brain cell I own zeros in on her touch, begging her to move a little to the left. Yes. One more swipe—a scrape against the tip. Fuck me, how I ache to take her. Here. Now, while we're surrounded by danger.

"Then do it."

The voice is in my head. I tense, then realize who it is and exhale.

"What do you want, Styx?" I send back to him.

The brush of his presence filters in, sucking more air from the stifling space.

Willow giggles. She glances up at me and then mumbles, "But he'll be even grumpier."

My brows lift. "Are you speaking to Styx?"

"Maybe." She swipes a fingertip across my tip. My cock jerks.

"Godsdammit. Stop that."

"Is that what you really want?" She lowers, sinking carefully onto her knees. "Help me understand, Bodin. Why did you sleep in the stables?"

"I—" I bite my inner cheek until it bleeds. The coppery taste triggers a primal hunger in me. My hands drop, slip under her arms, and wrench her back to her feet. I pin her against the frame and growl, "Stop courting danger."

Her worried eyes dart between mine. "You're actually afraid for me—that I'll get hurt."

It hasn't escaped my notice that Styx has gone quiet or left. Typical—he swans in here to ensure we're not dying, causes havoc, and then leaves. I squeeze my eyes shut, but I can't answer Willow.

"Is it something to do with your nightmare?" she prompts. "The one about the feathers?"

Somehow, I nod.

"Oh, Bodin." The pity in her voice doesn't have me fuming. It has me pushing against her until her nose hits my chest in some kind of bastardized version of an embrace. She inhales deeply. "*Crimson*, you smell so good." There is a beat of silence. Then, "I'm not going to break, you know."

It's my turn to gasp. How can she—? I frown at her soft, compassionate smile.

"I saw your nightmare, remember?" She rubs idle circles on my lower back. "Are you remembering things from your past?"

"Yes," I grunt. My frown deepens. "Since you, since I *tasted* you, fractured memories continue to plague me. You say you won't break, but you don't know how hard I can push."

"It's my fault." She tenses.

An apology?

"No." I take her chin a little too forcefully. "Don't think that. This is me—*my* feelings, Emrys's, Varen's, all of us. Our shared trauma is not your responsibility, nor is it your duty."

"I know." Her eyes glimmer in the shadowy light. "But it's my honor."

I blink. "What do you mean?"

She presses her lips to my heart. "I want to help you heal. I want to—" She inhales against my skin, sucking in my scent and groaning on the exhale. "I want to be close to you, to take care of you, and to serve you."

"Queens don't serve. They rule."

"*Mates* are equal." She slides down my body again, kissing my clenched stomach as she lowers to her knees. Fuck me, I let her.

I let her tongue swirl over my skin. I inch backward and greedily watch her reaction as she comes face to face with the bulge straining my breeches. Her eyes widen and fill with heady lust.

"You want me, Bodin," she murmurs, plucking open the buttons until the tip of my cock shows.

Don't look. Don't watch her fulfill your wildest fantasy.

Fabric scrapes down my hips. I squeeze my eyes shut when my erection springs free of its captivity, heavy and thick. I groan at the wet sound of her licking her lips.

"You can't deny it." Hot breath tingles the tip of my cock. "But you can tell me to stop. You have that power now. You have a choice."

I shake my head, braids clinking. "Not here."

"We have space."

"I don't."

I fist her hair and tilt her face upward. With the other arm braced against the doorframe, I hold my control by a thread. Can't she see that? But her golden eyes are fever bright as they meet mine.

Gold . . . so close to yellow. The color once gave me nightmares but now fills me with longing, with insatiable need. It feels right. Good.

She parts those fucking lips and sticks her tongue out. Waits. It is an offer, an invitation.

The castle still moves around us. It's slower, almost sluggish. She's right. We have room. My legs are braced wide. They'll be hit first. Not that the walls are closing in. It's almost as if the castle is her partner in crime, plotting to force us together, to obliterate my wall of resistance.

And Styx has seemingly deemed we're safe. He's deserted us.

"You have a death wish," I mutter.

She snorts. "Someone thinks highly of his dick."

Her breath teases the wet tip of my cock. It hurts how much I want to—need to—take my length and—*fuck it*. I let go of her hair and fist myself. Pleasure skates up my spine. Another drop of cum beads on my tip, and I growl out some kind of nonsensical noise. I lower the tip of my cock to her open mouth but then lift it when she tries to lick.

"No," I grate out. "No tongue yet."

Just those tempting lips.

A flash of sass. She swallows and opens her mouth—no tongue out, just the meek offering of a soft, wet, and tight space. I swipe the blunt tip of my cock along her lower lip, leaving a glittering line behind.

"Now, use your tongue," I growl. "Nice and slow along your lip. Taste me."

Her tongue darts out. Licks her lip. She groans. Pants and fidgets. Needy, I realize. The scent of her arousal is heady, blooming and growing within our cramped space. This need is animal. I have nothing to compare it to except the desire to hunt, claim, destroy, and consume. But I can't get to her pussy to sate my thirst. Not here. And she knows it.

Emrys would say she's manipulating me, that she's using my desire to break my resolve. She'll make me do something horrible for her in return. She'll warp my mind.

He couldn't be further from the truth. She's freeing me. She's showing me she's unafraid of my passion, my hunger. She wants us to be equal. It's terrifying and exhilarating all at once.

Gold eyes narrow. Harden. "Stick it in, or I'll take it."

I chuckle. "You think you can take it from me?"

She sinks her teeth into my thigh, clamping hard until I hiss. When I grab her hair with two fists, she smirks and takes my cock. Pumps. I am too overcome with pleasure to think of—

Licks.

Swirls her tongue.

Nibbles.

"Fuck," I grunt, and grip the doorframe to stop my knees buckling. She takes me a little deeper, over her tongue until my crown touches the back of her throat. She comes off me, and I almost weep from the loss. It was over too soon.

"Mmm," she hums. More pumping and licking as she contemplates my cock. "You might be right."

"What?"

"I'm not sure if I can take you all the way. You're so big."

I growl, hook my finger into her mouth, open her wide. The thought of not being able to fit drives me mad. My voice deepens. "You can take me."

Pure sensual mischief. Smug.

"You're teasing," I grind out.

"And you're holding back. Don't."

She takes me deep into her throat. My whole world lives inside her mouth, and I'm obsessed. I pull out and then thrust in. Again. Deeper. Harder. Longer. I fuck her mouth until she suddenly grips my ass and stops my hips from flexing back, forcing me to remain gripped in the tight channel.

That's all it takes, and hot pleasure explodes. I come hard, spurting my release. Stars burst in the shadows. Can't breathe. Can't—

She makes a choking sound, and my heart wrenches. I've broken her.

I try to yank out, but she snarls and fights me. Pumps me harder. I let her drink me up, milk every last drop, and groan at the cathartic satisfaction of submission. I worried I'd lose control, but that's impossible when she dominates. In this moment, I realize it's not me who has control. She does. Of me. I would do anything for her. Anything.

When there's nothing left for me to give, she wipes the corner of her lips with her thumb, flashing tiny fangs.

"What do I taste like?" I breathe, helping her stand.

"Good," she smirks. "See for yourself."

Her kiss releases more hunger within me. I'm about ready to devour her, to rip her to shreds with this new obsession of mine.

But the walls stop moving. A path opens to my right—blocks of stone clank and thud along the corridor leading to our private wing. Further down the hall, the door opens wide, and I see my bed. Willow laughs when the little beastie comes bounding out, running hard and fast toward her.

Her eyes meet mine, a mix of satisfaction, tenderness, and defiance. She jogs out, arms wide. The dragon leaps, half flying, half climbing up her body. She skillfully catches it as it licks her face.

"I missed you too, Hunt." She turns back to me, glances down, and says, "You going to stand there with your dick out, or are you escorting me back to my bed?"

My jaw clicks shut. I tug my pants back up and tuck myself in. "*Your* bed?"

"Well, Fox's bed. You were such a good little boy," she coos.

Not at me. "Attacking that big bad Nightmare to keep me safe." Another kiss on his bony skull. "You hardly scratched me this time too!"

Fucking little wildling, taking all the credit. "I should put you back in your cage."

She gasps and spears me with volatile eyes. "You kept him in a cage?"

"He . . . I . . ." I swear the wildling pokes its tongue at me.

She flattens her lips, then coos at the dragon, "You can sleep with me tonight in Fox's room. We don't need wool-headed mates sharing our beds until they learn to share their fears too."

What?

No!

But she's already tucking the dragon into her arms and striding down the hall. Harrumphing, I jog toward her, place my hand on her lower back, and keep walking.

Toward *my* bed.

CHAPTER 39

WILLOW

Frost crunches beneath our feet as we trudge toward the Nexus on this bitter Moonsday morning. Our breath clouds the air, a visible reminder of the biting cold. Geraldine and Max lead the way, nearly at the rope bridge, while Bodin stalks beside me.

As usual, panic knots my stomach the closer we come to the rope bridge. Last week, the moat river water wasn't quite frozen. I watch Geraldine and Max start crossing the rickety bridge, terror gripping me as they navigate such a treacherous path.

Fox saved me last time because he had full access to his powers. If I fall now and crash into the ice . . . no one will save me. I'll be dead, gone.

"Willow!" Geraldine shouts from the middle of the bridge. "It's frozen again! Look!"

I take a hesitant step forward, and some of the tension holding me captive releases. The moat's solid ice again. But once the fear enters, it's hard to eliminate. One look from me is all the excuse Bodin needs to gather me into his arms and murmur into my ear, "People can die from anything—at the hands of someone they trust, from someone they love. You

272

can't live your life worrying about accidents crossing a bridge."

"Rory didn't die by accident," I answer, a lump forming in my throat. "She died to save me."

His hand slides behind my neck, warm and large, guiding my gaze back to his. "It sounds like she cared for you a lot."

A memory flashes: Rory and I staring at the stars, our feet dangling outside the window in her high-level tower room. The smell of a diesel-soaked city wasn't so bad up there. We could almost imagine we were in another world.

"Apparently," she says, pointing to a star, "you can wish on those if you're lucky enough to see one fall."

"What would you wish for?"

She gives me a wry smile. "You first."

"Um." I gaze into the night, knowing my family is down there, refusing to let me come home. "I wish I could be a falling star . . . then maybe—" Maybe I'll be wanted. Lovable. Everyone will hunt nightly for a glimpse of me in the sky.

It hurts too much to voice. I dash a tear from my eye.

"Maybe what?" Rory prods her shoulder into mine.

"You'll just say I'm being emotional."

We sit silently for a while before she says in a small voice, "I'm not always right, Willow." Her arm slings around my shoulders, drawing me under her wing. She kisses the top of my head. "Sometimes, you need to listen to your gut."

"Hurry up, you two!" Max shouts out from the other side of the bridge. "Get it out of your system now because once we're there, no public displays of affection!"

"He's right, you know," Bodin murmurs, reluctantly letting go of me and stepping away.

"Can't anyone know?" I ask, frustration bubbling up inside me. "The idea of hiding how I feel for you is . . . maddening."

His expression darkens. "It's against the code. The consequences . . ." He trails off, his jaw clenching.

I blow a raspberry. "That's what I think of the code."

"Being facetious will get you turned to stone," he warns. "And that's only before Titania returns. Her punishments are far crueler."

"Fine," I concede, a chill running through me at the thought of being cursed again. "I'll be good."

But even as I say it, I feel a spark of defiance. I'm tired of hiding, of conforming to rules that don't make sense. Fox's sacrifice set my confidence back, but it didn't break me. It made me more determined.

If I'm going to lead and protect, I need to start questioning these outdated laws. The thought both thrills and terrifies me.

Bodin takes my hand, puts it on the rope railing, takes my other hand, and puts it on the other side. Then he moves to stand behind me, palms on my hips.

"Let's walk," he says, his touch both reassuring and electrifying.

I'm so conscious of the heat of his hands on my body that we make it halfway across the rope bridge before I realize how far we've come. When we arrive at the end, I turn to him and smile. "That earned you one night in my bed."

His brief arrogance is swiftly replaced by shrewd opportunity. "Let's cross again."

My smile explodes into laughter.

OUR FIRST CLASS for the day is in the House of Stone Tower. It's meant to be tactical warfare, but a little thrill skips in my stomach when I see Legion and the earl alongside him—still no Colin. Before I take a seat, I turn to Bodin. "Since Legion is here, will you do me a favor and look for Colin?"

The concern flashing in his eyes is directed at me, not the missing boy, but he nods. My smile warms, rushing through me. He inhales deeply, taking in my scent. I can tell he doesn't want to leave.

"I'll be fine," I assure him.

"If I'm not back when class ends, stay with Geraldine and Max until I arrive."

I sit in the front row beside my friends. Across the room, I recognize a few familiar faces: Corey, the new House of Stone Shadow, and beside him sit Alfie and Dahlia.

Legion walks to the center of the room, looking every bit the leader, even with the spectacles. Somehow, they make him look sharper. Behind him, Earl Larkspur is securing a map to the wall. When they place pins in specific locations, I realize what's happening.

"I saw this map," I whisper to Geraldine. "In Legion's study."

"And?" she replies, brow rising.

"The pins mark recent Nightmare sightings around Avorlorna."

Before I finish my sentence, the earl stands beside Legion, commanding the room's attention.

"Instead of the usual drivel they've given us, the Knight Commander and I have decided to give you something useful, something real."

Murmurs rise like the tide. Legion raises his hand. Everyone hushes. His aura commands the room, even with his true demigod self sealed.

He asks, "Who can tell us what's meant to happen to the watergates during the Gentle Interlude?"

Multiple hands raise in the air. He points to a random person I've never met—a female with dark hair and green eyes. "Yes, you," he says.

"They're meant to be frozen," she replies.

Legion gives a curt nod. "Now, who can tell us why?"

No one responds for a moment. Then another puts up their hand. "To stop the Nightmares coming through, of course."

Legion's stare hardens at the mocking tone, and the exhibitor looks at his feet, a blush staining his cheeks.

"Yes, they're meant to be frozen," the earl says, then points to the pins on various points across Avorlorna. "So these are—"

A hushed whisper catches my attention, drowning out the reply. Two students behind me gossip, their voices low.

"Did you see how haggard the earl looks?" one murmurs.

"I heard it's because of his wife," the other replies. "Apparently, she was a Never."

My breath catches. I strain to hear more, my heart pounding. "What happened?"

"They were caught. She's exiled to the Cabinet. They stripped him of magic for a year. He hasn't been the same since."

The weight of their words settles heavily in my chest. I glance at Legion, wondering if he heard. His jaw is clenched, eyes fixed firmly forward. But there's a tension in his shoulders that wasn't there before.

The earl's voice cuts through my racing thoughts. "These pins represent Nightmare sightings and known locations of water-gates. Now, who can tell me what's wrong with this picture?"

I force myself to focus, but the implications of what I've just heard linger. Bodin warned me not to be facetious about showing public affection to them, but I didn't think the consequences would be this bad.

"Nothing. That's normal." Alfie dismissively tosses his hand at the map. "In fact, it's not much at all compared to last year." A smug look crosses his features. He addresses the rest of the room and boasts, "I've served for multiple years. I'd know."

"Unless . . ." Geraldine starts. Everyone looks at her, and she lifts her chin. "Unless they're sightings from after the Gentle Interlude started, not before. Then it wouldn't be normal. It would be worse."

Legion smiles at her. "Correct."

The earl steps forward. "You'll notice most activity is concentrated outside the cities . . . where it's barely snowing, if at all. The queen's slumber should expand the Holly King's power across the land for the entire Interlude. Now, he can hardly hold the cities in his icy grip."

A chill runs down my spine as the implications sink in. The watergates should be completely frozen by now, but Nightmares are still getting through. Is this the same thawing occurring in Elphyne over the past few hundred years? The only problem with that theory is that the Well flourishing there is the reason why.

"What does the earl's revelation tell you?" Legion prompts the class.

"It tells me someone isn't doing his job," Alfie sneers.

My fists clench. I can't believe he has the nerve. Legion is one of the highest-ranked Radiants in Avorlorna. The Alfie I knew did anything for Nero's approval, but he now seems to have little respect for leadership. I look at him across the room and see a stranger.

My mind travels to the wisps Titania kept in jars in the temple and how they're now gone.

"It tells us," I call out, "that something is wrong with the magic keeping the gates frozen."

The earl gestures to the map again. "These are the Nightmare sightings since the start of this year's Gentle Interlude." He plugs in many pins around the Nexus, but even more around the city of Heliodor. "These are the Nightmare sightings since two days ago."

They've doubled.

"Titania's magical slumber is failing," someone mutters.

"War is returning faster than we expected," the earl admits. "We can no longer afford for you to remain inside these protected walls while Avorlornians are dying."

"What are you saying?" Alfie asks, eyes shrewd. "That you're canceling the exhibition?"

"I'm saying," the earl replies, "there might not be an *Avorlorna* if we don't do something now."

Gasps ricochet off the curved walls.

"For the following week," Legion announces, "the exhibitors will take a pilgrimage into Heliodor—the House of Stone's home territory. Goodfellow refuses to release the Baleful Hunt to patrol the area, so the exhibitors must do it instead. Return to your towers, pack your belongings for a long, cold journey, and reconvene here at noon."

Alfie starts to protest, as does Dahlia, but Legion silences them all with a dark, unbending gaze that scares even me.

"You will be traveling in small groups," he continues. "Each will have a Radiant taking point. Every dragon-bonded member of the Shining Host will be with us. Your mission is to scout and nothing further. You report to your leader what Nightmares you've seen, if any, and where. We aim to send more experienced soldiers to track the Terrors back to their watergate. Do not engage the monster, but if you're discovered, use your knowledge from the Nightmare Codex to exploit the Terror's weaknesses and escape. We wish you to remain alive and return with this vital information. Is that understood?"

A chorus of "Yes, sir" repeats around the room.

"During the expedition," the earl adds, "we are not guarding your dreams. Hence, you will face rogue dreamscapes from your fellow exhibitors. This is the perfect opportunity to receive schooling on tactics for evading or escaping them in preparation for the trials . . . or if war comes sooner than planned."

The acrid scent of fear starts to build in my nostrils. I look upon the sea of faces, draining of blood. It makes me sick to my gut that we've been spending this time lulled into some kind of false sense of security, content to spend our time partying, having fun, smiling. No one's smiling now. War is not glamorous. It could be here before Titania wakes. Before the trials and the Interlude end. And we're woefully underprepared.

CHAPTER 40
WILLOW

It doesn't take us long to pack travel bags stuffed with supplies, strap weapons to our bodies, and pull on furred cloaks and thick leather winter gear. Geraldine, Max, and I say goodbye to Peggy, Cricket, and Finch in the castle foyer near the entrance. Titania's portrait stares down at us from the wall, her painted eyes seeming to follow our movements. The air in the foyer is chilly, and the scent of old stone and faded tapestries fills my nostrils. Our footsteps echo off the high ceilings as we say our goodbyes.

Varen has already worked himself into a tizzy at our departure. He was napping when we returned to the castle, and now he appears more chaotic than usual, his hair sticking up at odd angles and his clothes askew.

"No," he says, shaking his head, refusing to let go of me. His grip is surprisingly firm, his fingers digging into my arms. "If the queen leaves a hive, the other worker bees don't know what to do."

"It's okay, Varen," I say, gently disentangling myself from his arms. His skin is clammy against mine, and I feel him trembling slightly.

"The colony can collapse without her pheromones to guide them."

"We'll be fine. Legion wouldn't send us on this pilgrimage unless he's certain it's safe. In fact," I pat his arm, trying to soothe him, "he's doing this to prepare us. We need it. My friends need it. It's a good thing."

But he keeps returning to how the honeycombs need repair. Usually, I make sense of at least half of his ramblings, but today, I'm stretching.

"They're broken," he says, slapping his hand on the wall. The sound echoes through the foyer. "The honeycombs are broken. They're looking, but I can't find it, and they won't find it unless she's here. The queen bee must *not* leave the hive, or the worker bees will follow her."

"Just a few days," I tell him, trying to keep my voice calm and reassuring. "I'll be back. Keep the honeycombs . . ." I shrug, thinking *I don't know* to myself. "Keep working on your plan. Show me when I get home."

Somehow, this seems to appease him. He nods, scrubs his face with both hands, and walks away, his shoulders slumped.

The baby Wild Hunt tries to follow me as I exit the castle, its tiny claws clicking on the stone floor.

"No, Hunt. Keep Varen safe. That's your job." It whimpers, its eyes big and pleading. But then I say, "He's got some yum-yums for you."

He's off, chasing Varen up the stairs. I shake my head, but I'm smiling. That dragon understands more than everyone knows.

We arrive outside the House of Stone Tower, and when I see Bodin standing with his hand on Colin's back, joy bursts from my chest. I can't believe it. He found him. Grinning from ear to ear, I stride up to them, Geraldine and Max at my back.

"Colin! I'm so glad to see you," I say. He looks at me strangely, his eyes darting around nervously. He probably doesn't recall me from Burn After Reading. So, I stick out my hand and reintroduce myself. "I'm Willow," I say. "This is Geraldine and Max."

He gives a shy nod but doesn't say anything. I look closer at him and see signs of a wounded animal—a twitch here, a flinch there—hypervigilant where he doesn't need to be. I wonder where he's been these past few days. I look at Bodin, but his jaw clenches, and he gives an almost imperceptible head shake. *Later*, his eyes seem to say.

True to his word, Legion organizes the exhibitors into small troops. He assigns a Radiant or a dragon-bonded to each and announces he's leading a unit I'm not a part of. Emrys takes another, while Styx takes a third. Bodin leads my troop. All the while this is happening, a slow excitement builds in my blood. Finally, I get to see Avorlorna. My heart races with a mix of excitement and apprehension. The chance to explore beyond the Nexus thrills me, but uncertainty about what we might find out there sends a shiver down my spine. I get to see if this land lacks wisps everywhere.

I suspect I know the answer. The Sluagh haven't given me any reason to believe the Well flows abundantly out there. But I still need to see it with my own eyes.

Before we leave, Puck charges in, flanked by a unit of green-cloaked city guards who start breaking up the groups, ordering them to return to their towers until further notice. The atmosphere charges with tension, and I can see the confusion and worry on the faces of the other exhibitors.

"They can't do that, right?" Max asks nervously. Geraldine and the rest of our troop murmur their concerns.

"Just wait." I nod to where Legion speaks with Puck at the center of the furor. "We don't leave until the Knight Commander tells us to."

Calling them knights doesn't feel so jarring anymore. It feels right.

Legion and Puck face each other through the commotion,

their bodies tense. Legion's face is a mask of cool indifference, but I can see the subtle clench of his jaw. Puck, on the other hand, struggles to maintain his composure. His eyes dart nervously, and his hands fidget at his sides as he speaks.

Bodin returns to my side, unworried about the turn of events. I think he actually yawns at one point, so I relax. Legion can handle a little politics, I'm sure.

I take the opportunity to assess the timid Colin. Something definitely happened to him. I tug on Bodin's sleeve to bring his ear closer to my lips and whisper, "I thought you said he could switch to learning to be a Phantom. Does he have to come with us?"

He looks down at me, his dark eyes intense. "Willow, training as a Phantom includes what you'll be learning while we're out there."

"It's just that he doesn't look—"

"We'll take care of him." He pets my arm, his touch reassuring. "Don't worry."

Legion and Puck's argument continues, escalating in tone and pitch. The green-cloaked guards stall, knowing their Knight Commander is unhappy with whatever Puck told them, and Earl Larkspur takes advantage of the lull. He renews assigning exhibitors to each troop.

Two more young teenagers join our group, and I'm happy to see Colin perk up. They must know each other, and from the look Bodin gives him, satisfied and relieved, I know Bodin had a hand in their assignment. I introduce myself and find out the perky female with curly blond hair is Maggie. Her friend with bangs and masses of brown hair is Ji-Soo.

We receive eleven exhibitors from various Houses. I don't know any except Becky, one of Dahlia's and Irisa's friends. She's not a Shadow herself, but she was there when they steered me toward Milford. Of course, she doesn't remember being part of that drama. Probably. We exchange polite greetings and then return our focus to where Puck's voice suddenly raises, tight and shrill.

"—blatant disregard and breach of protocol," Puck accuses Legion, his face flushed with anger.

"You broke protocol first," Legion points out coldly, referring to Puck's new stony gaze.

He stole the Baleful Hunt from the House of Stone—the traditional host of the dragon since the Shining Host was created.

Puck bristles visibly. He leans in close and threatens Legion with a hiss. "I could send you to the Cabinet immediately for your insubordination."

Legion doesn't even blink. He looks as bored as Bodin.

Puck adds, "Mark my words, Sluagh, there will be consequences."

I didn't think the temperature could plummet any lower, but the air turns icy. Legion's upper lip curls, and my heart races. Puck just said the S-word. No one here is supposed to know the true identity of the queen's knights. A flash of white cuts through the crowd like a shark's fin—Emrys approaches Legion. This time, when I glance at Bodin, he's not yawning. He's ready to charge in and do something. Worse, Styx is smiling like he knows something we don't.

"There already are consequences," Legion counters Puck quietly, taking a step away and dismissing him.

Why isn't he worried? I can't help but admire Legion's calm demeanor in the face of Puck's threats. But a knot forms in my stomach as I wonder about the consequences of this confrontation. What if Puck follows through on his threats? What would happen to the Six . . . to me? I push the thoughts aside, focusing on the present—one crisis at a time.

I search the faces of nearby troops. Most Radiants are busy organizing the rabble. Even the green-cloaked guards seem distracted and even . . . *helping* with the organization. When did that turn about? Could we be so lucky that none of them heard? I'm at least ten feet away, and I heard.

Then I see a guard shake his head as if disoriented. My gaze snaps to Styx. He stands back, arms folded, lips stretched wide, and eyes wicked as he sweeps the crowd. I remember that grin. I saw it in the temple the first time he met Puck.

He's the reason Legion isn't worried.

"You messed with their minds," I project my thoughts to Styx.

He turns to me and flashes a mouth full of sharp, monstrous fangs. The glimpse is so brief that I almost think I imagined it.

"You didn't imagine it," Styx purrs into my mind, eyes gleaming. The more I'm learning about him, the more I see he's the sort to get a thrill dancing on a razor's edge.

Puck mumbles something I miss.

Legion turns back from his retreat and gives him a withering glare. "I expected better from you. You were a good soldier once. But now look at you. What a waste."

"Be careful, Knight Commander," Puck warns. "I control the Shining Host now."

"I know. I'm the one who put you there, remember?"

"You didn't—" Outrage mottles Puck's expression. Something dark swims beneath his chalky skin. "Regardless of who voted me in, I have the controlling vote. All I need to do is—"

"You control nothing," Legion states, "if there is no Shining Host to cast a vote."

"Are you threatening me—us?"

Everyone is looking now. He's making a spectacle of himself in a very bad, un-faerie way. On the other hand, not a hair seems out of place on Legion's head.

"I'm simply pointing out," Legion drawls, "that every dragon-bonded Radiant has already agreed to this expedition."

"But I didn't!"

Legion simply stares at him until Puck reads between the

lines. No one counts Puck as one of them, not really. The veiled insult only riles Puck up.

"Why the sudden interest in the curriculum?" he asks, his voice dripping with suspicion.

"What are you afraid of?" Legion flicks chalky sand from Puck's shoulders. "That we'll head out there and find your leadership is lacking? Or that everyone will soon know the truth behind your dragon acquisition."

"Fine, leave the Nexus," Puck grinds out, stepping back to avoid another patronizing sweep of Legion's hand. "You won't find evidence to support a state of martial law. The exhibition will go on."

CHAPTER 41

WILLOW

We set off for Heliodor in mid-afternoon, heading west, following the Abhainn River beside the woods. We aim to cover as much ground as possible before nightfall and find a good place to camp. Fresh snow crunches beneath our feet, but the sky is a brilliant cerulean blue, and I'm still filled with barely contained excitement at finally being outside Avorlorna.

How can I not marvel at the winter wonderland? It reminds me of home, of the mountainous terrain surrounding my father's cabin. Icicles hanging from tree branches sparkle with an inner light. The snow seems to shimmer with a rainbow when the sunlight hits it just right. In the distance, I swear I hear the faint tinkling of bells, though there's no one else in sight. I half expect to see snow sprites flurrying around, proving me wrong about the lack of magic here.

I can't say my mortal companions feel the same thrill I do. I doubt half of them are used to trekking through the wilderness, but whether there is snow or grass, the wild is home to a wolf. This is where I feel most at peace. My eyes flutter closed, and I

inhale deeply, the crisp winter air filling my lungs. The scent of pine and frost mingles with something distinctly magical.

When I was little, I used to go on runs in the wild during a full moon with my father and older brother, Thorne. I smile fondly at the memories. Even though I couldn't shift all the way into a wolf—just my fangs, ears, and claws—it didn't stop me from tagging along. After returning to Elphyne as an adult and the twins were born, I envied their ability to become wolves. Even hated them for it. But now I'm here, I only feel joy at knowing they'll get to immerse themselves in that experience fully. They'll feel this exhilaration too.

A melancholy takes control of my heart for a moment . . . but only for a moment because I remember where I am and who is with me. I'm nowhere near done with Avorlorna. In Elphyne, I floundered for purpose. Here, I'm building it.

The snow crunches behind me, and I turn to see Bodin approaching. The white landscape sets off his dark form. His sleek, black military uniform accentuates broad shoulders and cuts an imposing figure. A shiver runs through me that has nothing to do with the cold or fear.

"Everything alright?" he asks, deep voice rumbling.

I nod, offering him a small smile. "Just remembering . . . and looking forward."

He studies me for a moment, his gaze intense.

"Stay alert," he says finally. "We don't know what we might encounter out here."

As if to emphasize his point, a distant howl echoes through the trees—too wild to be a normal wolf, too haunting to be anything but magical. The hairs on the back of my neck stand up, a mix of excitement and apprehension coursing through me. The Fever Hunt screeches and dives, a black streak against the sky. He crashes through the trees, and we lose sight of him. A few seconds later, he returns and drops a smoking carcass up ahead near Ignarius's troop.

"A Terror?" I ask a little too eagerly.

He squints ahead and replies, "Just a regular boar."

We walk in companionable silence for a few more minutes, the crunch of snow beneath our feet the only sound. I'm hyper-aware of his presence beside me.

To cool my hormones, I return to the magical winter land-scape, the Abhainn a ribbon of darkness slashing through the glittering land to our right. Its cascading waters should cause fear to ripple through me at being this close, but I'm not afraid. Not with Bodin, Legion, and Styx nearby. In the end, Emrys didn't come. I suspect Legion sent him off to keep an eye on Puck. I'll ask later when I get a private moment.

Something ripples in the waters, and my breath hitches. But then I see the shimmering scales of the Dread Hunt close to the surface and whip my gaze to Bodin.

His lips curve. "The dragons gain power from their elements. The Hollow Hunt will be out tonight."

"How does the Fever Hunt draw power?"

Bodin looks up at the sun.

"Ah." I shake my head. "I assumed it was fire."

"That too."

"The Wild Hunt?" I tentatively ask.

"Death, chaos, darkness—souls."

That makes sense.

Finally, I work up the courage to ask him, "What happened to Colin?"

He glances at me and keeps walking. He opens his mouth, shuts it, and then exhales through his teeth. "He and other young and inexperienced were tasked with tower chores."

"Okay . . . go on," I prompt.

"They had little time for the rest," he explains dryly. "He missed multiple classes and the ball. When I found him, his fingers were raw and blistered."

My gaze narrows. "He's from the House of Embers, right?"

He gives a curt nod.

"What about the other two young ones?"

"Found them the same," he replies. "House of Tides."

"Did Colin remember anything of the night at Burn After Reading?" I ask, although I know the answer.

"No, nor did he have the patch I handed to him. He was set upon the moment he left. He wasn't even aware of what his House members confiscated."

Anger and fury well within me, hot and potent. "We can't send him back to that after this."

His eyes flick ahead as he says, "I'm working on it."

The injustice of it all makes my blood boil. These kids came here for a chance, and instead, they're being exploited and abused. It's wrong, and I'm determined to do something about it. But how? The enormity of the task ahead feels overwhelming, but I push the feeling aside—one step at a time.

Our troop is one of seven walking along the river in a line, so it's not hard for me to see further down the train to where the House of Embers Lord, Ignarius, guides his troop. He barely blinked at the smoking carcass except to bark an order. Probably to claim the food rights, but I really hope he'll send some fresh meat our way. It smells good.

"He's not a good person, is he?" I ask Bodin.

"If you have to ask that question . . ."

"Yeah, yeah," I reply. "I know the answer."

No meat, then. Bastard.

Unbidden, my gaze tracks further along the train of walking troops and lands on Styx. Something tugs within my chest, uncomfortable and needy. He was briefly there with Bodin and me in that tiny wall cavity while the castle changed shape. I felt his wraith occupy the space, and he spoke into my mind, daring me to get down on my knees for Bodin. He overheard my thoughts, but contrary to my worry that he'd be dejected or jealous like he was on the dance floor, he wanted to join in.

Only for a moment before he thought better of it and disappeared.

The memory brings a rush of heat beneath my skin. The danger, the closeness, the way Styx's hoarse whisper in my mind gleamed with mischief and desire . . .

I'm still smirking to myself when Bodin tugs me toward the back of our troop and pulls something from his pack. The crisp winter air nips at my cheeks, but I barely notice, too intrigued by Bodin's secretive behavior.

"Here," he says, handing me a long, thin cloth-wrapped package. His fingers brush against mine as he passes it over, sending sparks shooting up my arm.

"What's this?" I ask, excitement bubbling in my chest.

"Something I thought you might need," he replies, a hint of gruffness in his voice. "A gift."

"A gift?" I blink.

"Yes," he says, a little frustrated. "Hurry up and open it before somebody sees."

Barely able to contain my grin, I hastily unwrap the package and have to stifle my gasp of surprise. It's my Elphynian bone sword—but shorter and refined. I turn the blade over in my hand. The elven strengthening glyphs are still there, glimmering blue on the blade. An onyx skull is the new pommel.

"How did you get it? How did you change it?" I ask, wonder in my voice.

Bodin's enigmatic smile makes my stomach flip. "I honed the blade but asked Styx for help with the decorations."

I twirl it in my hands. In its original form, the sword was chunky and a little barbaric looking. It suited Elphyne, but not here. More ornate jewels encrust the cross-guard. It could easily stand among Titania's glimmering Court and their obsession with pretty things. I swing it around, cutting the air like a pretend monster.

"It's perfectly balanced," I breathe.

"Stop drawing attention to yourself," he grumbles, but his words have no real heat. "Strap it on and forget about it. Hopefully, you'll never have to use it."

"Hopefully, I do." I smirk, excited. "Here." I shove my backpack at him. He makes an "oof" sound as he catches it while I flick open my cape and strap the belt around my waist, shifting the sheath to my right hip. The old sword was too big for my hips. I had to wear a shoulder baldric, which was great when I set out with deliberate intentions for hunting. But to wear around day to day . . . this one is—

"It's perfect," I gush, stroking the skull.

He grumbles something inaudible. When I look at his face, I'm sure I catch a blush darkening his cheeks before he quickly looks away.

"Thank you, Bodin," I say softly, stepping closer to him. For a moment, we're standing so close I can feel the heat of his breath on my face. "And please . . . thank Styx for me too."

I know he's watching somehow. I feel his presence nearby, despite his figure walking steadily ahead.

Bodin's eyes darken, a flash of possessiveness crossing his features before he schools his expression. "We added a few upgrades to it as well," he says, his voice rough.

"Oh? Like what?" I ask.

"You'll find out," he says cryptically, returning my pack.

As I refit my pack, I feel a sense of completeness I didn't realize I was missing. This isn't just a weapon; it's a symbol of my old life and the new life I'm building. The fact that both Bodin and Styx had a hand in creating it makes it even more precious. It's a reminder that I'm not alone in this fight and that I have people I can trust at my back . . . even if they might one day forget.

CHAPTER 42
WILLOW

On the first night, we set up camp beneath towering trees. The snow rapidly lessens the further we get from the city. Legion said something in class about the winter not being so brutal in the regional areas. I hardly believed it when we stepped outside the gates, but here, a mere day's trek from the city, not a single snowflake decorates a branch.

The ground is damp but not soggy. Evergreen trees are lush and filled with twittering wildlife. I notice more marked glyph trees—more signs of dissent amongst the people. Bodin said change was coming. I'm desperate to head out and hunt, but we're forbidden to leave the camp. Scouting expeditions start tomorrow.

Chaos reigns as we struggle to set up tents and organize supplies until the more experienced take charge, directing those who aren't. Most are older exhibitors or Chasers who've served in the military.

A pang of disappointment flickers through me as I watch the Radiants lounging while we work, leaving the task of setting up to us "mere mortals." Even Bodin leaves us to confer with Styx

and Legion in a decorated tent at the head of the train. But my mood refuses to sour.

As twilight descends, the forest comes alive with crickets chirping and the distant hoot of an owl. Tent poles clanging and canvas rustling mingle with exhibitors' chatter, creating a symphony of activity. The Fever Hunt returns to Ignarius's body, and the Hollow Hunt takes to the moonlit skies, a beacon of light as it guards our perimeter. The Radiants can be pompous assholes, but something tells me when the time comes, they spring into action to keep us safe.

It's not respect I feel. It's an acknowledgment that they know what they're doing. Even Nero protected his people to a point, but evil men want to keep their army bigger than their enemies. This knowledge makes it hard to reconcile their delight in watching us kill each other for sport during the trials.

It makes me wonder if they do enjoy it or if they're suckers for a good distraction. This oppressive world Titania has built would weigh on anyone. I don't know how Legion convinced the dragon-bonded to agree to this expedition. Something else must be happening beneath the surface, and I'm itching to find out.

I call for volunteers for a due-diligence perimeter sweep. Becky's hand shoots up. Despite my lingering distrust, I nod for her to join. I grab Colin, too, while Geraldine and Max stay behind to handle the food for our troop.

We head toward the tree line, and Colin's excitement is palpable. "I can't believe we're out here. For real."

I feared he had lost his spark, but he brightens each time I give him a task and encouragement.

"We're looking for signs of danger," I explain. "Animal tracks, anything out of the ordinary. Keep your senses open and your eyes peeled."

By the time we return to camp, dusk has settled into night. The aroma of something delicious bubbles from a pot over the campfire.

As I'm scraping my bowl for the last of the soup, wishing it was stew, I notice Bodin returning from the decorated tent. Our campfire casts flickering shadows across features etched in concern. His eyes, usually guarded, betray a flash of longing as they meet mine.

"Tonight, the troops sleep under the stars. Take turns keeping guard," he instructs. "The instant the guard recognizes a dreamscape, rouse the person it belongs to."

"We're not practicing entering them and escaping?" I ask, frowning.

"Tonight, we focus on recognizing them and obliterating them. This is as important as learning to escape, for it stops our secrets from getting into the wrong hands."

Oh shit. I didn't think of that part.

He wants to say more; I can see it in how his fingers twitch at his sides as if fighting the urge to reach for me. But duty wins out, as it always does with Bodin.

With visible reluctance, he retreats to his smaller decorated tent, the flap closing behind him.

My heart aches. I know how hard this must be for him. He's been dying to sleep beside me . . . to taste me again. A wave of heat runs through me, and I shuffle away from the fire.

The longing I feel for my mates is almost overwhelming. It's not just physical desire; it's a need for connection, for understanding. In this strange new world, they're my anchor.

At least the view is nice. I look up at the star-studded sky, a bittersweet smile tugging at my lips. But then I see the moon, almost full, and my smile drops. *Shit.* No wonder I've been feeling hot out here in the cold. In a few more days, I'll be in heat.

With any luck, we'll be back at the Keep. If I'm stuck out here, surrounded by hot-blooded males, animals, and potentially Terrors from the subterranean, who knows what trouble my scent will attract?

After I returned to Elphyne, I visited my aunt Kyra. My

father's sister is the Alpha of Crescent Hollow, the small village they grew up in. At first, she seemed like a gruff person, and I wanted to die of embarrassment when my fever came on. But then she told me a story of one of her early heats. She'd been in a tavern, gambling in a card game with strangers, and losing incredibly. But then her pheromones started releasing. One male gave up his hand to her and growled for another male to do the same. The other gamblers accused them of cheating. The entire thing ended up in a brawl. They were kicked out, but she went home with both males and had the best weekend of her life . . . before robbing them blind and walking home with a pocket full of coin.

Jaded and bitter then, I said, "*You were lucky they were good to you.*"

She smiled sadly. "*Yes, I was. That night could have ended far worse, particularly when I was overcome with a fever and incapable of seeing straight. That's why keeping an eye on the moon and your cycle is always important. But, Willow, there's another lesson in there too.*" She tapped her temple. "*Don't tell your dad I said this, but sometimes a female on her own needs all the tools she can get to protect herself. The truth behind that story is that we were starving and desperate, and your dad had already left to become a Guardian. I was on my own. But I learned to use the gifts the Well gave me, and now here I am, the first female Alpha of Crescent Hollow.*"

"*Are you suggesting I use my biology to influence males into protecting me?*"

"*I'm saying it doesn't hurt to surround yourself with good males when you're incapable of protecting yourself.*"

I still prefer to control the heat, to suffer in silence, and to avoid confrontation at all costs. But I can see her point. If I'm ever thrown into a situation I can't control, having a male around I trust can be good . . . and if it's a life-or-death situation, then I'm not opposed to using what the Well gave me to survive. I won't feel good about it, but I'll be alive.

And I want to live.

I'm not quite the giant ready to squash the spider yet, but I'm still Willow. And I'm stronger than I've ever been.

CHAPTER 43

WILLOW

The second day of the journey starts earlier than anticipated. I jolt awake, heart pounding, every nerve on edge. It's still dark. The camp is shrouded in an eerie silence, broken only by the whisper of wind through the trees and the occasional crackle from campfire embers. Becky should be on guard duty, watching for rogue dreamscapes, but I don't see her.

A barely audible rustle catches my attention. Small and quick shadows flit between the bedrolls. Goosebumps erupt as I reach for my sword. With practiced stealth, I wake Geraldine and Max.

"What's wrong?" she whispers, her hand already fumbling for her dagger.

"Intruders." I nod toward the moving shadows.

We creep forward, the damp earth muffling our footsteps. I make out several small figures rifling through our supplies in the dim starlight. Children—a boy and a girl roughly the same age. They can't be any older than six or seven. Their ribs are visible through tattered clothes, and their faces are gaunt with hunger.

One spots us, eyes widening in terror. They bolt, racing for the tree line, their feet barely making a sound on the forest floor.

"Wait!" I hiss, but the darkness of the woods swallows them.

Without hesitation, we plunge after them. The forest closes in, the scent of damp earth and rotting leaves filling my nostrils. Branches claw at our faces, roots threatening to trip us at every step. Tiny, ragged breathing echoes ahead, punctuated by soft whimpers of fear.

"We're not going to hurt you!" I shout, my voice seeming to bounce off the trees.

Geraldine, Max, and I jog together. When we spot dissenters' symbolic and crude carvings, I give a subtle gesture to my friends, urging them to cover my blind spots while I race ahead, knowing I can move faster. They coordinate silently and split—each moving to an alternative side of my rear.

Suddenly, the trees thin. We burst into a clearing filled with makeshift shelters—little more than piles of branches and tattered cloth. The acrid smell of unwashed bodies mingles with the smoky scent of dying fires. A baby's weak cry pierces the air, making my heart clench. Gaunt faces peer out at us, eyes hollow with hunger and desperation.

The children we chased tear through the camp, screaming, "Mama! Mama! They found us!"

And there, in the center of it all, is Becky in her exhibitor uniform—the dullest clothing at the Nexus, but here, it's a luxury. She's deep in conversation with a haggard-looking man. Her eyes widen as she sees us, weapons in hand. In an instant, she's handing her children to the man and charging at me, face contorted with rage and fear.

"You won't take them!" she screams, swinging a crude weapon at my head—a club of dead wood.

I parry with the flat of my blade, the clash cracking through the clearing. "Becky, stop! We're not here to hurt anyone!"

But she's beyond listening, attacking with the desperate fury of a cornered animal. Around us, the camp erupts into chaos. Geraldine and Max move in perfect sync, keeping other dissenters at bay while I focus on Becky. It's not hard—these people here are untrained and unhealthy.

"Think about this!" I shout, deflecting another blow from Becky. "You've seen me fight. If I wanted you dead, you would be."

She hesitates, just for a moment. It's enough. I disarm her, my blade at her throat. The clearing falls silent, save for the sobbing of children.

"Willow!" Bodin's voice cuts through the night. He bursts into the clearing, eyes wild with worry.

I step back from Becky, lowering my sword.

"It's okay," I say to both of them. "No one panic. We're all okay."

Bodin grabs my arm, pulling me aside and out of earshot. Becky and the other humans watch, afraid to breathe now that a Radiant has appeared. Her children break free from the haggard man and run to her.

Bodin sees none of it. His voice is low, tense, and solely focused on me. "What were you thinking, running off like that?"

"I was thinking I could handle it," I snap back, frustration bubbling up.

"You can't just—"

"Can't what? Make decisions? Fight my own battles?"

"That's not—"

"Then what? You don't think I'm capable?"

His jaw clenches. "Of course you're capable. But you're also—"

"Fragile? In need of constant protection?"

"Important!" he growls, eyes flashing. "To the mission. To the hive. To me."

I blink, taken aback. "Bodin . . ."

"It's me I don't trust, not you." He hits his chest. "*Me.*"

"I—"

"Let me finish. If anything happened to you . . ." He swallows hard. "Even without my memories, I know. Losing you would break me. Break us. More than we've ever been broken before."

My lips part, but he's done listening. His mouth crashes on mine. He kisses me with wild, desperate need, pinning my face between his hands. I can do nothing but submit to his tongue, his taste, his emotion. This is everything he struggled to say. It's that feeling I get between my ribs—the one when my mates are close. It's fate. It's home. It's also reckless with everyone watching, but at this moment, he doesn't care. I don't care. I drop my sword and cup his face, returning his kiss with the same unhinged passion.

A twig snapping breaks us apart. I rest a hand on Bodin's heaving chest, silently pleading for him to trust me. His eyes, usually so guarded, are wild with fear and anger. His hands tremble slightly as he grips my arms, betraying the depth of his concern. But he allows me to take him back to the others.

Geraldine and Max stand sentinel, shrewd eyes on the dissenters now gathering into a pitiful group around Becky and her children.

"Explain," I say softly. "Please."

Becky glances around, still looking for an escape. It draws my eyes to the carved marks on the trees, the same crude symbols we found outside the Keep on the way to the Nexus. A moon, a star. Now, they seem benign, like children's drawings. Like my sisters' drawings back home. Then I notice small trinkets hanging from branches—bits of cloth, twisted metal, even a child's toy. They're offerings, I realize, to old gods worshipped by the Folk. These humans cling to any hope they can find.

"What's going on here?" I ask, head spinning.

Max sheaths his sword at his hip and says, "They're old-worlders, Willow. Like me and Gerrie."

Geraldine's eyes are haunted as she looks at Becky's children clutching her with dirty fingers. "They're starving. We've been in their position."

"So . . . you're not dissenters?"

Becky glances at my palm on Bodin's chest. Her shoulders slump, and the fight leaves her. "We are, I guess. It's a long story."

"Tell me," I urge.

"I woke up in this time with my arms around my twins. The Folk . . . they wanted to split us up, enslave us. We chose to stay together, even if it meant starving. Last year, I joined the military, hoping to earn enough to send food back. They barely survived the winter. So this year, I volunteered for the exhibition, hoping to win, to at least find a way to feed my kids and—" Her voice cracks as she tugs one of them close—the boy. My heart leaps when his little hand clutches her shirt, displaying his webbed fingers. The abnormal trait is enough to have him sent to the subterranean.

My throat clogs as I ask Bodin, "Titania wouldn't send children down there, would she?"

His bleak look is all the confirmation I need. His gaze darts between me and the dissenters, his body tense like a coiled spring. His protective instinct is intense, but there's something else there too—a flicker of uncertainty, as if he realizes the world isn't as black and white as he thought.

My heart aches. These people are my responsibility, even if they don't know it. I want to tell them everything, to beg for forgiveness, but the words stick in my throat. Would they understand? Or would they hate me even more?

"We're not here to hurt you," I say, meeting Becky's eyes. "I promise."

"Why should we trust you? I've been nothing but rude to you."

More than that, I want to add. But there's only one question I need answered. "Do you hold any loyalty toward the other Shadows?"

Her eyes narrow. "I do what I must to survive, but the only people I'm loyal to are my kids—these humans."

My mind races to come up with a solution for them. Could we

smuggle them back to the Nexus? No, that's too risky, and there's not enough space. Maybe we could set up a secret supply line? But how would we keep that hidden from the other Houses? What if we found a way to petition Titania directly? I almost laugh at that thought—as if she'd care about the plight of humans. For a wild moment, I consider giving up my wish, but I know that won't solve anything in the long run. There must be a way to use my position, my connection to the Six, to help these people.

"Switch allegiance to the House of Shadow," I urge Becky.

"Willow," Bodin warns. "It was hard enough convincing Legion to allow your friends to stay at the castle."

"But what if it's the tower?" My wild eyes dart to my friends. "What if Becky, Colin, and the others all move in there? We can funnel food and supplies out."

"We'll figure something out." He sighs, scrubbing his face. "But we need to return to camp before our absence is noticed. The only reason it hasn't is because we're at the end of the line. The Hollow Hunt is due to sweep our airspace soon."

He tries to herd us back to camp, but Becky resists. I have to admire her tenacity, strength, and devotion. I see a flicker of the fierce competitor I know at the Nexus. Her shoulders are slumped with the weight of her responsibility, but a maternal fire in her eyes refuses to be extinguished.

"What assurances do we have you won't return and kill—" She chokes off her words, eyes pleading with me.

"Becky," I point out softly. "You saw me with Bodin."

Recognition flickers on her face, but then that shrewd viper returns. "You've hidden your relationship well so far. It's no secret Dahlia fucks Ignarius. He protects her from punishment."

I look at Bodin and hate how the stark fear in his eyes means Becky's concerns are valid. The Six would destroy anyone threatening to end our relationship. But the difference between them and Ignarius is that they won't—not if I ask them not to.

"Geraldine, Max, and Peggy have known for a while," I point out to Becky. "They're not dead."

The nods of encouragement my friends give melt my heart. But then Bodin responds with, "Yet."

Crickets chirp.

I laugh to fill the silence, as though it's a joke, despite knowing Bodin is deadly serious. "He's kidding."

"I'm not." He glares at each dissenter. "If any of you so much as whisper a threatening word about our Shadow, you'll be dead before the last syllable leaves your lips. Now, before I run out of patience, let's go."

I collect my sword, sheath it, and walk up to Becky. The little boy with webbed fingers looks up at me, his eyes wide with a mix of fear and curiosity. I kneel to his level.

"It's okay," I say, offering a small smile. "We're going to help."

The girl steps protectively in front of her brother. Her chin juts out defiantly, and her lower lip trembles. The children don't return my smile, but terror leaves their eyes. They've grown up too fast, forced to be brave in a world that shows no kindness. I couldn't do anything about the starving people in Crystal City, but maybe I can here.

"I'm Willow. What are your names?"

They look to their mother. She nods.

"I'm Ava," she says. "This is Arthur."

"Nice to meet you. Look. I'm a Nothing too." I swipe my hair from my face, intending to show them my scars. But my fingers brush the acorn clipped there. I haven't taken it off since the ball. "Here—" I pull it out. "I stole this from Titania's temple. I want you to have it."

I sense Becky's eyes widening . . . and Bodin's pulse skyrocketing, but I press on.

"This acorn is magical. It brings luck to the wearer." I hand it to the girl and tear up when she gives it to her brother instead. "I think you tap it three times and make a wish, but I'll be honest,

I'm not exactly sure if there's another wish in there. It turned my dirty clothes into a beautiful dress—"

"Like Cinderella?" Ava gasps.

I smile, although I don't know who that is. "But if there are no more wishes, I'm almost certain it still brings luck to the wearer. I can feel the magic buzzing in there."

"Can we keep it, Mama?" he asks.

Becky meets my eyes, then drops to hug her kids.

"Keep it hidden," I warn, and Arthur drops it into his dirty pocket.

Ava and he start bickering over pretty dresses, and Becky explains the importance of keeping it a secret. I give them space and return to Bodin. He's unhappy with me, but too bad.

The comfortable bubble of the Nexus has been shattered, and I can't unsee the harsh reality of Avorlorna. I know I'll never look at the exhibition, or my role in it, the same way again.

These people are desperate to win, each with a compelling reason. What makes mine more important? Why do I get to save Fox while they starve?

We make it to our bedrolls—with Becky—just in time before the Hollow Hunt's glowing form sweeps the territory above our heads. When it's gone, I see Bodin slip into his tent, and I finally let my exhaustion in.

Geraldine's bedroll is only inches away. I feel the weight of her eyes.

"You don't agree?" I whisper.

"The opposite," she replies. I open my eyes and make out her smiling face in the shadows. "Just when I thought your heart couldn't get any bigger, you do something like that."

"It's what anyone would do." I'm grateful her eyesight isn't as good as mine because then she'd see my guilt, my fear. If she knew the truth about me, she wouldn't think that. None of them would.

"I doubt it," she scoffs. "You're not just anyone."

I roll to my back and stare at the sky, hunting for stars behind the clouds. Maybe she's right. "I just . . . I just feel like I'm drawn to them. To you all. Even if I don't want to be"—my voice drops to almost inaudible—"a queen. Is that weird?"

"Not really." She yawns. "I mean, you're also part wolf. We're like your pack."

I stare at her in the darkness, waiting for more, but she's already asleep.

I close my eyes, but all I see are the dissenters' hollow cheeks and desperate eyes. Their silent pleas echo in my mind. I've always known I was different, caught between two worlds. Human, wolf, magic, then not. Maybe that's not such a bad thing. I identify with both sides. Maybe instead of trying to pick one, I could be the bridge between.

CHAPTER 44
WILLOW

The third day of our journey feels off. We continue our routine, checking for signs of Nightmare activity and fae creatures, but the lack of results is unsettling. Each scouting group returns empty-handed, the disappointment palpable in their faces. Even the dragons grow restless and return to their hosts more frequently.

Last night, only three from our troop projected dreamscapes, including Max. I managed to wake him before anyone saw his nude teaching escapade, but the incident leaves me uneasy. Why only three? Are we all too exhausted to dream, or is something else at play?

As we trudge through a rocky valley near Heliodor, the memory of Legion's map, dotted with sighting pins, haunts me. This doesn't add up. I make a mental note to find out at the first opportunity.

Suddenly, Heliodor emerges from the mist, a vision of gleaming white stone and intricate carvings. It's breathtaking, but the beauty can't mask the underlying sense of danger. Claw marks on the walls and crumbled turrets serve as reminders of the Baleful Hunt's presence—or should, at least.

Intricate carvings adorn the city's boundary wall, telling stories of ancient battles and long-forgotten magics. One particular deity takes the forefront. Dagda is a towering figure with a beard resembling a cascade of pebbles. He carries a great hammer that shapes mountains and a cauldron carved from a single, massive boulder. It's easy to tell he's a god because two polished gems are inserted into his eyes every time he's depicted.

What's stranger is the sound coming from the wall—whispers and the occasional song pitched too low to understand.

"It's . . . incredible," Colin breathes, his eyes wide with wonder.

Geraldine nods. "It's like something out of a fairy tale . . . if fairy tales had teeth and claws."

I grip my sword's pommel, its weight comforting. "It's odd how decorative it is when the House representatives dress so boring, don't you think?"

Max snorts. "Maybe they save all the flair for their architecture."

As twilight descends, we're instructed to camp outside the city gates while the Radiants decide what to do next. The looming walls cast long shadows over our camp, the intricate carvings now eerie in the flickering firelight. I shiver whenever I pass near them.

Suddenly, a screech pierces the air. I whirl around, heart pounding, and for a split second, I swear I see a Nightmare flitting between the trees. But as I blink, I realize it's only Styx, his dark form melting into the shadows as he walks the perimeter.

Geraldine sidles up to me, her voice low. "I don't like this, Willow. It feels like we're being watched."

"We probably are," Max murmurs, his eyes darting from shadow to shadow. His hand rests on the hilt of his weapon, mirroring my stance. It's remarkable how much he's grown on this journey alone.

I catch Bodin's worried expression as he enters his tent, the furrow between his brows deeper than ever. The desire to go to him, to seek comfort in his arms, is almost overwhelming. But I can't. Not here, not now.

As I help set up a campfire, my mind wanders to Emrys back at the castle. What is he doing? Is he taking care of Fox and Varen? Or has he forgotten without Styx there to remind him? The thought of the Six not remembering their true selves, their history with me, sends a pang through my chest.

Crouching to light the kindling with a flint, my eyes dart to Ignarius and another Radiant, their heads close together in conversation two camps further along. A chill runs down my spine as I consider the political implications. If we return empty-handed, both the earl and Legion will look foolish. And what about the whispers of martial law?

A terrifying thought occurs to me: what if someone intercepts the Nightmares before we can find them? Goodfellow couldn't manage that alone. He'd need help—perhaps from someone in our very camp.

My gaze lands on Styx again, now done with his perimeter check and approaching Ignarius with a deceptively casual stride. The tension in his shoulders and his gaze darting around the camp seems off. *No,* I think. Not Styx. He wouldn't betray us . . . would he? What would he gain? I dismiss the thought almost as quickly as it forms. If it was Styx, why would he have erased the S-word from everyone's minds back at the Nexus?

OUR MEAL'S RICH, savory scent lingers in the crisp night air, mingling with woodsmoke from the campfire. I scrape the last vestiges of gravy from my bowl, savoring the unexpected treat.

Finally, someone passed down scraps of the Fever Hunt's latest charred carcass for our stew. Bodin's overprotectiveness chafes; he won't even let me hunt. Earlier, I spotted a plump rabbit during our scouting mission, but I knew chasing it would earn his disapproval.

We've been waiting outside Heliodor for hours, but we've made camp, eaten, and swept the perimeter multiple times. It's a far cry from the chaos of three days ago. Now, we've settled into a natural hierarchy. If Bodin isn't barking orders at our troop, it's me. If I'm not directing, it's Geraldine or Becky. The rest of our eclectic band are first-timers in the exhibition, each bringing unique skills from their former lives.

Sarah, a former paramedic—some kind of traveling healer, I'm told—has already proven invaluable. Her steady hands deftly tended to Ji-Soo when she sprained her ankle on an exposed root. Jack, once a high school gym teacher, now leads our physical training. I catch snippets of his nostalgic chats with Max about their old vocations. Lena, an ex-librarian, has become our unofficial lore keeper, absorbing every scrap of information about Avorlorna with voracious curiosity. She and Geraldine have bonded over their shared thirst for knowledge. A former chef, Miguel has elevated our camp meals from bland rations to something almost resembling cuisine. I suspect he sweet-talked someone further up the line to score us tonight's smoked carcass.

As I watch them chatting around the campfire, their determination to survive—to thrive—in Avorlorna is clear. I almost believe in the certainty of their return to a happy life. But then Miguel's words to Colin make my ears twitch.

"You know," Miguel says with a sigh, his eyes reflecting the flames, "as much as I appreciate being alive again, I can't help but wonder if it would've been better to stay frozen."

Becky winces, her face a mask of barely concealed pain. "I keep thinking about my kids," she says.

"You have children?" Lena gasps. "Where are they? Wait. Are they . . . even alive?"

My gaze catches Becky's across the campfire. Once filled with suspicion and fear, her eyes now hold gratitude and uncertainty.

She answers, "We were separated after we awoke in Avorlorna, so I don't know."

Her voice breaks on the last word. I guess because it's true. Even though we saw her children yesterday, anything can happen to them.

"Or worse," Maggie chimes in, her tone bitter, "what if they're in that subterranean hellhole beneath us?"

Colin tosses his empty bowl at her. "Read the room, Maggie."

She gives Becky a guilty look. I stare mindlessly at my bowl, guilt coiling in my stomach like a serpent.

Geraldine clears her throat. "Come on, you lot. It's not all bad, is it? We're alive, aren't we? And we've got each other."

Max nods enthusiastically, though I can see the strain in his smile. "Geraldine's right. We've got to focus on the positives. We're in a magical realm! Who would have imagined that?"

"You were both Nothings a few weeks ago," Becky reminds them, acid in her voice. "Have you forgotten already how you were almost down below, too? Luck can change in an instant."

I know my friends were trying to lift the mood, to defend me without revealing my secret. But their words ring hollow against the weight of the others' losses.

Colin leans in, his voice low but carrying clearly in the night air. "I overheard something interesting earlier. Lord Ignarius was talking to Lord Styx."

The group falls silent, all eyes on Colin.

"What did you hear?" Ji-soo asks, her curiosity piqued.

His brow furrows. "Lord Ignarius said Legion was wrong to think Titania's power is waning just because the watergates are thawing."

"What does that mean?" Sarah interjects.

"Well, here's the kicker," Colin continues, his voice dropping even lower. "Ignarius said Titania was never strong enough to wake the dead in the first place. She can only make us slumber, dream."

A murmur ripples through the group. My heart begins to race, my palms growing clammy.

"But if Titania didn't wake us . . ." Miguel trails off, the implication hanging heavy in the air.

"Then who did?" Maggie asks, her eyes narrowing.

The silence that follows is deafening.

Finally, Becky breaks the silence. "Whoever it was, if I win the trials, I'll wish that person dead. Life has been nothing but heartache since we woke."

The words pierce me like a dagger, twisting in my gut. I struggle to keep my face neutral, desperately trying not to let the horror and guilt show in my eyes. This secret, this burden I carry, isn't just a ticking time bomb anymore—it's a wildfire, ready to consume everything I've built here. And when it explodes, the fallout will be more than devastating. It will be apocalyptic.

My mind races with terrifying possibilities. They'll all hate me. No, it's worse than that. They'll want me dead. The very people I've come to care for, to protect, will turn on me instantly if they know the truth. The warmth of their companionship suddenly feels like ash in my mouth.

Bodin ducks out of his tent, his broad shoulders stretching the canvas as he emerges. He calls me over, his deep voice carrying across the camp. I'm grateful for the distraction, anything to pull me away from the murderous wishes being casually tossed around the fire.

"After I speak with him, I'll take the first watch," I tell Geraldine, my voice low, trying to keep the tremor out. I place my empty bowl in her offered hand.

"Good." She smiles at Max, where he's drawing something in

the dirt and explaining it to Colin. I catch random words like "force" and "saber." The young boy's face is rapt with attention. I think they're discussing a famous battle.

"Tonight's the night I'm making my move," Geraldine says quietly, a mix of excitement and nervousness in her voice, "and I need to build up my confidence first."

"Sure," I say, far too interested in Max's burgeoning battle recap. But then her words soak in. "Wait, what? Tell me everything."

"Shadow!" Bodin's impatient bark cuts between us like a knife.

"Hold that thought," I point to Geraldine, fighting a grin that feels more like a grimace. "I want to know everything when I get back."

I jog over to the tent.

"Get inside," Bodin grumbles, his eyes darting around the camp.

The instant the flap closes, he wrenches me around and crushes his lips to mine. The kiss is so sudden and passionate that I'm thrown off-guard. He pins my head with his large hand, calloused fingers tangling in my hair, holding me at his tongue's mercy. I heat. I ache. I need more. But the moment I gather my wits enough to kiss him back, the bastard pulls away. My lips chase his but come up short.

He breathes through his nose, nostrils flaring, and holds me at arm's length. His eyes are dark, pupils dilated in the dim light of the tent.

"What was that for?" I breathe, my heart racing.

"The Radiants are heading into the city for the night."

"Okay," I reply, still a little dazed. "All of you?"

"Just the heads of Houses." He pauses, his jaw clenching. "And their Shadows."

"So . . . not you?"

He shakes his head, his braids tinkling. "Nor Styx."

"Why do you look worried?" I ask, studying the tense set of his shoulders.

A wry, disgruntled look slides my way. "Because, Calamity, I'd prefer you be within watching distance, so when disaster inevitably strikes, I will be there."

Did he hear the words around the campfire? Trying to hide my nerves, I fold my arms. "Are you expecting something to go wrong?"

After a moment, he concedes, "No. It is a diplomatic activity. Nothing more." But the furrow between his brows doesn't ease.

He tells me, rather grumpily, to get my things. When I emerge from his tent and pass on my news, the disappointment on my friends' faces is noticeable. I feel it too. Spending time together and watching them grow has been the best part of this trip.

"Bring us back a souvenir," Geraldine says, her smile not quite reaching her eyes. I give her a salute and return to the tent with my bag.

"Do I have to go?" The words tumble out before I can stop them. Bodin's scowl deepens, his fists clenching at his sides.

Heading into a triple-fortified city after days in the wilderness holds little appeal. Diplomatic discussions? Boring.

"Yes," he growls, closing the gap between us. His scent—leather and something uniquely Bodin—envelops me. "You'll be back tomorrow morning. Then we return to the Nexus."

His eyes flash with an unspoken promise: *Then you'll be mine.*

I sigh, rolling my shoulders. "You do realize we're mortals, right? Three days of marching equals blisters, sores, aching muscles."

"Would you prefer to sit idle while you recuperate?" One eyebrow arches in a challenge.

Three days. My heat approaches fast. I've stifled it before, but out here? The breeze might carry my scent. And who knows how potent it is in Avorlorna? At least Cait's pink elixir might help.

"Why not use portal stones?" I shake my head. "Seems obvious."

"The Folk cling to tradition."

Legion bursts in, startling me. He meticulously seals the flap, fingers lingering on the canvas. As he turns, the tent shrinks, his presence filling every corner of the already cramped space.

Lantern light glints off his brass spectacles, casting eerie shadows across sculpted features. Where Bodin exudes raw, primal strength, Legion's power is honed to a razor's edge— evident in his squared shoulders, tilted chin, and piercing gaze.

Legion's gaze flicks between us. For a heartbeat, I glimpse longing—or is it frustration?—before he clips, "Wait outside."

I blink. "Um . . . okay?"

"*Now*, Willow."

Still avoiding me. Fine. I need air anyway.

Outside, I tilt my face to the sky. Their muffled voices drift out.

"She has no idea how she smells," Bodin growls.

"Indeed." Legion's rich baritone drips with disdain. "I'd prefer to be anywhere else."

His words sting. I sniff my armpit and wince. Yeah, I reek. There are no showers out here, just icy river splashes. The Dread Hunt lurking in the depths doesn't encourage lingering.

"Leave her with me, then," Bodin demands.

"I would, but Puck insists all Shadows attend. For diplomacy and education." Legion sighs, heavy with . . . resignation? Regret? "I will endure."

Endure. The word slams into me. But as I process their exchange, I realize there's more to Legion's reaction than simple disgust. His rigid control, his insistence on distance—a male fighting his own desires?

Could Bodin mean my pheromones? Are they detecting them this early?

My ability to shift might not be the only wolfish trait they absorbed. The urge to mate, to guard one's partner, can turn aggressive when rivals approach a wolf's new mate. Mom once let slip that Dad nearly brawled with a bartender for merely serving her the morning after they first mated.

Maybe Heliodor is a blessing. One night away from judging eyes.

CHAPTER 45
WILLOW

We join other Radiants, their Shadows, Alfie, and the earl at Heliodor's gates. While we wait for them to open, I scan the camp one last time. Plenty of campfires flicker in the darkness, but no sign of Nightmares. The Gentle Interlude seems genuine. Was this all just an elaborate vacation?

As guards direct us through three sets of gates, my breath catches. The city spirals up a mountain in dizzying terraces. In the distance, the palace's crystal spires pierce the sky.

Only the waiting carriage reminds me of Avorlorna. It glides on fey lines, propelled by swirling, luminous giant wisps. As we settle in, I brave the silence beside Legion's brooding presence.

"Legion, did you—"

His razor-sharp glare silences me. "Know your place, Shadow."

Heat floods my cheeks. I look away, acutely aware of the other passengers. Dahlia sits ramrod-straight beside Lord Ignarius, the picture of Shadow decorum. The hawkish Radiant dismisses me with a glance before resuming his chat with the earl.

I know Dahlia and Ignarius are having an affair, forbidden or

not. But he maintains a professional façade in public. Occasionally, when no other Radiants are watching, he'll treat her with flowery delicacy. Still, it's not enough to violate the Old Code's strictures on Folk-mortal liaisons.

The carriage lurches into motion, bearing us deeper into Heliodor's stony heart. We jolt over a polished granite bridge, and Legion's hand grazes my thigh. It lingers—a heartbeat too long—before he snatches it back, fixating on the approaching palace beyond the window.

If only I could blame his coldness on social rules. But he's just as distant in private. Except for that raw moment when I knelt before him, his memories flooded back, and he gazed upon me as if I were the center of his universe.

We approach a colossal geode palace, its crystalline heart exposed to the moonlight. Cascading gardens adorn the palace walls, rare crystal flowers and bioluminescent vines pulsing with otherworldly light—the sight tugs at memories of Elphyne, a bittersweet ache in my chest.

Lady Nivene's reverent whisper to her Shadow Irisa catches my ear. "Dagda himself shaped the Adamant Palace from the mountain's core. His divine hammer struck the stone, and with each blow, the palace grew."

I lean in, careful not to draw Legion's attention.

"The Baleful Hunt's power echoes through every crystal, every stone," she continues. "On nights when it flies, they say the entire palace sings with Dagda's strength, a melody that fortifies the soul. Without the Hunt . . ." She pauses, her voice dropping lower. "Some fear the palace might crumble, taking all of Heliodor with it."

Her words stir something deep within me. Beyond the ache for the earl's loss of the Baleful Hunt to Puck, there's a profound sense of wrongness. The Hunt belongs here, with the House of Stone. It's an elemental dragon, needing to feed on stone as the others feed on their respective elements.

I glance at Legion, wondering if similar thoughts plague him. His face remains an impassive mask, betraying nothing. No wonder the Six kept their secrets in Elphyne for so long. He's unreadable.

A shiver runs down my spine as the faintest whisper of crystal song reaches my ears. But as the carriage rolls to a stop and we alight, I realize the sound comes from the wisps powering the line, echoing Lady Nivene's story.

I flush, remembering too late that our words in the carriage can be repeated. Legion, of course, never forgot. That's why he told me to be quiet. Somehow, this knowledge draws me closer to him while we walk toward the palace entrance.

The night presses close as the palace staff greets us at the door, their smiles professional yet warm. Their simple, gray attire reminds me painfully of Sylvanar, and I push the thought aside.

Earl Larkspur addresses us. "Our steward will show you to your chambers. Any requests should go through him." His gaze lingers on Legion. "You're welcome to explore, but please join us for breakfast in the grand hall at dawn."

As he walks away with his Shadow, the earl's shoulders slump, their footsteps the only sound in the hushed palace. The absence of Dagda's stone melody hangs in the air like an unspoken lament.

I search Legion's face for any reaction to the earl's distress. His features remain stoic, but there's a new tightness around his eyes, a barely perceptible twitch at the corner of his mouth.

The steward clears his throat as he addresses the remaining group. "If you follow me, I'll direct you to our finest accommodations."

Our group dwindles as we move deeper into the palace. Alfie is the first to go, shooting me a dark, unreadable look as he closes his apartment door. What have I done now?

The crystal walls pulse with faint light as if alive and watchful. I force myself to play the dutiful Shadow, letting Legion handle all communication. Even when Dahlia enters Ignarius's room while other Radiants take separate quarters from their Shadows, I bite back my questions.

Finally, only Legion and I remain. The steward directs us down a winding hall and then stops beside a small, unassuming door, his lips pursed with concern. "Are you quite certain, Knight Commander, you want this room?"

Legion's eyes narrow. "It is vexing to explain myself."

He dismisses the steward with a flick of his wrist, then places a palm on the door.

The steward gives me a nervous glance. "If you require anything—"

"Yes, yes," Legion cuts him off. "Pull the bell rope in the absence of the resonance network."

An awkward beat passes before the steward retreats. Legion's exhale is somewhere between relief and exasperation.

"Don't dawdle, Willow," he murmurs, pushing open the door.

I step inside, only to freeze after a few paces. My eyebrows shoot up as I take in our accommodations. Gone is the luxury of the palace. Instead, the room is small and simple, with a single window overlooking rugged cliffs and a vast ocean.

But it's not the view that has me rooted to the spot. No, it's the singular piece of furniture dominating the space . . .

There's only one bed.

CHAPTER 46
WILLOW

Legion steps inside, closing the door with a heavy exhale. I watch him cautiously, still unsure what to make of him in this unfamiliar setting. He doesn't look at me, instead taking a quick lap around the room. His graceful fingers traverse the wall every few steps as if listening for something. Curious, I mimic his actions, but it feels like an ordinary stone wall.

"Good," he murmurs to himself. "Good."

With another exhale, he crosses to the window and throws it open. A blast of cold air rushes in, carrying the tang of salt and the faint whisper of distant waves. Something in his posture relaxes, the taut line of his shoulders easing slightly. The wind tugs at his long, silken hair, sending it dancing around his face like living shadows.

I glance between Legion and the wall, then back to him. "What's the deal with the walls?"

He answers without looking at me, his voice tight, "I had to be sure the resonance network didn't extend to this room."

"Resonance stones," I mutter. "The bane of my existence."

It clicks into place—the whispering walls outside, the feeling of being watched. The stone must be mined here.

"Ah," I say, a slow grin forming. "You wanted privacy for us."

"Obviously," he says, his tone clipped.

"Right. But you also wanted privacy. For the one bed."

"Having anyone listen to our conversations is not an option."

His brow furrows as he eyes the bed. I'm just teasing, but still —it's a bed. I make a running leap and land with a bounce on my side, hand on my head, grinning. I watch his back as he glares out the window, his shoulders set rigidly.

"Our *conversation*," I tease, my voice taking on a sultry edge. "Is that what people are calling it these days?"

He does a double-take, looking at me strangely. Then, understanding dawns, and to my amazement, a faint blush colors his pale cheeks before he quickly looks away.

I gasp, sitting up. "Did you just blush?"

"No," comes his curt reply, but I know what I saw.

"You did!" I slide over the bed, getting to my knees. "You went all pinkish in the cheeks." I lower my voice conspiratorially. "What was it about what I said that made you blush? You, a Sluagh whose favorite pastime before I came along was watching people *'do it'* for research purposes?"

Legion's jaw clenches, a muscle ticking in his cheek. The blush deepens, spreading to the tips of his pointed ears poking through his black hair. He faces me, dark eyes glittering with an unreadable emotion.

"You misunderstand the nature of our . . . observations," he says, his voice low and husky.

I lean in closer, drawn by the sudden intensity of his gaze. "Then enlighten me, oh wise one. What exactly is the nature of your . . . observations . . . if it wasn't to learn how to, how did Fox say it—pleasure me?"

The air between us sizzles. He opens his mouth to speak, but a sharp knock at the door shatters the moment.

We freeze, staring at each other.

The second knock is more insistent. Legion grunts in annoyance, strides to the door, and flings it open. Earl Larkspur stands outside with the steward and two staff members.

"Knight Commander," the earl says urgently.

"Earl," Legion replies curtly.

"I brought comforts for you and your Shadow to enjoy during your stay." Legion's lips flatten; he clearly doesn't appreciate the intrusion. But there's something in the earl's eyes that strikes a compassionate chord within me.

I sit on the bed, waiting for Legion's lead.

"Very well," Legion says, waving them in. The earl glances around with barely concealed distaste before gesturing for the servants to enter. They bring food, drink, fresh clothes, and a wooden bathtub, which they place between the bed and the wall. They fill it with hot, rose-scented water and leave. I eye it warily —it's not too deep.

The earl hesitates at the door.

"Is there something more?" Legion asks impatiently.

After dismissing his staff, the earl confesses, "I would like a private word with my Knight Commander before the Shining Host gathers tomorrow for breakfast."

After a beat, Legion says, "As you wish."

The earl hands Legion a card. "If it pleases you, here is a map to my chambers. Wait a few minutes, then join me there. Ensure no one sees you."

"Understood," Legion answers. When the door closes, he studies the card briefly before collecting his jacket.

"I thought he said to wait," I remind him.

"Bolt the door when I leave," he instructs. "I should not be longer than one turn of the hourglass. It is late; we're all tired. In the meantime, enjoy the bath."

I stare at the water apprehensively. Didn't Bob once say that he saw a Nightmare crawl out of a puddle?

Legion huffs, but to my surprise, he doesn't berate me. Instead, he neatly folds his jacket, places it on the bed, and approaches the tub. He tests the water, swirling long fingers through the surface. When he brings two fingers to his lips to taste the bathwater, his expression is no longer bashful but dark and intense.

"Get undressed," he instructs, his voice low and commanding. "And into the tub."

I swallow hard, my heart racing.

Legion picks up a washcloth, turning it over before looking at me through lowered lashes.

"The earl is waiting, Willow," he says, his tone softening slightly. "And I'm not leaving until you are cleaned, fed, healed, and resting."

I nod, still fixated on the water.

"That tub isn't big enough for both of us," I observe, a hint of disappointment slipping into my voice.

He chuckles softly, a sound that surprises me. These glimpses of vulnerability feel like rare gifts, ones I doubt even his hive sees.

"Quickly," he says gently. He turns his back to me.

I undress and slide into the bath. A sigh escapes me as the heat soothes my aching muscles.

Before facing me again, Legion takes a deep breath as if steeling himself. He kneels beside the tub and dips his hand into the water, his eyes locking with mine. "Are you well?"

"I think as long as I'm not alone, I'm not afraid," I admit.

"You'll never be alone again," he murmurs, almost to himself. He gently massages my foot, healing the blisters and aches. I let out an embarrassingly blissful sound.

He bathes me with reverence, swiping the cloth over my body. The scrape contrasts with the easy glide of water. His scent blooms thicker in the steam—something sweet, floral, peppery, and with amber undertones. I wasn't aware a scent could feel warm, but it glides into my lungs like whiskey.

I don't want to ruin the beauty of this moment by saying something stupid or needy. Like asking why he keeps his distance from me. The worry seems so unfounded when he's like this. There's something sweet and unguarded in his eyes. The look on his face is hard to explain, but it's almost like taking care of me is refilling the well of his soul. He worships me. Is energized by me.

Once he's tended to all my wounds, the wall between us slowly rebuilds. He dries his hands and dons his jacket wordlessly. He holds out a towel for me, but his eyes don't meet mine as I step out. As I step into his arms, his gaze fixes somewhere over my shoulder, near the window. He wraps the towel around me. His hands rest briefly on my shoulders, tense with unspoken emotion. Then, the warmth of his body disappears, and he mutters a reminder about bolting the door before slipping out.

The room feels colder without his presence. I stand there, wrapped in the towel, water droplets running down my legs. The rose scent from the bath overtakes his lingering aroma, pushed in by the crisp night breeze. I shut the window with a frown, mourning the loss of his scent.

"Willow," he warns from outside.

I startle. "Yes?"

"Bolt the door."

I move to obey but pause, my hand on the door's surface. "What if I fall asleep and can't let you back in?"

"Then I will wait out here until you wake."

A smile tugs at my lips. When the bolt's heavyweight slides into place, I hear his footsteps recede. I dry myself and slip into the bed—the only bed—and try not to fall asleep, savoring the lingering warmth of his touch and the memory of his unguarded gaze.

CHAPTER 47

LEGION

This ugly thing crawling in my belly is sickening. All I've ever wanted and needed is within my reach, yet still so far away. I hear myself tell my hive time and time again to wait, my tone patient. I was confident that events would turn out precisely as Varen had predicted, in our favor, with happiness and peace.

And her at the epicenter.

But we never foresaw Titania's theft of her magic or the following cascade of events. In all potential futures, I never imagined wanting her like this—like my skin aches from holding desire at bay, like my blood roars in my ears so loud it competes with the wind.

I arrive at the location Larkspur gave me and rap swiftly on the door.

Waiting. It was once my source of comfort, but now it is a torture device. Waiting gives me the scent of her rose-kissed skin. It lingers on my fingers, wraps itself around my heart, my mind, and my cock. I inhale. My lashes flutter as I command my blood to cool. It will get much worse than this.

The battle has only begun.

The door opens. He lets me in. I look around, using every preternatural sense I own to check for danger—not that I expect it. Styx has crept through this Radiant's mind and scoured through the dark places. Larkspur is remarkably ignorant of everything endangering our safety.

"Knight Commander." The earl guides me to a comfortable settee in a drawing room facing the same cliffs our guest room overlooks. I scan around and recognize the same impotent walls. He has also chosen chambers far away from the resonance network.

"I prefer to stand," I reply. This meeting needs to be over quickly.

I have places to be, an impertinent Shadow to . . . sleep beside. The earl's jaw twitches, but he sits.

"Very well. I appreciate your time. I know it is precious."

"It is."

"I'll make this quick. Robin Goodfellow has—"

I hold up my hand, cutting him off. "Spare me the sob story. I am well aware of the rules he breaks and continues to abuse. As I have mentioned, I do not intend for him to retain custody of your dragon."

"Yet you voted him into the role."

Finally, he confronts me directly about it. I was beginning to think of him as spineless.

"Come now," I drawl. "Someone as intelligent as you can understand why I did this."

A muscle ticks in his jaw. "You also suspect the Hunt is feeding on him."

"I'm surprised the Baleful Hunt hasn't revealed this truth to Puck himself."

"The Baleful Hunt is a particularly . . . willful dragon."

"Aren't they all?"

He winces. "But this one has a tendency to, how shall I put

this delicately . . .? He has a habitual obsession with breaking free."

"But then the rightful custodians will swoop in and reclaim him." I smile flatly. "I'm not sure what you want me to do."

He bristles at my tone. "I am not asking you to do anything. That's not what I was insinuating before you made your assumption. Our expedition was foiled. Tomorrow's informal meeting with the Shining Host will no doubt end similarly."

Assumption? An uncomfortable feeling tightens my chest. I loathe not being able to delve into his head myself. The torment of remembering the skills I am missing is unbearable. If I had access to his mind, I would have anticipated his train of thought. Instead, I am wrong.

It is irritating yet also refreshing.

Before this, before Willow, we lived in a numbing vacuum of the ordinary. Even though I am eager to reunite our hive and claim our queen, I cannot escape the niggling feeling of being alive again. And it has been a very long time since that happened. Any time my fingers brushed her velvety skin while I washed her, sparks skipped into me.

Blushing. *For Nicnevin's sake.* Since when do I blush?

"What do you want of me, then?" I ask, fingers twitching to return to Willow.

"Information." He sits back with intelligent eyes and drinks from his stone goblet. "When the Folk woke from our long slumber, we found this world remarkably changed. But it is starting to dawn on some of us that—" He takes another sip as if to check himself before continuing—to check me, rather. "Have you noticed that none of the original dragon-bonded are present? The ones who entered the slumber bonded?"

Titania crafted a version of reality that suited her. If the original Shining Host were alive, they would know their true purpose —and their dragons' purpose—is not to guard the gates of Avorlorna against Nocturna, but to guard them against us, Sluagh, and our Wild Hunt. We were Oberon's greatest weapon before Titania bartered with the gods to create dragons strong enough to contain us. They couldn't. Not without the help of the Keepers of the Cauldron and their enchantment binding us to slaver queens.

"Titania said they perished during slumber," I reply.

"And you believe her?"

"Of course not."

"And this war . . . do you believe it is because Nocturna tries to steal our resources?"

"Again, no. But you already knew that." What does he believe?

"Yes, I knew that," he admits, gesturing to the Guardian teardrop beneath my eye. "Just as I know, your mark is not something neither the Folk nor the mortals have seen before. They have also never seen one like your Shadow—a mortal with fae ears and . . . interesting biology." A void opens within me. Is he threatening our queen? "Which leads me to believe you and the Knights of the Queen's Hive are the only members of our kind— apart from Titania—who know the truth about what happened to the original dragon-bonded."

"That's a leap. Are you accusing me of lying, or do you have a point?"

"I'm going to challenge Puck to a duel. The military must approve it in the queen's absence."

His proclamation is not a surprise, yet a relief all the same. The entire land knows about his intentions. And the Old Code states this request for approval is simply a formality. Very little can block a duel challenged under the gods.

If he is busy with this nonsense, I will have more work cleaning up the Nightmares escaping Nocturna. Oddly, they've suddenly cleared up, a fact I will investigate more thoroughly once I have the time. But at least Willow will be out of focus.

"And?" I prompt, knowing what he will say next, but I tell myself to reveal the appropriate surprise.

"And I will ask that you be my second."

"Me?" I place my hand on my chest. Raise my brows. Yes, I believe that was a convincing display of surprise. "Why not ask one of the Shining Host with whom a dragon actually takes direction?"

"Because the duel must be walked on two feet," he explains. "A dragon hosted within a person is technically more than two feet. No other Radiant is brave enough to risk walking a duel without a dragon, except for you knights."

"You flatter us with lies."

"Is it working?"

"No. However . . ." I shake my head. I can't believe I am about to say this. "If you need me, I will be there—for the right price."

"I'm listening."

Puck will expire soon, anyway. What's the rush? But perhaps I can use this to our advantage. "Obviously, if somewhat impatient, the duel is your elaborate plot to regain control of the Baleful Hunt."

"I don't think it's impatient. It's necessary."

"You are aware the Knight Spymaster has been petrified."

He stills. "Yes."

I don't address the unanswered question of why—he likely assumes it is for Sylvanar's death, even if Puck has not publicized it. It matters not to him since he benefited from inheriting the earldom.

"The House of Stone has hosted the Baleful Hunt since its origins," I say. "You must have an antidote for accidental petrification. A spell. A charm?"

"There was a mirror once. But I regret to inform you that it's long gone."

His stare lingers on me, and my heart sinks before he responds. He has nothing of worth. Not many are aware of the transference spell Fox used with Styx. Unless we wish to sacrifice an innocent soul, we are unfortunately without options apart from the mirror Cait already searches for. She has proven her loyalty to Fox, but I am not convinced.

"But," Larkspur continues, "when I regain the Hunt, I vow to use the Baleful Gaze and free Lord Fox from his stone prison."

A promise based on a dream.

"This conversation has ceased to interest me." I start toward the door, fingers twitching to be near rose-scented flesh again.

"Legion."

I halt at the use of my name without the title. "Your familiarity borders on disrespect, earl."

"Do I have your support?"

My anger swiftly rises. I face him. "It is not the time for duels."

"Quite the opposite. The Gentle Interlude is the most opportune time. And no one believes us about the Terrors or the thawing watergates. My reputation is being demolished." A plea enters his eyes. "You and I both know someone is covering up the sightings, sweeping them under the rug. Only the dragon-bonded, or Titania herself, have the—"

"Choose your words carefully." He includes us within this statement.

"I only meant to insinuate that this treachery comes from the Ivory Palace. And whoever is behind it has help from someone in power too."

If the duel eventuates, it's unlikely Puck will last until the end. I have nothing to lose in accepting his request but everything to gain, like a valuable alliance with the House of Stone. More importantly, a debt.

With my hand on the doorknob, I tell him, "You can trust that I want the Baleful Hunt back in his territory, cleansing it of Nightmares. I will accept your offer if the time comes."

CHAPTER 48

LEGION

By the time I return to our chamber, an ugly feeling has taken root in my belly, growing and multiplying with each step. Madness circles my mind like a hungry predator. There are too many variables and too many ways this could go wrong. I need Varen's insight, Bodin's strength, Emrys's wit, Fox's cunning, Styx's stealth, and gods-damn it all, I need the fucking Wild Hunt.

I tap on the door and wait, my heart pounding against my ribs.

No answer.

The crawling thing inside me expands, threatening to consume me whole—my heart races. I wasn't gone that long.

I tap again, harder this time. "Willow," I call, trying to keep the desperation from my voice.

Silence.

"*STYX!*" I bellow into the darkness with my mind. "*Come here now. STYX!*"

He materializes from the shadows beside me, a disgruntled look marring his features. From his shirtless attire, mussed-up hair, and puffy eyes, I've clearly disturbed him from sleep. The

332

helpless feeling inside me, the incapable thoughts whirling in my head, they give that crawling feeling a name I refuse to repeat.

"She's not answering," I say, gesturing at the door, hating how weak I sound. "It's bolted."

I said I would wait for her to wake up, but what if she's . . .

"She's fine," Styx projects into my mind, his mental voice tinged with annoyance.

"How do you know?"

"I checked on her three times already. She's asleep."

Something eases inside me, a knot of tension I hadn't realized existed. Then it tightens again. I didn't ask him to check on her. He's either very curious, murderously obsessed like Emrys or . . .

He *flickers* away before I can finish the thought. Inside the room, the bolt lifting grinds. The door opens, and Styx gives me an unreadable look before disappearing again. A little too quickly.

I'll deal with him later. For now, I ensure the door is closed and bolted behind me. Then, as quietly as possible, I slip off my jacket and unbutton my collar. My boots are subsequent, set carefully by the door. The spectacles stay on, always.

Her soft, rhythmic breathing is a lullaby to my fear. By the time I reach the bed, ease down and lay beside her, I've forgotten the name of that ugly, crawling thing. Bathed in moonlight, her face is all I see. I stare so long that at some point, I can't tell where the light comes from—her face or the moon.

She was right. I could have requested separate rooms. It would have made things easier. The decision to keep us together came out before I could stop it. I tried to reason away the choice, but the truth is, I want a night of indulgence. One night to lie beside her. One night for me, when every other night will be for them. At least until our hive is united.

Only then will I unleash the force of my longing on her.

I shuffle closer to her, but stare at the geodes glittering on the ceiling. I try not to use my lungs lest the noise obliterates hers and that ugly feeling returns.

She stirs.

I suck in a breath, holding it like a lifeline.

"Legion?" she mumbles, her voice husky with sleep.

Perhaps if I close my eyes, she will—

"What are you doing?" Her dubious tone turns my head. She leans on an elbow, golden eyes narrowed on me, silver hair looking as soft as the dandelion seeds filling our pillows.

"I was sleeping," I grit out, then return to glaring at the ceiling, my brows pinched together in a futile attempt at nonchalance. "Is it not obvious?"

Her soft snort hits my cheek like a caress. My insides quiver, and I want to touch her so badly that I tremble with the effort of restraint.

"Did Styx let you in?" she asks.

"Yes."

"Hm." The blankets rustle, and her unique floral and musky perfume blooms around me. It grows stronger every day. Harder to resist. I shuffle an inch away from her, but it makes no difference. The movement sends the wrong message to my body. It says it's time for action—pump the muscles with oxygen. My heart races. Blood rushes south. My cock hardens and throbs. Aches. Demands.

I should sleep on the floor.

I won't.

"Did you just get in?"

"Go to sleep, Willow," I manage, my voice rougher than intended.

Another snort. She settles, but after a few minutes, when her breathing fails to even out, I know she is still awake. And thinking. Even as a child, her thoughts were filled with open-minded curiosity. It had been easy for us to slip into her mind, to relate to her naivety with our own. As she grew, so did her natural ability to block us out. We slipped away, let her grow on her own, and tried to do the same . . . despite the darkest parts of us begging for us to do the opposite.

We are not good creatures, despite her hopes.

The enchanted spectacles weigh on my face. If I remove them, will my conscience disappear? That I've started considering this option is a sign I should move to the floor.

"Legion?" she asks, her voice soft in the darkness.

"Yes, Willow."

"We're mates, right?"

I nod.

"So why are you avoiding me?"

It hurts to exhale. That crawling feeling is back. In my gut. Churning and twisting.

"This might sound weird," she continues, "but is it something to do with a canary you once had?"

My breath catches. "How do you know about that?"

"Cait mentioned it. Then Bodin said something about the bloody golden feathers he kept seeing in his head. And I saw one of his dreams. I thought it was a pet bird, but . . . there was a queen involved."

The sound of her plucking blankets fills the silence, a nervous habit I've noticed before. As a child, she would shift out her claws and pluck and pluck and pluck. She would ensure her bedding was just right, and then she would slip into sleep.

"Are you aware of how the transfer of power works within the Sluagh?" I ask, still facing the ceiling.

"Maybe," she mutters. "Remind me."

"When any fae creature dies, their magic is reabsorbed through the Wellspring into the Cauldron, returned to the deities from which they originated—"

"Wisps. Manabeeze. Blots."

"Yes. But for us original sons of the Morrigan, we have evolved enough to return to our hive first."

She nods. "I think I remember Fox saying something like that. Or reading it."

"Did he explain why we have a rank?" At her head shake, I venture onward. "When our minds meld in the hive state, we think collectively and act as one. However, there are occasions where discord occurs. Rather than being thrown out of the state, potentially risking our survival if we are in battle, the decision travels up that chain of command until it reaches a tiebreaker."

"You."

"Yes. But also—" I swallow, the words sticking in my throat. Since the hierarchy of power inevitably falls to me, it also works in reverse. "I can slip into any of my hive's minds or bodies, controlling them."

"This is why you're called Legion." More plucking of blankets. "I don't understand why this means you reject me."

"I do not reject you." That muscle in my chest squeezes. Her shaky exhale cuts short on my next word. "However..."

"However?"

I clear my throat, pushing past the lump forming there. "I was not a good leader. Our Seventh died because of it."

"Oh, Legion." Her voice is soft, filled with misplaced compassion. "So now you're punishing yourself?"

"No. I'm correcting my mistake. I am the First. So with you, I must be the last."

At her silence, I roll to face her and wish I hadn't. Now, I have the picture to accompany the alluring smell. She is perfection, from her tiny scars to the sprinkle of freckles on her nose to her golden eyes and tiny fangs. I want them on my flesh. I want them biting hard, cruelly, and possessively. I want them making me feel only one thing.

Her eyes dart between mine, searching for something. She nods. Her jaw sets with determination. "I get it. You need them to trust you. It's admirable."

Rolling to her back, she tugs the blanket to her chin and

contemplates geodes in the ceiling. I almost see her thoughts ticking over in her expression. What does this all mean? Why won't I tell her more? How much pressure have I laid at her feet?

She glances at me, her eyes shining with determination. "I'll help you."

"With what?"

"With making sure you keep your vow. I won't ask about the distance between us again. I won't ask why you won't make love to me. I respect your vow and trust this is what you need. Thank you for telling me."

"I've hardly told you anything." Not really.

"I know there's more." She frowns. "But it's clearly too painful to speak about. You'll tell me when you're ready."

She tries to shove me away, and my heart wrenches. But it quickly becomes apparent she's tugging the blanket from beneath me. I lift my hips to allow it freedom. She raises it to make space for me beneath the shadowy warmth.

"I'm your mate." She yawns. "And . . . I can still hug you, even if I can't fuck you."

That word on her tongue. My lashes flutter. A wave of hot, hungry need hits me. Oh, what I'll do to her when she's finally mine. The pleasure I'll give her. The devotion I'll show her. The worlds I'll burn for her. Unable to resist, I slip beneath the covers and gather her to me. The Cauldron itself sighs as her body presses against mine. I frown when my palm runs down her bare back.

"Willow," I growl, my lips brushing against her hair. "You're nude."

She wiggles closer, sighing contentedly.

"I can see why you're the First. So clever," she mumbles sleepily.

My lips twitch. My fingers flex on her back, savoring the feeling of her warm skin against mine. I should really leave. Now.

"Relax," she breathes. "Punish me tomorrow."

"Now there's an idea."

Tomorrow will come sooner than we realize. The small reprieve from my vow will be over, and that ugly crawling feeling will return. Perhaps she is right. Perhaps this resistance of mine is a form of punishment. But she will agree it is warranted when she learns my crime. For now, though, I simply hold her, listen to her steady breathing, and feel a sense of peace for the first time in my very long life, knowing it won't last.

CHAPTER 49
WILLOW

Morning light filters through the sheer curtains, casting a soft glow across the room. I wake feeling more refreshed than I have in days, the weight of uncertainty lifted from my shoulders. As I dress for the day, I notice Legion's stilted movements as he sits facing the window, rubbing his temples. The only part of his tailored suit he removed for sleep is the jacket. Dark shadows smudge beneath his long-lashed eyes.

Standing before the mirror, I run a crystal-handled brush through my hair, the silver strands slipping through my fingers.

"Didn't you sleep?" I ask, catching Legion's reflection turning my way. "Was it because you didn't want to risk the spectacles falling off?"

He gives me a look that could melt stone, his obsidian eyes flashing. "You were naked, Willow," he grinds out, straightening his collar.

"Next time, I'll wrap myself in a sack."

In three long strides, he's beside me, taking the brush from my hand. "Excellent idea."

I grin, playing along. "Maybe I should start wearing Bodin's old socks. That ought to keep you at a distance."

"Brilliant," he deadpans. "And why stop there? A touch of the Wild Hunt's breath in your hair would add a lovely aroma of sour meat and decay."

Our eyes meet in the mirror, and for a moment, the playful atmosphere charges with something more intense. I turn to face him, suddenly aware of his closeness.

"You know," I say softly, "all this talk of hunts and socks . . . it's kind of hot."

Legion's eyes shutter, and he takes a deliberate step back. "We should focus on more practical matters."

I nod, feeling the loss of his warmth like a physical ache. Helping him keep his vow will be more challenging than I first imagined. He tugs the brush through his long hair, then tosses it onto the rumpled bed with a glare that could wither flowers.

"Right. Practical matters . . . like how I'm going to survive a morning of diplomatic meetings without falling asleep."

"I'd suggest pinching yourself, but you'd probably enjoy it too much," he quips.

"You're probably right."

For a heartbeat, I think he might close the distance between us. Instead, he clears his throat and orders, "Put your boots on."

I do as told while he shrugs on his jacket, the fabric whispering as it settles over his broad shoulders. The metamorphosis is immediate. I felt his powerful body against mine last night. It's not the bulky power like Bodin, but athletic and subtly explosive . . . almost like a dancer. If dancers could punch into a chest cavity and rip out a still-beating heart without breaking a sweat.

"Let's go," he says, his voice clipped. "We're late for breakfast."

"Wait." I get serious for a moment. "What's really happening out there? I want to talk about it before we leave. Why did we go on this expedition?"

His hands slip into his pockets, and he gives me an intelligent, sharp look. "The House of Shadow can impose martial law if danger is imminent."

"But we've seen no Nightmares."

"And therein lies the rub."

He yanks the door open with more force than necessary, muttering under his breath about how he has to now "eat mortal food and pretend to like it."

Even in his grumpy state, he exudes a potent aura of power and grace. His walk—each step purposeful and controlled—is dangerous but breathtakingly beautiful to watch. Staff scuttle out of his way—some blush and bluster when they look at his face. I know how they feel.

A group of servants round the corner, arms laden with trays of delicate crystal goblets. One young server stumbles upon seeing Legion's face. Legion pulls me tight against him, shielding me with his body as the servant careens past, barely avoiding a collision.

We're pressed together for a heartbeat, maybe two. I feel the solid warmth of his chest, the steady thrum of his heartbeat betraying his calm exterior. His dark eyes lock with mine. This close, I see flecks of white gold in their depths, like stars in a midnight sky.

As quickly as it happened, he sets me back.

"Are you alright?" he asks, voice rougher than usual.

I nod, not trusting my voice.

Legion turns to the still-trembling servant.

"More care in the future," he says, tone brooking no argument.

The servant nods frantically before hurrying away, leaving us alone in the quiet hallway. Legion continues walking, but now his posture holds tension.

"You know," I whisper as we near the Great Hall, "I think I prefer you grumpy. It's much safer than when you're being charming."

He raises a dubious eyebrow. "Perhaps I should practice scowling more often."

"Perfect." I smile. "And I'll work on my impression of dragon bait. Between the two of us, we'll be the least appealing pair in all of Avorlorna."

The Great Hall's grandeur immediately strikes me. The vast circular space is carved directly from the mountain, its walls adorned with intricate geode formations that catch and reflect the light streaming in from high windows. Crystal chandeliers hang from the vaulted ceiling, their facets casting rainbow prisms across the polished stone floor. At the center of the room stands a massive circular table. The Radiants are seated there, their faces animated as they converse, the clink of fine silverware punctuating their discussions. To the side, the Shadows occupy a smaller, less adorned table.

Legion's hand, a comforting presence on my lower back, falls away. He drops seamlessly into his persona of the Knight Commander, his handsome face an impassive mask. With a curt gesture toward the smaller table, he says nothing and moves to join the "grown-ups."

A staff member collects my bag and guides me to the only free chair. Unfortunately, it's beside Alfie, but not even his sour look can dampen my mood.

"You're in a good mood this morning," he sneers.

Sitting on Alfie's other side, Dahlia gives me a knowing smirk. "I wonder what put that blush on your face."

"You would know," Alfie shoots back at her darkly.

I ignore their continued bickering and help myself to food. The spread is a feast for both the eyes and the nose. Platters of glistening fruits are arranged like jewels, their colors vibrant against the pale stone dishes. Freshly baked breads release tendrils of steam, their yeasty aroma mingling with the sharp scent of aged cheese.

As I load my plate, I sneak glances at the Radiants, my eyes inevitably drawn to Legion. Even from here, I can see the tension in his shoulders and the way his jaw clenches as he listens to whatever the earl is saying.

I tune my shifter senses, hoping to catch snippets of conversation. Ignarius taunts Larkspur about the suspicious lack of Nightmares. Someone asks a pointed question about falsified reports. But before I can hear more, Alfie leans in, blocking my attention.

"There's only one reason why a Shadow shares a room with their Radiant," he says, voice low and accusatory.

I sigh, setting my fork down with a soft clink. "It's none of your business, Alfie."

His face flushes an angry red. "We're engaged," he hisses. "Or have you forgotten that?"

I pray to the Well for patience and look him dead in the eyes. "I know we're in the House of Stone, but have you grown rocks in your head? We're *not* engaged. We haven't been for years. Move on."

As soon as the words leave my mouth, I realize the table has gone silent. All eyes are on me, and I feel my cheeks heat. I replay what I just said in my head, hoping I haven't revealed secrets. Alfie's breathing grows heavier and more labored with each passing second, his anger palpable between us.

He's going to be a problem. Part of me thought he'd lose interest, but his attention is becoming an obsession. I'm not his biggest fan anymore, but I don't want him killed by one of my six possessive mates.

The earl stands abruptly, his chair scraping against the stone floor. He declares loudly his intention to challenge Puck to a duel when they return to the Nexus, the winner to receive custody of the Baleful Hunt once and for all. Then, to my surprise, he gestures to Legion, announcing that the Knight Commander will be his second.

A frown pulls at my brows. What does this mean? Legion stares stonily ahead, giving a slight nod of confirmation, but his eyes betray nothing. The earl sits, and the Radiants' conversation becomes more trivial—the next scheduled revelry on the Gentle Interlude's program, and something about a new challenge for the leaderboard.

I roll my eyes and turn back to our table. Most Shadows discuss the duel's implications in hushed, excited tones. Alfie has gone quiet, his thoughts turned inward. At least it's not me he's focused on anymore. He's tapping a Chaser charm on his thigh, a rhythmic pattern that sends a telltale tingle of magic brushing against my skin.

"What are you doing?" I ask, suspicion coloring my voice.

He drops the stone like it's hot. "Nothing," he replies too quickly. "It's none of your business."

"Whatever," I mutter, deciding to let it go for now. At this point, engaging in conversation with him is more trouble than it's worth.

I turn my attention to wrapping a few more delicious-looking cakes and treats from the table in crisp linen serviettes. Maybe I can sneak more into my bag. The troop will love them.

CHAPTER 50
WILLOW

The blistering cold bites through my cape as we return to the camp outside Heliodor's gates, making my cake gift seem inadequate. My friends nod along, feigning interest as I recount tales of the palace and the impending duel, but their eyes betray their weariness. When Bodin barks orders to pack up for the journey home, they spring into action with renewed vigor.

Bodin's gruff demeanor toward me initially seems part of the ruse, mirroring Legion's public stance. It suits me fine, considering the full moon's impending rise along with my temperature. Going into heat during this journey might even be a blessing. The crisp mountain air should mask most of my scent from Legion, preserving his vow. Bodin and Styx will sleep in a separate tent, and the exhausted mortals—even Alfie, far ahead with his troop—should pay me no mind.

As twilight paints the sky in muted purples, confidence swells within me. No accidental acts of calamity tonight. But as we huddle around the crackling campfire, steam rising from our bowls, Bodin's announcement shatters my peace.

"We'll salvage this pointless expedition by elevating your dreamscape training tonight." A chorus of groans ripples through the camp. Colin's hand shoots up, his voice tinged with fatigue. "Won't we be too tired to dream?"

"There are ways of inducing dreamscapes," Bodin replies, his tone brooking no argument.

Maggie scoffs, "Better not be me. I don't want you all seeing what I dream about."

Bodin's glare silences her instantly, a reminder of who's in charge. His eyes never meet mine as he outlines the evening's plan—we'll take turns jumping into each other's dreamscapes, finding exits without harm.

Panic claws at my throat. Nobody should see what I dream about. I could inadvertently reveal everything. What is he thinking? Glancing down the line of troops, I notice other Radiants issuing similar directives. We're not alone in this exercise.

When Bodin dismisses us and retreats to his tent, I count two thundering heartbeats before following. I find him rummaging through his pack, pulling out—of all things—rations of human food.

"Bodin," I say, struggling to keep desperation from my voice.

He straightens, fixing me with the same withering glare he gave Maggie. "Did you just enter my tent without permission, Shadow?"

I blink, mind reeling. What's happening here?

My eyes dart between his face and the food he's unwrapping, as if he intends to eat it. My heart plummets. He's forgotten. All day, I thought he was simply maintaining the ruse, but Titania's spell has ensnared his mind once more.

Didn't Styx reveal his Sluagh form to Bodin overnight? Is that method of combatting the spell not working anymore?

He stalks toward me, nostrils flaring. Frustration and something darker tighten his features when I fail to avert my gaze respectfully. Panic engulfs me. I stammer an apology, fleeing the tent to my bedroll, mind whirling. I need to find Styx. Legion needs to know too.

"Hey, Willow." Miguel's voice cuts through my spiraling thoughts. He holds out a steaming bowl. "I brought you seconds. I know you like my cooking, so . . . yeah."

"Um, thanks, Miguel, but I'm not that hu—"

"Take it," he insists, thrusting the bowl forward. Soup sloshes onto my fingers, leaving me no choice but to accept.

"Okay." I force a tight smile.

He doesn't leave, staring at me with a crooked grin. Is he waiting for me to eat?

Oh no. It's happening. I'm in heat. No, no, no.

"I'm just going to set this down for a moment. Is that okay?"

He scowls. "But I made it, especially for you."

"I need to see to my . . . female needs." I grimace, slowly collecting my cape while keeping a wary eye on him. It's not exactly a lie.

"Oh, sure." He nods, looking lost. "I'll just . . . wait over here."

I pull my cape tight around my shoulders, praying it blocks the pheromones radiating from my body. Geraldine sidles up, concern etched on her face. "What's wrong?"

"Smell me," I demand, fanning air from my neck toward her.

Her face scrunches in disgust and then realization dawns. "Oh, you smell kind of . . . nice. In a weird way. Did you get perfume in Heliodor?"

"No," I groan. "It's my heat."

"What's that?"

"It's my, um, cycle." I wince. "It only happens every other month. Unlike pureblooded humans, I get really . . . hot"—yeah, that's one way of putting it, Willow—"and smell kind of . . . attractive."

She presses the back of her hand to my forehead. "Shit, you're burning up. How bad is it going to get?"

"Bad enough that I shouldn't be around anyone. It's not just them. I also get very . . . turned on." I bite my lip, humiliation burning through me. "I might dream things I shouldn't. Actually, I'll *definitely* dream things I shouldn't."

"Oh no. Did you tell Bodin?" she whispers.

"He's lost his memory again," I reply quietly.

"Damn," she says. "That's not good. He'll get it back, though, right?"

"Probably," I mutter. "But I need to find one of the others."

Shit. Miguel's looking. He's noticed I haven't left.

"I gotta go," I mumble. "Cover for me?"

She nods. "Go."

I duck away, walking as fast as possible in the brisk twilight air. I make a beeline for the front of the long line of campsites. Why does Legion's tent have to be at the beginning? Anxiety knots my stomach. I'd hoped to avoid dumping this problem on him. He has enough to worry about without me adding to it.

Interested looks follow me as I pass, and I hug my cape tighter. It will be fine. I'm overthinking things. Miguel was just being friendly. They're all just wondering why I'm rushing. My scent isn't that powerful, surely. Bodin all but kicked me out.

I'm overreacting and underestimating the male ability to control their hormones. But as my fingers curl around the flap of Legion's tent, a memory flashes unbidden.

Alfie and I, on a bench in Nero's garden weeks before my eighteenth birthday—days before the big battle. Sick of suppressing my heat, desperate for attention, for touch. Alfie insisted we wait until marriage, and he was so rigid in that belief that he grew angry when I brought it up. But that night, when I decided I'd had enough of denying my need, I made my move. His control snapped. He became so aggressively aroused that it frightened me. I punched him, then fled. We apologized later, agreeing to wait until we were ready. He's always known about my fae biology.

The flap suddenly opens, revealing me standing there, horror painted across my face. Styx holds the tent open, Legion further inside at his desk, poring over reports, tension evident in his shoulders.

"Are you coming inside?" Styx asks. "Or are you going to loiter all night?"

Chagrinned, I mutter something respectful, catch the smile tugging at his lips, and rush inside. He drops the flap, blocking the exit, eyes raking over me with dark appreciation. Shit. My heightened senses make him smell ten times more alluring than usual. It's making my head spin. I fight the urge to bury my face in his neck.

"We have a problem," I say, voice tight. "They're—"

"You have a charm for this occasion, Willow." Legion's brows arch.

"Sorry." I slip my hand beneath my cape, brushing my fingertip over the stone they gifted me. I wait until magic flares outward, creating an itching silencing shield. Its range isn't great, so I ask Styx to stand beside Legion's desk with me. The change in them is immediate. Their eyes darken. Faces slacken with desire. Styx might even growl.

"I'm about to go into heat," I mumble, cheeks burning with embarrassment.

Legion says, "I thought that elixir—"

"Is birth control. Not a heat thing."

Legion swallows hard. Styx's eyes have gone wholly black—Sluagh black—and he's staring at me as if I'm his next meal.

"Did you know Bodin's lost his memories again?" I blabber to fill the silence. "I caught him about to eat actual food."

With visible effort, Legion tears his gaze from me and asks Styx, "When was the last time you revealed your Sluagh form to him?"

"Don't know," Styx replies vaguely, still staring at me in an entirely predatory way.

"What do you mean, you don't know?" Legion presses, alarm coloring his voice.

Oh shit. Has Styx lost his memory, too? This is bad. This is so bad.

"Stop panicking," he sends into my mind. *"You're ruining the vibe."*

"Are you messing with us?" I say. "Because I'm not in the mood right now."

He gives Legion a disgruntled look. "I'll shift before him tonight."

"You should be doing it multiple times a day." Anger flares in Legion's eyes. "You know how important this is to combat Titania's memory enchantment."

"I've been busy."

"Not too busy to visit Willow three times while she slept."

My brows shoot skyward. Wait. What? Has he been spying on me in his wraith form? Only when I sleep or—an intense wave of hot need washes over me, and I barely stifle a groan. The scent of my pheromones spikes in the air, and I see my mates' nostrils flare. Styx steps toward me, but Legion's hand flattens against his chest, holding him back.

"Enough," Legion growls, his voice strained.

I need to get out of here. My wild eyes dart around, searching for escape. I can't be like this around so many people; it will cause chaos.

"Return to your camp," Legion tells me. "Styx will see to Bodin. We'll isolate you and tell everyone you're unwell."

My eyes sting with relief. Legion places his hands on my shoulders. His touch sends a jolt through me, igniting nerve endings I didn't know existed. I see the struggle in his eyes—duty warring with desire.

"I might have my memories," he murmurs, eyes searching mine, "but there's still so much about you we don't know. You need to tell us about these things, Willow."

"I didn't want to bother you."

His jaw clenches, and I feel his desire thickening the air. "Is there anything else?"

Mortified, I shake my head. "I'll go. Thank you."

I let the silencing shield drop before he can question me further and stride back to camp, feeling like my skin is too tight. I want to rip my clothes off and roll in the snow, but it's still green here. Maybe we'll be lucky with rain tonight. It drizzled for half the day. I'm so caught up in my thoughts that I don't hear someone calling until they grab my arm. "Where are you going so fast?"

On instinct, I shove him.

"What the hell, Willow?" Alfie stumbles back.

"Sorry," I mumble and keep walking. "Didn't realize it was you."

His footsteps follow. "Wait."

"Not the time, Alfie." I wave him off over my shoulder.

The cold air balms my flushed skin as I break into a jog, providing momentary relief from the inferno inside me. The scents of the camp—woodsmoke, unwashed male bodies, and the crisp winter air—assault my heightened senses, making me dizzy.

My feet pound against the damp ground, each impact jolting my overheated body. I'm aware of eyes on me as I sprint past other campsites, but I can't bring myself to care.

I hate this. I hate this feeling so much.

The heat pulses through me, reminding me how different I am—not quite human, not fully fae. In moments like these, I feel like I belong nowhere. I haven't felt this different since Crystal City. *Freak*, they used to call me.

As I weave through the camp, I notice heads turning and nostrils flaring. A young soldier stumbles as I pass, his eyes widening. An older woman pulls her partner close, whispering furiously. The air feels charged as if a lightning strike is imminent.

What if people start asking questions? Most have kept to themselves, but our troop has been opening up the past few nights. I've seen Becky look at my ears on more than one occasion. Now that I know her secret, she might feel confident enough to ask about mine. If I tell them where I'm from, then I'll have to explain why I have no magic, and then—

A hand lands on my shoulder and wrenches me around.

Miguel.

It all happens so fast. One minute, he's about to offer me the bowl I left, and the next, Alfie's fist meets his face. Blood spurts from a nose. Soup flies.

"Miguel!" I gasp, trying to help him, but Alfie steps in my way.

"You okay?" he asks me with a wild look.

"You hit Miguel!"

"He attacked you."

"He was giving me soup!"

Behind him, groaning on the ground, Miguel clutches his nose. I try to push past Alfie, but he crushes me to his body, hand cupping the back of my head, fingers fisting in my hair. He buries his nose in my neck and drags in a deep inhale. "Fuck, Willow. I forgot how good you smell. I've been dreaming about this for years."

I freeze.

I'm not afraid. This is my warning system, telling me it's time to fight. But I can't add to the drama unfolding. This can be salvaged.

"Alfie," I grind out, face still smooshed against his chest. "You need to let go of me and walk away right now."

"Don't pretend you don't want this," he growls. "Enough with the lies."

"I don't want to hurt you." I squeeze my eyes shut. Curl my fingers into fists.

"When are you going to admit it?" His fist tightens in my hair, ripping strands at my scalp. "Ever since we were young, you've been flirting with me like this. Give me a little and then change your mind. You're mine."

He's roughly jerked to the side—hit. But I'm tangled up with him. I fall too. Another body is there, large and powerful, dominating Alfie. It takes me a moment to roll free and realize what happened. Bodin happened. His eyes are dark and murderous as he straddles Alfie, fisting his shirt, snarling in his face, "She's *ours*."

Multiple sets of eyes watch us: Styx, standing to the side with an amused look; Lord Ignarius striding over, his dragon's red eyes flashing as his own; Dahlia; Becky; Geraldine; and Max. Styx must have *flickered* to Bodin's tent and shifted, restoring some of his sense, but now Bodin's gone and done this—because of me.

He pins Alfie by the throat and repetitively punches him in the face. A snarled word punctuates each hit. "Touch. Our. Mate. Again. I. Dare. You."

"Bodin," I gasp. "People are watching."

He shoves off. Alfie flops back, but he's laughing despite his rapidly swelling face.

"You just broke the Old Code," he gurgles through blood. "Twice."

Bodin advances on him, jaw working. Every muscle in his body is tense, twitching, and ready to unleash. Instead, he rips Alfie's charms from his chain and tosses them into the darkness. Every glamour, illusion, and magic trick disappears. The perfect symmetry of Alfie's face, the virility, the godlike physique—gone. Even beneath the new wounds, it's obvious. He ages in an instant. Not old, but not obscenely perfect. Dark circles under his eyes. A jagged scar runs under his chin. He should have been classed as a Nothing, but he found a charm to hide his imperfections. That's why he was so convinced I could do the same.

Shock ripples around the spectators.

Ignarius arrives with Legion, demanding to know what's happening. All the while, Styx's eyes glimmer with humor.

"Inside the tent. Now." Bodin's voice rumbles low, a predator's growl. His eyes, dark as the night, never leave mine. "Before I forget we have an audience, Calamity."

CHAPTER 51
WILLOW

I pace the confines of Bodin's tent, my heart racing. Shit. Shit. Shit. I've really stepped in it this time. Way to go, Willow, queen of calamity.

Escape beckons, but the consequences of my actions loom large. And Alfie—a Nothing. The revelation stings.

Styx enters, his face a mask of reluctance. "I have to take you back to the Keep," he grumbles, as if the words taste of bile.

Despite the inferno raging beneath my skin, I wrap my arms around myself, seeking comfort that eludes me.

Bodin returns with my pack and sword in hand. His eyes mirror my own sense of loss.

"I'm sorry," I mumble, strapping on the blade.

"Don't be," he replies, his tone softening. "You're our queen—"

"Mate," I correct reflexively.

"—let us handle this."

Styx reaches for my hand, a pained noise escaping his lips. "You need to get closer," he reminds me, voice strained.

Bodin's lips part as though he wants to say something but thinks better of it. His palm finds the space between my shoulder

blades, gently urging me toward Styx. The contact sends shock-waves through us both, and suddenly the world blurs. My stomach lurches as reality shifts, and we *flicker*.

I stumble, finding my footing in glorious snow. Confusion sets in as I survey our surroundings. This isn't the Keep, but somewhere nearby. The air carries familiar scents.

"I can't take you further," Styx rasps, doubled over and panting. His eyes are wild and unfocused. "I'm not touching you anymore." He shakes his hands as if to rid himself of my lingering touch, then vanishes into the night.

Fucking bastard.

I kick the snow, biting back a scream. Alone in the darkness, I force myself to focus. Where am I? The towering walls of the Ivory Palace loom nearby, recognizable trees dotting the vast grounds. East should lead me to the Keep—there must be a connecting gate. My only other option is to scale the palace wall, potentially fall into the moat, still circle back to the Keep's front entrance, and then cross the moat again.

Nope.

I close my eyes, inhaling deeply. Damp earth, ancient stone, and the faint crackle of magic. The familiar scent helps ground me. But underneath it all, I can still smell them—Bodin, Styx, even Legion—their essence clinging to my clothes, my skin.

A wave of molten desire rolls through me, pulsing beneath my skin. When it recedes, arousal lingers—my nipples, breasts, and pussy aching for relief. These fever waves will intensify over the coming days before breaking. With a groan, I force my leaden legs forward. I need sanctuary, a place to weather this damn condition without wreaking havoc.

Homesickness lurches in my gut. If only I had my pack, other wolf shifters who understand, I wouldn't feel like a pariah. Tears sting my eyes as I trudge onward.

Guilt gnaws at me. I left Geraldine and Max without explanation. Was Alfie right? Will Bodin face consequences for claiming me so publicly? Or can they "Styx" their way out of this mess?

I shake my head, trying to clear the fog of lust and worry. *Focus, Willow.* One step at a time: Get inside. Find a room. Lock the door. Pray to every deity in the Cauldron, the Well, and everything between them that I'll survive this cycle without shattering all we've built.

One step at a time.

The mantra echoes in my mind as I walk, occasionally grabbing fistfuls of snow to cool my feverish cheeks.

The full moon, shrouded by storm clouds, casts an otherworldly glow. Tracks in the pristine white catch my eye. My breath hitches. These aren't human or beast—but tiny, repeating pinpricks.

My hand finds the sword at my hip. The whisper of bone leaving its sheath shatters the eerie silence. I force my scattered mind to focus, scanning the snow-capped trees. I've ventured deep into the woods now, and the palace wall is no longer visible.

A bone-chilling shriek pierces the night, far too close for comfort. A Nightmare. It has to be. My pace quickens as I mentally flip through the Codex, trying to match the sound to a known Terror. Ethershrieks produce a cacophony of voices—not this. Screamhawks circle from above, leaving victims in constant fear. Their bird-like nature could match the tracks.

Another set of prints appears, slightly different. Dread pools in my stomach as I push on, but doubt creeps in. Have I traveled far enough? Should I double back and try the opposite direction?

My traitorous body chooses this moment to unleash another wave of heat. With a groan, I crouch and touch the snow, desperate to anchor myself as I breathe through the onslaught. Need surges through me like liquid fire, setting every nerve ending ablaze—my skin prickles, hypersensitive to even the lightest touch of fabric. The world around me sharpens, colors more vivid, scents more potent. It's intoxicating and terrifying all at once.

Fuck Styx for abandoning me here, so close to safety. Was I truly that difficult to touch? His self-control that fragile?

The wave passes, leaving an insistent ache of unfulfillment in its wake. If I were home, in the privacy of my room, I'd slide my hand inside my pants and satisfy this pulsing need. Instead, I press on until voices reach my ears—male. Alert, I try to pinpoint their location in the misty woods.

The palace's inner wall comes into view again, a pale sentinel in the gloom. I spot a path winding through the trees just before shadows swallow everything. The strange tracks lead there, likely toward the palace or the Keep. Keeping my breath controlled and my steps light, I move closer.

Another burst of conversation pricks my ears up. Is that Emrys's distinctive rasp? I lift my nose, inhaling deeply. Absinthe and tobacco—yes, it's him. But there's something else . . . something animal, with a tang of rot. A faint scratching reaches my ears, like claws on wood. It could be horses, but something about the rhythm sets my teeth on edge. My grip tightens on my sword as I approach the path, keeping to the cover of trees.

Carefully peeking around a trunk, I see Emrys in his military uniform, facing away. He gestures at a long structure with boarded-up windows, speaking to someone just out of view. As he adjusts his stance, I glimpse Puck.

The tracks lead to the door. The scratching intensifies inside, joined by low, guttural growls that no earthly animal could produce. Every instinct screams at me to run. But why would Nightmares be there?

Emrys and Puck disappear inside the royal stables, taking their conversation with them. I stand frozen, weighing my options. Something feels very off. Emrys looked guarded, secretive. With Bodin's memory lapse, could something have happened to Emrys too? Is this paranoia, or is the fever addling my mind?

If I return to the Keep, I'm just sitting around feeling sorry for myself. I've powered through my heat before. It's natural. I'm not dying. Ignore it. Think of something else to occupy my time. It'll pass.

Something to occupy my time—this is it. My mind whirls, trying to piece together Emrys's behavior. His hatred toward me, his preference for staying at the palace. That first moment in the Knight Inquisitor's chambers, when he was mid-interrogation.

Legion expected Nightmares to roam free, yet they were suspiciously absent. Is this Legion's doing? Or is Emrys working against him? The latter seems more likely, given Legion's plans for martial law.

If I walk away now, I'll never rest easy. Seeing is believing. I creep closer to the stables, pressing my ear against the rough wooden door. My pulse thunders as I strain to hear through the barrier, praying those inside can't detect my presence. The sounds are more evident now—snarls, shrieks, and something that might be laughter if it weren't so twisted. The wood vibrates against my cheek with the force of their frenzy.

I close my eyes, inhaling deeply to parse the layers of smell. If only my racing heart would quiet, and the continuous screeching would cease, I might catch the conversation. I press harder, willing my shifter hearing to penetrate the thick wood.

"...said this was the last..."

A gust of icy wind snatches away the words, bringing another whiff of that rot-tinged scent. I stifle a gag, refocusing my efforts. I can't shake the feeling that I'm on the precipice of something monumental, something that could change everything.

Even as possibilities race through my mind, my body reminds me of its urgent needs—sweat beads on my forehead despite the cold. I fight the urge to pant like an animal and dig my nails into my palms, using the sharp pain to anchor myself.

I can do this. I can control myself long enough to uncover Emrys's secret. I have to. Because if I can't trust one of the Six, how can I hope to be the queen they need me to be?

CHAPTER 52
PUCK

A rustling, like fabric caught in the wind, pricks my ears. My eyes dart to the stable doors.

"Emrys, check it out," I command, my voice echoing off wooden beams.

His upper lip curls, flashing teeth. "Since when do I take orders from you?"

"Let me out," the Baleful Hunt whispers, its voice a cold tendril slithering through my mind. *"I'll investigate for you."*

My fists clench. *"Stay put. Until after the trials—after I've secured my leadership."*

Emrys narrows his eyes, scrutinizing me.

"Fine. I'll go," I snap, irritation crawling under my skin.

"I'm only helping you, Puck, because it aligns with my goals," Emrys drawls.

I scoff. "Which are?"

His lips twitch. "For a moment, I almost laughed."

The Hunt's whispers grow more insistent, demanding respect. It hisses that the new King of Avorlorna would never tolerate such insolence.

"Hush," I tell it. *"The sooner we finish this, the faster you'll have*

your wish. I'll release you, but first, I must cement my position. For that, Titania needs to vanish."

Murdering her in her chambers is impossible with the Keepers hovering about—they've barred me entry, claiming I'm unpredictable with a dragon inside. But if I unleash the Hunt prematurely, who's to say it will return to host within my body? I need the crown first.

"Why not let me turn those wood-faced demons to stone, then?" The Hunt's voice purrs seductively.

"The Keepers? I've explained why." Their masks repel magic— not foolproof, but long enough to raise the alarm. Guards could potentially blind me, negating the Baleful Gaze. It is difficult, but not impossible if they cooperate.

The Keepers are here to control the Shining Host. They have contingencies.

I rake my fingers through my hair, frowning as fine dust sifts onto my shoulders. My joints creak as I brush it away, muttering, "Damned drafty palace . . . can't keep the sand out."

"Is something wrong with your head?" Emrys asks, gesturing at my face.

"He's mocking your eyebrows," the Hunt jeers. *"Turn him to stone. Let me out!"*

I glare at Emrys. "Are you insulting my appearance?"

"Simply stating you're looking rather . . . gray," he observes, eyes narrowing.

I wave dismissively. "It's this blasted lighting. Everyone looks half-dead."

The Hunt chuckles. *"Trouble with your complexion, Puck?"*

"Shut the fuck up," I hiss, pacing. "I can't focus with your incessant nattering."

My boots crunch on straw. An itch crawls beneath my skin like sand, burrowing deeper with each step. I scratch absently, nails scraping oddly rough flesh.

Howling wind rattles the foundations. Nightmares in their

pens shriek and growl, a hellish chorus. But they can't escape—I had the doors rebuilt floor to ceiling.

"Double-check their pens," I order Emrys. "We can't risk a single escapee."

These creatures slipping through must mean something is amiss between Titania and Oberon's bargain. But I can't allow the knights their martial law. My power would evaporate.

Emrys tugs on his gloves, striding toward the exit. How dare he ignore me?

"Stop!" I command. "I gave you an order."

He reaches for the doorknob. A gust of frigid air carries the scent of frost and fear . . . and a figure stumbles in. A cape. Silver braided hair. Female.

Their Shadow, the—

"Danger! He betrayed us!" The Hunt roars, clawing for control.

Emrys's surprised expression baffles me. Is this betrayal or something else? Either way, I don't wait to find out. I bolt for the opposite exit, slamming the door behind me before my grip on the Hunt slips.

I stumble back, releasing the pressure building inside. The Hunt's gaze erupts from my eyes, striking the stables. Wood crunches, transforming into solid rock before me.

"Fuck, fuck, fuck!" I pound my forehead. "Look what you made me do!"

The Hunt's laughter grinds like stones in my skull.

"Turn it back then," it taunts. *"Or don't you know how?"*

"Fuck, fuck, fuck." I need those monsters for the trials. My plan to claim the crown relies on moving the trials forward. If I can't kill Titania in her bed, sending bloodthirsty exhibitors to murder her dream form is the next best option. The result might differ if she projected in Avorlorna. But Oberon—her ancient, twisted mate—has bound her to Nocturna for the Gentle Interlude.

Any harm done to her astral form outside her own dream-scape is lethal.

Everyone believes she slumbers to freeze the watergates, but that's only part of the bargain. The other half: Oberon grants her people a reprieve from war if she returns to satiate his sick desires. I was so in love with her—so in awe.

Until the Hunt revealed her warped reality, including my wish. She does all of this for greed because she wants to have all the riches of Avorlorna for herself—without her mate's influence. They've been fighting like this for eons.

I force myself to breathe. To think. The weight of my schemes threatens to crush me. My limbs grow heavier each day, as if gravity's intensifying. But I can't falter now—not when I'm so close to true power.

The stone stables loom, a monument to my lapse in control. Emrys and that silver-haired witch—Willow—are trapped with the Nightmares.

The Baleful Hunt's laughter echoes in my skull, a constant reminder of the precarious balance I'm trying to maintain. I grind my teeth, forcing myself to focus.

"Alright," I mutter. "Think. How do we salvage this?"

Willow.

The one Titania fears.

"*Why?*" I ask the Hunt. "*Why does she fear this mortal?*"

"*Finally, you ask the right question.*"

Chalky flakes dust my sleeve. I brush them off, staring at my nails. They seem harder and slightly discolored.

"*Just stress,*" the Hunt soothes. "*Lack of sleep and this dusty palace—that's all.*"

Yes, I lack sleep. As I pace, the Hunt reveals more of Titania's secrets. A plan crystallizes—risky, potentially disastrous, but what choice remains?

I turn back to the stone stables, a grim smile twisting my lips.

"Well, my dear Hunt," I say, "it seems you'll get your wish sooner than expected."

CHAPTER 53
WILLOW

The door flies open, and I tumble forward, tripping over someone's feet and landing flat on my face. I look up, up, and up, realizing in horror what's happened.

Emrys looms above me, a dark figure silhouetted against the dim stable light. As my eyes adjust, his features sharpen into focus, shadows dancing across the planes of his achingly handsome face. Black brows arch high, coppery eyes wide, rosy lips parted in surprise.

Fuck, he's so attractive—my first thought.

Shit, I'm dead—my second.

He releases the door. It slams shut, trapping me inside. Movement behind him catches my eye—Puck's auburn hair receding as he flees, kicking up the straw. He escapes through the door at the far end, slamming it behind him.

Emrys recovers quickly, his face twisting into a mask of fury. He grabs my shirt, yanks me to my feet, and slams me against the door.

"Ow." I scowl.

"How much did you hear?" he snarls, his breath hot on my face.

"Enough," I reply, struggling to keep my voice steady despite the fear coursing through me.

His eyes flash dangerously. "Enough what?"

I meet his gaze defiantly. "Enough to know something's very wrong in here."

For a moment, I see the promise of death in his eyes. This is my last minute on earth. But then a deafening crack splits the air, wood splintering around us.

The Nightmares rattle their stalls, their unearthly shrieks piercing the chaos. I catch glimpses of writhing shadows through tiny gaps beneath and above the doors.

I don't realize how close I am to a structural pole until Emrys yanks me away just before it turns to stone. We stand there, stunned, as the outer building morphs from wood into solid rock. When the booming transformation finally ceases, even the Nightmares fall silent. Emrys's eyes drop to where his gloved hand still fists my cape. He gasps and lets go, stepping back.

"What just happened?" I whisper, my heart pounding against my ribs.

"That fucking prick," he spits, his expression a mix of rage and disbelief. "He seeks to trap us in here together."

I take in the tense set of his shoulders, how his gloved hands creak, clench, and unclench at his sides. His eyes dart around the room, assessing our situation with a predator's keen gaze. Despite the dire circumstances, there's a part of him that seems almost . . . aroused by the challenge.

Or by me.

"Why would Puck trap us?" I ask slowly.

"Oh, Willow," he says, tone dripping with sarcasm, "you have no idea what you've stumbled into."

Emrys turns his attention to our entrapments. His gloved fingers trace the newly formed patterns in the stone walls—swirls and symbols that seem to shift when I look at them directly. The straw carpeting the floor beneath our feet rumbles subtly, as if the magic is still settling.

"What have I stumbled into, Emrys?"

"Somewhere you're not welcome." His hand pauses mid-swipe along the existing doorframe. "But since you're here, maybe it's time you learned a few things about the world you're so eager to rule."

I gape at him. "I don't want to rule it. Is that what you really think of me?"

"Rule, save, destroy. It's all the same to you queens."

"Not a queen," I remind him dryly. "A mate."

The look in his eyes is a mixture of anger, frustration, and something else—a hint of dark curiosity that makes my breath catch.

A low, ominous groan echoes through the stables. The stone walls shudder. Hairline cracks form along the seams of the solid stall doors. Sensing weakness, the Nightmares begin their cacophony anew, their cries more frenzied than before.

"Those doors will hold, right?" I ask. "We're safe?"

"You're never safe with me."

His bitter laugh sends chills down me, shaking loose a tingling between my legs. With a gasp, I realize I'm attracted to this side of him—the cruelty, the danger. It calls to that dark place inside me, the deep reservoir capable of destruction. It wants to be filled, to have a companion, just like the other, warmer parts of my soul.

A wave of heat chooses that moment to punish me. Scorching desire builds under my skin, my nipples pebbling beneath my shirt. The friction is torture. I release a strangled groan, trying to suppress it, and have to lean against the very door Emrys inspects. Suddenly, there's nowhere to look but into his striking eyes. They roam over my face, his expression a battlefield of conflicting emotions. His nostrils flare as he catches my scent. I glimpse an echo of my yearning on his face before the hard glint of suspicion swallows it.

He slams his palm against the frame beside my head.

"What is this?" His snarl is a husky, volatile mixture of hunger and contempt. "You think to seduce me with your little queen bee pheromones? How delightfully naive. Tell me, does it sting to be so unprepared for the game you're playing?"

I try to steady my breathing and remain passive while fighting against my feverish urges. My hormones demand I rip his clothes off and explore the hard slabs of muscle, to see if those curious tattoos cover every inch of his flesh.

"This isn't a game, Emrys," I groan.

His laugh is sharp and mirthless. "Oh, but it is, little moth. And you're fluttering right into the flames." His demeanor grows quiet and reflective as he trails the back of his gloved fingers down my throat. "Do you know what happens to moths dancing too close to the fire?"

"For someone so cruel, you're remarkably poetic."

He blinks, taken aback. That I've surprised him gives me the strength to push on.

"Styx tried to scare me away, too, but I'll tell you what I said to him. I'm not afraid of you."

"No?" His genuine smile transforms his face into poetic beauty, matching his silver tongue.

"No."

"Perhaps you should be scared," he murmurs.

"He said that too."

"There are fates far worse than death, and I've tasted them all." He leans in closer, hot breath against my ear. "Tell me, sweet Willow, have you ever wondered what it feels like to have your soul flayed open? To have every secret, every desire laid bare and found wanting?"

I suppress a shudder, both repulsed and intrigued by his words. But I wonder ... "Is that what happened to you?"

"You have no idea of the depths I've plumbed, the horrors we've endured. And yet, here you stand, offering salvation like some misguided saint."

"I'm not offering salvation," I retort. "I'm offering understanding."

Maybe. He's working my last nerve right now.

"Understanding? How quaint." He inhales my scent deep into his lungs but is careful not to touch me. "What do you understand about the monster before you?"

"I understand pain," I say softly. "I understand what it's like to be used and seen as nothing more than a tool." My throat closes up. "To stand by helpless and watch as someone you love dies."

The realization that I know about his Seventh hits him like a physical blow. He pulls back to look into my eyes. Legion didn't tell me the details, but the experience had to be harrowing. They must have all witnessed it, been helpless to stop it.

Emrys's thoughts play out on his face. Who told me? How much do I know? What does this mean? How will I use this information against him?

"You understand nothing," he hisses, stumbling backward, spearing a hand through his white hair.

"Then help me," I plead, stepping toward him.

The Nightmares shriek in their cages. Their malevolence seeps through the air, making me shudder. It reminds me of why I followed Emrys here in the first place.

"You're conspiring with Puck. Why?" My heart wants to say he's doing it for us, for his hive. But my gut warns me it's the opposite. "Why foil Legion's plan to instate martial law?"

A flicker of something—surprise? amusement?—passes over his face before it settles back into seething hatred.

"Clever little queen," he murmurs, "but you're only seeing the pond's surface, not the depths beneath."

"Not a queen," I mutter. "Why don't you want martial law? It would give you control of Avorlorna."

"You think that's the answer? More false promises, more fake smiles, more playing pretend?"

"What do you mean?"

As I stare into his manic eyes, I'm struck by the realization that I'm missing something crucial. His words and actions don't align with what I thought I knew. He's playing a more complex game than I'd imagined, with rules I don't understand. And it scares me.

A muscle in his jaw ticks, and for a moment, I think he might lash out. But then his shoulders slump, and he laughs bitterly.

"You want to know why I align myself with him? Maybe it's because I don't want to be saved. I don't want a queen at all. I want the oblivion the gods robbed us of when they gave us you."

"Again, not a queen," I grind out. I stare. "Puck promised you that?"

His smile is hollow. "At least with him I know where I stand. With you . . ." He trails off, his eyes roaming my face, lingering on my lips. "With you, I don't know if I'm losing my mind or finding it."

Somehow, my words fail me. The air in my lungs thickens. Even from where he stands a good yard away, I feel the heat of his body and smell his intoxicating scent. Part of me wants to reach out to him, but another part knows that doing so could be incredibly dangerous.

"So what now?" I ask, my voice barely above a whisper.

Emrys's eyes darken. "Now, little moth, we wait. And you pray that your precious mates find us before the Nightmares break free. Because trapped in here with me . . . well, let's just say I might not be as noble as the others when it comes to resisting temptation."

CHAPTER 54
WILLOW

I take my sword and sit down with my back against the door. There's no chance of falling through again. The solid stone has melded it closed.

Emrys does the same, but first, he walks across the partition down the center of the stables, distastefully kicking straw out of his way. He sits with his back to the door, his hate-filled eyes never leaving me.

I untie the laces on my cape to let the air in as I look around. Numerous doors stretch from floor to ceiling, hiding the inhabitants of each stall. Two lanterns dangle above, casting the only light. I don't feel a breeze, which makes me think the boarded windows are the primary sources of airflow. Now they're solid stone.

Hissing, shrieking, and doors rattling grows in intensity like an oncoming thunderstorm. The beasts know something is wrong. They want out with a renewed passion.

My gaze returns to Emrys. His face doesn't seem so scary now. Maybe it's because I've realized why, despite all his cruelty, I'm still attracted to him. Like each of my mates, he satisfies a different need in my soul. Or maybe his scowl is not so scary

372

because my little sisters give the same look when I take some-thing of theirs or tell them no when they really, *really* want some-thing. It's the kind of look one gives to mask the pain inside.

I close my eyes and fall into the past, back to when I was alone and aching—sobbing in my Crystal City room, desperate for someone to share my pain with—someone who would under-stand. But I'd returned to Elphyne and lived amongst heroes.

When I open my eyes, Emrys's black brows knit together. He looks ready to run across the room and strangle me. Instead, I point my sword at one of the thick stable doors. "Why don't you tell me about the Nightmares you've trapped in there?"

"Why would I tell you anything?" he spits. "You're a brief, transient visitor in my very long life. Soon, your light will be snuffed out, and we'll forget you as we do the rest."

"Sure. Keep telling yourself that." I smile, unperturbed. "We're mates. We're destined to be together."

"The only way we would be together is if you crawled on your knees to me."

I stare at the expanse between us. "It's not that far."

His lips part, I guess, to explain that's not what he meant by us being together. But then his jaw clicks shut with understand-ing. "Your attempts at wit are as feeble as your grasp on our reality."

"Come on, Emrys," I press, ignoring his barb. "Just tell me about the Nightmares. What if one of them gets out? Will you face them by yourself?"

His jaw works, eyes flashing as he contemplates my words.

"We're stuck in here, aren't we?" I say. "May as well fill the time. What else can we do? Unless of course"—I drop my voice to a husky whisper—"that offer about not resisting temptation stands."

He balks. "It wasn't an offer."

"Sure sounded like an offer to me."

I can't bear to sit still, so I start pacing beside each stall, listening to the unique sounds and sniffing the air. A strange clicking comes from one. Is that even an animal?

I yank off my too-hot cape, toss it on the floor, and tap a door to test the creature inside. It slams its body against the door, and I step back. Interesting.

"You're either mad or stupid to think it was," Emrys continues. "I would rather sink my fangs into your juicy heart to drink up that persistent song before it gets stuck in my head."

"Aww," I reply with an exaggerated pout. "You say the most romantic things. Tell me more."

I rattle my sword on another door, incensing the beast within. When its screeches die, I start reciting poetry to myself and inspect the next stall. "Oh, Willow, my Willow, how does your skin glow?" *Clang clang.* More ticking and tapping answers me inside. Curious. "With silver bells and moonbeam shells, I'm making this up as I go."

I pivot, grinning at him, waiting for an applause.

He grinds his teeth audibly. "Fine. I'll tell you about the Nightmares. Anything to shut you up."

"Excellent. What's this one?" I tap the door of a quieter stall. "It smells familiar, like rotting flesh."

His eyes narrow briefly as if I surprise him, and he doesn't like it. He's probably forgotten I grew up around the undead. I made them.

"It's a Graftspawn," he explains, then gives me no more.

"Okay . . . if you're not elaborating, then I'll just make up something. Hmm. What would a Graftspawn look like and do? Graft-spawn. Grafts-pawn. Graaah-fftah. Spooorn." I play with the words on my tongue as ideas run through my head. "Ooh. Does it look like a winged monkey with poop for eyes and—"

"Sit down before you hurt yourself."

I don't sit.

He gives me a disparaging look, but I see a hint of amusement in his eyes. "Imagine, if you will, the most grotesque amalgamation of flesh and bone, driven by an insatiable hunger for more parts to add to its patchwork body." His voice takes on a dark, almost reverent tone as he continues. "Born in the House of Flesh, they represent the fear of bodily corruption, of losing one's identity to a monstrous transformation. Each seam, each mismatched limb, is a testament to the fragility of our physical forms."

I suppress a shudder. "So definitely not a monkey with poop eyes."

His lips twitch.

"And you're definitely good with your words. I'll bet you read a lot too."

He shifts uncomfortably at my observation. Inwardly, I'm fist-pumping the air in triumph. His awkwardness means my Christmas gift for him is suitable. I continue my path along the partition to give him a moment. Each stall I pass, the Terror inside throws itself at the door. I don't even antagonize them. It's almost as if . . . they scent my pheromones. The doors are solid, from bottom to top—except for that thin gap below and above. It's enough for me to smell them and vice versa.

The fever curdles in my stomach, making me feel sick. I startle when the crash against a door is so violent that a whiff of coppery blood washes out from the crack beneath it.

"A Chimera." Emrys's voice is now so close that his breath tickles my skin. "A shapeshifter."

My eyes flutter closed at his nearness. I didn't hear him move from his spot by the door. His very scent wipes out all fear—sweet, tobacco, pepper. My body recognizes him as my mate despite his desperation to be something else. Awareness ripples through me, pulsing that need again.

Gloved fingers brush my neck as he shifts my braid to the other side, away from my ear. The rasp in his deep voice is a direct line to every feminine instinct I own.

"It takes on forms," he says, "tailored to your deepest,

unspoken desires and uses seduction to lure its victims closer. It fulfills your favorite erotic fantasy and then warps it into something terrifying right when you're about to—" He nips my ear lobe. Pleasure shivers through me, and I gasp. Or maybe it was him.

"How do we kill it?" I ask, trying to maintain focus.

Leathery fingertips swipe down my neck and curl around my throat. "Did you know the inspiration for their creation came from us Sluagh? From the sexual cravings we instill in our victims?"

"So you understand, then. This thing inside me I can't control?"

His fingers flex against my throat, gentle but firm—a reminder he has me caught—much like his prey behind the stone door. My head drops back to his shoulder. Our bodies are flush. Every haggard breath he battles pushes against my spine, forcing me to inhale. I sense him looking over my shoulder, down my front, watching my breasts surge beneath my gaping shirt as I breathe—Legion did the same thing when Bodin licked my cleavage. The memory kindles heat in my blood, making me ache for release. A needy moan slips from my lips.

"Look at you," he murmurs hotly. "So desperate for my touch."

"Yes," I breathe, eyes fluttering as his other hand lands on my waist.

"Where?" he grunts.

"I..."

I can't concentrate because his palm glides around my hip, aiming between my thighs. He stops short of where I need him most and growls in my ear, "Beg for it."

"Please," I whimper, my hips flexing forward, shamelessly trying to connect. He teases me, lifts his hand, and then lowers it until I feel his heat. I have no sense of logic. My brain is drowning in a haze of need. My control snaps. I take his gloved hand and use it to cup my pussy through my clothes. Instant pleasure zooms into me, and I gasp, "Yes. More of that."

"More what?" He rubs the seam between my legs, first slow and tentative until I beg, plead, whimper. "This?"

My body answers for me, melting against him as I pant hard. His fingers grow confident, fast, and firm. I cry out as bliss builds, hot and demanding. I hear his lips part—maybe to speak or to scold, but when I reach up to cup his nape and steady myself, his breath hitches. His grip tightens on my throat, courting me with pain. When I make a needy sound in response, his erection digs into my lower back. He groans, low and deep and hot, into my ear. But he doesn't pull back. He barrels toward this violent end alongside me, lungs heaving with mine.

I feel as beastly as the creatures on the other side of the door. I feel wrong. But good. This is not the place to lose myself. Except with Emrys, it's the only place.

There's no other way to explain this paradox except to steal the words from his mouth. With him, I can't tell if I'm losing my mind or finding it. He forces my chin up, throwing my head back so our eyes clash. Upside down, the effect is dizzying. He bows over me, white hair spilling, shrouding his lust-filled eyes. I am wet, soaked through and into his gloves. He works me relentlessly, gauging the rise of my pleasure through the silent plea in my eyes until I lose focus, lose air. Finally. My orgasm builds, the tease of ecstasy growing closer. I'm about to—

He lets go. Steps away from me. Cold air rushes in. My release dies miserably, unfulfilled. I collapse to the ground, my mind a whirl of agony and empty joy. Tears sting my eyes, but I refuse to let them out.

"Why?" I croak, swinging my gaze up to him.

He stands above me, eyes wild, jaw clenched. "I lied."

"About what?"

It hurts to breathe. I have no answer as he crouches, coming eye-to-eye with me.

"I lied when I said I would be with you if you crawled to me." Darkness swims over his features. "You're just like the rest of them: a manipulative slut, through and through. I wouldn't be with you if you crawled, begged, or bled for it. I'd rather pluck out my entrails and string them on the mantle—save Legion the trouble."

"I hate you."

"Good."

A strangled scream rips out of me, but I don't engage. He's not worth it. Instead, I turn my back and search for my sword and dignity in the hay. Nightmares rattle their cages, screeching and raging. I know how they feel. What an asshole. Fucking *floater*. Stupid, big fat—my fingers wrap around the hilt. Instantly, my mood calms. Something about the familiar touch of the grip is comforting.

Closing my eyes, I slowly count to ten in my head. Then I climb to my feet. I want nothing more than to shove my blade in Emrys's gut—to help him realize his dream, Legion's, or whatever he's on about—but getting angry at each other won't solve anything. We're still mates. Eventually, we'll have to find a way to live together. At the very least, I can pretend to get along until we escape.

A stall's inhabitant throws himself against a door behind me. The bang is so loud and violent that the entire structure shudders. I whirl around and come face to face with Emrys.

"I'm so sorry," he says. "Forgive me. I've left you unfulfilled when you need it most."

"Forget it." I try to push him away.

He grabs my shoulders. "Willow, let me soothe you."

I shove him. "Enough with the games."

He's suddenly in my face, all hot male angles and broad shoulders. Eyes dark and eager and unguardedly hungry. That bond connecting us in my chest vibrates like a warning. This is wrong. My gaze darts to the hands gripping my shoulders—no gloves.

"Come now, little moth," he purrs. "You know you want relief. You need me to fill your aching, empty, dark places no one else dares to tread. You need me to fuck you so hard it hurts." His voice drops to a whisper. "We're two peas in a twisted pod, both sick fucks reveling in self-flagellation. Why not hold each other's whips? Suffer together."

A groan on the ground behind him, a flash of white hair amongst the hay. The stall door is wide open and—oh shit. This is the Chimera in my face, not Emrys. Instinct takes over. My wrist flicks up. The tip of my blade sinks below his ribs. I push to the hilt with two hands until the blade pierces the other side. Warmth spills over my hands. His skin shimmers and flows like liquid metal. It struggles to hold Emrys's appearance, morphing into something hideous—monstrous teeth and misshapen bones. Itching magic scuttles from the sword onto my hand, tingling so intensely it hurts. With a gasp, I realize it's me disrupting the Nightmare's shift, or rather, the skull charm Bodin added to the pommel.

The Chimera's warped rippling stops. It looks at me, shocked, and then it spills in a cascading gush of blood and viscera to the straw-covered ground. The stench of death blooms as inky blots form in the puddle and drip upward. I step back to avoid being hit, but they're not as wayward as wisps. They spill toward the ceiling, splash on the stone, and leave dark stains.

With the creature gone, I see Emrys on the ground a few paces back, clutching his head. That bang must have been the stall door opening, and he was hit. Terrors throw themselves at their enclosures. They know one escaped, and now each attempts the same. He lifts his gaze to me, then to the mess, then back to me. A flash of vulnerability, of something profound, flickers in his eyes.

Some kind of awareness bounces between us. Moments ago,

he was cruel, wicked, and hateful toward me. I don't trust him, but we're in this together. I rush to offer him my hand. He takes it before realizing what he's done. I help him to his feet, and then he lets go like I'm lava.

"Yeah, I still hate you too," I grind, gazing at the blots splashing onto the ceiling. They rot the stone and wear away at it like acid. In time, a hole will form. But will it be enough for us to climb out?

Emrys gives my sword a dubious look, curses under his breath, then stalks down the partition and gets on one knee. He swipes the straw aside, yanks open a hatch, and shoots me a death glare. "Are you coming?"

"You mean to tell me that was there the whole time?"

His lips flatten. Nostrils flare.

"Little moth . . ." He points at the shuddering stall doors. "Meet the flames."

A door cracks down the middle. Spindly, arachnid-like legs poke through the gap, trying to escape. They make a clicking sound.

Oh shit. Oh fuck. Oh shit. Screw waiting for the blots to make a hole. We'll be dead before that happens. Heart leaping into my throat, I pivot and run to Emrys. The clicking and shrieking follow me, louder and closer. *They're out!*

I drop, skidding boots-first along the floor as Emrys descends into the hatch. Sharp bits hidden beneath the straw cut into me as I slide. I twist to my stomach, hoping to know what's coming so I can defend myself—wrong move. Fear obliterates my logic. My momentum slows. I do nothing but stare in horror as multiple shadowy entities crawl along the walls and ceilings, their eyes glittering like cold, distant stars. Some kind of web spurts out from them, latching onto surfaces.

Strong hands grip my waist and tug. I'm dragged down the hatch, acutely aware of Emrys's larger body behind me, his presence both a comfort and a threat. He maneuvers us, making space to reach up. With a swift, sharp motion, he slams the trapdoor shut. He murmurs something under his breath and traces arcane symbols on the hatch's underside.

When he's done, he turns and does something I can't make out in the darkness behind us. A whooshing sound breaks the silence, startling me. Emrys's tall, broad-shouldered silhouette grows darker as torches ignite along a long, endless tunnel before him.

He faces me, firelight dancing in his stark eyes. As I study him, a realization dawns. This tunnel leads somewhere he wants to keep a secret—a secret big enough to keep that he was willing to wait in a stable filled with Nightmares.

<h1 style="text-align:center">CHAPTER 55
WILLOW</h1>

Emrys stalks down the tunnel at a breakneck pace. With nowhere else to go, I follow. After a few strides, he glances over his shoulder, eyes flashing. "Why are you following me?"

"Where else am I supposed to go?" I shoot back.

He continues walking, ignoring me. After a few more paces, he rips off his jacket and hurls it at me. "Go away," he bellows.

I dodge it, fire blazing in my veins. "There's nowhere to go!"

Torchlight catches his eyes, making them gleam with an unhinged intensity. I step back instinctively. But then he spins and keeps walking.

"Why did you save me then?" I shout after him. "You hate me so much. Why not finish on a high after humiliating me and leave me with the Nightmares?"

He doesn't answer.

The longer we walk, the more my fever rages. Shivers rack my body despite every inch of me burning up. Embarrassing squeaks escape as I suffocate my urges. Sweat slicks my spine. Hot need pulses between my legs. Eventually, Emrys whirls around so fast it startles me.

"How did you do it?" he demands, voice raw. "How did you manipulate the Chimera to your will?"

"What. The. *Fuck* are you talking about, Emrys?"

"You made it look like me." The word *me* drips with disgust. "Like you actually desire me."

"I didn't *make* it do anything. You said so yourself. It takes the form of my most erotic fantasy."

"You only fantasized about me because I left you wanting."

I jab my finger in his face. "For the record, that was *not* okay."

"Turning your desire against you?"

"Manipulating me," I shout. "Humiliating me. Playing with my heart!"

He smiles bitterly. "I did warn you I liked its song."

"Fuck you," I choke out. "Just because someone hurt you once doesn't mean you have the excuse to pass that pain onto others."

I storm past him, leaving him in my dust. Another queen hurt him, but I refuse to be his punching bag. I have no idea where I'm going or where this tunnel leads, but I'm walking first.

He overtakes me, muttering about losing his mind.

As we stubbornly continue alongside each other, the tension between us ebbs and flows like a tide. At times, he slows his pace, allowing me to catch up. I almost think he's doing it to check on me. Other times, he speeds up, as if trying to outrun his thoughts.

"Mates," he scoffs after a while. "Another pretty lie to chain us."

His steps become less sure, his resolve wavering. He keeps throwing glances my way, each one lingering longer than the last. At one point, he stumbles, and I reach out to steady him. My fingers latch around his wrist—above the glove. Skin-to-skin contact. A jolt of electricity passes between us.

He jerks away as if burned, but not before I see the naked desire in his eyes—and the agony.

"Don't," he growls, but it sounds more like a plea than a command.

"Emrys—"

He backs away, shaking his head. "This isn't real. It can't be. You're in my head, influencing me like the others."

The pain in his voice is palpable, and I realize how deep his wounds go. This is trauma, like my fear of water. Something happened to him, and it won't be easy to heal. After Rory died, I had five years supported by a loving family. What did he have?

"I'm sorry," I mutter. "The pheromones are always more intense among mates, especially when I'm in heat."

For a long moment, he stares at me, conflicted. Then, with a sound that's half growl, half groan, he surges forward, pinning me against the moss-covered wall. The scent reminds me of Fox, and my heart breaks.

"Prove it," Emrys clips, his lips a breath away from mine. "Prove this isn't just another trick."

The challenge hangs between us, charged with tension and unknowns. I look into his eyes and see a man teetering on the edge, desperately wanting to believe, but terrified of being hurt again.

"I thought I was proving it," I whisper.

"You've proven nothing." He rolls to the side, revealing a door. We're at the end of the tunnel.

He leans back, appraising me down his nose, waiting for something. He is the picture of predatory nonchalance, a wolf in sheep's clothing. Fox joked about the gods making me specifically for them. I never believed it. But as I stand here, raging inside over Emrys's behavior and somehow still fighting my urge to rip his clothes off and lick him all over, I think Fox is right. What if we have no power in our fate?

"Where are we?" I ask. "Where does it lead?"

"The Clock Tower."

Whispers of conversation filter through the door, coaxing me closer. I press a tentative hand against the surface. A tornado of magic burns against my skin. I gasp and pull back, stung.

Curious, brave, or perhaps foolish, I press my ear to the door. The voices whizz by, but the harder I concentrate, the easier it is to identify individual sounds: Bodin's deep rumble, Legion's velvety confidence, Emrys's rasp, and more. The whirling magic steals them away again. Then I hear something that chills me to the bone.

Me. My voice when I'm younger.

I round on Emrys, and puzzle pieces start clicking into place. He never seems to have memory slips, even though he spends so much time at the palace. His seething hatred of me is because I'm yet another queen in a very long line of them. And back at the stables, when his hand dipped between my legs—unlike Bodin, he knew how to pleasure me. He knew so well that he sensed when I was close to climax and pulled away to hurt me most.

"You have your memories," I accuse him, looking at the door. "You found them in there."

His lips twist into a knowing smile.

Fury pumps my fever to new heights. I launch at him, slam my palms beside his head, and snarl, "How can you betray your brothers like this?"

His humor dies, replaced by something agonized. Sweat glistens on his skin, sparkling under the torchlight, but hungry desperation is on the verge of snapping in his gaze. His broad chest heaves. The black tattoos on his neck seem to writhe, to ripple in response to his inner struggle. When I glance down the length of his body, I see the evidence of his arousal bulging his breeches. I wish seeing him didn't affect me, but I am powerless against my attraction, my need—and this close, our breaths mingle. My mouth goes dry.

I can't tell if I want to kiss him or kill him. My hands slide down the dirty wall, and I step back.

"Through the tower is the only way out of here," he says, voice rough.

"Why haven't you shared this information with the rest of your hive?"

"Why do you think?"

I think about Legion's vow, their Seventh's death, and Bodin's overprotective tendencies and shame over those feathers. Fox truly believed I was to be their salvation, their freedom. According to him, they all thought that. Varen sacrificed his sanity for it.

"They wanted me from day one. But you didn't." I glance down. "Because you think I want to control you?"

His head leans back against the wall, and he fists himself through his pants. "This is what you do to me. All I have to do is breathe the same air as you, and this happens. It sickens me. You sicken me. You are not freedom. You're another cage."

"I'm sorry you think that."

His shoulders slump, and he lets go of himself. "You can either go in there, walk through all our darkest memories, risk insanity . . . or stay here and prove I'm right. But I'll still make you crawl to me. Beg for it."

"That's not really a choice, is it?"

"Now you're catching on." His long lashes flutter, and he sighs. "There's no point denying it. No one controls their fate. You can't go in there any more than I can resist you out here."

"You think I won't do it?" I spit back at him. "You think I don't have what it takes to go in there, witness who you all really are, and still love you afterward?"

A cruel laugh escapes him. "This is not about love. It's not about enduring the suffering. It's about the pain," he says, "and the fear. You think you know us, little moth. You think you want to be with us because the gods threw us together. You have no idea what we've done. You have no idea what we still want to do. But if you walk through that door, you'll see what it's like to be with us . . . and it won't be love," he says, his voice full of pity.

"We'd destroy you, pull you apart. It is in our nature. This is what we're made for."

We stand there, staring at each other. He's waiting for me to make the first move.

"Why don't you go in first?" I suggest. "Or is this all a lie?"

"I've already been in." He lifts his chin. "If I go twice, I might end up like Varen."

I gasp. The Clock Tower, the moving castle, Varen's insistence that the honeycombs are broken and need to be repaired . . . Emrys always telling Varen to shut up, ripping his scribblings from the walls.

"All this time," I growl out, "you knew this castle is linked to your bindings, to the seals stifling your powers. This is what Varen has been trying to tell us."

His eyes glitter, nostrils flaring.

"Styx found out, didn't he?" I say. "And that's how he ended up getting turned to stone. You didn't want him to tell everyone else, so you told Titania he knew." My mind races, eyes darting to and fro as information bombards me. "He was confused and forgetful when he came out of the stone. But he insisted he was set up. He must have remembered recently. He dropped me near you, hoping I'd learn your secrets."

That glitter turns into a wicked grin. "Don't look so surprised."

"But you haven't broken the seal on your powers, have you?" I challenge. "Otherwise, you'd have *flickered* us out of the stables."

He grinds his teeth, clenching his jaw.

His reaction tells me I'm right. Something different happened with Styx. Maybe it has something to do with being turned to stone. I have to tell the others. My hand grips the doorknob when something else occurs to me.

The Nightmares were rounded up so fast it surprised Legion. I glimpsed a Nightmare in the woods but then realized it was only Styx doing a perimeter sweep.

"Styx is at the end of your hive's chain of command." Disappointment leaks from my soul. "Legion said he was a bad leader once, so he's vowing to put his happiness last to prove you all can trust him. But you—you *know* Styx is afraid of you. He holds no power where all of you are concerned, and instead of making him feel safe, you used him to betray us. You're as bad as the queens who manipulated you."

I must hit a chord because he has no reply. Shaking my head, I turn the doorknob.

"I should warn you," Emrys says, "it will hurt less if you stay and fuck me."

"You think you're the only one who's made friends with pain?" I growl. He opens his mouth to speak, but I continue. "I've had to kill my friends. I've had to kill strangers. I've had to kill animals. A madman manipulated me. I've watched innocent people be murdered because of me. I raised an army of the dead. My magic was stripped and then used to curse me. I watched my aunt—a victim of cruelty—sacrifice herself for me. I watched the look in my parents' eyes change from love to pity to helplessness. I watched my only friend, my protector, jump before a Wellhound to save me and die. I watched the blood of my new friend cool because I was too late to save him from a cruel world I summoned." My throat closes up. Tears burn my eyes. My next words are a harsh whisper. "Since I started going into heat, I've been stifling my urges because I'm different. And that made me feel so alone. Not once have I let someone else touch me to ease the agony. Not once have I felt safe enough to explore these desires until you—and we were surrounded by Nightmares!"

"Willow—"

"I'm not done!" I am shouting now. Shaking and blind with tears and rage. "I watched Fox sacrifice himself, become stone, to *protect* me. Because you lied about this! Pain comes in all shapes and sizes, Emrys. Anything you want to throw at me, I can take."

I fling open the door and charge into the hurricane.

CHAPTER 56
BODIN

It has been two hours since Styx *flickered* Willow away, and I remain consumed with thoughts of her. I pace the tent, my muscles tense with the need to act. Every moment she is gone feels like a failure on my part. I should be there, protecting her . . . seeing to her needs. My eyelids flutter when I recall her scent, heady and intoxicating. I want to consume it, to soak in it. But I'm here, useless, waiting for word. The urge to take control, to do something, anything, is almost overwhelming.

"Stop pacing," Legion mutters, eyes roving over papers on his desk. "Sit down."

His tent is larger than mine, and he has a small table with chairs beside his bedroll. Grumbling, I sit quietly, although I'm still annoyed he refused to allow me to attend the trip to Heliodor with our Shadow. Still, I understand this rabble of exhibitors needed to be corralled.

"Ignarius is appeased?" Legion queries, looking over his brass spectacles at me.

"It didn't take much to convince him to cover for me," I reply. "After all, he breaks the Old Code himself with his Shadow."

We spend the next hour brainstorming ways to avoid continu-

ously slipping into this horrible state of false identity Titania gave us.

"There are no viable options," Legion says, "apart from begging our mother, the Morrigan, for assistance."

I bristle at the idea. "No. We can do this ourselves, as we always have." The words sound hollow even to my own ears. "Have we asked her for help before?"

He shakes his head. "We disowned her after the first deal she made with Oberon to contain our power."

I remember none of that. "My answer stands. We avoid the gods at all costs."

My fingers drum an impatient rhythm on the table. "Where is Styx? It has been hours."

Legion sighs, his dark eyes troubled. "Hopefully, seeing to Willow's comfort. But with him, anything is possible these days. I don't know what's going on inside his head. He reminds me a little of . . ." He pauses, then continues, his voice low and intense. "Bodin, I must tell you something. Perhaps you won't resist the memory flashes so much if you understand what you're trying to push away."

Our eyes lock. If I recall the bloody feathers when Willow is not here, I fall deeper into the false identity. The ugly pain attached to the memory feels unbearable without her by my side. Everything feels intolerable without her. How did I come to be in this position? She has destroyed me thoroughly and addictively.

My fingers resume tapping on the table. "You think this pet—this canary—is why I slip more frequently?"

He winces. "It can't hurt to test the theory."

A part of me recoils against finding out the truth. But if it avoids another situation where Willow is hurt, then I'll do it. "Tell me."

"There were once seven of us," he explains quietly, his steady eyes watching me for signs of . . . I don't know. Collapse? Breaking? "And that Seventh had golden feathers."

A cold stone sinks in my stomach. "Canary."

"Our nickname for him."

"Why do I always see blood on my hands?" I ask, the coppery scent suddenly vivid.

His lips flatten, almost like he doesn't want to relive the memory. It's as painful for him as for me.

"Did I kill him?" I ask, eyes wide.

"We all played a part," Legion admits, "but the act was by your hands."

"How?" I gape. "I thought we were immortal."

He cocks his head, studying me. "You are aware of our hive's chain of command."

I nod, but I don't like where this is heading.

"Death is possible," he continues, "if it is by the hand of a rank above. Canary was the Seventh."

You'll never escape your true nature.

"I killed someone I was meant to protect—worse, the weakest among us?" Self-loathing twists my features into something ugly. I can hardly get my words out. "Yet you allow me to be the . . ." I can't even say the word. It is a mockery.

"As I said, we all played a part." The haunted look in his eyes deepens, and I see the crushing weight of leadership. If I, the Second, killed the Seventh, then the only one who could have physically stopped me was the First.

And he didn't.

"This is the source of your vow," I state.

"In part." He runs a hand through his long hair but doesn't meet my eyes. "I am telling you this now, so you know it is not a burden solely on your shoulders, but on all six of us. When your memories return, you will understand. Until then, I ask that you trust me."

"Always," I reply on instinct.

But the words feel foreign. And I don't feel any better. The intensifying, squeezing, and dizzying sense of mortification only grows. "I should be dependable, lethal, loyal, and adaptable. I should blend into society's vital surface and never—"

"Reveal your true nature?" Legion finishes, eyebrow arched. "How many times have you told yourself that? Those aren't your words."

"Whose are they?"

He tells me his theory about the enchantment being an amalgamation of fears designed to separate us. I realize how much I've come to rely on his strategic mind—even when he also suffered under this affliction. Memories or not, we each bring something unique to our hive. I can't do everything alone. He trusts me to protect, even knowing our past. The thought both comforts and unnerves me.

But if he doesn't blame me for our Seventh's death . . . then perhaps I must trust him too.

"Titania wants us divided," Legion continues, "because then we cannot host the Wild Hunt. It cannot grow in power and size. She cannot control it. Not like Willow."

"So then we glue ourselves back together," I suggest.

"Agreed."

Something uneasy, along with the sickening feeling of failure, turns in my mind. "Titania and Willow are both tied to us, but only one can control the Wild Hunt. The other has all the power. What happens if they face each other in the flesh?"

Concerned eyes flick to mine. "They will feel the uncontrollable urge to obliterate each other until one is left standing."

"Then we must kill Titania."

Legion folds a letter, swiping his fingers along the crease. "I expect Puck will soon take that responsibility from our hands." His lips purse. "At least he'll try."

"And if she survives?"

His eyes meet mine. "Then I hope by that stage we have our hive back in one piece."

"Tell me one more thing about Canary, and then I will put it to rest."

A nod. "You will never put it to rest, but I pray you will learn to forgive yourself—as we have."

"Was it before we received—" I gesture to the glowing blue mark beneath my eye. The teardrop shape is fitting, considering it is the source of our sense of shame.

"Yes," Legion replies, swallowing hard. Something about the memory brings a sheen to his eyes that I rarely see.

Styx *flickers* into the room. We stand, our chairs scraping against the ground.

"Where have you been?" I growl. The scent of guilt rolls off him in waves.

"Is she back at the Keep?" Legion demands.

Styx doesn't seem to hear us. He paces the small space within the tent, hands running through his dark, unruly hair, and his eyes are wild.

"I don't know what to do," he mumbles.

A cold feeling of dread wraps around me. He hasn't answered the question.

"Where is Willow?" I repeat.

He stops, his eyes locking with mine. The chaos I see there makes my soul cringe. Flashes of bloody golden feathers hit behind my eyes, ratcheting up my panic. If I could kill my own brother . . . it's entirely possible Styx could kill his mate, right?

It's an incredible leap, but my current state of mind can take me nowhere else.

I don't voice my fears. There's no time. Styx starts muttering about Emrys, memories, and feeling bad that he left Willow in the snow. With every word, Legion's expression grows darker. Styx says he returned but found Emrys trapped in a tunnel after escaping with Willow from a stable full of Nightmares Puck ordered collected.

The tent walls close in on me.

Styx and Emrys have betrayed us? They're working behind our backs, colluding with the enemy? Styx put Willow in danger —abandoned her?

A war rages inside me. Part of me wants to lash out, to punish him for leaving her alone. But another part recognizes that I can't control everything. And what if this rage cost our Canary his life?

It's a bitter pill to swallow.

"What tunnel?" Legion demands, voice tight.

"Beneath the Keep," Styx confesses, his eyes downcast. "Outside the Clock Tower. Or rather, she *was* there—"

I grab him by the collar, ready to choke him. "What are you talking about? The Clock Tower?"

"It's filled with our memories," he explains. "It's where Titania's . . ."

"Spit it out before I break your neck."

His blue eyes flit with sadness. He shakes me off and replies, "The Clock Tower holds our memories."

Shadows flicker in the tent—Legion's fragile grip on his control slips, but it's me who feels like my world is collapsing. Am I the only one, apart from Varen, who doesn't have his memories?

"How long have you known?" I growl.

"Since before the Baleful Gaze hit me."

"And your full Sluagh powers?"

"They came when I started turning to stone." He rubs his forehead. "Emrys already knew about the tower. He didn't want anyone else to find out because . . . because he was trying to make a deal. But I found out, got my memories, and he . . . it took me a while to remember who betrayed me, and when I did, Emrys— he threatened me. Everything is mixed up."

"Deal with who?" I shake him. "Puck?"

"Where is Willow?" Legion interrupts, eyes wide.

"Emrys dared her to enter the tower or to stay with him, knowing they wouldn't be able to resist her heat." Styx's eyes widen with disbelief. "She went inside, knowing that if she stayed . . ."

"Emrys would never trust her again," Legion finishes.

"Take us, Styx," I demand. "Take us to Emrys."

Everything around us flickers. We travel through darkness and arrive inside a torch-lit tunnel. Emrys sits on the ground, head against the wall, staring at the Clock Tower door. The air is thick with the scent of fear, guilt, and something else . . . desire.

As I take in the scene, my fists clench at my sides. The burden of our tragic past—the betrayals, the pain—comes crashing down on me, and I have no defenses without my memory. But one thought rises above all others: Willow is in there, facing our darkest moments alone.

If only a glimpse of a memory can undo me, what will they all do to her?

I don't pound my fist into Emrys's face like I want to. Maybe once, I would have. I don't know. But right now, I cling to what I know to be real. I am still the protector, and Willow is ours. My role, my duty, pulses through my veins like a second heartbeat. I point to the door, my voice low and controlled despite the storm raging inside me. "That's the entrance?"

Emrys nods, his eyes haunted and hollow.

"If I go in there, will I regain my memories?" I press, the urgency in my tone barely concealed.

He gives another nod. "There's a possibility of getting lost in there—of never coming out. And you can only go through it once. Otherwise, you could end up like Varen . . . at least until all of us have our memories returned to their rightful owner."

"How long have you known, Emrys?" Legion demands, his voice as sharp as a blade.

I don't wait for his response. I grab the doorknob and yank, the hinges groaning in protest. I hesitate, but only to brace myself because once I enter this whirlwind, I will relive the moment I killed my brother.

Everything in my past has led me closer to Willow. If I erase it, then she disappears too.

Air rushes out of the Clock Tower, carrying a faint trace of her feminine scent, ozone, and something deeper, more primeval—the essence of our shared past. I hear whispers, echoes of voices both familiar and strange, calling out from within. Magic pulses inside, a living thing eager to invite me in.

I cast one last look at my brothers—Legion's face set in grim determination, Styx's eyes wide with regret, and Emrys . . . he looks broken. Varen is lost. Fox is stone. I am on the brink of losing control. Willow recklessly entered the tower.

Because she cares. Because she is our skin, our glue.

Maybe the slaver queen was right. Maybe darkness cannot understand sunshine. But one cannot exist without the other, and together, they create something beautiful.

"I'll find her," I promise.

With that, I step into the swirling vortex of memories and magic. As the door closes behind me, cutting my brothers from sight, I allow my thoughts only one focus: Find Willow. Protect her. Bring her home.

BODIN

From the outside, the Clock Tower appears as a circular building made of stone, a few yards wide. But the moment I step inside, I enter a new, endless realm. Its landscape is an expanse of sunshine and rolling hills, birds tweeting in the distance. For a moment, I think I've made a mistake. I've stepped through a portal and ended up elsewhere. But then I hear voices further down by a river—arguments. The sky darkens—thunder rolls. I'm swept down into a memory, a boy in my past.

But I was never a boy. I don't think.

The younger version of myself is carefree and unburdened. He sits by a crystal-clear stream, carefully cradling something in his hands. As I approach, I realize it's a small bird with golden feathers.

The young Bodin looks up at me, his eyes bright with an innocence I've never had.

"Isn't he beautiful?" he asks, gently stroking the bird's feathers.

I want to warn him, to tell him to cherish this moment because it won't last. The mortal bird will eventually die. But

before I speak, the sky grows gloomy. The acrid smell of brimstone replaces the sweet scent of flowers. The stream runs red with blood.

The boy is not me, but an innocent child. He is mortal, dead beneath my obsessions and hunger. He is a tasty meal, yet my curiosity is not sated. I am a monster. Shame and despair clamp around my mind, urging me to turn back. Escape now while I can —sink back into the oblivion of false memories. These are not worth the pain they bring.

Oberon appears, towering over us, his eyes glittering with malice. He is the definition of darkness, one of the Folk—magical beings born after us, the first seven sons of Morrigan. He is an imposing male with harsh, angular features that seem carved from stone. He did not have the freedom to destroy and conquer as he desired, so he used us.

"Obliterate everything that dares defy me," he commands, his voice booming across the now-barren landscape.

I am hunting, chasing, devouring. This is the first glimpse of myself I am not repulsed by. This energy, this feeling of capturing and taking—this, I love. It settles in my bones like a sigh. Then it brings something darker and hotter to life, as I recall Willow testing my patience when we sparred. How I flipped her onto her back, clamped my teeth on her neck, and held her down like prey. The thrill in my blood, the excitement unfolding. I warned her not to squirm, but she did anyway. She welcomed this part of me, and my hunger multiplied.

This memory does not exist within this hurricane, but in my heart. With her.

Just as I am sinking into rightness, the scene shifts again.

I am hit with memory after memory, pelted like arrows. They wound me all at once, dragging me further into darkness from the small place of joy.

The Canary is no longer a small bird but our brother in his Sluagh form. Long ago, we were more avian than man, but we have changed. We swallowed the darkness, yet the Canary retained his brightly colored feathers. He was unique like that. Stubborn, challenging, curious, refreshing, a spark.

He and I watch milling mortals from a city rooftop many years in the past.

"Do you know," he asks, lips curving, "what it means to play games?"

"Idle distractions," I grumble.

"Are they?" He gestures at the mortals moving a ball with their feet. Back and forth. Back and forth. It's elementary. They cheer and celebrate when the ball goes in a particular direction. Boo and hiss when it goes in another. Canary cocks his head. "I think games are where their hearts receive flavor. Perhaps we should start thinking of our hunts like games. We could compete and cheer each other on." He grins. "Boo and hiss when you miss your target."

"I never miss," I scoff. Then consider his suggestion. "Competition will divide our hive."

"Perhaps." He crouches, intent on the milling mortals below. "But, oh, what if it's fun?"

"Fun?" I frown at the foreign word.

"Something that feels good, even an idle distraction." Canary turns to me, black eyes glittering. "I hear them use the word all the time." He inhales. "Fun."

The scene shifts. Now, I am in Queen Maebh's opulent throne room in Elphyne.

She moves among my hive, her voice a poisonous whisper. "Legion is the First," she murmurs, her lips curving into a cruel smile. "Do you think he won't come for you all, one by one? He has the power. He has the right. You're nothing but toys to him."

Doubt flickers in each of my brothers' eyes. It creeps into my heart.

Canary begins to pace. His golden feathers are ruffled, his eyes wild with paranoia. "He's going to kill us," he mutters over and over. "Legion will absorb us all. We're not safe. We're never safe so long as we are linked like this."

I watch as my past self struggles with the decision, torn between protecting the hive and saving our brother. But Maebh's whispers are too strong, the fear too deep. My past self finds our Canary pacing the length of a hallway, hands ripping out golden hair as he mutters repetitively, "He will come for me first. They all will."

"You are a distraction," my past self whispers to him, fingers reaching for his throat.

"No!" I bellow, trying to stop the scene from unfolding. But this has already happened.

And now I am no longer watching it but living it, feeling it as it sinks into my bones.

"I'm protecting us," I hear myself say as my hands close around Canary's throat. "I'm protecting the hive."

My brothers are bystanders. Their watchful silence is permission, an accessory.

There is a fight. A struggle. A will to live. But I am the Second. Golden feathers float in the air, stained with blood. As the light in Canary's eyes fades, I feel the hive fracture under the influx of his soul filling us with power. But we do not feel good. That is not *fun*.

This is a cruel mistake. The trust we have shatters, replaced by suspicion and guilt.

I stumble away from the memory, my heart pounding and bile rising in my throat. What we've done—what *I've* done—threatens to annihilate me.

I catch a familiar musky floral scent through the haze. Willow.

It's faint but unmistakable—hope. She is a glimmer in the distance, dimming by the second under the weight of our darkness. She came here, knowing what she walked into. Varen's voice surrounds me, hardening me and giving me armor.

Catch our falling star, give her your heart, and she will guide us home.

I push forward, driven by a need to find her, to protect her from the horrors of our history, and maybe, just maybe, find redemption in her love. But the more I am pelted with memories from the past, the more I am torn between rage and regret.

Suddenly, I'm there again. The Morrigan's primeval domain, eons ago. The acrid smell of brimstone and rancid ink fills my nostrils. Oppressive heat pushes at my skin. I watch, helpless, as our younger selves are forced to devour the souls her sister Danu births, each one burning like acid down our throat until we find the one that tastes like something else—the one set apart, an innocent mortal with heartache. We do anything we can to enhance that ache, so the sweet flavor is strong enough to coat our tongue. It is the closest we come to understanding the other side of our coin.

Screams echo in my ears, a storm of agony I once found so sweet. Now, it turns my stomach.

I continue to hurtle from one hideous memory to the next, watching myself commit unspeakable acts. In one, I'm tearing a village apart, reveling in chaos and destruction. In another, I'm standing over a battlefield, drinking in the despair of the dying, licking their blood from my fangs. The hurricane of time threatens to suck me under, to keep me lost in the world I once lived.

That was before Willow.

Another whiff of her scent. *Mine. Ours.* I latch onto the only part of me I know she is unafraid of. I hunt.

Her taste. Think about her taste.

But I am thrown into another memory, this one more visceral than any other.

WITHIN THE SAFETY of my bedroom, I watch through our shared hive mind as Fox pokes at a mess on the kitchen counter with his black-stained talon. It's his third attempt at cooking People Food, which resembles a disemboweled muskox's intestines.

Styx's voice drips with disdain. "I don't think it's supposed to look like that."

Fox's determination pulses through our link. "I must begin again."

Emrys's voice rasps into our collective consciousness. "*Let it go.*"

But Fox can't. "We want to please our fated queen."

Emrys's disquiet ripples through our shared space. Despite his disparaging attitude, he can't overcome the curiosity we all harbor for our one true queen.

We share fantasies—longings. Only his are buried deeper.

She'll be the first to belong to all of us in a way we've only experienced second hand. And then there was that one time Fox lived the experience himself . . . the whore who tasted like the beginning of addiction. But she tasted wrong. Not ours. Not deserving of the magic his tongue wrought between her thighs. That gift alone will belong to our true queen. On this, we all agree. We are hers, and she is ours.

I join Fox and Styx in the old kitchen.

"How will we know it is any good?" I ask, approaching Fox at the counter.

"Simple," he replies, swiping his finger through the pulpy mess. He sucks it into his mouth. I watch as he tastes. I know it's not the same as between a female's thighs. That was nectar—I am told. This is blood no longer warmed by a beating heart. This is . . . dirt.

Emrys's cruel laughter echoes through the house. Fox's tail lashes irritably, and I'm reminded that we are not people. Our queen is people.

"Look here," Styx points to the book Fox pilfered from the Order library. "This reads you must tenderize the meat first."

"Huh." Fox sweeps the pulpy mess from the counter into a trash can. It slops against his other failed attempts—time to start again.

As he strides to another room, I flip through the book, searching for more information. It all seems tedious. Elementary. He looks at me when he returns with a fresh slab of meat. "What is tenderize?"

I find the answer. "You must hammer the flesh with a mallet, a spiky corrugated tool."

Styx grins as he forms a fist and punches the flesh with his spiked knuckles. When he's done, the meat fibers are well and truly separated. Fox gingerly lifts the slab, but it falls apart into wet, sloppy chunks.

"Perhaps our queen will sup on souls like us," he suggests hopefully.

"*Meat,*" Varen dryly corrects through our hive mind. "*She will eat People Food. But most importantly, meat.*"

A wicked glint sparks in Styx's eyes. He grasps the appendage between his legs. "Perhaps she prefers this flavor."

"That is not the sort of meat she ingests," I growl, though the idea of putting my cock in her mouth stirs an unfamiliar heat in my core. Perhaps that is because it will be *fun*—it will feel good— a game.

Fox lifts the slop and releases a long-suffering exhale. "We are doomed."

"No," Legion replies with melancholy from the living room. "Our Seventh was doomed. With our queen, we are saved."

NOT ALL OF my memories are painful. It seems impossible, ridiculous, and irrational to believe a single soul can affect me so completely. But Willow has infected us with her light. I refuse to return to darkness.

I use all she is and means to hunt and chase her down. She is here in the hurricane somewhere.

I think of her mischievous smile, the little sounds she makes when asleep, and her feminine grunts when she trains with me—she refuses to concede. She is stubborn, willful, and refreshing. Loyal.

The golden twinkle in her eyes, the way she enjoys watching me squirm as I do her. I recall the little collection of strange items in her room. Each means something special to her. I found one of my hair beads there.

I see her holding Varen's ear to her chest. See her protecting the wildling from my ire. See her eyes flashing when we threatened to send her friends away.

"Come on. Let's dance. It could be fun!"

Her voice is my lifeline.

I think about her scent, her intoxicating scent. How it makes my body ache for her, even when she's not in heat. I see her eyes heavy with reciprocated lust as she looks up at me, those lips wrapped around my cock and taking me deep into her throat. Pushing. Testing my limits. Desire is the heat of life, the opposite of cold and chaos and the oblivion we wished for.

I chase the fading star until I land in a memory, standing behind our silver-haired hope as she watches the last of my shame unfold.

Maebh's voice is silk and poison as she speaks to us, kneeling at her feet.

Six, no longer seven.

"Oh, my dear, sweet monsters. Don't look so perplexed." Her hand cups my past self's face, and her eyes fill with pity, making my skin crawl. "You are Sluagh—harvesters of heartbreak. You are drawn to suffering because you do not understand it. Did you ever ask yourselves why? Why do the mortals feel so much pain when the wound seems so small?"

I see the confusion in my old self's eyes. We didn't understand then. We couldn't.

"It is because love is not something you see," Maebh continues, her words weaving a spell around us. "It is something you feel. Love is not something you consume. It's something you earn. If you were to suddenly understand that pain, well, then cruelty would not be so delicious. You would starve, would you not? And so, my dear unfortunate souls, you are destined to hurt those closest to you for eternity." She pauses. "The day you stop is the day you cease to exist."

Golden feathers float in the air, stained with blood.

Willow spins to face me. Disgust glimmers in her water-logged, red-rimmed eyes. She hates us. She abhors us. A calamity against my heart. How will we ever . . .

"Bodin?" She reaches for me, her bottom lip trembling. She runs into my arms, almost bowling me over with the force of her hug. "You came for me. Even though you had to relive this tragedy." She glares at the memory—her disgust aimed at Maebh, not me—as my shameful past fades and swirls into a bright, sunlit meadow. "How did you find me?"

"With this." I place her palm on my chest, where my heart beats hard—where it sings to be in her presence again. The wind changes, and her intoxicating scent hits me anew. Our bodies are pressed together. Need and desire violently surge within me. I want to kiss, taste, and know she's real. *Ours.* She gives me a mischievous grin, then squeezes my aching erection with her hand. "You sure it wasn't with this?"

A laugh erupts from deep in my belly. I've never felt this much . . . joy. At something so . . . It was a joke. Fun. This is what Canary wanted. For us to live.

I recall all the other hotter ways to live. Most of them revolve around her taste, her body—my hunger to swallow her star whole.

"We need to get out of here," I growl, then take her hand and search around the meadow.

She points. "There." In the distance, we see a door. "I can sense the magic."

Together, we run. Time moves differently. It colors the grass beneath our feet, raises the sun over our heads, and shifts the sky from dusk to day.

We push through the door and stumble into the stairwell inside the Keep—the padlock clatters to the ground. I close the door behind us and crouch to pick it up. Memories sink into my soul and settle, finding a home. I piece together the past and the present. Rage simmers in my blood.

"Emrys knew," I grind out. "He fucking knew."

She makes a little sound—that breathy one caught between a grunt and a whimper. I glance up, and she's wincing, doubled over with sweat dappling on her upper lip. Pheromones leak from her pores, a heady aphrodisiac.

I feel unleashed and hungry. Complete, even without full access to my powers.

She must see the change in my expression. She backs up the steps to the hallway, but I launch at her, taking us both down. My face buries into her, seeking around her stomach for the source of that delicious scent sparking such passion within me. She gasps and tries to slow me.

"Bodin!" she cries as my nose digs under her shirt. Sweet, sweet, smooth flesh. I lick her stomach. Good. This is good.

"You need relief," I groan against her flesh and head south to where the nectar smells strongest. "I am here, my Calamity. Tell me what you need."

My nose roams over the crotch of her pants and finds the damp center. I bite her mound. She moans but then tries to shove me off. "Stop."

"Why?" I nuzzle her sweetness. Lick over the fabric. Can almost taste it.

"I don't want to manipulate you into—"

"Manipulate me?" I growl, eyes flashing as I stare up the length of her body. "I have fantasized about you since before you were born. All we want is to please you." My voice deepens. "To pleasure you."

Her lips part. A blush hits her pale cheeks.

Fucking Emrys. His insecurities have hurt her. I ease off her body and step down the stairs until she is above me, where I hope she feels safe.

"Your suffering ends now," I declare. "You will never have to explain yourself, fight for yourself, or save yourself again. You are our queen, Willow."

She smirks. "I think you mispronounced that word."

"Mate," I correct, proving I remember everything, including our time here in Avorlorna. "And mates provide for their mates, especially when they are in need."

"Do you mean you or me?"

"Both." I put one foot on the step above, testing her reaction.

She gives me a reproachable look. "I said no."

"Did you?" My lips curve when I see her eyes sparkle. "Is that what you really want?"

She backs up, nodding, biting her lip to stop her grin.

"I'm going to run," she teases.

"And what if I warn you not to?" I lick my lips, my mouth already watering. "What if I chase you?"

"Then you'd better catch me."

Our eyes lock. My heart swells. Then she turns on her heels and runs.

CHAPTER 58
WILLOW

I'm running full pelt down the hallway, adrenaline pumping. Logical thought has abandoned me. I must be crazy. I grin to myself and dare peek over my shoulder, then stumble when I meet Bodin's dark, hungry eyes.

Inches behind me.

I squeak and surge forward, but he's on me in a heartbeat, spinning me to face him and pressing me against the wall. The cool stone at my back is a shock against my feverish skin. Hungry lips claim mine in a punishing, greedy kiss. It's a balm to my suffering. Bodin echoes the animal in me. He knows what I need because he needs it too. The floodgates open on my biology. Lust ignites in my veins. Suddenly, I'm so ready for him, so wet and aching to be filled that I can wait no longer. The empty, hot part of me has waited so, so long.

"Get this shit off," I snarl, ripping at his clothes. I yank anything in my way until I find smooth, muscular brown skin. His taut lower abdomen is mine to explore. He groans into my mouth, the sound vibrating through me. He captures my hands, slamming them against the wall above my head, and grunts,

"No." Pain flashes over his features. "Don't you dare put my pleasure before yours again."

"I just want you inside me," I moan.

"First," he promises darkly, "you feel good."

I whimper, arching into him, craving more. We kiss. He takes. Then, driven by some primal instinct, I shove him off me and renew my escape. I want him to pin me like he did that time we trained. I want him to take me, to claim me the way wolves do. It feels natural—what I've suppressed. Doors fly past me in a blur. Walls. Paintings hanging on hooks.

The scent of leather and spice fills my nostrils.

He catches me again, growling with satisfaction. He tosses me through a doorway, like a rag doll. I stumble, grinning, feeling more alive than ever.

A glance tells me I'm in his private chambers. Somehow, I knew exactly where to go—or maybe he herded me here. Seeing his vast bed sends a fresh wave of fever coursing through my body. But from the look in Bodin's dark and wild eyes, I'm unsure we'll make it that far.

The air between us is thick with the scent of our shared arousal. My skin feels too tight, every nerve ending alive and singing for his touch. Shirtless, Bodin stalks toward me. His movements are fluid and predatory. This is it—the moment everything changes. And despite the small voice in the back of my mind warning me about consequences, all I can think is: finally.

This acceptance is what I've been chasing since Fox left, what he'll bring when he returns.

We don't make it to the bed. Bodin is atop me, flattening me with his heavy body, biting me and nipping me as he tears clothes from my limbs. I think we're on a rug. I'm unsure, but it's rough against my spine when I twist. Each little spark of our touch builds to something bigger. And then he's ripping my pants with his bare hands, burying his face between my naked thighs.

His first lick glides up my seam from bottom to top. I'll never forget the groan he makes. Never. It sounds the way I feel. Overcome. Feral. Hungry yet satisfied at once. His inhale against my sensitive flesh makes me tingle. He holds my scent in his lungs, savoring it, then pauses as if he needs to restrain himself. When he lifts his head, smoky eyes clash with mine.

"If you think to keep me away when you're needy . . ." A snarl. A plea. Then he drops, and he's eating me out with a frenzied, expert mouth. Pleasure barrels through me, stealing my logic.

"I wouldn't dream of it," I breathe, moan.

My first orgasm is wrenched from somewhere deep in my soul. The sound I make is animal. The fever heat amplifies the ecstasy, combusting every last nerve ending I own. I barely have the sense to push his head back from my pussy when he snarls and chases for more. I try to crawl backward. It's too much. Wicked eyes meet mine as he pins my hips with large, capable hands.

"You're not going anywhere, Calamity." He ensures I understand, shoves off me, and stands, looming as he unbuttons his leather breeches and shoves them down. I watch, slightly unhinged and with desire building again, as his hard slabs of muscle tense and twitch with restraint. Every inch of him is defined and luminous with his lust. It's sweat, I realize. It glitters over him like stardust. He fists his long, thick erection and strokes.

"You're not going anywhere," he repeats, a slow smile splitting his handsome face. "Except to my bed."

"As if you can stop me," I tease.

He lifts me off the floor, throws me onto his bed, and flips me onto my stomach. He raises my hips and notches the blunt head of his cock to my swollen pussy. It's odd. He's about to fuck me hard, dominate me. I should feel afraid, submissive, or like prey. This only feels safe. Thrilling.

But he hasn't entered me yet. First, he crowds my smaller

body with his. A trembling, tentative touch at my neck as he brushes aside my hair. The press of his teeth is delicate at first. Hesitating or questioning?

"Do it," I moan, panting and breathless with anticipation. "Mark me hard, Bodin."

He clamps down, spearing sharp needles into me. I cry out, squirm, need.

"Don't squirm," he growls against my flesh and glides his shaft along my wet seam, teasing me. But it makes me writhe and need more. Another growl, another warning not to squirm. I can't help it. One little wiggle, and he loses himself. He thrusts in hard, filling me so deep, stretching me so deliciously that I release a hoarse cry and claw at the blankets. Every instinct in me sighs at the same time it seizes. This is what I need. This is what I've been fighting all these years. Waiting.

I'm only sad Fox missed this first too. The thought of him being here, taking turns . . . I groan and push back.

"I—*fuck*." Bodin rolls his hips, savoring the feel of me. "Told you." Fingers flex on my hips. "Not to squirm."

"You did," I pant. Wiggle some more. Tease. Grin when his breath hitches.

He fists my hair and rips my head back to kiss me.

"Your cunt takes me so good," he rasps deeply, breathing against my lips. "But I like your mouth more. I'm fucking that next."

He breaks away and snarls as he renews his efforts, pounding into me from behind. I am a hot, sweaty, prickling ball of plea-sure, fire, and contentment. I am his to do with what he will. And it feels so good. So right. I moan into the sheets. Maybe I wiggle some more, but he pulls out and slams in so hard that I climax with a sharp, sudden electrical burst—wave after wave of bliss shoots through me.

"Fuck, you're gripping me," he gasps at my back. "So tight. So—"

He seats himself, utters obscenities as he comes, and then stays there fitted to me from behind. I can't see him but hear him trying to catch his ragged breaths. Then he pulls out. Pins me there. I feel his release leaking down my thigh.

"This belongs inside you here," he mutters, sliding it back into my pussy. He swipes more cum and brings his fingers to my mouth. "Or in here." I moan at his taste, remembering the last time he spilled into me there.

He pulls back and pauses. I feel the heat of his gaze on my behind as he uses his thumbs to spread my cheeks. I almost giggle, vulnerable, awkward. But then his fingers slide up my thigh, catching more dripping release and guiding it to my back entrance. "Or here," he adds gruffly, almost to himself, rimming my tight hole.

My body reacts eagerly, hot and prickly at the new pleasure. On instinct, I push back. His fingertip slips past the first ring of muscle, and I moan. The sensation is different but good. It's another empty place eager to be filled. Especially now that I remember Styx's promise to me.

Biting my lip, I brace for another feverish contraction of need. When it comes, I groan. Bodin keeps his finger there, spits to add more lubricant, slides his other hand around my front, and works my clit until I climax again, clenching around him in a gasping, pleading mess. He curses, utters something inaudible, then nips my butt cheek and falls onto the bed beside me.

I didn't realize I'd collapsed long ago. Facing each other, I have nowhere to look but the snare of his deep-brown, long-lashed, and wholly sated eyes. He leans in to whisper hotly against my lips, "You have destroyed me."

"Better not have," I pant, another wave of need building. The helpless look I give him falls upon hooded eyes.

"Again?"

I nod. "This can last days."

He growls with triumph, almost to himself. "I'm not done either."

I find his cock already getting hard. I stroke him, making little pleading noises to hurry the fuck up.

"You need to be filled, don't you, Calamity." It's a statement, but I nod all the same. "Next time you go through this, there will be more than one of us, understood?"

I nod again, breathless with desire as he positions himself behind me.

"Good," he grunts, cock slipping into my channel. He hooks his finger into my mouth and turns my face so he can kiss me, hot and rough. "Because your pleasure comes first, but I want to feel your throat around my cock again. So we'll need help."

Part
Three

CHAPTER 59
WILLOW

Predawn light filters through arched windows in Bodin's room. The sun's not up yet, but soon. One or two turns of the hourglass, perhaps. My body still hums with residual heat—its needs woke me. Beside me, Bodin's bare chest rises and falls in shallow breaths, his smooth, muscular body twisted in rumpled silk sheets.

I prop myself up on an elbow and take in the room. Dark, polished wood panels line the walls, inlaid with intricate filigree that seems to writhe in the dim light. Weapons of various designs hang on the walls—swords, daggers, and things I can't name— their blades gleaming with a sinister beauty. A whetstone rests on a nearby table, its surface worn smooth from countless blades honed.

The air is thick with the mingled scents of leather, spice, and sex. Our torn clothes lie scattered across the floor. The massive bed has four posters. I never noticed that last night. Its dark wooden frame is carved with arcane symbols. Torn silk hangings drape limply from the canopy, bearing the brunt of our lovemaking. I remember clutching them at some point.

As I turn, another wave of heat ripples through me, igniting a fresh surge of desire. I bite my lip, suppressing a groan. "Well—dammit," I whisper, "how long will this last?"

I give Bodin a needy look, my gaze tracing the sharp lines of his face, softened in sleep. I resist the urge to run my fingers through his braids. The sight of this brutal warrior, vulnerable and at peace, stirs something profound within me. Shaking my head, I roll away, but his arm snakes around my waist, tugging me back. I feel his muscles contract and flex as he fits his body flush to mine.

"Where do you think you're going?" he grumbles, breath hot against my ear.

"I should clean up," I manage to say, my voice breathy. "We can't stay in bed forever."

"Why not?" Bodin licks my new mating mark, and I shiver. His hand glides down my stomach. "You're still burning up. Let me take care of your needs."

"I'm fine." A wiggle of anticipation. A groan.

His fingers curl between my legs and swipe through my slick folds.

"Fucking liar." He nips my ear and I shiver. "So wet for me."

The head of his cock is pushing between my thighs, nudging closer to my entrance. He raises my leg to accommodate a quick thrust. I gasp at the sudden fullness. Groan as he pulls out and drives back in. Pleasure scores my insides. Each punishing thrust hits me hard, deep. He locks me in against him with one arm, fondling my breast, while the other braces my thigh, lifting it higher.

"Touch yourself," he growls. "My hands are occupied."

I let go of embarrassment over my insatiable desire sometime last night. He doesn't care how badly I need this. Watching me touch myself makes him harder. I slide my fingers down, groan when I connect with my clit. He watches over my shoulder, fucks me harder. When his teeth clamp down on my neck, adding to the sense of being owned, my orgasm hits. Hard. I lose all sense of time, my body, my life—except where he connects with me, grinding against me, filling me with his release.

We lie there wasted—gathering our breaths and feeling so good.

"What a fun way to wake up," I mutter, smiling at the delicious ache.

"Get used to it," he replies, lips against my upper spine. "I am devoting myself to exploring this . . . fun with you."

His words bring a flurry of memories from last night. His brother, the Seventh. His shame. His heartache. Theirs. I roll to face him and find raw anguish on his face. I cup his jaw, and he leans into my touch.

"I'm so sorry," I murmur, rubbing my thumb over his Guardian teardrop. "That was so cruel of Maebh to do."

His brows meet in the middle, but he doesn't speak. He is tense and still.

"Are you okay, Bodin?"

I don't think he's even breathing. He won't open his eyes. Maybe he can't with me staring at his face. I duck my head beneath his jaw and kiss his neck.

"It's okay if you're not," I whisper. "I'll hold you until you are." And then, because I haven't said it, I add, "I love you."

His harsh exhale tickles my hair. Strong arms wrap around my shoulders and squeeze. I hear his sharp inhale a few times, as if he's trying to say something.

"You don't have to say it back." I pat his abs. "I just want you to know how I feel."

"It's not that I can't say it. Love is not the right word for us. Love is . . . a single muscle pumping in the body, tiny and insignificant at its core."

I snort. "Thanks for shitting on my—"

He growls and rolls on top of me, cupping my face with his large hands so I look directly into his wild, dark, and expressive eyes. "We spent eons trying to understand love. We ripped bodies apart, flayed them to pieces, devoured hearts, and were so disappointed. This was the apparent home of love—yet it was . . . nothing. I would keep trophies of those parts, pieces of my obsessions, and hang them in my room to remind myself that love does not exist." A sharp, incredulous laugh huffs out of him. "And it doesn't. Not amongst the pieces, but . . ." His gaze hardens on me. "It comes *to* the pieces. From the *feeling* of being surrounded, contained, safe, accepted, and wanted. It comes from the thing stopping those pieces from falling apart. You are our *skin*, Willow. And if we ever lose you, we—"

I press my lips to his, stopping his train of words. I don't want to talk about maybes. I don't want to talk about loss. Not now. He tenses at first, but then melts into me. Our kiss is tender, sweet, and all those things he explained. In his weird Sluagh way.

A throat clears, and we both freeze. I turn to find Legion standing in the doorway, his imposing figure silhouetted against the dim hall light. I scramble out from under Bodin and find a sheet to cover my naked body. It's not fair he sees this when he can't partake. His vow means so much more now that I know why he made it. His dark eyes flick between us, a fleeting look of longing, and then his usual mask of stoic control.

"I hate to interrupt," he says, sliding his hands into his pants pockets. "We have a situation."

"What's happened?" Bodin sits up, tensing.

Legion steps further into the room, the shadows seeming to cling to him. "Puck has triggered the countdown to the trials. Willow will forfeit her place if she doesn't arrive at the arena before sunrise."

The words hit me like a bucket of water, temporarily dousing the heat. Bodin leaps from the bed, his naked form rippling with barely contained energy as he strides toward Legion. *Well-damn,* his butt is fine. Two perfect, muscular globes of—I need to nibble.

No. I blink, shaking off my train of thought. It's time to focus.

Not fuck-us.

Focus, Willow. *Focus.* This is serious. I fan my face.

"This ends now." Bodin's growl takes on an inhuman quality that sends shivers down my spine. "We take out Puck."

Legion holds up a hand, his expression grim. "It's not that simple. The signal's been sent. All of Avorlorna knows. The fort stadium is filling, and the magical timeline has been triggered. You know as well as I do once it starts, it can't be stopped until the final trial is complete—or time runs out."

Bodin begins to pace, his movements fluid and predatory. The floorboards creak ominously beneath his feet, and the weapons tremble on the walls. He shoots rapid-fire alternatives, each cut down by Legion's calm logic.

As they argue, my mind races. The trials. Emrys. My friends. Fox. The heat still simmers beneath my skin, demanding attention. It's all too much, yet I know I must face it head-on.

I take a deep breath, steeling myself.

"Geraldine and Max?" I ask, my voice more assertive than I feel. "The final leg of the pilgrimage went okay?"

"Well enough." Legion's eyes soften almost imperceptibly on me. "Cricket is rousing them. They will eat and prepare in their quarters. Prepare and meet us in the upper-level dining room. We will have sustenance ready for you. A little over one turn of the hourglass remains before you present yourself at the fort."

I nod, throwing off the sheet the moment he leaves.

I wash and dress quickly, but my skin burns with residual heat. My thoughts keep derailing to places they shouldn't go. Bodin paces the room like a caged beast, his muscular form taut with tension. He rattles off information he thinks will aid me in the trials, his deep voice a constant rumble in the background.

"Remember, the first trial is always about facing your fears.

Don't let their illusions trick you," he says, then abruptly stops, growling. "I'm going to tear Emrys apart for this." His eyes flash dangerously before he resumes his lecture.

After securing my belt and fitting my sword, I flick my silver hair out of the way and stop his ramblings with another kiss. The tactic seems to work quite well.

"I won't retain this information," I murmur against his mouth. "There's no point wearing yourself out. If I don't know by now, I don't know."

He pulls back, his brow furrowed. "You're underprepared."

"So is everyone else."

Bodin grips my hips hard enough to hurt. "You could forfeit. You could withdraw from the trials."

"Is Peggy even officially out yet?" I meet his gaze. "We could also win, right? And then I can bring Fox back earlier than planned. We can all be together."

As long as we remain alive.

Having clothes on now is stifling, trapping my heat. But at least I don't feel so unsatisfied. I fan my face to cool down. His nostrils flare, picking up my scent.

"Fox wouldn't want you to go in like this," he grumbles.

"I can't not turn up because I smell like a sex meal. There will be consequences, surely."

His flash of annoyance means I'm right. He doesn't elaborate; he just moves on to the next idea. "Cait could still find the mirror."

"Do we want to take that risk?"

Then he hits me in the heart. "What about your parents? You said you wanted to talk to them. We can activate your portal stone and go."

"You bastard." I take a deep, shuddering breath. "I can't—not before the trials. It will feel like I'm saying goodbye."

"Willow," he sighs, gathering me into his arms. "I just want you to be sure."

His question is loaded with more meaning. I search his eyes and see the anguish and fear. His identity revolves around his need to protect, and he can't be with me during the trials.

"I will have my team with me—we have each other." I pat his shoulder. "Come on, I'm starving. This wolf can't start slaying without food in her belly."

CHAPTER 60
WILLOW

We enter the dining room, and a riot of scents and colors assaults me. The table groans under the weight of a feast fit for kings—roasted meats dripping with savory juices, fresh bread still steaming, and fruits so ripe they look ready to burst. The Yule decorations are still up, evergreen boughs and glittering ornaments lending a festive air that feels oddly out of place given our current predicament.

In the corner, Fox still stands in his statue form, a silent sentinel watching over us. Someone has draped a chain of flowers over him, the delicate blooms bright against his stone. My heart clenches at the sight.

To my surprise, the entire hive is seated around the table. Legion is at the head, his imposing figure radiating authority in his official House of Shadow military mandarin-collared coat. Long, raven-black hair spills over his broad shoulders as he dips his chin to meet my eyes. "We don't have much time," he warns.

"Eat fast. Got it."

I tense when I lock eyes with Emrys. His fingers drum an agitated rhythm on the table. His pale skin seems to glow, making the dark circles under his eyes more pronounced. He, too, wears his official military coat—black, tailored, and cut to intimidate.

Styx perches on his seat like a bird, ready to take flight. His mood seems to shift with each moment—scowling and then curious. I feel like he's been unintentionally caught in Emrys's machinations. But what do I know? He keeps his walls up with me.

The baby dragon huddles beneath the table and gnaws on what looks like a whole roasted chicken. His scales shimmer with an iridescent sheen, changing color slightly with each movement.

And then there's Varen. He sits beside the window at the end of the long table, looking more refreshed and alert than I've ever seen. A sharp clarity has replaced the haunted, faraway look usually clouding his eyes. But there is a strain around the edges, a reminder that he's not entirely well. Yet.

His long, elegant fingers are wrapped around a steaming mug . . . and he's not muttering about bees.

"We fed," he explains quietly, almost nervously. My heart swells, hardly daring to believe it. Emotion fills his eyes as I walk toward him—recognition, wonder, and something deeper I can't quite name.

I kneel and place my hands on his knees.

"Hi," I whisper, looking up at him with a tentative smile.

His lips twitch. "Hi."

That look is everything. My lashes lower, and I drag in a big lungful of his honey-and-jasmine scent. I'm overwhelmed with emotion, hot and needy. I want to ask if I can kiss him. I need to feel his lips on mine. But if I do, my control might unravel, and I might really do what Bodin asked and forfeit the trials. Maybe run off to Elphyne.

"Yes," Varen whispers. It takes me a moment to realize what he means. He's not reading my thoughts.

Is this his psychic ability? Has he seen me ask the question?

A grin splits my face. I leap onto his lap, cupping his jaw. His whole body tenses when our lips meet, and then he melts into the kiss with a soft groan that sends shivers down my spine.

"You have no idea," he whispers hoarsely against my lips, "how long I have yearned for this moment."

"Aww." Styx's mocking voice breaks the moment. "Do we all get a kiss?"

I twist to glare at him and flip up my middle finger.

"Feeling left out?" I quip, arching an eyebrow. "I thought you preferred your affection with a whole lot of deceit."

His smirk falters before returning full force. "Come now, fangs. You already know what hole I prefer."

I squirm and blush. How dare he make me feel . . . I don't know, like I'm the bad one here. Sort of. I don't hate him. I just want him to trust me. I want to trust him. "You and Emrys knew how to restore your memories for years, and you said nothing."

"Technically, I knew for weeks," he points out.

"You knew in the temple when Fox took your place." I glare at him, blood going cold. "You lied to me—pretended not to know me."

His lips part. Close. A blush creeps up his neck. "I was disoriented. It took me a while to realize the truth."

"You and Emrys worked together—"

"Don't lump me in with that wastrel," Emrys snarls. "My reasons are—"

"Your *reasons*?" I cut him off, anger flaring. "You helped Puck capture Nightmares. You betrayed us all. What possible reasons excuse that?"

The room falls silent, tension thick enough to cut with a knife. Emrys's eyes flash dangerously, but there's a flicker of remorse behind the anger. Styx's eyes lower, and he frowns.

"We have made mistakes," Legion interjects, his authoritative voice cutting through the tension. "But now is not the time to rehash grievances."

I take a deep breath, forcing myself to relax. I'm furious. I'm not ready to forgive. I didn't experience every memory they had in that tower, but I know they are family to each other. I know their ranking system would severely affect Styx's state of mind. I know Emrys is traumatized. And they are my mates. I can no more send them away than I could forget about them. They feel the same way about me. It's probably why they're being such assholes. They're finding it hard to deal with, considering how long they've fought against a female in their lives. Emrys was cruel, but he pulled me away from death. Styx has been helpful as much as he's hindered. Trust will be hard to claw back, but not impossible. We will find a way through this.

Bodin growls, "Eat quickly, Calamity. We don't know what the first trial will entail and should get there early."

I stay perched on Varen's lap but reach for the table, loading a plate with an assortment of breakfast foods. The rich aroma of freshly baked bread and sizzling meats makes my stomach growl.

Styx ponders Bodin's remark. "My bet's on something delightfully cruel. It is Puck we're dealing with, after all."

"Or his dragon," Emrys points out. "The Hunt has infected his mind."

"This isn't a game for your amusement," Bodin snarls, his fingers leaving shadowy scorch marks on the polished table. "Or have you forgotten what's at stake?"

Legion clears his throat, silencing the brewing argument. "Willow needs our support, not our squabbles."

"Support?" Emrys scoffs, a bitter laugh escaping his lips. "What support can we offer when we're bound by Titania's—"

"Enough," Varen interrupts, his tone soft but firm. His arms tighten protectively around my middle. "We may be bound, but we're not powerless. Styx, you will shadow Willow into the below."

"But isn't that cheating?" I ask.

"Fuck cheating," Styx scoffs. "This whole exhibition is a joke."

"What if you're caught?" My eyes widen. "I'll get disqualified. Maybe executed."

"I never get caught," he counters darkly. Holds my gaze. Then shrugs. "If I have to be seen, I blend in."

"We won't let anything happen to you," Legion promises. "Don't worry."

"I should do this alone," I tell them slowly. "If everyone exhibitor is mortal, we're all in the same boat. Surely, Puck won't set up a situation where we're all expected to die. You need soldiers for the war. He needs subjects to fawn over him."

No one looks convinced. None of this is normal.

The wildling chooses this moment to poke his head above the table, shadow curling from his skull's nostrils. His black, liquid eyes lock onto my plate, far too intelligent for a mere beast.

"Don't even think about it," I warn, but cave and toss him a piece of bacon. He snaps it out of the air with surprising grace, then licks my fingers. "Such a good boy."

"Charming," Styx mutters.

I grin at him with a mouth full of food. He grins at me with fangs, plucks a twig from the Christmas tree, then rips it apart. My gaze swings to the tree, to the unopened gifts. I twist to ask Varen, "Do I have time to—"

"Yes."

I shove more food in my mouth, so Legion and Bodin can see me multitasking, then race to the tree. I load up with gifts and drop one on the lap of each of my mates, then fork another mouthful of food into my mouth and say, "Happy belated Yule-Christmas."

No one moves. The only sound is my mouth, masticating food. I swallow and look around at their stunned and concerned faces.

"You open them," I explain. "They're gifts. But hurry."

They look to Legion, who purses his lips and tugs the ribbon from his gift. It is the signal for the others to begin. I can hardly contain my excitement as they unwrap and reveal an item I made or stole. Styx has a collection of charcoal from Varen's fireplace. Emrys scowls at his book of poetry, but he flicks through the pages. Legion has a new brush—bejeweled, ornate, and stolen from the temple. It might have a magic surprise. I should warn him. Bodin has hair beads. Varen has a jar of honey. He turns it over in his hand, catching light in the amber.

"I know they're dumb," I mumble, "but I had to give them now."

At their continued silence, I take a drink.

I think I broke them. They don't know what to say, but I can see their gratitude on their faces. It's enough for me. Legion clears his throat and announces that it's time. Everyone files out of the room. Varen and I are last because I collect two more gifts from under the tree, and he lingers by the door.

"Got them," I say, smiling fondly and jogging to him.

He grabs me, pushes me against the wall, and steals my breath with a crushing kiss. His taste is heady and oh-so-good. It's over too fast, and I'm left dizzy and hot. So, I almost miss his whispered words against my lips. "One will betray you. One will try to kill you."

CHAPTER 61
WILLOW

Varen stares at me, unblinking. Our lips still almost touch, but his words have already fled my mind.

"Did you say something, Varen?" I ask, my voice barely above a whisper.

His eyes seem blank, as if no one's home. Fear wraps itself around my heart and squeezes. I don't like this look.

"Varen, honey?" I gently touch his face. In an instant, the madness flashes in his eyes like a festering wound.

I try to keep my expression passive despite the urge to scream at the injustice of this affliction torturing him. His hands, which moments ago touched me lovingly, now grip my shoulders painfully.

"False queen," he snarls in my face.

Tears sting my eyes. "Do you mean me?"

He shakes his head, frustrated—at him or me, I'm not sure.

"The honeycombs are still broken," he says. "They need to be fixed."

"But you all have your memories."

"They're broken!"

"I know," I tell him softly. "We'll fix them, don't worry."

"No, you don't understand!" His voice rises in pitch as he shoves me, eyes wild with panic. "If we don't fix them, there is no honey!" His voice takes on an eerie quality. "Without honey, the colony starves. Worker bees die within weeks, and the entire hive collapses. It's a slow, agonizing death for all."

"But I thought Styx gave you bee bread."

His hands claw at me, but he's not listening.

"Yellow jackets." He's rambling again, the monotone persisting. "They invade weakened hives. They slip in unnoticed, mimicking the scent of the colony. When the bees realize the intruders' true nature, it's too late. The yellow jackets slaughter them, steal their honey, and leave nothing but destruction in their wake."

I don't know what to do. My feet are frozen to the floor, my mind a blank canvas.

"I have to go," I mumble stupidly.

Something snaps inside him, and he shouts, "The queen's scent attracts drones for mating, but it can also lure in predators. Wasps, hornets, even rival colonies." His tone grows almost angry and accusing, making my emotions well up until I'm sobbing. "The yellow jacket sting is more potent, their hunger insatiable. They will consume everything in their path, leaving nothing but hollow shells behind."

"Varen, you're hurting me."

"First, they send scouts," he barks in my face. "Then they attack in force, overwhelming the guards at the hive's entrance."

"Ren, hush." Bodin is there, gently prying Varen's clawed fingers from my bruised shoulders. But Varen won't let go.

He growls and snarls at Bodin, then comes back to me. "They *decapitate* the bees with their powerful mandibles."

I can't see through my tears now.

He gives my face a withering look and snipes, "A strong queen's scent might repel invaders, but a weak or corrupted—"

Emrys arrives and covers Varen's mouth, muffling his words.

"Enough with your incessant ramblings. Can't you see you're frightening her?"

Varen bites him. Scratches Bodin. It shocks them enough to weaken their hold. Varen lunges at me, once again shoving me against the wall.

His manic eyes bore into mine, his voice dropping to a chilling whisper. "And the worst part? They have pheromones too. They leave a trail leading their entire nest to the weakened hive. It becomes a massacre, a complete and utter destruction of everything the bees have built."

The fight leaves him. He has nothing left but sadness when they pluck him from me and drag him out of the dining room. I slump against the wall, my mind reeling. How much of that was relevant? How much was madness?

Styx finds me first. I'm a trembling mess, leaning against the wall for support, tears streaming down my face. My body is a mix of feverish hormones and dismay. Sitting on Varen's lap moments ago felt comforting, safe, and even alluring. Those sensations have now been corrupted, twisted into a sickening helplessness and fear.

Styx, usually so quick with barbed words, asks gently, "Are you okay?"

Those three little words hold the power to open floodgates. My emotions break free. I launch into his arms, clutching him like he might float away on a Dandelion Drift.

His arms circle around, holding me as tightly as I do him. He says nothing, but I feel it in his firm touch. He *feels* for me even if he can't act like it. We will be okay. We have to be.

"Willow." Legion's voice cuts through, insistent yet respectful. "If you don't leave now, it will be too late."

I pull back from Styx, dashing tears away with my hand. Nodding, I manage, "I'm coming."

Rory's dagger is at my feet, the wrapping torn. Max's gift is there too. I pick them up and follow them out. I have to bury the doubt worming its way into me. My friends can't see this weakness. I must be strong to show our enemies not to mess with us. So I use the cool castle air to anchor me. It gives me the strength to suppress any rogue attempts of fever trying to rise up.

By the time I reach the foyer, I've composed myself enough to dismiss my blotchy face as an aftereffect of my biology. My womb, however, is clenching in tight cramps. It's as though all my doubt, fear, and worry has collected there and knotted. I give Geraldine a trembling smile and hand her the gift. I hand Max his.

"These might come in handy," I explain.

"Open them on the way," Legion says gruffly.

Cricket and Finch give me quick hugs and wishes of good luck. Peggy holds me tight, using her strong arms to trap me as she whispers, "Do it for Bob."

"You don't have to go?" I ask, hesitant.

She glances at Legion and replies, "He fixed it, so I don't."

Then we're off, walking at a breakneck pace out of Shadowfall Keep and back into the Nexus. The sky is already purple. The wind is harsh. Sunrise is minutes away.

We're in the woods when Geraldine opens her gift and finds Rory's dagger. She turns to me, her voice thick with emotion. "You stupid cow, you were supposed to keep this!"

"It's yours," I tell her. "At least for this trial. Whether or not the steel remains afterward is up to the Guardians."

"But it means so much to you," she whispers, her eyes glimmering.

I take her hand and squeeze it tight. "You mean more to me."

Legion and Styx stride ahead. I guess Bodin and Emrys will catch up once they settle Varen.

"Open your gift, Max," I tell him. "I think you'll like it."

He's too nervous to reply, his hands shaking as he unwraps the package to reveal the thin gloves I took from Titania's temple.

Max gives me a dubious look. "They look a little girly, no offense."

I laugh. "Maybe, but they won't act very ladylike once you put them on. Trust me."

Something in the magic tells me they're for protecting the weak.

"Do I put them on now?" he asks.

"Wait until we start."

The curved walls of the fort come into view between the trees. The sounds of the crowd fill the air, cheering between music designed to make hearts beat faster. Tension knots in my stomach —or maybe it's the cramps.

"We're going to be fine, guys," I tell them, tugging at my collar. "Believe it or not, we have prepared."

Legion gives me a look as we arrive at an arched entrance and explains loud enough for my friends to hear, "You'll be signed in and kitted out with supplies. Remember, it is an exhibition. The Folk enjoy extravagance. It's not just winning. It's performing. Don't hold back."

"We should still destroy the cunt," Styx grumbles, meaning Puck, I guess. His eyes narrow on the other stragglers running into the fort.

"It won't make a difference," Legion returns.

A raven caws up ahead in the branches. Styx *flickers* and then disappears. Legion's jaw clenches. He checks around to see if anyone notices, but only a few people ahead are nearby.

"Why won't it make a difference?" I ask.

He gives me a grim look. "Puck has used the entire temple-load of wisps to fortify the trials so the events will continue no matter what happens to him. Usually, this failsafe is a collective effort from the Shining Host while Titania slumbers. Once you begin, you cannot stop until the last trial is complete, or dusk arrives, and then the survivors are transported back here."

"Can't stop—like when they forced my feet to keep walking?"

He frowns. "I don't believe your feet will be compelled now, but something else will ensure the timeframe."

"Like a ticking time bomb," Max mutters.

A shiver runs across my arms, lifting the hairs.

"One last thing," Legion says, pulling me aside urgently. He stares at Max and Geraldine until they head through the arch, giving us a moment. Then he retrieves something from his pocket —a pink skull charm. "To block your pheromones. It's all I could come up with at the last minute."

He attaches it to my chain. I cover it with my hand and activate the magic. While I don't sense a difference, the tightness in his posture eases a little. He inhales and nods. "Good enough."

"Thank you."

His hand lifts to my face, eyes searching mine. "The Dreamscape and Nightmare Trials will be held here in the fort, but the subterranean infiltration will be captured on resonance stones pinned on your bodies. Nothing you do or say will be private. Remember that. Even the silencing charms we gave you won't block the resonance stones. But it is also for this reason that we believe the trials will progress as they always have." His tone goes quieter. "This is not a massacre. This is entertainment."

Not a massacre. Then why did Varen mention one?

CHAPTER 62
WILLOW

We arrive just in time to join the line of exhibitors forming around the arena. Glancing up, I spot faerie nobility occupying each House loge. Their faces are alight with joy, hands clutching goblets of fairy wine that slosh about in their excitement. Further in the stands, Folk of all kinds gather to be entertained. Even green-cloaked guards wander the tiers with wide grins. Is Briar up there, ensuring everyone wears their smile?

Sunrise peeks through the top of structural trees forming the fort. Leaves shimmer gold against the pinkish-blue sky. No dragons perch on buttresses. Instead, their eyes gleam from within their bonded Radiants prowling around their troops, issuing last-minute instructions.

Ladies-in-waiting, dressed in extravagant attire matching their hair, bustle along the line, assigning and pinning resonance stones. For once, I'm in the correct uniform to match the others. Mustard Seed pins my stone to my chain with an arrogant smirk before moving on.

Another lady-in-waiting, Cobweb this time, hands me a scroll before continuing down the line. Finally, Moth takes my hand and stamps my palms with something that sears. When I cry out, she flashes me a cruel smile and moves to the next person. My palm burns and itches with the power of a magic circle covering it.

"What did she do?" I ask, but no one responds.

Those ahead on the challenge leaderboard are called forward to the center of the arena to receive a blessing from the Keepers of the Cauldron. All Shadows. What a surprise. Everything happens so fast it's hard to stay calm. Only Geraldine and Max stand in the House of Shadow section. We didn't have time to bring Becky, Colin, and the other youngies in. My heart races as I realize how unprepared we are.

Bowls of water are placed before each exhibitor while I'm rushed forward to meet one of six masked druids standing around an enormous rock. It's flat and wide. It wasn't here during the Pageant of Prowess and hums with familiar magic.

I hunt the House of Shadow area for one of the Six and lock eyes with Legion. He stands in the shadows under the archway, hands in pockets, eyes on me with an unreadable expression, then looks pointedly at something over my shoulder—to the druid.

My Keeper holds out a water-filled bowl and bids me to pull out a blessing, clearing their throat. It sounds feminine. My eyes snap to theirs, hidden behind slits in the wooden mask, but it's impossible to determine an identity. Until I lean into my shifter senses and take a long, slow inhale that fills my lungs with a familiar, sweet scent.

"Peablossom?" I whisper.

She lifts the bowl, insisting I hurry up. The brand on my palm burns and itches, compelling me to obey. That must be what Legion warned about—the magical enforcement ensuring we proceed with the trials. So I stick my hand in.

Other Shadows pull out strange weapons or magical items

ranging from a long, dark wooden staff wrapped in rune stones to glittering orbs. Anything, any size, can come out of the water.

The water is cool as it swims around my fingers, a balm to the brand. I fumble about until something small, round, and smooth knocks against me, tingling vibrantly. I pull out . . . nothing.

"Ah, nothing for the Nothing!" Puck announces over a broadcasting stone, waltzing into the arena. "Who would have predicted that?"

Nothing? But I feel something. The Keeper winks at me, and I gasp.

It *is* Peablossom. I'm sure of it. She draws the bowl back to her center and, like the other druids, walks toward one of the arched entrances to the arena. All around us, other exhibitors have their hands dipped into bowls.

Robin Goodfellow struts toward me, his eyes twinkling with mischief and malice as he takes me in. The crowd hushes, anticipation crackling in the air. It's hard to look away from his face. It's covered in ribbons of stone—like Fox's did when he exchanged places with Styx. But it's more than that, more than a statue forming. Puck is a living monument. Ripples of stony scales swim beneath his skin. His auburn hair is dull and stiff. It's almost like I'm not looking at Puck anymore but the Baleful Hunt.

"Go on," he rasps, shooing me with his hand. Dust crumbles from his lips as he speaks. This close, his voice sounds more gravelly and less lilting. "Run along now, Nothing."

Every word amplifies around the arena. Laughter erupts as though he's made the most hilarious joke in the world. I shoot him daggers and belatedly return to our troop, clutching the invisible round thing in my fist, using the sting it causes against the brand to ground myself. Does anyone else see what's happening to him?

"My dear Good Folk," Puck shouts as he steps onto the large central rock. It must be a resonance stone. His words amplify, echoing through the tiers of trees. "What a glorious morning.

The bad weather teasing us earlier has evaporated. We are smiling, are we not?"

The responding cheer trembles the stands, sending a cascade of botanicals floating down. I dust off my head, reaching my friends with a sick feeling rolling in my stomach. I flick water from my fingers to catch Geraldine or Max's attention. They're standing stock still, eyes forward, dutifully listening to Puck's performance. I glance along the line of exhibitors backed around the arena wall. They're all watching avidly. Every single bowl is gone.

That was fast.

When the noise dies down, Puck adopts a more somber face. "As you can see, this year's trials are not quite what anyone expected. But then, where would the fun be without a little chaos? I know Glen agrees." He points somewhere in the tiers, and more cheers erupt.

Goodfellow grins, basking in their attention. "Are you ready to hear what other surprises we have in store?"

He pauses dramatically, letting the suspense build.

> "Listen well, Fair Folk, for I bring you riddles three,
> Of trials and truths, of dusk and dreams you'll see.
> Three challenges our brave exhibitors shall face,
> Three lies unraveled in this very place."

The crowd leans in, captivated by his overly dramatic words.

> "First, through a nightmare dreamscape, they'll flee,
> While we watch enthralled with their struggle to break free.
> Next, their nightmares will come alive,
> As we witness their courage, will they survive?
> The third, my personal touch, a special treat,
> Deep in Nocturna's heart, their deepest fears they'll meet."

Murmurs of excitement ripple through the arena. Goodfellow's grin widens as he continues.

> **"But hark! There's more than meets the eye,**
> **For three great truths hide behind a lie.**
> **One speaks of war, its purpose unclear,**
> **Another of our queen's slumber, oh so dear.**
> **But first, a secret long concealed,**
> **A mortal truth shall be revealed."**

He pauses, letting the weight of his words sink in.

"Is he threatening to reveal the truth about the war?" I project my thoughts toward Styx, hoping he hears me. *"Are you all in danger?"*

No reply. Silence. Crickets in my mind.

My hand moves to my sword at my hip. The other clenches the smooth, invisible thing in my stinging palm. I don't know what it is, but Peablossom hasn't let me down yet. The arena's arched exits are gated shut, trapping us in here. The early morning sun shines through the fort's opening above, blinding my eyes and creating shadows, hiding faces—all except the show pony standing on the rock in the center of the arena. A single ray of light lands directly on him, amplifying his beauty and presence where he appeared so dull before.

"Who is ready to hear the truth?" Puck grins. "A lie so tricky, one would have thought our dear Glen was involved."

Laughter explodes. A dark suspicion of danger coats my tongue, and my heartbeat rapidly increases.

"It was not Titania," he announces, "a lazy queen with an ailing dragon, who woke us all from the long slumber," Puck reveals, pointing his finger at me. "But the House of Shadow's Shadow. A last-minute stranger arriving at Avorlorna's gates, a Nothing who woke armies of undead in her land, killed innocents with her bare hands, and was trained by the evil man who bombed the old world, destroying all we loved and held dear."

Shocked gasps suck the air out of the arena. It feels like a vacuum. My lungs won't work. My ears ring. All around me, hate-filled eyes pepper me through the heart like arrows. Alfie told Puck everything. I look for my mates, but can't locate them. Instead, I see Becky—horror and disgust on her face. I see so many eyes looking at me like I'm a monster. I turn to Geraldine and Max and see betrayal in their eyes.

"I can explain," I say, stepping forward.

"The man who raised you destroyed our world?" Geraldine's face contorts.

"Kidnapped me," I hiss. "He forced me to—"

"It's true," Puck continues, his loud voice drowning out my words. He taps his temple. "The Baleful Hunt has revealed this secret, and I, your only trustworthy and loyal soul, once mortal and now dragon-bonded, simply could not keep this worrisome news to myself. The gods punished this agent of chaos, confiscating her magic for such cowardly acts. And what did she do?" He starts pacing toward the wings, scoffing, "She didn't invite you to her abundant realm, where mortals are free, that's for sure. No, she came here to steal the prize of a dream come true from mortals whose suffering *she* created. Times are changing, my friends." He pauses beneath the last open archway. "Secrets have been kept for far too long. I promise you that everything will be revealed in due time. But first, let us enjoy the spectacle before us!"

The crowd's shocked silence feels like a physical force pressing against me. I fight the urge to run, to hide, to disappear. But I can't. I won't. I square my shoulders and lift my chin, ready to face whatever comes next. The truth may be out, but it's not the whole story. And I'll be damned if I let Puck's twisted version of events be the last word.

CHAPTER 63
WILLOW

Ironically, Nero's forced training keeps me calm as a herd of vengeful mortals strides toward me across the arena. Alfie approaches, his glamour restored, a pistol—an old-world weapon I haven't seen since Crystal City—swinging at his hip. How did he find one in Avorlorna? Becky, wild-eyed, draws her sword from behind her back. I may have kept her children's secret, but I'm the reason they're starving. More come for me, every Shadow, and every exhibitor. A deadly cocktail of hate, fear, and disgust gleams in their eyes. But worse is the betrayal radiating from my friends.

"You keep lying to us," Geraldine accuses, eyes glistening as she retreats.

"I'm sorry," I choke out, stepping forward.

Max interposes himself between us, palm outstretched. "Don't go near her."

"Max!" I plead. "Please—let me explain."

"What is there to explain?" He shakes his head, voice cracking. "We trusted you—were willing to lay down our lives for you, and you lied."

"I'm ashamed, okay?" I cry, pounding my chest. "I hate myself for what I did, what he made me do. I did it so much that I started wondering if I liked it. Maybe I do. Fuck, I don't know. I just know that I'm on your side. You're my friends."

His hand lowers, and I take another step. The gloves are missing from his hands, a detail that sends a chill down my spine.

"Why haven't you put on the gloves, Max?" I ask, gesturing to his bare hands. I'll never forgive myself if he dies because he doesn't trust my gift is for his protection. My gaze flicks to Geraldine, and I wince. She clutches an ordinary dagger—not even steel. "Gerrie, where's Rory's dagger?"

Footsteps grow louder, faster, as exhibitors break into a run. "Kill her!" someone shouts. "She's stealing our wish!" another barks. "She's not even human!"

They sound seconds away, but I ignore them all because something is wrong—Max frowns at his hands. "Why would I wear gloves?"

"For the trial!" I shout, desperation clawing at my throat. "The first trial is about to start."

They don't listen. My mind races, desperately trying to find the missing piece of this puzzle. Something felt off earlier, *before* Puck's damning announcement. I'm out of time to think. A muscular exhibitor—pale, tall, dark-haired—charges at me, sword raised. I parry one-handed, twist, and boot him to the side. He goes flying into the wall.

Dahlia is next, shrieking like a Nightmare, sword held high with both hands. The blade chops down but doesn't connect. Another blocks it—Becky.

Alfie saunters in, green eyes flashing with malice. "Your lies were bound to catch up with you, Willow."

"Did you tell them your lie, too, Alfie?" I shout. "I was Nero's prisoner. You were his aeronautics captain!"

"Lies!" he bellows. "Everyone knows I've been here for years —same as them."

"I must have sent you here." I gape, hardly believe it. "Or Titania stole you when she summoned—"

I cut myself off. There's no way I can refute his claims without damning the Six, and he knows it. I'm fucked. The other Shadows —Irisa, Heath, and Corey—arrive with a mix of caution and aggression in their eyes. Exhibitors swarm behind them. Having surprised Dahlia with her block, Becky is the only one between me and the mob.

"Let her explain," she shouts.

"Fuck that," Irisa spits out. "She had her chance."

"Get out of the way, bitch." Dahlia rotates her sword. "I'm ready for a little payback."

I back up until my spine hits the wall, mind reeling as I try to piece together how we got here. One moment, Legion was warning us to be wary of being recorded. The next, we lined up. Resonance stones were pinned to us. Scrolls were placed in our hands, and brands seared into our palms.

Wait.

I glance down at my hands. One grips my sword, and the other is wrapped around the invisible round thing, itching and tingling in my palm. No scroll. I don't even remember unfurling it and reading it. I look up at the tiered stadium, leaves rustling around the balconies. I should be able to see faces, especially those in the loges. The sun blazes bright and high in the blue sky, but shadows linger everywhere. It's cold. Freezing. When did the weather shift from brisk and frigid to a beautiful, cloudless day? The sun had barely risen.

A cloying, sickly sweet scent drifts in the air like rotting flowers. Buzzing under my feet.

The puzzle clicks into place.

Through a nightmare dreamscape, they'll flee. While we watch enthralled with their struggle to break free.

We're already in a dreamscape—a nightmare.

In both Elphyne and here, water is a magical gateway. I entered the dream when I put my hand in the bowl. I'd wondered how they'd cleared all the bowls so fast. I'm probably slumped on the floor, sleeping with the other exhibitors. The other Shadows pulled out elaborate, magical weapons as their blessings. Our weapons are figments of our imagination, but the injuries inflicted here will be real. I can still die. We all can.

Becky won't move out of the way. Dahlia lifts her sword, growling, "I warned you."

"Stop!" I shout. "We're dreaming. Wake up!"

It's too late. Swords clash. Pandemonium erupts. I shout for Geraldine and Max to hear me, to believe me, but they're also fighting. It seems as if disgruntled exhibitors can't reach me, they're going for my friends.

But how do we wake with no one standing guard while we're asleep?

More exhibitors break past Becky and Dahlia's battle, faces mottled with fury—the ground tilts. The air presses in on me. I can only defend so much one-handedly. It's either drop the round thing in my palm or die.

The round, invisible thing.

My brain clicks, and I glance down at my seemingly empty palm. I don't even see the brand, but it stings. It's there. That's my way out, my anchor. Peablossom gave me something that won't transcend the dreamscape. Everything else is an illusion so real that it takes form.

Angry exhibitors charge me, but I drop the sword. I focus all my attention on the invisible ball in my hand—feel its round surface, cool and smooth. That's real. Not this. I glance up as someone swings an ax at me, the blade arcing toward my face, and I crush that object in my fist until the brand burns so painfully I scream.

I wrench awake, lungs heaving, heart galloping. The taste of copper lingers on my tongue, a remnant of the dream or a warning of what's to come. I'm slumped against the flat rock at the center of the arena, cool wind whipping my face, a small steel ball in my hand.

Shivering, I dust the light snow off myself and climb to my feet. The sun is high in the overcast sky. Time passed swiftly in the dream. Around me, by the central rock, four Shadows sleep. Some have blood pooling in places and welts forming on their skin—their dream injuries made real. Glowing spectral figures battle each other—swords clashing, fists flying, faces contorted with rage and desperation. The one with the ax has already stumbled past me, looking around, stunned.

"Where did she go?" he growls, looking my way.

I tense, but his gaze swings past as if I'm invisible. Not me—the metal ball. Now that I'm awake, it's keeping me from being dragged back into the dreamscape. Maybe. Hopefully.

Voices swim in and out of earshot on a breeze. Becky—screaming at Dahlia and Irisa as she fights them both off. Blood oozes from a wound on her face. And Geraldine, Max? They're fighting exhibitors who've come for them since I've gone. Death by association—their worst fear.

"No," I breathe and bolt to the House of Shadow's arena section, swerving around stray arms swinging, ducking under swords. Each near miss sends a jolt of electricity across my skin. Even with the magic-cutting ball, if one touches me, I still might be dragged back into the dreamscape. Nothing is certain.

Geraldine and Max are slumped against the wall, sleeping with their heads together. But their faces are pinched with dismay. I fall to my knees beside them, the ground beneath me shifting like sand. Their skin is clammy and cool to the touch, unlike the feverish heat radiating from my skin, from the brand on my palm.

"Max! Wake up." He groans but doesn't rouse.

I move to Geraldine. Do the same. Then I slap her face.

Her brow furrows and her lashes flutter, but she doesn't wake. She jerks as though hit, and a welt forms on the side of her face. Shit—did I disrupt her focus in the dream? I glance over my shoulder and scour the specters. There. Her ghostly figure clutches her jaw, pointing a sword at someone I can't see.

I hunt around her body. Behind her on the floor is a scroll and Rory's dagger. She must have put it down when she put her hand in the bowl. I place it in her palm, pressing it hard against the brand mark and shouting in her face, "Fucking wake up, you stupid cow!"

She gasps awake, eyes wide. "What the fuck?"

Relief punches a laugh out of me. A sob. She's awake.

"That was a dreamscape," I blurt. "Quick, help me wake Max. The gloves."

Thank the Well, she doesn't fight me. I fish into Max's pockets and pull out the lacy gloves. They hum with power, with violence. I hand her one, and she tugs it onto his hand while I fit the other hand.

"I hope this works," I mutter, pressing the glove where his brand is. Pain seems to be some kind of grounding force. He roars alive like the undead, body pulled to his feet by an invisible force. We duck in time to avoid his flailing fists, and he stumbles forward. "You were dreaming, Max!"

He pivots, eyes wild, sees Geraldine, then glares at me.

"She woke us up, Max," she says, about to sheath her dagger.

"Don't!" I shout, palm out. I show her the silver ball. "Metal and the pain keep us from being pulled back into the dream-scape. Don't let go, just in case." I look at Max. "The magical gloves must be enough to keep you grounded in reality."

He winces, nodding. "They fucking hurt! But it's good. They feel strong. Like I can Hulk smash."

Geraldine quickly redraws the dagger and opens her palm. "The brand—it's a big circle welt. Kind of dusky."

"It's our connection to the trials," I reply. "It's where the compulsion to put our hands in the bowls came from."

Her eyes lock with mine, and I see confusion and pain swimming in the depths.

"I'm s-sorry," I say, tripping over my tongue. "I'm sorry I didn't tell you about Nero. I did so many bad things for him. I never planned on raising the army of undead or everyone here. Didn't even know I could until the taint and—" I scrub my face, distraught. "We don't have time for me to explain. We have to wake the others or the dream will spin and evolve. Everyone will find reasons to attack each other. Will you help me?"

They stare at me for a heartbeat, then nod. A blood-curdling scream pierces the air—sharp and real.

"What was that?" Max blurts.

"I don't know," I murmur. "Is anyone else awake?"

A bad feeling prickles over my skin. I start running, saying, "I'll wake Becky—you find Colin and the young ones."

Max calls after me, "But how will we wake them if they can't let go of—"

Geraldine hits his chest, eyes wide. "Chaser chains. We'll put them in their branded hands."

"Genius!" I shout, grinning, dodging two brawling specters. A shoulder brushes mine, zapping me with electricity. I wasn't dragged in. Good. I find Becky on her side by a wall, blood oozing from her ear. My throat clogs. She defended me. I should have come here first.

I fall to my knees and grab her palm, slap it to the chain dangling across her uniform, and push hard. "Wake up, Becky!" She moans. Lashes flutter, but then she jerks and spits blood. Fuck. She's in the midst of a fight. Instinct takes over. I draw my sword, pierce a meaty part of her thigh, and push her palm into the chain again. "Becky, wake up! Your kids need you!"

She lurches forward, eyes opening, and vomits onto the ground—bloodstained bile.

"You're okay," I say, dropping my things and taking her face. I bring her disoriented eyes to mine and repeat, "You're awake. This is real. I've got you."

Tears leak from her eyes, and she nods. "I'm okay."

Exhaling, I collect my sword and steel ball. I give her a quick rundown of what I told the others while I search the arena, trying to ensure Geraldine and Max are okay. I spot them further down, shaking someone.

"You saved me," Becky rasps.

I turn to her and smile. "You saved me first. Thank you for trusting me."

Wincing, she climbs to her feet and wipes her mouth with her arm. "I figured anyone who protects children is more trustworthy than someone like Puck."

"He told the truth," I whisper. "I'm responsible for waking everyone up."

Her eyes widen. "For real?"

"It's a long story we don't have time for. Let's help get more up. I think the more awake, the less power the dreamscape has."

She stops me by the shoulder as I move. "Are you with Titania or us?"

Red fills my vision. Rage. Death. Revenge.

"She's dead," I promise through gritted teeth. I don't care if all of Avorlorna hears. I'm done hiding.

"Good," she exhales, then falls to a knee, head lolling, body swaying. "Give my kids a chance."

"Becky!" I drop and grab her shoulders, holding her up. "What's wrong? Where are you hurt?"

She groans and spits blood. "Everywhere."

I start searching her for a wound, but she pushes me off. "It's inside me."

"Shit." I scrub my face. "There's no triage for this."

"I know, bitch." She smiles weakly.

"Then you'll have to survive," I fist her collar and shout in her face. "Parents shouldn't give up on their kids. They shouldn't stop protecting them. Never! They shouldn't—"

My voice cracks. I sob. Tears stream down my face.

Becky whispers, "Is that what happened to you?"

"Yes. No." I close my eyes and cover my face. "They left me with an evil man so that I would survive. It broke them. It broke me. I can't even be angry at them. I can't be angry at *anyone*." I bite the inside of my cheek before I reveal something I shouldn't. But it's so fucking hard not to feel this now that it's out. "I don't know if I'll ever be at peace with the injustice of my life. There's no one to blame."

But the gods.

Her sticky hand covers mine and squeezes. "Willow, knowing who to blame won't give you peace. Believe me."

"What will?" I ask, opening my eyes.

"I'll let you know when I find out." Her sharp laugh erupts into a cough. I watch her with concern, one hand gripping my sword, the other on the steel ball. She can't die. I won't let her. When she's done, she smiles again and says, "Fine. I won't give up."

"Good." I stand.

Her gaze lifts with me but then drifts somewhere over my shoulder. "What the fuck?"

My gaze shifts higher, following Becky's line of sight. The blood-curdling scream echoes again, sending vibrations through my chest. Perched on the flying buttresses, an army of Nightmares looms. Some of their forms shimmer and twist as if struggling to maintain solidity in our world. Some are flesh. Some are just blood.

"Next," Becky whispers, "their nightmares will come alive."

I have to warn Geraldine and Max. My gaze drops, seeking them out. They're still working on waking that first troop. They don't see the solitary figure walking around the arena, getting closer by the second.

Only four Shadows were still asleep by the rock when I woke up. One was missing. I should have stopped to work out who. Alfie strolls along, systematically eliminating his sleeping competition, piercing his sword into their chests.

CHAPTER 64
WILLOW

"Stay here," I tell Becky, urgency tightening my voice. "Remember what I said."

"About the metal?" She groans, reaching for her sword.

"About surviving."

Our eyes lock. Understanding clicks between us, a primal connection forged in this nightmare's crucible. She knows I'll do everything to help her, and I won't stop trying. Each obstacle, each person hurt, fuels my need to protect them all. Maybe Geraldine's right—I'm building my pack. Either it'll be the biggest this world has seen, or I am what the Six keep calling me, what I keep denying.

A queen.

I instinctively search for my mates in the tiers and locate them immediately. A rush of warmth flows through me. I lock eyes with Bodin, Legion, and Styx. Emrys is gone. Whether he's with Varen, I don't know. But his absence cuts me.

Bodin scowls at my inaction. Styx starts gesturing something, pointing to a spot in the arena. He hurt me, too, but I know my claws are already worked into his heart. He's here and trying to warn me to pay attention. Smirking, I blow them a kiss and sprint across the arena. My boots kick up dust tasting of ash and despair. It feels empowering in a way I can't explain.

I have one target—Alfie.

The fool.

By killing his competitors, he's decimating our strength in numbers.

Rory always joked I was more snake than wolf. I don't scream or snarl when my prey's near. No war cry bellows from my lips. I'm light-footed. Silent. Sneaky. Calculated. They never see me coming.

So when Alfie looks up, I'm already within reach. I've cataloged his weapons. I know my chances. The dream pistol's gone —only a bloodstained sword in his hand. I torpedo his waist, tackling him to the ground. His charms rattle as we hit and slide along the sand, grit scraping my skin.

"What the hell, Willow!"

I use the jarring impact to disarm him, but I'm not free. His arms wrap around me in a chokehold. The scent of his sweat, tinged with fear and adrenaline, fills my nostrils.

"You're an idiot," I hiss, headbutting him with a satisfying crunch.

Somehow, I'm on my feet, facing him in a crouch, ready for another round. My forehead throbs, but he's worse. He covers his nose, stemming the blood flow. Bright-green eyes glare at me over his hand, filled with pain and betrayal.

"I can't believe how far you've fallen," he spits, words muffled.

"Me?" I laugh, drawing my sword. Elven strengthening glyphs flare to life, casting a soft blue glow on my face. "Look at you, cowardly killing them in their sleep."

"How else do you think we win?" He wipes his nose and spots his sword on the ground beside me.

I step in front of it, blocking him. Sand shifts beneath my feet.

Disgust laces my voice. "What can she possibly give that's worth this?"

"Anything I want!" he sneers, giving me a pitiful look. "A fucking dream come true."

"Oh, Alfie." I shake my head. "You've always been a sucker." I move the resonance stone on my shirt closer to my mouth. I want everyone out there to hear this. "Titania can't make every dream come true, only what's within the limits of her power. And in case you haven't noticed—her power's dwindling, even after she stole mine. Puck had to use hundreds of jars of wisps stolen from Titania's temple to activate the trials."

I drop the stone. Above us, in the tiered stands, mouths and eyes widen. Faeries turn to each other, their whispers lost on the wind like ghostly echoes. We can't hear them down here, but I've made them think.

Doubt flickers in Alfie's eyes before he glares at me. "Guess I'll just wait and see when I win."

His eyes dart to a scroll on the ground. "You're not the only one destined for greatness, Willow. This trial is just the beginning."

"What are you talking about?" I narrow my eyes, suddenly alert to the calculated gleam in his.

He chuckles, a sound devoid of warmth. "The subterranean holds more than just Nightmares."

"You're delusional. There's nothing but death below."

"That's where you're wrong." He collects the scroll with his bloodied fingers. "This map tells a different story. And when I meet her, I'll have everything you were too weak to take for yourself."

Her? The pieces click into place. Alfie's desperation for status, his willingness to kill—it all stems from his need to be more than a nobody. If he can't have me, he'll find power another way.

"You're playing with forces you don't understand," I warn, but my words only seem to fuel his determination.

"I know exactly what I'm doing."

"Hate to burst your bubble." I point at the Nightmares waiting on the buttresses, their twisted forms mocking life. "But you won't make it to the end if you keep killing your competition."

Fewer specters flicker in the dreamscape now. My heart sinks, knowing it's not just because they're awake, but because he made it so.

A shriek pierces the air like a physical blow. Alfie looks for the source. I could kill him right now. My sword's already in my hand. His back is turned. He's unarmed. But, fuck it. We need him—at least for this next challenge. So I kick his sword across the dirt. It hits his boot with a dull thud, and he glances down.

His shoulders tense, his lips flatten, and he stares at my gift.

"Big mistake," he mutters, picking it up. "They'll drop as soon as enough are out of the dreamscape. And we only need to kill one Nightmare for the final trial to begin."

A wicked glint enters his eyes. I catch his almost imperceptible glance to the ground, to a fallen scroll on my left side. I point my sword at his neck and prowl around him. The glyphs pulse in time with my heartbeat, each symbol a conduit for magic. It courses through my veins, itching and turning my blood to liquid fire.

"If you kill these people," I warn him, "all my attention will focus on you."

Movement near the center rock draws our attention. Heath is awake and rousing Corey, their figures silhouetted against the eerie light. They've allied. *Interesting.* I scour the arena to see what else I've missed. Geraldine and Max have managed to wake Colin—my heart swells as I see him jogging to join Becky. She's woken one of her troop members, and is working on another, but her movements are sluggish.

This troop is dead—eight lives snuffed out by Alfie's greed.

My eyes sting as I recognize Miguel's face among them, his once-vibrant features now slack and lifeless. The last time we spoke, he offered soup, and Alfie punched him. I hate that it was our last interaction.

"Fuck you, Alfie," I choke out.

There's nothing I can do for the dead, so I run from the corpses before I start remembering bad things, the scent of death clinging to my nostrils. Corey sees me coming and steps in front of Heath, sword drawn and muscles hard. They're together, I realize. It's more than allies. Sometime over the past week, they've developed feelings for each other. Heath scrambles for something at his belt—but he's no warrior like Corey. He's a Never. But he's still a Shadow. Lady Selene chose him for a reason. He is kind, compassionate, and maybe more.

Dahlia and Irisa are still asleep but murmuring, rousing somehow.

I sheathe my sword and hold my palms up. "I'm not here to hurt you." I glance at Heath over Corey's shoulder. "Becky needs your help—" I nod in her direction. "She's bleeding inside. I don't know what to do. We need every able body to survive the Nightmares." I point up. "They'll start dropping as soon as enough exit the dreamscape."

"How do you know that?" Corey's eyes narrow, suspicion etching every line of his face.

"Alfie told me." I glance in his direction. He stands back against the wall near the people he killed, reading the scroll. "But I don't know how much of that is true. He was murdering exhibitors in their sleep until I stopped him."

"You stopped him?" Corey asks, knuckles whitening on the sword's grip. "Or did you kill them?"

"No, it wasn't her." Heath pushes Corey aside, knowing eyes taking me in. "I saw her take him down when I woke. Is Becky coughing blood?"

"Yes."

Something flickers in his eyes that I don't like, but he says, "I'll see what I can do."

"Wait." I stop him. "There was an old-world emergency healer in my pilgrimage group. Can she help?"

"Sarah?" he asks, rubbing his jaw. "She was a paramedic. She could help."

Corey gives me a wary look. "You would wake your competition?"

"We already are." I point to my friends. "Use metal from chains or weapons and push it into the exhibition brand on your palm—metal blocks magic. It's enough to disrupt the dreamscape."

They share a tense, brief hug. Corey mumbles something in Heath's ear that they don't think I can hear, but I do: "Go be a hero."

I drop to Dahlia's side and expose her branded palm—Corey's hand locks around my wrist, stopping me.

"They're in it for themselves," he warns me, eyes flashing.

"Maybe," I reply. "But I can't leave anyone to die in their sleep. That makes us as bad as the Nightmares."

He lets go and drops to Irisa. They don't take long to rouse, and after explaining the situation, I'm surprised they join us on our mission to wake the rest of the exhibitors. Dahlia was almost friendly to me in Burn After Reading when she thought we had no reason to be competitors. I'd like to think if things were different, she wouldn't be so vicious. I'm sure once this trial is over, it'll be every exhibitor for themselves again. But I'll cross that bridge when I get to it.

I wake Sarah and a few others I recognize. Alfie, the fucker, refuses to do anything but read his scroll, his eyes darting across the parchment with feverish intensity. We instruct anyone awake to rouse those caught in the dreamscape. With Sarah and Corey at my side, I run toward Becky but can't see her through the growing group of exhibitors. I'm pleased to see her blond head at eye level when we arrive. Heath must have worked some kind of magic—I didn't think it was possible for a Never, but a Shadow would undoubtedly have a few tricks up his sleeve.

The relief squeezing my heart is so powerful that I hug her. Tight. "I'm so fucking glad you're okay."

She hesitates but then returns my embrace. "Me too."

Nodding, I pull back and search for the next person I'm worried about. This exhibition isn't over yet. I see him huddled with some youngies, their faces pale with fear.

"Colin," I shout. He turns to me, eyes rimmed with red. It's the same gangly frame, too-large hands, and an awkward smile. Alive.

"Are you okay?" I ask, pushing past an older exhibitor to get to him. I can't see blood on his dull uniform.

"I knew you wouldn't forget us," he mumbles, voice hoarse. He turns to his friends. "See? Didn't I tell you guys? Goodfellow's wrong."

My throat clogs. "He wasn't wrong."

"What?" Colin gasps, betrayal flashing in his eyes. "But—"

"You're not wrong either," I quickly say, holding his stare so he knows I'm telling the truth. "I might have a past I'm not proud of, but I'm not going to leave you all to die."

I recognize Ji-Soo with the bangs, but I've not met the nervous male with olive skin and deep-set eyes. She's holding an arm to her chest as though it's hurt. He's favoring one leg.

"Where's Maggie?" I ask Colin.

His expression curdles my stomach. It's fear, grief, and a step away from madness. This is too much for him—for anyone. I need to give them something to do—a distraction.

I turn to every exhibitor in earshot and shout, "Start cataloging the Terrors. Know their weaknesses so we're ready when they attack." I point to the closest buttress where a Terror matches Emrys's description. I never imagined something this grotesque was behind that stall door. A furry hindquarter is crudely stitched to a skinless ape-like torso. Its eyes swivel independently. One reptilian slit focuses on me while the other bulbous and insectoid eye scans the crowd. The stench of decay wafts from its patchwork body. A string of drool dangles from its mouth. Maybe it recognizes me from the stables.

My hand covers the charm Legion gave me just before entering. It's supposed to hide my pheromones, but my usual scent would still penetrate. Interestingly, I haven't felt the crippling effects of my heat since I put it on. I have at least another day of fever in me. If I lose this charm, my pheromones will leak again.

An idea forms in my head.

"That's a Graftspawn," I say, gripping my sword. "It's mine."

"Fine with me." Colin gives a little hysterical laugh.

"Colin." I grab his shoulder. "Start listing all the Terrors you recognize. Stay with your youngies. Safety in numbers, okay?"

"I don't know."

"You've got this. Bodin wouldn't have offered you a traineeship as a Phantom if he didn't think you were capable. Make sure your friends are all doing the same thing. I need you to keep watch for me—to shout warnings for those of us fighting, okay?"

He nods vehemently. "Yeah. We can do that."

"We only need to kill one to trigger the next trial. Until then, everyone just needs to survive."

Ji-Soo nods, her eyes wide but determined. The olive-skinned boy swallows hard but squares his shoulders. Their fear is evident, but so is their resolve. These kids are tougher than they know.

"Good," I say.

"We woke everyone we could," Max announces, panting as they reach us. No sooner are the words out of his mouth when the brand on my palm burns like fire. I hiss and hear a chorus of others doing the same. We all feel the pain. When I glance down, the raised welt has changed a shade darker. No longer pink, but blue.

A ripple of tingling air filled with the smell of rotting flesh gusts over us. The arena shimmers, and reality warps like a mirage. The ground grows colder, frost crystals spreading in intricate patterns across the sand and grass. Clouds form from our breath. A torrential downpour of nightmarish shrieks lifts the hairs on the back of my neck.

The second trial has begun.

CHAPTER 65
PUCK

I stand at the edge of the Court of Dreams box, my fingers curled around the ornate railing covered in botanicals. Gasps and laughs ripple around us. The crowd loves it. They love *me*. Below, chaos unfolds in a symphony of screams and clashing weapons. The second trial has begun, and with them, my ascension to power.

"Look at them scramble," the Hunt whispers, its voice a cold caress in my mind. *"Like ants beneath your boot."*

I smile, ignoring the twinge of pain as my lips crack. "Soon, they'll be *my* ants."

Exhibitors battle not just each other, but the very fabric of their fears made manifest. At first, I'd been furious about that pilgrimage to Heliodor, but it forced my hand. We ended up with more Terrors than expected, sooner than later.

In the center of it all, that silver-haired witch rallies the others. How quaint.

"She thinks she's saving them," I chuckle, absently scratching at my arm. More dust flakes away, but I pay it no mind. "If only she knew."

My gaze finds Alfie, that eager pawn, as he scans the scroll I

planted. Good. Let him think he's discovered some grand secret. Let him lead the charge into the subterranean, straight to Titania's vulnerable form.

A jolt of excitement courses through me, and for a moment, I swear I can feel the Hunt's wings lashing beneath my skin. Soon, that power will be mine. Titania's essence, the very magic that has kept Avorlorna thriving, will flow into me.

"You're certain?" I ask the Hunt, my thoughts barely a whisper. *"When she falls, her power transfers to the next ruler?"*

"The land demands a conduit," it purrs. *"You've orchestrated this perfectly. Who else but you could be worthy?"*

I preen at the praise, even as another piece of me crumbles away. It doesn't matter. This failing form is merely a chrysalis. Once I have Titania's power, I'll be reborn. Perfected.

The fool Larkspur waits in the wings to declare this duel before the gods after the trials. It will be so satisfying to wipe that smile off his face when he realizes I am no longer falling apart.

Below, the first of the Nightmares breaks free. Screams intensify as a twisted creature lashes out, its mismatched limbs a blur of violence. I should feel something—fear, perhaps, or remorse for unleashing such horrors. After all, I was once down there, fighting for my life. Instead, a laugh bubbles up from my chest.

"Your masterpiece," the Hunt croons. *"Watch how they dance to your tune."*

"Lord Goodfellow?" A hesitant voice breaks through my reverie. I turn to see one of the lesser fae nobles regarding me, his eyes wide with concern. "Are you . . . well? Your skin, it's—"

"Never better." I cut him off with a wave. Flakes of what was once flesh drift to the polished floor. "Simply the excitement of the games. You understand."

He doesn't, of course. How could he? These simpering courtiers, with their petty intrigues and meaningless titles. Even the Shining Host lacks the truth. They can't fathom true ambition. True power.

I turn back to the arena, drinking in the carnage. Willow has managed to organize a group, fighting back against the Nightmares. It's almost admirable, in a futile sort of way.

"She'd make a formidable ally," the Hunt muses. *"Or a satisfying meal."*

"In time," I reply in my head, my eyes tracking my Shadow as he edges toward the center of the arena. *"For now, let her play the hero. It makes the fall all the sweeter."*

A tremor runs through the stadium as something massive stirs beneath. The next phase is beginning. Soon, they'll be forced into the below. Soon, Titania will fall.

I grip the railing tighter, feeling it crumble slightly beneath my grasp. My body may be failing, but my spirit soars. Let them think me mad. Let them whisper and stare. In mere hours, I'll hold the power of a god.

"The board is set," I murmur, a manic grin splitting my deteriorating face. "The pieces are in motion."

"And the crown," the Hunt whispers, *"is within reach."*

As if in response, a crack echoes through the arena. The ground begins to split, spraying water like a geyser. This spectacle is why I wasted all those wisps. Screams of terror mingle with the Hunt's laughter in my mind.

I spread my arms wide, welcoming the chaos. "Let the true game begin."

CHAPTER 66
BODIN

Chaos churns in the arena below, a vortex of fear and violence that twists my gut. The ancient stone walls of the faerie fort seem to pulse with anticipation, every crevice leaning in to witness the spectacle. But I can't look away. Not when Willow's down there, fighting for her life.

Her silver hair flashes like moonlight against the shadows, a beacon in the madness. She darts between Nightmares, rallying the other exhibitors. Pride swells in my chest, quickly smothered by dread. She's exposed. Vulnerable. More Terrors drop from their perches, prowling the arena floor. My lip curls. The scent of their rot and decay wafts up, mixing with the crisp pine and ice from the surrounding forest. They'd be dead instantly if our powers were unlocked, us functioning as a hive. Our impotence drives me to the brink.

"She's holding her own," Legion mutters, knuckles white on the ornate railing of our box.

I grunt, not trusting my voice. The air thrums with magic, making my skin prickle. Willow's sword pulses with strengthening glyphs, but they can't protect her from everything. A

464

Graftspawn lunges, mismatched limbs blurring. She dodges. Not fast enough. Claws rake her side.

My roar of fury drowns in the din below. I surge forward, every instinct screaming to protect her, to rend anything that dares harm her. Legion's iron grip holds me back. We're being watched. Every eye in Avorlorna is here, from the luminous aristocrats in their private boxes to the wild faeries with dormant wings and entwined horns. They come out of the woodwork for a taste of their old world. The druids too.

Peablossom is among them, but her identity is a fragile secret we hold close to our hearts. She has worked quietly in the trappings of her role to assist where she can. But her aid comes with a risk.

"We can't interfere," Legion growls, dark eyes flashing. "Not yet."

Willow stumbles and falls. She presses a hand to her bleeding side. The Graftspawn circles, readying another strike. My heart hammers against my ribs, echoing the distant drums still playing in the fort. She's mortal. Fragile.

"Come on, Calamity," I whisper. "Be that force you were born to be."

For a moment, she looks directly at our box. Determination blazes in her golden eyes, visible even through the mist creeping into the arena. I silently urge her to remember the sword's upgrades, hating that I can't reach into her mind and show her. She rises, sword arcing with a blue slipstream. The Graftspawn falls, dissolving into a bloody mist.

My relief evaporates as the arena floor cracks. Fissures spider out, the sound of splitting stone echoing off the fort's walls. Leaves rustle. Water bubbles up, forming a swirling maelstrom. The scent of damp earth and algae fills the air. Exhibitors scramble for footing as the ground gives way to a churning pool.

"A watergate?" Legion balks. "How?"

Puck's gravelly cackle draws our gaze toward his loge. The imbecile is more stone than flesh now, his laughter grating like rocks in a tumbler. Larkspur waits nearby, ready to capture the Baleful Hunt when it breaks free. But what good is that to us now?

"The wisps," Styx mutters. "From the temple. That's what he used them for."

"No," Legion rasps as Willow loses her balance. She tumbles into the water, swallowed by the portal to the subterranean. The crowd's gasp is a physical force suffocating against us.

"Willow!" My bellow tears out, raw and agonized. I strain against Legion's grip, ready to leap after her, rules be damned. The branches of the Hawthorn trees above seem to reach down as if they, too, want to pluck her from danger.

"Stop!" His voice cuts through my panic. "We can't—"

"I don't care!" I snarl, rounding on him. "She could be—"

The word sticks in my throat. Dead. Our mate, our queen, lost before we ever truly had her. The thought chills me more than the icy wind that's picking up.

Styx paces behind us, muttering. His agitation fuels mine. The beauty of the botanical balconies and the majesty of the Hawthorn tree columns mock us with their serenity.

"This isn't right," I growl, running a hand over my braided head. "We should be down there."

"We can't always protect her," Legion says, his tone calmer now. "She must face this on her own."

I know he's right. She needs to prove to these people—to herself—that she can be their queen. She might be our whole world, but we're not hers. Her light is destined for everyone. We know it. But it doesn't hurt any less. The memory of our training session flashes through my mind. I told her the watergate would be no deeper than a puddle. I was wrong.

She'll be terrified.

"I've failed her," I grind out. "I should have known something like this could happen."

Watergates can open anywhere with the right amount of magic. All that is needed is a single drop to amplify. We never expected Puck to have the power.

"Willow has seen our darkest moments," Legion reminds, eyes scouring the water. "And still, she's willing to take a chance on us. On you."

His words hang in the air, and I realize they're directed not just at me but at Styx, who's still pacing behind us.

"Where's Emrys?" Styx interrupts, his voice tight and anxious. "He should be back by now."

Legion's eyes narrow. "Go find out what's taking him so long."

Styx freezes, guilt flashing across his face. "I . . . I can't."

"What do you mean, you can't?" I demand, turning to face him fully.

He shrinks back, looking more like a cornered canary than the powerful Sluagh he is. I've never seen him like this. It's too familiar. My jaw hardens. My fist flexes with the need to shake sense into him, but I exhale and force myself to relax. Legion has made a sacrifice for the sake of our trust. I must prove to Styx I am doing the same.

"Losing her should be the only thing you fear," I tell him. "Our natures have changed."

When the bees realize the intruders' true nature, it's too late. The yellow jackets slaughter them, steal their honey, and leave nothing but destruction in their wake.

I freeze with the memory. I'm not sure what it is about that rant, but it fills me with dread.

"What?" Legion asks, seeing the look on my face. I relay Varen's panicked rambling.

"Emrys tried to shut Varen up again," Styx points out, then resumes his pacing, eyes wild. "Is he the yellow jacket?"

"Styx," I say, my voice low and dangerous. "What do you know?"

He swallows hard. "I tried to tell you, but you didn't listen. He

. . . he was talking about making a deal. Not with Puck, but with someone worse."

A rippling aura of darkness enshrouds Legion. "Titania?"

"No," I growl, the pieces falling into place. "Someone else."

An emptiness enters Styx's voice as he stares at the swirling whirlpool; no soul is left swimming. "He's the Third. I'm the Sixth. I know my place."

"Haven't you learned a single thing?" I grip his shoulder for attention. "We can't be a hive again until we start acting like one."

Legion nods slowly. "Remember what Varen said, Styx. You're meant to be in the subterranean for this final trial. We can't join you down there, but you can stay connected to our minds."

"Fuck you both." Styx shakes me off, determination and menace returning to his eyes. "I'm done taking orders."

The whiff of rot and despair rising from below makes my stomach churn. But beneath it all, I catch the faintest trace of Willow's scent. She's alive. She has to be.

"So don't," I tell Styx, my voice steady despite the storm raging inside me. "Do what you think needs to be done. We trust you."

He disappears, and I meet Legion's steady gaze.

"Well handled," he intones, bracing the railing.

I join him and consider the past twenty-four hours. I was with Willow, seeing to her needs while he walked through the Clock Tower with Varen. Our Fourth is not the kind to waste an opportunity.

"Varen was lucid for hours," I remark. "He must have warned you about this."

"Naturally."

Tension releases from my shoulders. That's why they were so calm at breakfast.

"You know how this will end. Why haven't you shared it with me?"

"When did we have time?"

My eyes narrow on him. He had time when he found Willow in my bed. Unless Styx's wraith form was around, listening in. At breakfast, Emrys was there. Whole. Unpunished. He sees me calculating, and his lips curve briefly in that arrogant way of his.

"I see through your machinations," I remind him wryly.

"I know." His lips twitch. "But I trust you, and you trust me."

"Invariably."

"Styx and Emrys must learn to do the same . . . without us interfering."

"And you believe this is the right time to test such loyalties?"

"Believe me, Bodin." His gaze turns grim as he regards the watergate. "Now is the best time."

Flickering images appear above the central rock as water drains, sluicing off the large resonance stone. The restless crowd cheers as the spectacle continues. Shimmering pictures of exhibitors manifest in the air, broadcasting from the subterranean.

"I'm with Styx," I mutter darkly to Legion, searching for a sign of silver hair. "I'm done taking orders."

I feel his eyes on me, hard and penetrating. But then he sighs, no doubt realizing I don't refer to him. I trust him. It's this situation we've been trapped in for eternity. Whether it was Titania, other queens, Oberon, or the Morrigan herself. We've always taken orders. Willow is our first glimpse of freedom—something bright, chaotic, and uniquely ours.

I know Styx feels the same. Emrys too. He's just too stubborn to admit it. But we're a hive. We are one soul in six bodies. And now that we've found our queen, reuniting is inevitable. It matters not if Styx is down there being the one to protect Willow. Where there is one, there are six.

"Hold on, Calamity," I whisper into the void. "We're coming for you."

CHAPTER 67

WILLOW

One moment, I'm wrenching my sword from the Graftspawn's grotesque body. The next, it explodes into a crimson mist, splattering my face with warm, iron-tinged droplets. Before I can wipe the gore from my eyes, the ground beneath me lurches.

Fissures spider across the arena floor, water gushing forth in violent geysers. My gaze locks with Geraldine's, terror mirrored in her wide eyes. Max clutches the youngies close, their faces pale with fear.

Then we plummet.

Water engulfs me, a roaring, arctic embrace that steals my breath. My body instinctively seizes, lungs burning as they fight the urge to inhale. The current drags me down, down, down, my silver hair billowing around me like specters in the murky depths.

For a heartbeat, an eerie calm washes over me. The icy water numbs the throbbing gash in my side, almost soothing. Then gravity shifts.

I'm caught in a maelstrom, tumbling end over end. Electricity crackles across my skin, setting every nerve alight. Bile rises in my

470

throat as nausea rolls. My fingers clench desperately around my sword's grip, the only anchor in this watery hell.

Just as my vision starts to darken, I breach the surface. Air floods my starved lungs as I gasp and sputter, blinking furiously. Shadowy walls loom around me, their surfaces pulsing with otherworldly purple bioluminescence. Most of the light, however, emanates from beneath the water's surface—crisp and bright, like liquid starlight.

My limbs flail as I fight to stay afloat, panic clawing at my chest. Then my boots scrape against something solid. Sand. A ledge. Hope surges as I drag myself through the shallows, finger-nails digging into gritty sand.

I twist around, still half-submerged, and freeze. Above me— or is it below?—I glimpse the shimmering image of the fort, its trees and columns impossibly inverted. My mind reels. This isn't some underground cavern system. It's as if reality itself has been turned inside out.

Splashing draws my eye. Others are coming through.

"Over here!" I call out, my voice echoing strangely off the cavern walls. Relief floods me as familiar faces break the water's surface. Geraldine's dark hair plasters her skin as she swims toward me, Max close behind. He helps pull out Colin and his friends. Those gloves give him abnormal strength. It's so good to see him embracing them. The youngies cling to each other, their frightened whimpers carrying across the water. Becky emerges, coughing violently, supported by Heath.

As I help drag them to shore, movement catches my eye. Looking more feral than I've ever seen, Alfie scrambles to his feet and bolts down a shadowy tunnel without a backward glance.

"Coward," I mutter, the word tasting bitter on my tongue.

I turn my attention back to the group and conduct a frantic headcount. Several exhibitors, clearly deciding they're better off alone, dash off in various directions—notably, different from the one Alfie chose. Their departures leave us with about forty remaining.

"You're bleeding," Geraldine says, her voice tight with concern. She gestures to my side, where the Graftspawn's claws raked me earlier.

I glance down, surprised to see the wound knitting itself closed before my eyes. "That's . . . strange," I murmur, running my fingers over the newly healed skin. "In Elphyne, water is a rich source of magic. It has healing properties, but . . ."

"Our wounds aren't healing," Max points out, wincing as he examines a nasty gash on his arm.

A chill runs down my spine. Is this another sign that I'm not entirely cut off from the Well? But why would my mother let me believe I was mortal? Unless . . . she foretold this moment years ago. She knows I'll be allowed in this exhibition if everyone thinks I'm mortal. Her psychic abilities showed her my arrival in Avorlorna. She even knew I would be at Shadowfall Keep.

I push the thoughts aside as the other exhibitors gather around me, their faces a mix of fear and expectation. "What's next?" Becky asks, wringing out her sopping hair.

Their gazes settle on me, heavy with unspoken trust. We're supposed to be competitors, yet here they are, looking to me for guidance. The realization sends a flutter of both pride and terror through my chest.

"The scrolls," I say, remembering Alfie's fixation. "Does anyone have one?"

Geraldine produces a scroll from her sodden pocket, carefully unrolling it beside a patch of glowing moss. Max leans in, his eyes widening. "It's a map of Nocturna—the subterranean," he says, voice hushed with awe. "But it's . . . it's Avorlorna in reverse."

I peer at the parchment, my breath catching as I take in the familiar yet alien landscape. A sinister structure labeled "Court of Nightmares" looms where the Court of Dreams should be. The Nexus has been replaced by something called "The Schism."

"I assumed the subterranean would be tunnels or something," I say. "I've never seen anything like this before."

"Maybe this is where the Folk slumbered for all those years," Geraldine suggests.

As we watch, the map comes to life, glowing faintly. A pulsing dot shows our location—inside the Schism—and a line snakes across the parchment, leading to a spot marked with an X.

"That must be the treasure we're supposed to steal," Heath says, then points at another symbol—a second watergate. "That's our ticket back to the Nexus and safety."

But something nags at me.

"Alfie ran in the opposite direction." I point toward the tunnel he disappeared down. "Toward the Court of Nightmares."

A heated debate breaks out among the exhibitors. Some argue we should follow the map to the treasure, while others insist we need to investigate why Alfie had different information. The underlying current of fear is visceral—no one wants to venture deeper into enemy territory if they don't have to. Heath pointed out the watergate is just after the X.

"Willow," Geraldine says softly, her eyes meeting mine. "What will you wish for if you win?"

I hesitate, acutely aware of the resonance stones broadcasting our every word. I can't voice my desire to rescue Fox, not with all of Avorlorna listening. Instead, I deflect. "What about you?"

"Your magic," she replies without hesitation. "You should wish for your magic back."

Her words trigger a memory—Alfie's cryptic statement about seeing "Her" in the subterranean. A chill runs down my spine as a terrifying thought occurs to me. "What if Titania is down here?" I ask, my voice barely above a whisper. "What if she's in a dreamscape down here? How much do we know about her slumber?"

Before anyone can respond, a bone-chilling shriek echoes through the cavern. Horror dawns on us all simultaneously—if we fell through the watergate, so did the Nightmares from the arena. An exhibitor breaks free from our group and runs for the pool.

"Wait!" I shout, but it's too late. Something darts out from the shadows and snags his ankle, dragging him clawing and screaming into the water.

"We can't go back the way we came," I say, my mind racing. "We need to move. Now."

We run, splashing and inhuman growls spurring us on—a flash of light in my periphery. I spin, slicing with my sword—it cuts through something gelatinous that explodes in a slime shower. Damn, this sword is good. I'll have to thank Bodin again. Each splat emits a dark, inky blot that floats upward toward the cavernous ceiling.

Shit. Blots.

I glance over my shoulder. Exhibitors bottleneck at the narrow tunnel. More shadows move in the cavern. I hear a clicking—like those spider things. We're out of time. There's only one choice left.

I turn to Geraldine and Max, my heart heavy. "Lead the others out," I say, my hand moving to the charm hiding my pheromones. "I'll lure the Nightmares in the opposite direction."

Geraldine's eyes widen in protest. "No, Willow. You can't—"

"Maybe I'll be lucky and catch up with Alfie before they reach me."

"It should be you finding the treasure," she insists, her voice breaking. "You've lost so much already. Don't sacrifice yourself for us."

I manage a smile, touched by her concern. "Maybe this is where I'm meant to be," I tell her, conviction growing with each word. "You'll make the right wish."

Before she can argue further, I rip off the charm. The effect is immediate—my scent, amplified by my heat, fills the air. The Nightmares' shrieks take on a hungry edge, just like in the stables with Emrys.

"Go!" I yell, already sprinting down the tunnel Alfie disappeared into. I don't look back. The pounding of my heart is matched only by the thunderous footfalls of the Terrors as they give chase, drawn inexorably to my intoxicating scent.

The others will be safe. Triumph surges until I realize the bioluminescence is fading, and I plunge deeper into darkness. I hope I haven't made a terrible mistake.

CHAPTER 68
WILLOW

Big fucking mistake.

As I run full pelt down a dark tunnel, death screeches at my heels. Whose great idea was this? My wet boots squelch. A rapid click near my ear. Pungent, rotting breath. Mold. Something catches my hair, ripping my head back with needles. I break free. Run. Terror fills me. So does euphoria, a thrill.

I'm insane. I'm dead. Hot. What an idiot move to make. I'm—

Something white flickers ahead of me.

"Get down." A growl in my head.

I drop. Air gusts over me, through me, and I land on my stomach, skidding forward. Dirt and gravel cut into me. I'm sliding so fast that I drift sideways. All I can think is to move the sword away from my face. Blue glyphs flash in the darkness. Behind me, strange sounds reach my ears. Shrieks cut short. Squelches and wet thuds. Gurgling. I can't comprehend anything until my shoulder hits something, and my slide ends.

Breathing hard, I stretch my senses. Too many things happen at once, too many sounds and smells. I don't understand. I check to see what I hit. It doesn't feel like a wall—too much air around me. The wall is a boot belonging to a shadowy figure now stepping over me. I track the shape and see darkness spread, filling the expanse of the tunnel and blocking my view. What is that? Wings?

Little blobs of darkness drip upward and sizzle against the ceiling.

The knowledge hits me all at once—the voice in my head, the flickering light. It was a skull.

"*Styx?*" I shout with my thoughts.

"*Being greedy as usual,*" he taunts.

Wincing, I use the sword and push to my feet. My eyes only pick up flashes of shadow on shadow. I can't catch anything clear, even with my enhanced sight. He's one Sluagh, but there are so many Nightmares. Limping forward, I adjust my grip and prepare for more danger. It doesn't come. Within seconds, the monstrous death rattles die down. The dripping hiss of blots meeting rock is the only sound left.

I open my mouth to call out, but Styx's warning in my mind stops me.

"*Your resonance stone.*"

Shit. I slap my hand to my chest, feeling for the stone. It's there, burning hotly on a chain.

"*Turn around,*" he orders.

Gravel crunches as I pivot so fast I'm left dizzy. There is a rustle of movement, and a hard, warm body presses against my spine. Hands wrap around my middle. He drops his nose to my neck, tugging me closer. His masculine scent blooms, good and real.

"*You smell so fucking good.*" His mental voice is more of a groan.

"*You saved me.*" I want to sink back into him, to turn and kiss him, to be with him in every way, but this tournament isn't done. I can't betray him by revealing his face to everyone watching.

His teeth clamp on my neck. "*Did I?*"

A rush of warmth blooms in my chest, and I smile . . . then

realize he's not hugging me. He's stiff and tense. Something barbed and twisted wraps around my heart, squeezing. I pull back, but he won't let me go.

"Styx? What's wrong?"

"You're about to find out." His arms lock tighter around me. *"When you see him, tell him this is payback."*

The world around us flickers. We stumble into a room in an instant, and he lets go. It takes a moment for my eyes to adjust, but when they do, my world shifts.

Obsidian walls veined with crystal surround us. An overripe, sickly sweet bouquet of something floral is in the air. The ceiling rolls with a never-ending shadow storm. People—people everywhere. Human, old, young, different. Faerie like I've never seen. Some are like the Nightmares we've studied, like those we've seen, but others are almost indistinguishable from normal.

I'm standing at the foot of the steps leading to a dais. It's not the two thrones of patchwork limbs atop it that shift my world, but the people sitting in them—a tall, dark-haired male I recognize from the Clock Tower memories. With sharp cheekbones and angular features, Oberon has the kind of stare that could wither stone. But it's the queen beside him who steals my attention. I've dreamed about killing her for weeks. But when I envisioned her, she was the vibrant, powerful brunette who cursed me in my dream—the effervescent lady in the portrait hanging in the castle.

Her pale dress is made of squashed petals and hangs wilted on her frail body. A tarnished gemstone tiara slips on her matted brown hair. She looks wild and unhinged as she takes me in, knuckles whitening on the throne's arms.

"What have we here?" Oberon purrs, standing and looking down at me. Something is off with his skin. It's stretched too tightly over his bones. No—something is too big beneath the skin. His bones move like they're alive.

"Styx?" I shout in my mind. *"If this is a joke, I'm not laughing."*

Each step Oberon takes down the steps is punctuated by some kind of wet, squelching sound. The air before him shudders with his approach. The closer he comes, the better I see what his footsteps leave behind—dark, viscous blood. He's not bleeding. Not wounded.

Just evil.

Ancient.

His aura tries to suffocate me as he takes my jaw, tilting me to inspect my face. My insides revolt at his touch. It's cold and clammy, and his magic feels like a scrape—not an itch.

"I thought you said she was ugly," he muses to someone at the side.

Footsteps approach. Absinthe. Tobacco. A raspy drawl. "She was."

Oberon lets go of me as Emrys arrives at his side. His coppery eyes lock with mine. A jolt rips through my heart. *One will betray me. One will try to kill me.* Well, at least we can cross that first one off the list. Oberon circles me, inspecting me like an offering for sale. I twist, trying to keep my eyes on him, but also Emrys. Which villain is more dangerous?

Fighting tears, I whisper, "What are you doing here, Emrys?"

"I would ask you the same, little moth."

"He's finally come to his senses," Oberon drawls, as if it's obvious. "He's ready to be rid of queens, once and for all. But what I want to know is, how did you get in here unnoticed?"

My eyes widen. They didn't see Styx? He must have *flickered* in and out too fast. My palm burns suddenly. I hiss and glance down, opening my fist to see. The circular welt is deepening to a dusky color. I feel compelled to move. What does this mean? Are the trials over?

"What is this?" Oberon's hand snakes out and wraps around my wrist. He lifts my palm upward, then shows it to Titania. "Darling, did you know they started your trials without you?"

She makes some kind of incomprehensible sound.

"How charming," he continues, a teasing lilt to his voice. "The distraction you crafted works so well. They don't even care you're not there." He flicks the resonance stone on my chest and lowers it so his face is captured. "Hello, Good People of Avorlorna."

I step away from him and stumble up a step. I look more closely at Titania and see something more disturbing than her disheveled appearance—bruise marks around her neck. Her visage shimmers. This is her dream form, her specter.

"I thought you were slumbering," I say.

Her eyes widen. She tries to respond, but her lips are sewn shut—with flesh-colored vines. They crawl like maggots in and out of her skin. Bile rises in my throat.

"Oh, she is," Oberon coos from somewhere below me. "As she has every winter for the past five years."

"I don't understand."

I take another step up, away from him. He doesn't seem to care. He's not even bothered that I still have my sword. He just smirks.

"You don't truly think I would simply pause war because she's sleeping? She stole my legacy." He gestures at Emrys, then back at her. "That tiara is the cost of her Gentle Interlude . . . unless, of course, she returns what is rightfully mine."

Pity rolls through me. Titania might be cruel. She might have lied horribly to her people about the reason they died in droves. But she's suffering to give her people a few months of peace.

Movement to the side of the dais catches my eye. Alfie's copper hair. A glint of steel. That's not a look of rescue on his face. It's murder. If he kills her here, she's dead in her bed at the palace. Any hope of reclaiming my magic evaporates. Fox's face flashes in my mind.

Do I kill her . . . or save her?

Alfie's green eyes meet mine, then dart to Titania, weighing his chances of reaching her before me. He lunges, breaking free from his hiding place. I intercept Alfie mid-leap, my body slamming into his. We tumble across the dais in a tangle of limbs and crash into Titania's throne. Chaos erupts in the throne room— shouts, the scraping of talons, swords, the thunderous footsteps of guards, and Oberon's bellow.

"What are you doing?" Alfie snarls, his face contorted with rage as we wrestle. We clash with Titania's throne again. He turns his dagger on me, pointing the tip to my throat. My lower back hits the throne's arm, and I'm forced to bow backward to avoid being cut. Titania's scream is muffled. She's trying to tell me something. I grab Alfie's wrists and hold him off, but he's strong. He snarls in my face, "You should have killed me. Now I'm going to kill you."

A force rips him off me, and he is tossed to the side. I have a moment to register Emrys's panicked and murderous face, and then Titania screeches something muffled. I pivot to find her thrashing on the throne, fingers scrabbling at the jeweled band on her head. But she can't reach. It's like an invisible string keeps yanking her hands back. Her eyes hold a silent plea.

Alfie rises behind her, thinking the same thing I do. *That tiara is the cost of her Gentle Interlude.*

If we remove it, she wakes. This is all over. One of us wins.

CHAPTER 69
TITANIA

I gasp awake in my bed chambers, disoriented and wrapped by wayward vines. The Weaving Hunt rouses nearby, an anchor for relief. I am alive. The tiara is off. The nightmare is over. Or is it? Panic claws at my mind. Is this another of Oberon's sick, twisted games?

"Welcome back, Your Radiance." Peablossom's sweet face is revealed, hovering over me as she lowers her druidic hood. She recites the ritual words announcing the end of the Gentle Interlude. "Tell me what you have learned, my queen—three truths hidden behind a lie."

My fractured mind scrambles to piece together my time with Oberon—the lie of which she speaks. But to cement myself in reality, I must separate what is real from figment. I must find three truths within the lie.

"Puck has turned against me," I rasp.

"Yes." She rips vines from my body, freeing me. "And the second?"

"The exhibition has a winner."

She pauses. "And the third?"

"Willow must DIE."

482

About the Author

OMG! How do you say my name?

Lana (straight forward enough - Lah-nah) **Pecherczyk** (this is where it gets tricky - Pe-her-chick).

I've been called Lana Price-Check, Lana Pera-Chickywack, Lana Pressed-Chicken, Lana Pech...*that girl!* You name it, they said it. So if it's so hard to spell, why on earth would I use this name instead of an easy pen name?

To put it simply, it belonged to my mother. And she was my dream champion.

For most of my life, I've been good at one thing – art. The world around me saw my work, and said I should do more of it, so I did.

But, when at the age of eight, I said I wanted to write stories, and even though we were poor, my mother came home with a blank notebook and a pencil saying I should follow my dreams, no matter where they take me for they will make me happy. I wasn't very good at it, but it didn't matter because I had her support and I liked it.

She died when I was thirteen, and left her four daughters orphaned. Suddenly, I had lost my dream champion, I was split from my youngest two sisters and had no one to talk to about the challenge of life.

So, I wrote in secret. I poured my heart out daily to a diary and sometimes imagined that she would listen. At the end of the day, even if she couldn't hear, writing kept that dream alive.

Eventually, after having my own children (two firecrackers in the guise of little boys) and ignoring my inner voice for too long, I decided to lead by example. How could I teach my children to follow their dreams if I wasn't? I became my own dream champion and the rest is history, here I am.

When I'm not writing the next great action-packed romantic novel, or wrangling the rug rats, or rescuing GI Joe from the jaws of my Kelpie, I fight evil by moonlight, win love by daylight and never run from a real fight.

I live in Australia, but I'm up for a chat anytime online. Come and find me.

Stalker Links
www.lanapecherczyk.com

facebook.com/lanapecherczykauthor

instagram.com/lana_p_author

amazon.com/-/e/B00V2TP0HG

tiktok.com/@lanapauthor

goodreads.com/lana_p_author

patreon.com/lanacreates

ALSO BY LANA PECHERCZYK

THE FAE GUARDIANS WORLD

Fae Guardians - Elphyne

(Fantasy/Paranormal Romance)

Season of the Wolf Trilogy

The Longing of Lone Wolves

The Solace of Sharp Claws

Of Kisses & Wishes Novella (free for subscribers)

The Dreams of Broken Kings

Season of the Vampire Trilogy

The Secrets in Shadow and Blood

A Labyrinth of Fangs and Thorns

A Symphony of Savage Hearts

Season of the Elf Trilogy

A Song of Sky and Sacrifice

A Crown of Cruel Lies

A War of Ruin and Reckoning

Fae Devils

(Fae Guardians Sluagh Spin-off)

Castle of Nevers and Nightmares

Trials of Dusk and Dreams

THE DEADLYVERSE

The Sinner Sisterhood

(Demon-hunting Paranormal Romance)

The Sinner and the Scholar

The Sinner and the Gunslinger

The Deadly Seven

(Fated Mate Paranormal/Sci-Fi Romance)

The Deadly Seven Box Set Books 1-3

Sinner

Envy

Greed

Wrath

Sloth

Gluttony

Lust

Pride

Despair